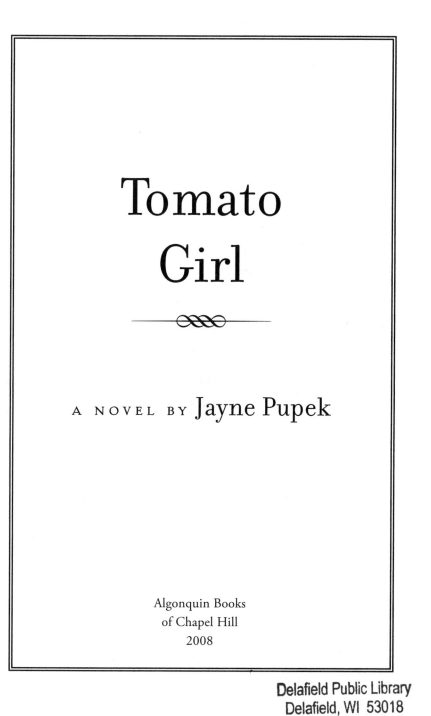

Tomato
Girl

A NOVEL BY Jayne Pupek

Algonquin Books
of Chapel Hill
2008

Published by
ALGONQUIN BOOKS OF CHAPEL HILL
Post Office Box 2225
Chapel Hill, North Carolina 27515-2225

a division of
WORKMAN PUBLISHING
225 Varick Street
New York, New York 10014

Library of Congress Cataloging-in-Publication Data
Pupek, Jayne.
    Tomato Girl : a novel / by Jayne Pupek. — 1st ed.
        p. cm.
    ISBN 978-1-56512-472-1
    1. Mothers and daughters — Fiction.   2. Mental illness — Fiction.
    3. Fathers and daughters — Fiction.   4. Problem families — Fiction.
    I. Title.
    PS3616.U65T66 2008
    813'.6 — dc22   2007801867o

10 9 8 7 6 5 4 3 2 1
First Edition

To Dora, who would be proud.

PROLOGUE

Jars line my cellar shelves. Some are filled with fists of yellow-veined tomatoes. Others hold small onions and chopped leeks, white pearls floating in an opaque sea. Sometimes the light falls on a jar of boiled quail or the slick, dark meat of a rabbit. There are unexpected moments when I see the slit of an infant's mouth, or the curl of a tiny fist behind the glass, and I run up the steps, back into the open light of sky. I gasp for air and tell myself the past is a distant thing, no longer able to reach me or hurt me. And yet, at times, it seems the past will always send its long thin fingers toward me, reminding me of all I want to forget.

Today I carry my notebook and pen down the cellar steps. I stand on a chair and screw in a lightbulb to wash away shadows. Then I sit. The notebook on my lap waits like an expectant child.

Long ago, a woman stood by a river and taught me the power of release. She would say I have held things and now I need to let go.

I pick up the pen. I need to tell what I remember. I need to tell the story of a girl whose world unraveled like a torn scarf . . .

ONE

MARKET DAY

TODAY IS MARKET DAY. Not because it's Tuesday. Not because fresh tomatoes were loaded into the wooden bins this morning. Today is market day because Daddy sent money.

The blue envelope came in yesterday's mail. Inside, there was no letter like there had been for awhile, only three twenty-dollar bills folded into neat halves. I sat on the step and traced the paper spine with my fingers. I imagined Daddy's thumb making the perfect crease, the oil and dirt pressed under his nail like a dark line. Now that he was hauling pulp wood, his hands would be splintered and red from rubbing against bark. Maybe another worker would let him borrow gloves. He'd left his one good pair in the shed.

Waiting for the mail is my job. Mama doesn't want to see the letters from Daddy or even the envelopes. When the first one came, she stood in the middle of the sidewalk and ripped the paper into pieces. The day had been windy and sharp and the blue and green shreds floated on the air like insect wings. I chased each piece, then shoved them deep into my pocket and ran to Clara's house.

Clara is a colored woman. And a clairvoyant. Some even say she's a witch. Clara laughs at what people call her. She says if you get to be as old as she is without learning a trick or two, you haven't been paying attention. For sure she knows magic. Not the rabbit-in-the-hat magic, but real magic. The kind that raises dead spirits and makes handsome men swoon over plain women. The magic that causes plums to ripen despite a hard frost. Magic that lets her see your future spelled out in brown tea leaves or in the lines crisscrossing your palm.

Even though Clara doesn't live far, I'm not supposed to walk there alone, through the colored part of Granby. It's not just a rule at my house, but one that everybody knows. We go to school with black children, and sometimes shop at the same stores, but most things are done as they always were, separately, with doctors and churches for whites and a different set for coloreds. No black man in his right mind would walk into a church full of whites. No white woman would dare let a colored doctor see her naked, or even let one give shots to her children to keep them safe from measles and smallpox.

"A white girl isn't safe in a neighborhood full of colored boys," Mary Roberts told me on the playground. I didn't ask what black boys might do that white boys wouldn't. I didn't want to hear any stories to scare me away from Gratton Street. Mary doesn't understand that when you need somebody the way I need Clara, you don't care two sticks what color skin they live in.

Before I go to Clara's in the afternoons, I sit on the front porch steps until the postman comes. While I wait, I rest my satchel across my lap and practice fractions in my notebook or recite my spelling list: *SORROW: S-O-R-R-O-W; TOMORROW: T-O-M-O-R-R-O-W.* I go over my words until I can spell them by heart. Sometimes I read my lessons, sounding out the words I don't know because I'm afraid to ask Mama. Her nerves are wound tight as a watch. I don't want to upset her. She might cry or take off her clothes. I'm always afraid she'll drop the baby.

Sometimes Mama does things to hurt herself. She gets carried away. Once while sitting at the kitchen table to write a grocery list, she scratched her wrist with the pencil until it bled. The more it bled, the deeper she pressed the lead point into her skin. Daddy had to wrestle the pencil from her, then bandage her wrist and give her a shot to calm her. I'm not strong like Daddy, and might not be able to stop her. Besides, now all the needles and medicines are gone. The sheriff took them when he came looking for Daddy.

Where Mama is concerned, preventing her bad moods is the key. "If we keep everything around Mama even and safe, she won't sink too deep," Daddy had said. A lily caught in a hurricane was how Daddy described Mama. If we calmed the winds around her, she would be fine.

Remembering what he taught me, I walk on tiptoes and speak in a low, soft voice. When washing dishes, I make sure not to let the pots and pans bang together. No running through the house or slamming doors. When the phone rings, I answer it before the third ring. I don't ask for lunch money or help with homework. Because Mama is prone to headaches and the light makes them worse, it's important to keep the lamps burning low and the curtains drawn shut. If someone comes to the door selling *Grit* papers or vacuum cleaners, I send them away in a hurry.

Most of all, I try not to mention Daddy, not even when his letters come. I put the money in her purse or in the cookie jar on top of the fridge, and keep his letters in a box under my bed. She never asks where the extra money comes from. Maybe she doesn't even notice how we run so low only a few dollars are left, then there is suddenly money for the market. It is hard for her to know real from make-believe, so Mama makes sense of things in her own way.

On Saturdays when there's no homework to keep me busy, I sit on the porch steps and wait. No matter how bored I get, I don't go inside before the postman comes.

People walk by. Sometimes they wave, speak, or nod at me. Granby is a small town where everybody recognizes you. It's common to stop and ask about the little details that make up a life: How is your garden? What do you think of the rain we've been having? Are you keeping up your grades in school? How is your mama getting on?

I don't want them to ask about Mama or about Daddy. When they do, I just wave real small and look away. I can't let them know about Mama's moods, or how she keeps Baby Tom in a jar. I can't tell them about the bad night with the spoon, or how Daddy ran off with Tess. Mary Roberts says people already know more than they say.

I keep to myself now more than ever.

To pass time, I gather the acorns that fell from the oak tree in our front yard. I count how many black ants cross the deep crack in the sidewalk. I say my ABC's backwards or recite the names of flowers I know: *aster, buttercup, daisy, pansy, tulip, snapdragon, rose* . . . Sometimes I make up stories about girls with magic powers, girls who can fly over mountain peaks and bring lost fathers home.

Most days the mail brings bills, advertisements, and coupons — even free samples of soap — but no word from Daddy. On the days no blue envelope comes, I pretend Daddy is on his way back home, driving in his yellow Pontiac with the windows down and the radio playing loud.

When another day comes and I see the blue envelope, I go hide in the shed to cry because I know Daddy is not coming home that day.

Nearly all the mail still comes addressed to my father. Somebody sits at a desk and types "Mr. Rupert Sanders," not knowing that he left. Even the newspaper carries his name. I'm saving the papers for him, stacking them in his toolshed where he'll want to read them when he comes home. I've saved forty-one papers so far.

Sometimes it's as if Daddy died, but there wasn't a funeral. There's no grave to visit.

Mary Roberts said mail came for her grandfather long after he died. "Papa even got Christmas cards," she said, "and that was three months after we buried him."

Mary gives me advice because that is what she does best. In the cafeteria this week she said I should tell people Daddy died because that would stop the rumors. People might even feel sorry for Mama and me. "You wouldn't have to go over to that colored woman's house anymore or eat her colored food. The church would take up an offering, and white ladies would bring cakes and casseroles," she said.

"But I like going to Clara's house. Besides, if I say Daddy died, how will I explain when he comes home?"

"My mother says your Daddy's not coming home," Mary whispered.

"He is, too!" I moved to another table and slammed my tray down so hard the red Jell-O spilled into the buttered corn.

Mary Roberts isn't my friend anymore.

IN THE MARKET, Mama buys stale bread and brown eggs. She buys cabbages as twisted as a man's fist. Red radishes the size of a doll's heart.

I follow Mama as she weaves her way between the vegetable stands. If I stay close enough, and keep my arms to my sides, maybe I can disappear behind the dark curtains of her coat. Like a girl on a stage, I pretend my life belongs to someone else. *This is not my life,* I whisper.

But of course, I can't even convince myself. This is the only life I know, this one that started when Daddy left. My old one is as far away as the stars. Maybe this new life is the real one and the life before only make believe.

Mama's shoulders slump. She holds her elbows too far from her body. Her knuckles are white knots clutching a dirty handkerchief.

The skin of her fingers is red and cracked because she has stopped buying bottles of Jergens. "Only the things we need," she reminds me, rubbing her hands with spit.

But all this is about more than doing with less. Mama has stopped combing her hair. She wears dresses that need hemming and stockings with holes. She doesn't bathe, sing, or pay the bills anymore. At night, she paces the floor with Baby Tom in her arms and tries to nurse him at her breast.

Mama lifts a yellow squash, then tosses it aside. "Too ripe," she snaps. She picks up another, presses her thumb into its pale skin, then drops it on the floor. Its narrow neck splits open to show raw, seedy insides.

I squeeze my eyes shut. These are pictures I don't want to see: the yellow squash broken on the floor; Mama's thin, bitten lips spilling dirty words; the other shoppers staring with wide eyes and open mouths.

I want to tell them that Mama won't always be this way, but I say nothing. Gradually, the other shoppers turn away. They can't keep staring; that would be rude. They return to their own shopping; they move to other aisles, carefully stepping around the smashed squash, choosing plums or cucumbers to avoid the bins near us.

For a moment, I think maybe someone will walk over and guide Mama to a quiet corner. Maybe someone will lead me to the red bench in front of the market where the newspaper is sold and the metal horse lets children ride his back. Maybe that same somebody will bring me a vanilla ice cream and tell me not to worry, that Mama will be back to her old self in the blink of an eye.

Wishing doesn't make a thing so. No one comes forward to comfort Mama. No one asks her what's the matter.

I nudge my mother. "Let's leave, Mama." I want to go home. I don't want Mama to act this way in front of other people. It's bad enough when there is no one but me to see. I don't want everyone else to know. What if she mentions the baby in the jar? I can't explain him away.

Mama motions me aside.

I follow her over to the dairy products where she frowns at the cartons of milk and the small blocks of cheese. She asks for half a pound of cheddar, thinly sliced, then demands the sheets of paper separating the slices be removed. "I can hardly afford the cheese," she complains. "I won't pay for your stinking wax paper."

We go back to the produce section, where Mama squabbles with the vendor over the price of his tomatoes. "Look at these bruised skins! These soft spots gone to rot!"

I stand beside Mama and look down at my saddle shoes, the once white toes now scuffed and dirty. I'm embarrassed by Mama's shrill voice. "Mister, your damn tomatoes are no good!"

I feel sorry for the vendor. His dark eyes narrow as he defends his prices. "There are no finer tomatoes in this town," he cries. "And no fairer prices!"

It's not your tomatoes, I want to tell him, but I can't take his side. I remember the fight in the kitchen, and the girl with tomato lips who waited in Daddy's car.

TWO

THE GREEN CHICK

GOD DOESN'T LIKE selfish girls. Mrs. Roberts says so. And if anyone knows God's likes and dislikes, it's Mrs. Roberts. She sings in the choir, directs the Christmas pageant, and teaches Vacation Bible School the third week of every July. Her name tops the prayer chain, which means she is the first to know when trouble hits somebody's life.

The pastor calls Mrs. Roberts a virtuous woman. I don't know what that means, but she works hard to earn his praise. She reads through the entire Bible each year, following a schedule she keeps taped to her refrigerator. When I visit Mary, I check the schedule to see which chapter Mrs. Roberts is reading. Sure enough, if you look inside her Bible, the red ribbon bookmark is always on the right page. Even when she has the flu, or the electricity goes out in a storm, a virtuous woman does not neglect reading the Scriptures.

Mrs. Roberts passes on what she knows to anyone who will listen. I've learned a heap of things about God in the time I've spent at the Roberts's house. For instance, when you disobey God,

He sends bad things like plagues, locusts, and floods. "That's to get your attention," Mrs. Roberts says, "and to make you think twice."

If you don't take heed, the next time God might kill your baby. The only way to stop Him is to paint blood on your doors.

If you are a selfish and stubborn girl, God might send away your daddy, the way He did mine.

There is no end to what God can take from you.

I try not to be mad at God. I know I'm to blame. It's my fault Mama twisted her back and the tomato girl came to stay. I didn't help Mama like she asked. I'd only wanted to be left alone so I could hurry to the store to pick out my new chick.

My selfish ways turned God against me. Mrs. Roberts would say so.

AFTER LUNCH, MISS WILDER, my teacher, sits at her desk and reads aloud, mostly stories about orphaned deer or ship-wrecked families. These stories are sometimes sad, but hold my attention. I can imagine being right in them.

Fridays are different. On Fridays, we write our own stories. "Every story," Miss Wilder explains, "is like a circle. Every story has a beginning and an end. The secret is to close your eyes, see a picture, then open your eyes and write what you see. Find the beginning and the rest of the story will follow."

When I close my eyes, I see Mama standing at the stove, a clean white apron tied around her waist. This is where my story begins, with Mama making beef stew for Sunday's supper.

WHILE THE RADIO announcer shouted out unbeatable deals at Emory's Buick, the beef bone boiled in the big black pot. Mama chopped carrots, potatoes, and celery stalks. The knife made a tapping sound on the cutting board, but Mama wasn't in one of her too-fast moods, so I didn't have to worry that she might cut her finger. There are days when Mama shouldn't handle knives, and Daddy used to sometimes wrap them in newspapers or towels and hide them. There hadn't been any days like that in quite some time.

"Ellie, can you run downstairs and fetch me an onion?"

I stood at the back door, pulling my sweater over my head. "Mama! The new chicks are coming today! I'll miss the truck if I don't get down there."

Mama turned down the radio and smiled. "Oh, all right! Such a tomboy I've raised. What kind of wife will you make, Ellie?"

"I'm never getting married, Mama!" I hated boys. They smelled bad and liked to spit in the bushes behind Daddy's store. I could hardly believe my father had once been a boy, but Mama showed me a picture of him at age twelve. He had too many freckles, short greased hair, and large teeth shaped like border stones.

"Oh, I see. You say that now, but you wait . . ."

"Mama!"

"Go on, then." She swatted my behind with her dishrag. "I'll get the onion myself. And tell your father not to be late for supper." She opened the top cabinet above the stove and handed me an empty oatmeal box.

Mama saved every kind of box, jar, and can. She used these as hiding places for her special things. Sometimes Daddy found her treasures and took them back to the store because she hadn't paid for them. Mostly she kept ink pens, stockings, and sewing goods. He ignored those because they cost so little, but the jewelry, perfume, and fur stole had to be returned. Sometimes she'd cry hard enough that Daddy would work out an agreement with the shop owner to pay for it, but usually, Mama just pouted, or said she hadn't really wanted the thing anyway.

"Have Daddy saw this in half," Mama explained, "and poke holes in the lid. Put some brown paper in the bottom. It should do nicely for your chick."

I kissed Mama's soft, warm cheek and ran out the door.

Overhead, dove-gray clouds hung in the sky. A few cool rain-drops hit my face.

If I ran as fast as I could, I'd make it to the store before the Easter chicks arrived.

DADDY WAS STACKING cans of paint in a pyramid along the wall when I plowed through the front door. "There's my girl," he said and smiled at me.

Back then nobody else in the world was his girl. Only me.

I locked my arms around Daddy's thick neck and kissed his rough, salty face. "I haven't missed the truck, have I, Daddy?"

"No, should pull up any minute. Here, you help me sort the new brushes until Mr. Nelson comes." He pointed to the card-board box on the floor. An open flap showed a box full of red- and black-handled brushes, their fine white bristles wrapped in clear plastic.

I loved Daddy's store. He didn't really own it, Mr. Morgan did, but Mr. Morgan hardly stopped by anymore because of his arthri-tis. Daddy ran it for him, and I thought of the store as ours. I spent hours after school sweeping the narrow aisles, sorting shiny nails and bolts into their bins, hanging new paint brushes on hooks. Sometimes I closed my eyes and wandered the aisles like I was blind, naming things just by touch and smell. This was a world where I felt safe, like being wrapped in a favorite blanket. Here everything had its own special place, and no one broke into tears for no reason or hurt themselves on purpose. This was a place like school, where things happened the way you expected, and the day at hand was much like the day before it. Each spring I watered seedlings and pulled dead buds. I arranged snapdragons in rows near the counter where we sold seed packets. We carried green hoses that hung on the wall like vines, and shiny watering cans with thick gray spouts. As soon as the frosts passed, we stocked more gardening supplies, and right after that the first produce came. Daddy bought from local people: flowers from the colored women on Gratton Street, corn from the sheriff's brother, and fancy mushrooms from the minister's wife.

Most everything else came from the tomato girl. She kept Daddy's store stocked in fresh vegetables all spring and summer. In the fall and winter, she brought in jars of sweet pickles, corn relish, and tomato preserves. Whenever she showed up with more produce, I placed it in the baskets so the nicest vegetables were on top, throwing away any with worm holes or bruises. In the front window, the sun ripened her tomatoes, turning them a deep red.

Everyone in town loved her tomatoes. Rumor was she spread blood and coffee grounds on her garden every full moon to make her tomatoes ripe and extra sweet. Other folks said it was her tears that gave them their unusual taste. She was rumored to be orphaned and infirm, but nothing people said about her made much sense to me. I listened to what people said, but wasn't sure which parts to believe.

Sometimes when the store wasn't too busy, Daddy let me work the cash register. I remembered to thank folks for shopping at Morgan's General, but often made mistakes giving them change. Most of the customers helped me when I lost count, but I still almost gave up. "There's too many ways to make a dollar," I complained. Daddy made me keep at it though. "You can't quit when things get a little tough, Ellie. You must keep at them until you get them right."

A job he never had to tell me to do twice was tending the Easter chicks.

They usually arrived one week before Easter. One hundred of them. Most were dyed blue or pink, because people like things to make sense that way, blue for boys and pink for girls. But some of the chicks were purple, orange, and green, and those were my favorites. Daddy called them the Life Savers chicks because they matched the candies.

My father had built a special glass display case at the front of the store, tall enough for small children to see into, but not reach inside. The display case stayed there all year, but we changed it each season. During the summer, Daddy filled the case with white play sand and added toy buckets and bright beach balls. In the fall, we placed pumpkins and leaves inside. When December came, we set up a village snow scene with a train and painted houses, some with tiny wreaths pinned to their front doors. Daddy always said I had Mama's knack for making things look pretty.

In April, Daddy cleaned the display case and lined the bottom with newspapers and pine shavings for the Easter chicks. My job was to feed and water the chicks, then change their dirty newspapers and bedding. Each chick had to be cleaned with a soft cloth or brush if it got dried corn mash or poop on its down feathers. Their tiny nostrils had to be kept perfectly clear, so they could breathe, which was sometimes a hard job because chicks are messy when they eat, dipping their little heads too far into the bowl.

I loved the way the chicks smelled, like corn and baking soda, and how they stood on pipe-cleaner legs while they pecked at my hands with their little orange beaks. Whenever I came near them, they chirped, fluffing up their soft down. Within a few days, they took me for their mother, peeping when they heard my voice or footsteps.

As Easter neared and mothers and fathers scooped up chicks to fill baskets, my brood became smaller. Any that were left, Daddy bartered away. Sometimes he traded them for birdhouses made by the blind carpenter on Gale Street. Once or twice he'd given them to shopkeepers who overlooked Mama's borrowing without asking. Most often, my unsold chicks went to the tomato girl, a trade for her spring produce.

This year, Daddy said if I kept his secret, I could keep a chick for my own.

THE BIG BLUE farm truck pulled up in front of the store. "They're here," Daddy called to me as he walked outside. I left my paintbrushes in their cardboard box and followed him.

He and Mr. Nelson stood on the stoop and talked about the weather for what seemed like forever. Mr. Nelson explained that on his way there he'd had to stop to wrap tarp around his flatbed to keep his turkeys from drowning. "They turn their heads right up in the rain," he said, tilting his head to show us. "The only thing dumber than a bird in rain is a man in love," Mr. Nelson joked.

My father didn't laugh.

A few minutes later, Daddy and Mr. Nelson carried in four wooden crates, each holding twenty-five dyed chicks. Daddy turned on the heating lamp and left me to move the tiny chicks into their new home. They would go on sale tomorrow, and I knew that immediately my little brood would begin to dwindle. For the rest of today, though, they were all mine. Daddy never sold them until he saw that they could stand and eat on their own. Any that seemed too weak would be kept in a box in the back office and fed a special gruel with powdered vitamins mixed into it.

While Daddy locked the cash register, I knelt next to my chicks. They felt a bit damp from the rain, and I quickly moved them to their place under the lamp to prevent a chill from settling into their small, thin lungs. I'd never lost a chick, not even last spring when the shipment arrived during a late frost.

As I finished moving the last of my brood, a tiny green chick stumbled over his feet and brushed against my hand. He wasn't bright green like a lime or lollipop, but a softer shade, the color of pistachio ice cream. Daddy said he'd climbed out of the dye too soon for the color to deepen.

The chick pecked at my thumb, and then stepped onto my finger. He wobbled, but caught his balance as his tiny clawed toes gripped my skin. With his head tilted, he chirped as if to say, "I did it! I did it!"

I laughed and kissed his soft head.

I knew then that this chick would be mine, and today I would carry him home.

"WE BETTER GET to the house," Daddy said, looking at his wristwatch. He rolled down his sleeves, buttoning the cuffs.

"Don't forget the holes," I reminded Daddy, handing him the box lid.

Daddy took his knife from his pocket and poked six or seven holes in the cardboard lid. With his thumb, he brushed the openings clean so that no dust would fall on my chick's head.

I scooped up my green baby and tucked him inside his oatmeal box. All the other chicks were warm, dry, and fed. Only two had seemed too small and weak to eat all by themselves, so Daddy and I fed them with a dropper, then placed them in a box in the office. In a day or so, they'd join the others.

DADDY AND I walked the four blocks to our house. The rain had stopped, and the clouds that had hung overhead like plump mushrooms a few hours earlier were thin and distant now.

A pale pink light softened the sky as we crossed Elm Street and turned onto Grace. I hugged the box in my arms and hummed to calm my chick. I hoped he wouldn't be afraid in a new place.

We passed the small brick post office and the row of painted houses where mostly renters lived. Mama sometimes talked about renting one and turning it into a coffee shop for artists and writers. She wanted to paint the walls bright colors, hang spider plants from the ceiling, and place matchstick blinds in the windows. Writers could sit at small round tables and drink coffee with cinnamon on top while artists gathered at the back to sketch nude women. Mama had said her own figure was good enough that she could even model herself. I worried that Mrs. Roberts would find out about the naked women and stop Mary from being my friend, but Daddy said not to give it a thought. He'd already warned the landlords and banks about Mama's behavior. *Erratic* was the word he'd used with other people, but I knew Daddy meant Mama has her moods. To make her happy, Daddy let Mama keep dreams that would never come true.

Daddy once said he'd picked the best house in Granby considering Mama's moods. Having boarders for neighbors meant there were fewer regular folks who saw the odd things Mama did. Transients, Daddy had explained, are not as nosy as townsfolk, and I guess he was right. None of the boarders ever asked about anything Mama did; most folks only knew she suffered headaches and crying spells.

As we neared the row of dark hedges marking the edge of our yard, I walked faster. I couldn't wait to show Mama my new chick. She'd help me name him. Maybe she'd stand at the kitchen sink and mix warm water and cornmeal to make his bedtime gruel, then press a handkerchief with her iron so he'd have a warm blanket in the bottom of his box. I'd seen her do these things when I'd once brought home a wounded sparrow.

Mama, like me, loves fragile things, but she can hurt them when she's troubled. Sometimes something comes over her, and she doesn't realize what she's doing, or how it will turn out bad. She once poured bleach in the fish tank because she'd dreamed the black mollies grew wings and teeth. The fish all went belly-up, and Daddy had to flush them down the toilet. Later, Mama stared at the empty tank and cried, but Daddy wouldn't let her fill the tank with more fish.

Another awful time, Mama wound tape around our parakeet's beak because the bird wouldn't be quiet. Each time Paco chirped, pain shot through Mama's eyes like swords. She'd only meant to quiet him, but she wrapped the tape up too high on his beak, covering the holes where Paco breathed. The little blue parakeet died. I'd found him that evening when I came home. Daddy dug a small grave in the yard to bury him, but explained we could not mark it or ever talk about the parakeet again. "It will upset Mama when she realizes what she's done," he'd said. "And other people wouldn't understand. This is best forgotten." I'd nodded then tucked away my sadness, like a handkerchief in my pocket. Keeping secrets came easy after so much practice, but some things you just can't forget no matter how hard you try.

Mama had been in a very bad mood then, but lately she'd been better. I couldn't imagine her hurting my chick. Besides, I was older now and knew to look after him. If I covered him with a blanket when I was at school, he would be perfectly quiet and Mama wouldn't even notice him.

"Slow down, Ellie, before you fall," Daddy warned from behind. But I was already up the steps and through the front door.

"Mama! Mama!" I called, leaving the front door open as I hurried to the black-and-white-tiled kitchen where my mother would be setting out the heavy bowls for supper.

A sharp, burning smell stung my nose.

The pot sat on the stove. Dried broth spotted the front of the oven where the stew had boiled over. The knob had been left on, scorching the pot and spilling grayish white threads of smoke.

Mama was gone.

The onion.

I remembered the onion.

Fear shot through my body. It reminded me of the time the dentist's drill slipped and hit my gum. The jolt had sent my body forward in the chair.

The box with my new chick slipped through my fingers and hit the floor.

"Mama!" I ran out the screen door toward the basement steps.

At the bottom of the stairwell, Mama's body lay folded in half like a paper doll.

Dark red blood stained her face.

THREE

GOD PROMISES

I STOOD AT THE TOP of the basement stairs and screamed until Daddy came and pulled me away.

I wanted to go down the steps and sit with her, but my legs wouldn't move.

An ambulance came. Its spinning red light sent splashes of color through the trees and made me dizzy. If the siren sounded, I knew my heart would split open and bleed.

I watched from the top of the stairs as a short man with reddish-brown hair and glasses knelt beside Mama and placed a mask across her face. A colored man with white wool hair helped the other man lift my mother onto a long stretcher. They strapped her in place to bring her up the stairwell.

Mrs. Roberts had shown me a picture of the risen Lazarus walking out of the tomb after Jesus rolled the stone away. I prayed to see Mama rise from the stretcher and walk up the steps on her own. I wanted her to laugh about how she'd tripped, and tell me the gash in her head didn't even hurt.

But she didn't speak and she didn't move.

She isn't dead, I told myself. Daddy had said she was just hurt. But maybe he didn't know. Or maybe he couldn't tell me. Daddy always wanted to make a bad thing sound better. He'd never tell you to be worried or afraid, even if there was good reason to be.

The men slid the stretcher into the back of the ambulance. They made it look so simple, like sliding a pan into an oven.

"You'll follow us to the hospital?" the red-haired man asked.

Daddy shook his head. "We don't have a car."

He didn't tell the man how the last time we owned a car Mama had taken off for three days. Sheriff Rhodes had found her parked near the river just sitting in the car, with no food, no belongings, only the nightgown she'd worn the morning she left. "I drove and drove and just couldn't remember the way back," she'd explained. Daddy said he couldn't see how a woman could forget her way around a town she'd lived in for years. He'd wanted to know what man she'd been with and held her by her wrists to make her tell. That only made her cry. Daddy said he was sorry and cried, too. He sold the car the next day.

"I could call a cab," Daddy offered.

The man scratched his cheek and said, "No, that's fine. I can let you ride with her. But you'll have to find a way home. They never release a patient with head injuries. They'll keep her under observation for at least a day."

Daddy nodded and gripped my hand as we climbed into the back of the ambulance.

I sat on Daddy's lap. He pressed my face to his chest to keep me from looking at Mama's bloodied face. The siren blared when we came to the stop sign. I covered my ears with my hands. The red light flashed on top of the vehicle, sending swirls inside the ambulance. I closed my eyes to block out the light, but the red kept flashing behind my shut lids.

I knew I should keep my eyes open, pay attention. Mary Roberts would want to hear all the details. This would be the sort of tale to impress even the toughest boy in class. But I knew I'd never want to talk about it.

At the hospital, we sat on an ugly plaid sofa in the waiting room while doctors tended to Mama. By then, I'd started to believe that Mama wasn't really dead. People came to the hospital to get well.

An old man slumped in a lounge chair in the corner near the television. A string of drool ran from his lips to his chin.

In the opposite corner, a tank of guppies gurgled on top of a bookshelf. I pitied the fish who had only this awful room to look at day after day. They must have seen more sadness than any fish on earth.

A nurse walked over and offered Daddy coffee in a Styrofoam cup. Her thick legs bulged in her stockings and made a swishing sound when they rubbed together. She handed me a coloring book with seven dwarfs on the cover.

"I don't want to color."

"Here's a nice picture of Snow White. You look a little like Snow White yourself with those blue eyes and dark hair." She turned the page. "And here's the witch with her apple." She pulled out a fat red crayon and put it into my hand. "Don't you want to color the witch's apple?"

I took the crayon, broke it in half, and shoved the coloring book back to her. "No, I don't."

Daddy wrapped his arm around my shoulder and pulled me close. He whispered to the nurse that I would be fine and thanked her again for the coffee. My father has always been kind and understanding. He's a person with too much love inside.

"I'm sorry for being rude, Daddy," I said after the nurse went away.

"It's okay." He pulled me closer. "People say things they don't mean when they're upset. The nurse understands, really."

I buried my face in Daddy's warm neck, and stayed there until I fell asleep.

When I woke sometime later, a man in green pants was talking to Daddy. I figured he must be Mama's doctor because a stethoscope hung around his neck.

"Your wife suffered no permanent damage, Mr. Sanders. She's regained consciousness. We stitched her forehead, gave her a muscle relaxant and something for pain. Her back is sprained, and she'll need to spend the next few weeks recovering. No bending or lifting. No heavy housework, laundry, or cooking." The doctor cleared his throat. "And I'm sorry to have to tell you that the odds are not good that the baby will survive the trauma."

Daddy nodded. He rubbed his head with his hand, and his fingers disappeared in his thick, dark hair.

"What baby?" I asked. No one had told me Mama was going to have a baby. I'd always wanted a brother or sister, somebody smaller than me to help look after. I thought about my mother's belly rising like a soft loaf under her apron and knew what the doctor said could be true.

Daddy hushed me. He asked the doctor if my mother knew.

"No, we haven't told her. She's still a little incoherent."

"Doc," my father said, then paused. He seemed to be searching for words. "My wife, well, she's prone to moods. And this baby, we didn't think we could have more, so this will be real hard on her. I'd rather not tell her until we know for sure. Let her get a little stronger first."

"I understand. Certainly," the doctor said.

"When can we see her?" Daddy asked.

"You can go in for a few minutes now. Then you both can come back tomorrow during visiting hours."

"I want to see Mama, too!" I jumped off the sofa and tugged on Daddy's sleeve.

My father was firm. His large hands picked me up and sat me back on the sofa. "Tomorrow I'll bring you to see Mama. I promise. For now, Ellie, you'll sit right here until I return."

There was no point in arguing. Sometimes *no* means *maybe*, but not this time. Daddy was seldom firm with me, but when he used that tone of voice and stared at me without blinking, I knew he would not budge.

I sniffed back tears, folded my hands in my lap, and watched Daddy disappear down the long hall.

Waiting alone was almost as bad as the ambulance ride. The hospital scared me. The old man coughed, pulled a wadded bandanna from his coat pocket and spat into it. The nurse drifted up and down the hall. A woman came in holding a baby with blisters on its fat legs. The baby screamed so loud it made a dull drum sound inside my head. I thought about how Mama sometimes curled up on the sofa with her hands pressing her temples when her migraines came.

The worst part about the hospital was the smells, a mixture of medicines and sour milk and bleach. My nose wrinkled.

I thought about my green chick, how I'd dropped him on the floor. *Where is he now?* I wondered. *Walking on the cool kitchen floor, or alone in a dark corner with the smell of scorched stew burning his small lungs?* I felt bad for him, left alone and hungry on his first night in a new place. When we went home, I'd fix him something warm to eat, and I'd give him clean bedding.

I wanted this awful day to disappear. I wanted to go back to the day before, when Mama was home and well. I didn't want to be in this bad place. I didn't want to be alone.

I slipped my hand into my pocket to rub the soft rabbit's foot Mary Roberts gave me for my tenth birthday. "It's for luck," Mary had said as she pressed the furry foot into my hand. "You rub it and make wishes." I felt bad that a rabbit was left to hop on three feet just for me, but I needed all the luck I could get.

Sitting on the hospital sofa, I closed my eyes and grasped the rabbit's foot. Then I prayed, "Please God, let Mama live, and let my baby brother or sister live. I will be good forever, I promise. I won't make fun of the blind man on Gale Street. I won't touch myself down there anymore. I'll give back the blue marble I stole from J. D. Wilson. And I will always stay home to fetch onions for my mother. I will cook, sew, and wear dresses like a regular girl, so I can grow up to be a good wife like Mama. Amen."

After what seemed like a long time, Daddy returned to the waiting room. He hugged me and told me not to worry, but his furrowed brow said he was worried himself. He kissed my cheek and said, "That's from Mama."

My throat felt raw and tight, and I locked my arms around Daddy's waist and sobbed into his shirt.

"Don't cry, angel. The doctor gave Mama something for pain and she will sleep all night. We'll come back to visit her tomorrow. You'll see. Everything will be fine."

With Daddy's arms around me, I believed everything would.

Since we hadn't eaten supper, Daddy bought us grilled cheese sandwiches in the hospital cafeteria. Mine tasted like rubber, not warm and buttery like the ones Mama made. But I remembered my promises to God. I ate the sandwich, washed it down with a bottle of soda, and said it tasted good.

Afterwards, we rode in a yellow cab to our house on Grace Street. Through the cab windows, I watched dark branches that reached up into an even darker sky.

I found my little green chick huddled in a corner, his tiny feet tangled in cobwebs. I scooped him up and held him close, whispering in his ear. "Poor baby. I'm sorry for leaving you, little one."

"He must be hungry," Daddy said.

I nodded and held the chick close to my chest. "And cold."

Daddy mixed cornmeal and warm water in a bowl. While the corn mash cooled, he used pliers to bend a teaspoon, making a little funnel.

After touching the mixture to make sure the temperature was just right, I spooned the cereal into his small beak. He gobbled down three spoonfuls, stretching his thin neck to swallow more.

With my chick fed and fresh paper placed in the bottom of his box, Daddy carried us to my bed. He pulled off my shoes and socks, lowered me onto my mattress, and tucked the covers under my chin. I cradled the box with my tiny chick inside, placing one hand inside the box to warm his small body. The evenings this time of year were cool, and my little chick mustn't get chilled.

"I'll turn up the furnace before I go to sleep," Daddy promised. He sat next to me on the edge of my bed, his body strong and warm beside mine. His rough, wide hand stroked my hair until I drifted to sleep.

The night was filled with bad dreams. In them, Mama's face was streaked with blood and the hospital nurse kept circling the room, saying, "Would you like to color the wicked stepmother? Would you like to color Snow White?"

I was glad when the warm sun on my face woke me. I blinked my eyes. My lids felt thick and sore, as if salt had been rubbed in them. When I sat up in bed and pulled away my covers, I saw I was still wearing my jeans and red sweater. I tasted what was left of the grilled cheese in my mouth. The hospital and bad dreams came back to me.

I wanted Daddy.

Grabbing my box with the chick inside, I hurried across the floor. As I opened my bedroom door, a girl's voice rose from the kitchen.

FOUR

TOMATO GIRL

D ADDY LAUGHING. A girl's voice. Sounds that were familiar, but so unexpected. Then I remembered the voice. It
belonged to the tomato girl. She and my father were in the kitchen.
Why was she here? She'd never been to our house before.

I crept downstairs and tried to be invisible behind the railing.

The two of them stood at the sink, making coffee. Daddy
spooned dark beans into the grinder while the tomato girl turned
the handle to crush them. He teased her, spooning the beans faster
than she could grind. I watched her scoop spilled beans into her
hand and shove them deep inside my father's pants pocket.

"Daddy?" I called from the bottom step. Being invisible sometimes means seeing things you don't want to see.

When he heard my voice, my father stopped laughing and
pushed the girl's hand away. "Ellie, you remember Tess, don't
you?" Daddy quickly filled a glass with water at the sink, then
drank it.

The tomato girl smiled at me. "Hello," she said, her voice so
small and airy it made me think of butterflies and garden fairies.

I nodded. I'd arranged her produce in bins at Daddy's store. Tomatoes and sometimes yellow squash, ears of corn, a few pumpkins. I never called her Tess, though; I knew her only as the tomato girl. She usually came in the mornings, while I was in school, but I'd seen her a few times on Saturdays. Even without seeing her, I always knew when she'd been to the store, because her baskets would be filled with tomatoes as red as her lips. Each time she visited, her honeysuckle perfume lingered behind, filling the store. Sometimes, even the gloves and paintbrushes smelled like honeysuckle.

Because I'd seen it, I knew that when the tomato girl came to the store, Daddy ran out to open the truck door for her. He held her hand while she stepped down, easing her onto the asphalt as if she were a princess. He hauled in her produce and placed it near the front store windows, checking to see if she was pleased with how he'd arranged the baskets. He hovered over her as if she belonged to him. Sometimes Daddy took her by the arm and led her to the back office to pay her for her goods. If there were no customers, he might lock the door, and they'd stay in the room a long time. Occasionally I'd hear them laugh, but mostly, they were quiet. I figured Daddy gave her special attention because of her hard life and her infirmity. People talked about it, but no one ever told me the details. They only shook their heads and said something like, "That child has had a time of it." I understood how Daddy could feel sorry for her, but I still never really liked her. I resented the easy way she leaned into him, and how his face became happy when he saw her.

One Saturday a few weeks ago, as the tomato girl was leaving, Daddy carried out the lumber she'd bought for her father's chicken house. Daddy had told me to refill the jars of penny candy and arrange the new shipment of yardsticks, but before I even got started, the telephone rang and I had to go to the front of the store to answer it. Someone wanted the price of a gallon of oyster-white paint, which I knew would be listed in the special catalog Daddy kept on a hook by the window.

That's when I saw what my eyes weren't meant to see. They were both inside the truck, and Daddy lit a cigarette, then placed it between Tess's lips. She drew on the cigarette, then leaned close to him, her mouth only inches from his neck. Very slowly, she blew little smoke kisses against my father's neck.

I felt a kind of panic run through my body as I stared, not accepting what I'd seen. Daddy's neck didn't belong to her. He belonged to Mama. And to me. Why didn't he make her stop?

After she drove away, Daddy returned to the store, whistling when he came inside. Then he noticed me by the front window, and he stopped. He knew I'd seen them.

I kept staring at the spot where her truck had been, deafened by a roaring in my ears.

When Daddy called my name a second time, I turned toward him. His face took on a worried look, his eyebrows coming together in one tight line. He squeezed my hands in his and warned me not to tell Mama. "You keep quiet about this, Ellie, and when the Easter chicks come, you can choose one for your very own."

I didn't want to keep Daddy's secret, but it seemed the only thing to do. I knew if I told Mama, she'd get upset and maybe try to leave Daddy or even hurt him. She might even hurt herself. Keeping the secret seemed the right thing. And I did want that chick.

I looked around the kitchen and held the box with my chick inside close to my chest. We almost never had visitors in the house because of Mama's moods. It was impossible to predict when Mama might do or say something that might frighten or shock someone, so Daddy mostly kept people away. I could probably count on one hand the folks who came to our house to visit in any regular way. Daddy always told folks that Mama wasn't well, and not up for much activity or visitors. Sometimes that made for a very lonely house.

So it felt strange seeing the tomato girl in our kitchen, wearing Mama's apron as if it were as ordinary as toast for her to be here. Turning back to the sink, she wet Mama's sponge and cleaned the stove where stains darkened the oven door.

I felt confused. How did the tomato girl get here? And why was she in Mama's kitchen, laughing with Daddy? Why were her thin fingers touching Mama's things as if they were her own? She'd never been here before, yet she acted as if this were her home.

And then I thought, *Isn't this what happens when your mama dies?* I'd read about this in many fairy tales. A new woman moves into your home and takes your mother's place, and she is very mean to you because you are not her child. She makes you wear hand-me-downs and work your fingers to the bone. Sometimes, you lose your father, or at least your father's love. Then one day, you are sent away, banished to another place entirely.

But the tomato girl was too young and too pretty to be an evil stepmother. And if Mama had died, why was Daddy laughing?

Seeing the confusion on my face, Daddy placed his hands on my shoulders and guided me to a chair. "Let's leave the chick here for a minute," he said. He took the box from my hands and set it on the table.

While Daddy talked to me, Tess knelt on the floor and scrubbed away the brown stains. Her skirt slid up her legs as she moved, but she didn't try to pull it down. The harder she scrubbed, the higher her skirt rose on her thighs. Didn't she know we could see her bare legs?

"Tess is going to be staying here with us for awhile, to help out," he explained.

"Is Mama dead?" I asked. Tears filled my eyes.

"Of course not," Daddy insisted. "Mama will be fine. And after you eat breakfast and get dressed, I'm taking you to see her, just like I promised. But we'll need some help around here while your mother recovers, and Tess kindly agreed to stay and pitch in."

"But *I'm* supposed to help Mama. I promised. And if I break my promise, God will let Mama and the baby die!" It felt all wrong to me, that someone else would do Mama's work when I was meant to do it. I was supposed to make up for my mistake. I hoped God might overlook my selfish ways if I worked hard and helped Mama.

My father squeezed my hands and smiled. "Don't worry. There's plenty to do around here. Dishes to wash, floors to sweep, laundry, cooking. Tess will see that you help, too. Now listen to me, nothing's going to happen to your mother, Ellie. I swear to you. And the baby, well, the doctor said we will have to wait and see, but if the baby doesn't make it, it isn't your fault. It's because your mother fell."

I couldn't tell Daddy that Mama's fall was my fault. If I'd only taken a minute to walk down the stairs and fetch an onion from the bin by the door, my mother would be home making oatmeal or bacon for breakfast. The tomato girl would not be in our house scrubbing my mother's kitchen floor.

"Now how about some breakfast?" Daddy offered. He poured cereal and milk into my morning bowl and handed me a spoon. Daddy sometimes boiled hot dogs for supper to give Mama a break, but he never cooked breakfast.

I was hungry, and the cereal and cold milk tasted good. Daddy let me scoop on all the sugar I wanted. I swallowed gulps of sweet milk to wash away the bad grilled-cheese taste that still lingered in my mouth. I tried to pretend that Mama was in the next room sewing, or out in the yard weeding her flowers.

Daddy sat next to me while I ate. He opened the newspaper and began to read, but I could tell he was pretending. His eyes drifted to the girl on the floor, to the back of her legs, where the edge of her white panties showed.

FIVE

KOTEX

WHILE DADDY WATCHED the tomato girl, I finished my cereal, giving a pale pink Froot Loop softened with milk to my chick.

"All done," I said, showing Daddy my empty bowl. I'd eaten all my cereal and drank the last drop of sugary milk.

Any other Monday, I'd be getting ready for school, rushing upstairs to brush my teeth and trying to get the barrette in my hair straight, but Daddy had said last night that I could play hooky just this once. He'd promised to take me to the hospital so I could see with my own eyes that Mama was alive. I needed to hear for myself that she wasn't angry at me, that she still loved me even though her fall down the basement steps was my fault. What if her baby died? Would she tell Daddy I was to blame? If Daddy knew, would he make me give back my chick? My mind swarmed with worries.

Daddy looked at me with a pleased smile. He didn't know how selfish I could be. He reached across the table and wiped the milk from my lips. "Good. Well, let's get ready to go. I need to shave and change my shirt. Why don't you take Tess upstairs? She'll be sharing your room. You can show her where to put her things."

I nodded and picked up my chick.

The tomato girl followed me upstairs.

"I'll bring Tess's suitcases up in a minute," Daddy called from downstairs. I heard water running and figured he must be rinsing out his coffee cup or my cereal bowl.

"You won't mind sharing your room with me, will you?" Tess asked.

I shook my head and walked up the last few steps. I didn't know how I felt about sharing my room. It could be fun, like a sleepover, but not if she upset Mama or made Daddy act like a fool.

The small mirror at the end of the hall reflected Tess's pale face and blonde hair. She looked delicate, like a fine lace doily.

If I'd known I was going to have company, I'd have cleaned my room. My dirty clothes spilled over the edge of my laundry basket and onto the floor. My bed was unmade, the covers shoved up against the footboard. Candy wrappers covered the table beside my bed. Atomic FireBalls and Tootsie Rolls filled a jar next to my reading lamp.

I placed my chick on the bed and pulled the yellow bedspread over the sheet, so at least it didn't droop on the floor. As I shoved the candy papers into the wastepaper basket, I felt thankful that Daddy had painted the walls buttercup yellow a few months earlier. With the new gingham curtains Mama sewed for me, my room looked nice even with the mess. Mama wasn't real strict about things like making the bed, picking up clothes, and dusting furniture. I started to apologize, but I decided not to, hoping maybe Tess wouldn't notice the mess if I didn't mention it.

"The colors are really nice," she said, looking at the yellow walls.

"Daddy painted the room for me."

"Your daddy is a talented man. I bet there's nothing he can't fix or do." She said this with so much pride it made me feel proud of my father, too. Tess touched the wall, lightly, almost like a caress. She smiled to herself as if she had a secret.

Just then Daddy walked through the partially opened door. "Making a delivery," he said as he set two suitcases beside my bed. "I'll leave you girls alone to get to know each other." He shoved his hands inside his pockets as if he didn't know what to do with them. "I'll go shave."

Tess stood in the middle of the room and twirled a strand of her hair in her fingers as she watched Daddy leave. I felt like snapping my fingers in front of her face.

Instead, I went into the bathroom to mix water with the cornmeal Daddy had left for my chick last night. The tap water was hot enough to make a soft gruel. Satisfied I'd stirred away all the powdery lumps, I returned to my bed and fed my chick while Tess unpacked her larger suitcase.

No one had ever shared my room with me. Mama sometimes had bad dreams and wandered in my room to sleep beside me, but that was different. Those were fretful nights with Mama clinging to me, her fingers digging my skin.

It looked like Tess must have planned to stay awhile. She'd brought everything a girl could need. She pulled out jeans and cutoffs, a short denim skirt, and three dresses. She hung them in the closet beside mine. Her bras and panties went inside the dresser drawers with my socks and leotards, her pink nightgown on the hook on my door. She placed a stack of paperbacks, drawing pad, and photo album on the nightstand by my bed.

Tess had a second, smaller suitcase for makeup and perfumes. I'd seen these cases in the Sears catalog, but didn't know anyone who had one. "You can borrow this whenever you want," she said.

"I can?" At first I thought she meant the suitcase itself, then realized she meant the items inside.

She nodded. Tess turned the suitcase over on my bed, spilling tubes of lipsticks, a powder compact, plastic barrettes, silver loop earrings, hair combs with silk daisies glued to them, a bead bracelet, spray bottles of perfume, and pots of skin cream.

"I love makeup," she said, sitting next to me on the bed. "I want to go to cosmetology school one day, or maybe sell Avon door to door. These are samples," she explained as she folded her thin legs under her. "They give you these so you can try the shades at home, and when the Avon lady comes back, you tell her you want a full-sized tube of the color you liked best."

I watched Tess open the compact and trace her mouth with red lipstick.

"Do you think I'm pretty?" she asked.

I nodded. She had blue-green eyes and long, pale blonde hair, almost as white as a winter moon. Her red mouth stood out like a summer poppy against her fair skin. She didn't have a single freckle or mole on her face, just a tiny scar above her left eye. Without thinking, I reached out to touch it. "What happened here?" I pulled my hand away, remembering it was rude to be nosy.

Tess ran her finger along the scar. "I fall sometimes on account of my epilepsy. I hit the edge of the coffee table a couple years ago. Left a scar."

"Does it hurt?"

"Of course not, it healed up a week or so after I fell." Tess put her compact back on the bed and tucked her hair behind her ears.

"No, I don't mean the scar. I mean epilepsy. Does that hurt?" I knew epilepsy was some sort of disease, but I'd never known anyone before who had it.

Tess didn't answer right away. She looked straight ahead as if the answer hung in midair. "No, I can't say epilepsy hurts so much. Sometimes I have a headache afterwards, or bumps and bruises from the falls. Those hurt. But the seizures don't hurt. It feels sort of like falling in a dream, or floating too long in water, and then it feels like nothing at all. Mostly it's a scary thing because I never know when a seizure might happen, and I don't like to be around people when it does. It's embarrassing to wake up on the floor and know that strangers have seen me like that."

I nodded. That's how I feel every time I have to work math equations on the blackboard with the rest of the class watching me get the answer wrong. Sometimes the backs of my legs feel like they'll collapse and my hands shake so hard my numbers look squiggly. I wondered if solving too many equations could one day bring on a seizure. Maybe that's what caused epilepsy in the first place, just being so nervous so long you can't stand on your own two feet.

"It's okay if you have a seizure around me, Tess. I won't mind." I patted her arm. Tess looked as fragile as porcelain. Part of me wanted to take care of her and make sure she didn't break. Another part of me wanted her nowhere near our house.

"I better finish unpacking." Tess shoved her cosmetics and toiletries into a pile in the middle of my bed.

She turned over a pink and white box. The letters *K-O-T-E-X* were printed on the front of the box.

"You can borrow these, too, if you need one," she said.

I knew what they were for, but not how to use them. "I don't need one." The idea made me press my legs together tight.

"No, not yet. But you will when you're a little older, and when you do, you'll have one."

I remembered a sixth-grade girl on the bus who stood up one day and everybody had laughed at the rust-colored stain on the back of her pink dress. "You shit your pants," the boys yelled. But Mary Roberts, who knows about these matters, whispered in my ear, "It's blood, not shit. My mother says it's the curse. It's written in the Bible. It only happens to women."

Mama hadn't told me much about the bleeding curse. When I asked her, she said it was like wearing a bra, that the time for those things would come. "Mary Roberts shouldn't be telling you things she knows nothing about," she had said, and since the subject seemed to upset Mama, I didn't bring it up again.

But now, with Tess, I had a chance to find out something that even Mary Roberts didn't know. "How do they work?" I asked.

"Well, every month, a woman bleeds a few days, and these are like sponges that soak up the blood."

"Does it hurt like a cut?" It sounded awful. I pressed my legs together even tighter. Maybe I didn't want to know more.

"Only a little, up here," she said. She pulled up her shirt and placed my hand on her warm belly. "But not where the blood comes out. That doesn't hurt."

I nodded like I understood.

"Okay, then I'll keep one." I tried to sound brave and curious.

"Sure." Tess opened the box and pulled out a cigar-shaped tube wrapped in white paper.

"Thanks, Tess." I wrapped my fingers around the paper and hoped my moist palms wouldn't ruin it. Mama might not want me to have it, and I wasn't sure how much Daddy knew about women things. I'd have to hide it.

"Do you have a special boy at school?" Tess asked, her voice interrupting my thoughts.

"No! Yuck! Boys are gross. Although there is one nice boy, Michael Sullivan. He has red hair and eyes so blue you almost wouldn't believe he could see through them. The first time I saw them, I thought he was blind. That's just how blue they are. He carried my books from the library once, and then said he'd carve our names in a tree if I let him kiss me." I felt myself blush as I spoke.

Tess smiled and lowered her voice. "So did you? Did you let him kiss you?

He was twelve, a whole year older than me, and might tell his friends if I kissed the wrong way. "No."

"Why not?"

"I don't know how." I looked at the floor, suddenly feeling sorry I'd said so much. What if Tess told Daddy?

Tess must have read my mind. "Don't worry, I won't tell. We can keep secrets, yes? Besides, when I was your age, I used to practice kissing."

"You did?" I thought about the smoke kisses she'd blown on Daddy's neck, how her lips had formed a perfect red *o*.

"Yes, mostly in the mirror, but there was an older girl who used to live next door to us and she gave me kissing lessons."

I tried to imagine kissing Mary Roberts, but somehow, it just didn't fit. Mary would surely stand with her hands on her hips explaining that girls are not supposed to kiss each other. If there was anything in the Bible against girls kissing girls, Mrs. Roberts would have covered it.

"Want me to show you?" Tess asked.

"Well, maybe someday. Not today," I whispered.

"Suit yourself. Just remember, you need the right shade of lipstick. Mulberry Pink is perfect, I think." Tess opened a small white sample tube and told me to purse my lips.

I sat back on the bed and did my best to follow her directions. Holding still was hard. My mouth twitched as she colored my lips.

"When you kiss, you always close your eyes. You never kiss with your eyes open. That's a very important rule. Go ahead, close them."

I closed my eyes tight. Why was I listening to her? I hardly knew Tess, and part of me didn't even like her. Part of me hated the way she looked at Daddy, and the way he looked at her. But she had the kind of voice that made a person want to follow. Before I knew it, I felt my eyes warm behind closed lids. Would I see bright lights and swirling colors like I did when I pressed my thumbs against my eyes?

The mattress shifted a little as Tess leaned forward. Her breath smelled like coffee and peppermint.

"Now, open your mouth."

Nervous and unsure, I did as she said. I felt my lower jaw drop and knew right away I had opened too wide.

Tess sighed. "No, more like half-opened. Pucker up your lips like you do to blow bubbles."

I closed my mouth partway and felt my face go warm again. I felt suddenly silly and ashamed.

Was I supposed to take a deep breath? I wanted to ask, but everything happened too fast. I smelled honeysuckle perfume, felt her breath, moist and delicate against my face, and in an instant broken by only the sound of breathing, Tess's lips pressed mine, warm and soft like taffy. Butterflies stirred inside my stomach, and then their lace wings fluttered inside my throat. I could feel them fly through the pores in my skin and circle my head.

Tess's mouth pulled away from mine. "There," she said. "How was that?"

Finally, I remembered to breathe. I opened my eyes. The room blurred before coming back into focus. My face grew warmer still. I felt grown up and two years old at the same time. Since I didn't know what to say, I smiled and changed the subject. "I have to clean up my chick now before Daddy is ready to go."

"Did you like your kiss?" Tess asked, her voice lifted in a curious and light way.

I couldn't answer. I felt small and shy as I climbed off my bed with my chick in one hand and Kotex in the other. This much I knew for certain: I would never be able to kiss Michael Sullivan and remain standing on two feet. Kissing a boy, I felt sure, would bring on something worse than epilepsy.

My third dresser drawer held a shoebox half-filled with popsicle sticks I was keeping to make a birdhouse. Mary Roberts and I had been saving them for nearly six months and would soon have enough. Scooping the sticks to one end, I buried the Kotex and closed the drawer.

At the bathroom sink, I wet the corner of a cloth and wiped my chick's face and beak clean. I looked in the mirror and pursed my lips. Did I look any different now, having kissed a girl? I strained to see any difference, but noticed only the pink color in my cheeks where I'd blushed. I wondered what kissing a boy might really feel like. Would it taste and feel the same, or like something else entirely?

I wondered if Tess had ever kissed a boy.

• • •

DADDY CALLED TO US from across the hall to hurry up, it was almost time to go to the hospital.

Tess helped me get ready. She pulled my lime green dress from the closet, slipped it over my head, and buttoned the three back buttons. She held my saddle shoes while I pulled on clean socks and rolled them down around my ankles to let the lace trim show.

"Are you coming to see Mama, too?" I hoped she would say no. Mama would not want to see her.

"No, sweet. Your daddy wants me to mind the store while the two of you go to the hospital." Tess sat beside me on the bed while I tied my shoes.

"Will you be sure to feed the chicks and turn on their heating lamp?" They should have been fed by now already, and would be scared their first day in a new place. "And don't forget the ones in the back office. They didn't eat on their own and need to be fed."

"Yes, of course. Want me to keep your chick, too?"

"No, I'm taking him to show Mama," I explained. "If Daddy will let me."

Tess frowned, then said, "Well, okay. Sure. I understand." She picked up her brush and ran it through my hair. "By the way, what's your chick's name?"

"I haven't named him yet. My mother is good with names. I was going to let her pick one, but then she fell."

"Well, I'm pretty good at names, too."

"You are?"

"Yes. When I have a baby, I'm going to name it Vanessa if it's a girl, and Rupert if it's a boy. Don't you think those are good names?"

I nuzzled my nameless chick. "Rupert is Daddy's name."

Tess smiled. "Yes, I know."

SIX

HOSPITAL

D ADDY TOLD ME to wait for the cab on the front porch.
He wanted to talk to Tess before we left for the hospital.
Tess was supposed to finish the breakfast dishes, then walk to the
store to tend to the chicks and mind the cash register while we
visited Mama at the hospital. He'd already gone over this twice
with her before he called for the cab. Why did he need to talk
to her again? I started to complain, but then remembered my
promise to stop being selfish. All that mattered was to see Mama
well and for her baby to live. I said, "Yes, sir," and did as Daddy
told me.

Rather than sitting down and risk messing up my dress, I
hopped on one foot then the other, up and down the length of
the porch.

Sheriff Rhodes drove by in his car and waved. His dog, Bubba,
rode with his head hanging out the window, and I imagined
myself on a police chase, hunting down famous bank robbers.
I'd wear a big white hat and have rhinestones on my boots and
holster. Mary says my idea of deputy clothes sounds more like a
cowgirl outfit, but that's how I'd like it. What's the use in make-
believe if it can't be the way you want it?

I'd worn the sheriff's hat a few times when he came to visit Mama for drawing lessons. After leaving his wide-brimmed hat on the table, he'd crack his knuckles, then sit at Mama's easel with charcoal sticks in his hand. For a man who handled criminals, you'd never guess how blank paper and charcoal made him so nervous. His brow shone with sweat and he blushed as Mama leaned over him. "The secret is to capture the shape and the shadows," she'd explained as she put her hand over his to guide the charcoal's path.

A car horn broke my thoughts, and I turned as the yellow cab pulled up in front of our house. I tapped on our door to let Daddy know it was time to leave. He cracked the door and told me to go ahead and wait in the cab, that he would be out in a minute. His face looked red and glossy they way it did at the store when he'd lifted a lot of boxes.

I did as Daddy said. "My father will be out in a minute," I told the cab driver. He held a fat cigar between his lips and grunted. The cigar smoke burned my nose and didn't smell sweet like Mr. Morgan's cigarettes. I didn't like the tilted way the cab driver looked at me in the rearview mirror, lids too heavy over his deep-set eyes. With my thumb in my mouth, I chewed the end of my fingernail and turned toward the window. Why was Daddy taking so long?

Finally the front door opened. Daddy walked out. Just as he stepped off the porch, Tess ran to him and grabbed his arm. She was giggling and trying to pull him back inside, tugging on his sleeve. Daddy laughed and shook his head as he peeled her fingers from his arm.

Before opening the cab's rear door, Daddy turned and blew her a kiss. That made me feel strange inside, but I didn't quite know why. It was only a friendly thing, but still it felt wrong. I looked quickly to see if the cab driver had seen the kiss, but he puffed his cigar and stared straight ahead, so I didn't think so.

Tess stood on the porch and waved. She looked small against

our house. A pair of crows settled on the porch railing near her, their blue-black wings folded at their sides. I'd never seen crows, or any birds, perch so close to someone.

The inside of the cab felt safe with Daddy beside me. As we rode to the hospital, I rested my head in the crook of his arm. He smelled clean, like Old Spice and Colgate. He had dressed in his good clothes, the gray trousers and white shirt he usually wore to church. Sweat circles had formed under his arms, but those would fade by the time we reached the hospital. Daddy pulled out his handkerchief and dabbed his forehead. "A warm day," he said to the cab driver.

Mama would be pleased to see him dressed up. She likes nice things, and is sometimes disappointed with the plain things in her life. I've heard Mama say there is nothing more disappointing than an ordinary life, but I don't know. Sometimes an ordinary life is what I want most in the world.

I buried my face in Daddy's shirt and played with the button-hole on his sleeve. "You lost your button, Daddy."

He looked at his sleeve. "So I have. Guess I'll need to leave this with my little seamstress." He winked at me.

I smiled. "I bet I have a button that will match just right."

A few years ago, my parents gave me a sewing basket, just like Mama's, only smaller, filled with buttons, needles, and spools of thread. Mama had shown me how to thread the needle and tie a knot. I'd practiced until I'd gotten it right, and eventually I'd learned how to sew on buttons and even repair simple hems.

After I'd sewn on a button, Daddy would dig into his pocket and pull out a shiny coin to pay for my work, saying, "This is for my little seamstress."

I kept the coins in a glass jar under my bed. It was my sewing money, I'd told Mary Roberts, holding the half-filled jar in my hands. I had plans for my sewing money, but never could settle on just one idea for long. Sometimes, a new red record player like the one in the window at Montgomery Ward's topped my list. Other times I wanted a nice set of oil paints, or a stack of hardback books that wouldn't have to go back to the library because they were mine to keep.

Another jar held the buttons I collected to sew on Daddy's clothes. After sweeping the floors in the store, I checked the dustbin for any lost buttons. When we went to church, I searched the pews. In the market, I checked shelves near the cigarettes and dirty magazines where men most often lost their buttons.

Sewing Daddy's shirt was a job I loved almost as much as tending the Easter chicks. When I held his shirt in my hand, I believed Daddy was mine for keeps.

THE CAB PULLED in front of the hospital entrance and while Daddy paid the driver, I counted six floors of windows. Babies were born on the second floor. I knew this because we'd sent a card to my third-grade teacher when her son was born. Fifth floor was for people who hurt themselves on purpose, which I knew because many times Daddy had reminded Mama that she didn't want to end up there. I didn't know which floor was for people who fell down basement steps, but I hoped Mama was on the first floor so I wouldn't have to go too high up to see her.

I'd been born inside this hospital, but that was too far back for me to remember. I'd been back there at age three to have stitches in my chin after falling against a saw in Daddy's toolshed. I don't remember the accident, only Daddy carrying me with a towel pressed to my face and the bright light in my eyes when the doctor stitched my cut. Daddy had been angry at Mama for letting me play in his shed. After we came home, he'd put a big padlock on the door and then sat out on the front porch, drinking so many beers he stumbled when he stood to come inside.

AS MUCH AS I wanted to see Mama, the hospital scared me. Daddy must have sensed how nervous I felt. He held my hand as we walked toward the large glass doors, which opened like magic when we stepped on the black mat in front of them.

While Daddy held one hand, I carried my pocketbook in the other, my sleeping chick tucked inside. I whispered to him to stay quiet so Mama would be surprised. I hoped that bringing him wouldn't get me in trouble. This morning, Daddy had said it was against hospital rules for animals to visit, but Tess found my straw purse in the closet and told him, "Here, the chick will be able to breathe in this, and no one will ask to see inside a girl's purse." Daddy threw up his hands, which meant Tess and I had won.

Just inside the door, Daddy stopped in the lobby and knelt in front of me. "Ellie, I don't want you to talk about the baby around your mother."

"Why?" I didn't understand Daddy's serious face or why he didn't want me to talk about Mama's new baby. "If she thinks about the baby, maybe that will make her get well faster."

"But the doctor thinks Mama's baby might not live, and that will make her very, very sad. Just because the baby is all right now doesn't mean that it's out of the woods yet. Remember when Nana and Grandpa died, how Mama's sad mood came on?"

I nodded. I had been only five when it happened, but I remembered, and I knew I'd never forget.

WE'D BEEN EATING supper when the telephone rang. Mama answered the phone and then only listened. When she hung up the phone, she screamed and dug her fingernails into her face, leaving red trails. Daddy had to hold her down on the floor to make her stop, and she kicked and screamed, biting his hand so hard blood came.

I remember I hid in the corner. Mama was scarier than any bad dream I'd ever had.

Daddy had called for a doctor to come and give Mama a shot to make her sleep. This was before he started giving her shots himself. Maybe it's where he got the idea.

The next day, Mama walked around the house mumbling to herself, a wad of tissue clutched in her hands.

Daddy and I drove her to the train station so she could go to the funeral in Georgia. I asked Daddy why he and I didn't go, too, and he said something about my uncles not being on speaking terms with him. We never visited them and they never came to Virginia, and I don't remember ever seeing a Christmas card from them. Daddy said some people carry grudges to their graves.

A week later Mama came home wearing a black dress that she wouldn't take off. She didn't want to talk or eat or play. That's when I started going to the store with my father, or staying at Mary Roberts's house.

One day we came home and found Mama sprawled on the kitchen floor, a bag of flour in her lap and a tablespoon in her hand. Mama was spooning flour into her mouth, and with each scoop, dough clumps stuck to her lips where the flour mixed with her spit.

The doctor came back. This time he brought a nurse and a colored man who made Mama get into the back of their car. They took her away, and I didn't see Mama for months.

She wrote me, printing her letters so I could read them. She told me how sorry she was, and said that losing a mother and a father was very hard. She said I would someday know for myself, and then I would forgive her.

Just before she came home, Mama wrote and told me how wonderful things were going to be. How she would sew me beautiful dresses and make angel cookies. We'd cut paper dolls from the Sears catalog, and at night, take our thick blankets and sleep under the stars.

We did do all those things. But only for a little while.

THE HOSPITAL SEEMED to have grown larger since last night. Or maybe Daddy's warning made me feel small.

"I won't say anything about the baby," I promised.

"And let me tell your mother about Tess," Daddy added as he took my hand again and led me deeper into the hospital.

We passed through the waiting room where I'd sat last night. I was glad to see that the old man was gone, and a fat lady squeezed into a green dress had taken his place. The bad ammonia smell hadn't gone away though.

At the nurse's station, we stopped to find out which room was my mother's. "Julia Sanders is in 311," the nurse said.

"How was she last night?" Daddy asked.

"You'll have to check with the nurse on the third floor."

WHEN WE REACHED the nurse's station, Daddy stopped and asked about Mama's condition.

"Let me check her chart," the nurse answered. She reached for a metal clipboard and read a few notes. "Mrs. Sanders seems to have slept well and her vitals are all good. No change in her status. Appears to be doing quite well."

The nurse looked up to see if Daddy had another question.

"And the baby?" he asked.

"No change."

"Thank you," Daddy said, and took me by the hand.

"No change is good, isn't it, Daddy?"

"Yes," Daddy said without looking at me.

We found room 311 and Daddy pushed the dark door open, a little at first, then wider.

"Good morning," he said, nudging me toward Mama.

She looked small and thin in the big metal bed. Fragile, too. Her skin was so white. Her brown hair spread out like a fan on the pillow.

When she saw me, she smiled. She put her elbows behind her and tried to sit, but then winced.

"Should I get the nurse, Julia?" Daddy asked, rushing to her side.

"No, no, I'll be fine," she insisted, motioning him to sit in the overstuffed chair beside her bed. Mama wore a faded floral-print hospital gown with blue piping around the neck. A gauze bandage covered the stitches on her forehead. Brown dots of iodine seeped through the bandage so that it looked almost like a tea bag pasted to her skin. A blue-black bruise darkened the right side of Mama's face.

I stepped closer to the bed, lay my purse on the blanket, and reached out to touch her bruise. It was an ugly, dark stain on her pale skin. I wanted to wash it away. "Does it hurt, Mama?"

She took my hand between hers and rubbed it the way she did on cold days to make the blood flow. "Only a little."

I pulled Mama's smooth hands to my lips and kissed them. They had a strange lemon smell, almost like cough drops. I wrinkled my nose.

"I know, it smells awful," Mama said. "I asked the nurse for hand lotion and she brought this horrible cream." She turned to my father, and added, "Rupert, do you think you could bring a gown from home, and some Jergens?"

"Of course. I should have thought of that myself, that you'd be more comfortable with some of your own things. I'm sorry."

"No need to be sorry. It's been a difficult time."

"I brought something from home," I whispered to my mother.

"You did?" Mama's eyes widened in surprise.

I unhooked my purse lid and lifted my chick for her to see.

"Let me take a closer look," she said. Mama patted the mattress, motioning me to sit beside her.

I climbed onto the edge of the bed, careful not to hurt her, and placed my green chick in her hands.

Mama cupped her palms around the fluffy chick and smiled. "Oh, Ellie, he's adorable! What an unusual green color. Did you name him?"

I nodded. "Jellybean."

"That's an interesting name . . ."

"Tess thought of it. She knows good names."

"Tess?" My mother's thin eyebrows rose, making small arrows across her forehead.

"Tess is Daddy's tomato girl." I smacked my hand over my mouth. I wasn't supposed to tell.

"Isn't she Mason Reed's girl, the one who has epilepsy?" she asked my father.

"Well, yes, she has epilepsy, Julia," Daddy said, shifting in his chair. "But she hasn't had an episode in months. Doctor's got her on some new medicine. She'll be a big help to you, cleaning up around the house, cooking. The doctor said you're not supposed to do any lifting or bending."

"I know that, Rupert, but I don't think a teenage girl with her own infirmity is what the doctor had in mind." The muscles along the edge of Mama's jawline stiffened, making the veins in her neck rise. I watched Jellybean in her hands.

"Julia, there's no need to get upset. Just trust me on this. Tess will work out fine."

Mama didn't answer. Her lips narrowed into a straight line.

Jellybean peeped. Mama's hands were too tight around him.

I nudged my chick's small body from Mama's tight fingers and put him my back inside my purse.

The rest of the visit with Mama felt as heavy and slow as a sermon. No one said another word about Tess, but her presence hung in the air like smoke you couldn't fan away.

Daddy worked the crossword puzzle from the newspaper and talked with Mama about the landscaping company opening up just outside of town. "They placed quite an order last week," he said, and gave Mama details about the wheelbarrows, levels, spades, and spools of twine he'd sold.

I stood by the bed and combed Mama's long hair. Little flecks of blood had dried on her scalp and peppered her pillow.

We stayed with Mama until her tray came, a bowl of pot roast, mashed potatoes, and oily green beans. We kissed her good-bye, first Daddy, then me. As much as I hated the hospital and wanted to leave, I would have done anything to stay with Mama. I wanted to sit by her side and spoon smooth mashed potatoes into her mouth. I wanted to hold the milk carton to her lips and urge her to drink it all. And then after her meal, I'd curl beside her and tell stories until we both fell asleep.

Daddy placed his hands on my shoulders and made me step away from Mama's bed. We promised to come back the next day and bring a few things from home.

Mama smiled, then turned toward the window. The corners of her eyes were moist with tears.

BACK ON THE FIRST FLOOR, Daddy was quiet while we sat in the hospital lobby and waited for the cab. He looked out the door as cars slowed by the entrance. A woman in a wheelchair rolled across the floor, then an elderly man in a gray suit walked in and nodded to Daddy. I'd seen the man in the store, but couldn't remember his name. If we sat there long enough, we'd run into customers who knew us. Daddy didn't say anything, and I didn't feel like talking either.

Something about Tess troubled Mama. Daddy knew it. So did I. Still, neither of us said a word, as if by keeping quiet, we could ignore what we knew.

Kissing Tess now seemed like a bad thing. Somehow, I felt I'd betrayed my mother.

When I got home, I'd wash out my mouth with something awful like dish-washing liquid, and I would never, ever kiss her again.

SEVEN

LITTLE SEAMSTRESS

INSTEAD OF TAKING ME home or to the store, Daddy dropped me off at Mary Roberts's house. Mary was in school, but her mother was home. When Daddy asked if she'd look after me, she smiled and said, "I'd be delighted, Rupert." Mrs. Roberts is always delighted to do her Christian duty, which means helping when she can. "How is Julia?" she asked. "I couldn't believe the news when you telephoned. One always worries about the elderly falling, but I guess it can happen to just anyone, now can't it?"

Daddy smiled as Mrs. Roberts babbled on. "Julia's going to be fine. Just fine," he said and patted my shoulder.

"And you said you found a girl to stay while Julia recovers?"

"Yes, Tess Reed has agreed to stay."

Mrs. Roberts raised an eyebrow. "I see. Well, you know, Rupert, I would have been delighted to find a girl from the church. The Reeds don't have the best reputation."

"I appreciate that, I really do, but don't trouble yourself. Tess will work out just fine. She's got a lot of energy and is happy to help. Now, I need to get to work. Expecting a shipment of paint today."

"I want to go to the store with you," I begged, tugging at Daddy's arm. I didn't understand why I had to stay with Mrs. Roberts.

"You missed school today, Ellie. You'll need to get your notes and homework from Mary. There will be other days to go to the store."

I could tell that was a made-up excuse. Daddy didn't want me at the store today. But why?

While I tried to figure things out, Daddy kissed my head and reminded me to be home for supper. We lived only four houses down from Mary Roberts, so I was allowed to walk.

"Thanks again, Charlotte," Daddy said to Mrs. Roberts before he left in the cab without me.

Mrs. Roberts made me lunch, and I ate my tuna sandwich quickly, washing it down with cold milk. I tried hard to answer Mrs. Roberts's questions without telling her too much. As Daddy has said, "Be careful what you say at Mary's house. Mrs. Roberts tells everything she knows and half of what she doesn't." I watched my words and did not say anything about either Mama's baby or Tess.

"God certainly was looking after your mother, Ellie. Why, plenty of people have broken their neck in falls half that distance."

"Yes, ma'am," I agreed, even though I didn't know of a single person with a broken neck. I wasn't so sure God was looking after Mama either. If He was, why did He let her fall in the first place? But not being up to a sermon from Mrs. Roberts, I kept quiet.

After lunch, I played on Mary's swingset, waiting for her to come home. While I twirled on Mary's swing, Mrs. Roberts swept the front porch and carried letters to her mailbox. She smiled and offered to get me more milk or something each time she stepped outside. I wondered what it would be like to have a mother who checked on you. Mama so often needed me that I couldn't imagine it being the other way around. Until I started spending time at Mary Roberts's house, I never knew how other mothers acted.

Before long, the yellow bus slowed and Mary stepped off. She squealed when she saw me, and we jumped up and down, holding each other's hands. Later, we rested in the warm grass and I let Jellybean walk around between us.

I told Mary about Mama's fall down the basement steps, and how the tomato girl had come to take care of things while Mama got better. When I whispered in her ear about the makeup and the Kotex, Mary squeezed my hands and said, "Oh, you are so lucky," just like I knew she would.

Some things I left out on purpose, like the kiss and Mama's baby. Keeping secrets is a lot like telling lies, but sometimes you just can't risk everything. I wanted to tell Mary how I worried about Tess being in our house when Mama came home, but I knew she'd tell her mother. And then Daddy would be mad at me for sure if Mrs. Roberts said something about Tess.

Before I left, Mary wrote down my homework assignments, and then I put Jellybean into my purse, and thanked Mrs. Roberts for lunch and tea.

"Why, you are so welcome," she said, and reminded me to give my mother her best. "We'll all be praying for her."

I thanked Mrs. Roberts again, but knew Mama wouldn't want to hear about the congregation praying for her. Although she sometimes went to church with Daddy and me, Mama thought most churchgoers were gossips and bores.

Even though I felt sad about Mama, a part of me filled with hope. Mama would get well, and we'd have a new baby in the house. There would be strollers, rattlers, and teddy bears in every room. With a new baby, maybe Mama would be glad Tess was there. She'd help Mama with all the chores and be my make-believe big sister. I'd bring over Mary Roberts and she'd play Avon, too. Maybe I'd be an Avon lady like Tess, instead of a teacher. My sewing money would pay for lipsticks to get me started. I'd take them to nearby houses and practice the way Tess had told me. "Hello," I'd say, "My name is Ellen Sanders, please call me Ellie. Would you like to try some Crimson Rose? It would look lovely with your fair complexion."

At our house, I stepped onto the front porch and set my purse down, freeing my hands to smooth the front of my dress and pull up my socks. I noticed bread crumbs scattered on the porch where Tess had stood this morning. Had she fed the crows that had perched on the railing? Black ants nibbled at the crumbs that were left.

I picked up my purse, careful not to swing it because Jellybean was asleep inside. I wasn't sure if chicks suffered motion sickness like I sometimes did.

I opened the door and walked inside the house. And then I stopped.

Daddy was leaning back on the sofa, beside Tess, his bare feet resting on Mama's coffee table. The dark hairs along his chest showed over the scooped neck of his white undershirt.

Tess held my father's dress shirt in her lap, her thin fingers sewing the missing button back on his sleeve.

When I saw her hand pull the thread tight, I forgot about Jellybean and threw my purse.

"Ellie, what's the matter?" Daddy asked, his face a puzzle.

How could he not know? He'd always understood everything about me.

"I wanted to sew your button back on. I told you in the cab this morning. Sewing on your buttons is my job. Not hers!" I bit my lip and tasted blood.

"Ellie . . ." Daddy moved toward me.

"Jesus Christ!" Tess muttered with a sigh. She rummaged through my mother's sewing basket until she found a pair of shears. Snatching my father's shirt by the sleeve, she singled out the button and gripped it between her forefinger and thumb.

With one quick snip, she cut the threads that held the button she'd sewn on my father's sleeve. "Happy now?" She stared at me with cold eyes.

The button rolled across the living-room floor and landed under my mother's rocking chair.

Daddy looked at Tess and frowned. "It's been a hard couple of days. I'm taking Ellie out for a hamburger and fries."

"Suit yourself." Tess pulled the tan afghan from the back of the sofa and wrapped herself in it. Then she curled up on her side and stared at us from inside her knitted cocoon. Her face went blank, like a chalkboard suddenly wiped clean.

"You can come if you want," my father offered.

"No, you two go ahead. I'm better off alone."

Daddy knelt beside me, picked up my purse and placed it back in my hands. "Go wash your face, Ellie, and bring me another shirt from the closet," he said, nudging me forward.

Upstairs, I moved Jellybean to his box. I checked his little wings and legs to make sure he hadn't been hurt in the fall. Relieved that nothing seemed to be swollen or broken, I kissed his tiny head. How could I have risked hurting him that way? Was Daddy right when he said that it was only because so much had happened in the last few days? Or was something the matter with me like with Mama? Mary Roberts said bad moods are like blue eyes: they come in a person's genes. That meant Mama's moods could pass on to me.

In the bathroom, I washed my face, and as I scrubbed, I talked to myself: "You are a bad, stupid girl, Ellie Sanders. It was only a button. Tess didn't know sewing was your job."

She didn't know, but Daddy knew. I tried not to think about what that meant. I kind of understood letting Tess help with the housework while Mama was sick, but why should she do my jobs?

Maybe I deserved it. All the wrong things I'd done in the last few days crossed my mind: how I'd refused to get Mama's onion; I'd dropped Jellybean on the floor, twice; I'd told Mama about Tess after Daddy warned me not to; now I'd gotten angry at Tess and Daddy. "You've got to do better, Ellie. You've got to!" I told myself. "Remember Mama's baby and the promises you made to God."

I stepped into my parents' bedroom to get my father a clean shirt. On the way to the closet, I noticed the quilt shoved to the floor and the sheet wadded on the bed. As I smoothed the wrinkled sheet, my hand touched a moist spot, and I pulled back.

On the floor, curled like a snail, lay Tess's pink nightgown.

EIGHT

JOE'S DINER

When I came downstairs, Daddy was trying to coax Tess into coming with us to Joe's Diner. He whispered in her ear to make her laugh. She wriggled and squealed, "Okay, I'll go!"

She went upstairs to change her clothes. I thought about her nightgown on the floor of my parents' room, and my stomach felt queasy.

A few minutes later, Tess came back downstairs wearing a short denim skirt, red tank top, and silver spoon earrings.

Daddy kissed her cheek. "Beautiful," he said.

And she was.

There's a donut shop in town that also sells sandwiches, and a bar that serves food on weekends, but Joe's Diner is Granby's only sit-down restaurant. I felt grown-up whenever we ate there. I loved the black-and-white-checkered floor, the tables with ashtrays and plastic flowers in slender bottle vases, the blue gingham curtains, the paper place mats with treasure maps and word scrambles printed on them.

At the diner, all the men looked at Tess. With her long blonde hair, red lips, and red nails, she looked like a girl a prince would marry.

We ordered Monday's special: hamburgers, french fries, and pie with ice cream for dessert. The waitress chewed gum and tucked a short pencil behind her ear. The name tag on her chest read "Betty."

"Betty needs to wear a lighter foundation," Tess explained after the waitress left our table. "Did you notice how orange her skin looks, and that line under her chin where her skin and makeup meet? That's a common mistake," Tess added. "A demarcation line."

That sounded serious. I nodded in agreement, but hadn't actually noticed a thing wrong with the waitress's face. I had so much to learn.

Daddy ordered a beer with his food. Tess kept stealing his brown bottle and taking a sip. "You know you're not old enough to drink," Daddy scolded her.

"I'm not old enough for a lot of things, but I don't hear you complaining."

They both laughed, and my father held the bottle to her lips to let her drink his beer. Her red lips made a perfect seal around the bottle's mouth.

I laughed along with them, but didn't understand why.

EVERY TIME I'VE been to Joe's Diner, I've seen someone I know. Tonight was no different.

Miss Wilder, my teacher, sat three tables away, where she ate pizza with the librarian, Miss Franklin. Mary Roberts claimed they were in love, but could two girls really be in love? Mary said yes, that the word for that was *lesbian,* but not to tell a soul, because if anyone heard me say it, they might think that of Mary and me. "Then," Mary had explained, "we would have to stop speaking to each other, at least in public."

I may have made better grades, but Mary understood all the things that really mattered. She knew about God, the blood curse, lesbians, and even how to tell if two people were in love. I guess when your mother doesn't have moods, she has time to tell you things.

While we ate, I watched the two teachers share a pizza and laugh. Miss Wilder reached across the table and wiped something from Miss Franklin's face. Maybe a hair, or smeared tomato sauce? Did that mean they were in love?

I nibbled the last of my fries, my mind full of questions about Tess. I knew so little about her really. Where in Granby did she live? What about her mama and daddy? Did she have any brothers and sisters? What was she like when she had seizures? I had a lot of things to ask her, and with her sleeping in my bed I'd have a chance to ask her.

Music played from the jukebox in the far corner, a country and western song. A boy in jeans danced with a girl near the jukebox, his hands holding her close as he rested them at the small of her back. Nobody else in the diner was dancing, but they seemed not to care. They were what Miss Wilder would call "oblivious" to the rest of the world.

While we waited for the waitress to bring the tab, Daddy twirled a toothpick between his lips. Tess dabbed at her mouth with a napkin, then put on more lipstick. Blotting her lips on the folded napkin, she explained how that was a trick to keep lipstick from smearing on your teeth.

Daddy put a wad of money on the table and asked if we were ready to leave. Just then a man wearing coveralls and a plaid shirt walked in the door. I wouldn't have thought anything about him except for Tess. She squinted when she saw him and said, "Shit!"

I didn't know the man, but both Tess and my father recognized him. Tess said more curse words. Daddy patted her arm, told her not to get upset, that he would handle everything. I wondered if the man had stolen from Daddy's store or if he was one of the cripples who live with Mildred Rogers.

The man saw us and threw up his hand. He walked over and greeted us with a wide grin. He seemed friendly. "Well, hello there, Rupert, how're you doing?" he said, his voice harsh and loud.

Daddy extended his hand, just as he did to his customers. "I'm doing all right, Mason. Just brought the girls out for dinner."

"And the little wife, she's on the mend, I hope?"

"Yes, Julia's much better. We saw her today."

"And how's my Tessy darling?" He touched her shoulder. The grooves in his fingers were dirty, and his thick yellow nails were dirty, too. Maybe he had been in the store and I just couldn't remember him.

Tess gave a half smile. "I'm fine, Papa."

"You taking your medicine, girl?"

Tess nodded and folded her arms across her chest. Her shoulders curled forward a bit, and she lowered her head. It was like watching a flower wilt.

I couldn't believe this man was Tess's father. It seemed impossible. He was nothing like Tess.

Daddy introduced me. "I don't think you've met Ellie. This is my daughter. Ellie, this is Mr. Reed, Tess's father."

"Hi," I said.

He leaned over to shake my hand. He smelled like the men who slept on the bench by the post office. I couldn't believe that this dirty, smelly man could be kin to someone as beautiful as Tess. I shook his hand and pulled back as quick as I could, wiping my hand on my napkin under the table where no one could see. No wonder Tess wanted to be near my daddy, who smelled as clean as soap.

"You sure are a pretty little thing," he said as he grinned at me. His teeth were small and dark, like kernels of dried corn.

"We were just getting ready to leave, Papa," Tess said.

My father pushed back his chair and stood up. Tess and I did the same.

Daddy offered his hand again. "We'd better be getting home. Nice seeing you, Mason."

Before we left, Mr. Reed touched Daddy's sleeve. "My girl, she's working out then, not giving you any trouble?"

"She's working out just fine, Mason. There's no trouble. Tess is a godsend to me."

"Well, don't count on keeping her forever, Rupert. I got lots of things at my own house that needs tending. I only let her come to help out while your wife's laid up, you know."

"Yes, I understand." Then Daddy's jaw locked together the way it does when he is angry.

I held my breath until we were outside again.

TESS DIDN'T SAY much during the walk home, and Daddy kept his arm around her shoulder. I didn't know what was wrong, but figured it had something to do with her father. The few words she did say were bad words that I'm not supposed to say.

When we got home, I tried to cheer up Tess. I offered to let her feed Jellybean or play Scrabble with me. I suggested we play Avon Lady and I'd be the makeover girl.

Tess didn't want Jellybean, Scrabble boards, Avon, or me. She only wanted my father.

DADDY TUCKED ME IN bed and sat Jellybean's box beside me. Then he kissed me good-night. "Kiss Jellybean, too!" I begged.

He uncovered the chick and kissed his downy head.

"Will Tess be all right, Daddy?" I snuggled under the comforter, suddenly feeling very tired.

"Yes, she's just a little sad. But she'll be fine." Daddy patted my head.

"Why does she have to take care of things at her house? Doesn't she have a mother?"

Daddy looked down at the floor then turned back to me. The lines in his forehead seemed deeper in the soft lamp light. "Tess's mother died when she was little, so her father has raised her alone. She's had things hard, and needs us to be good to her, understand?"

I nodded, my chin digging into the thick quilt. "But what will happen when she has to go back home to Mr. Reed?"

"I'm not going to let that happen." Daddy kissed my forehead once again and left my room.

Thinking about Tess without a mother made me feel suddenly sad for her. She'd had no one to cut out paper dolls, kiss her skinned knees, or braid her hair. Instead, she'd lived with her father who looked and smelled bad, with no woman at home to make him take a bath. I pictured Tess as a girl my age, standing at the kitchen sink while trying to figure out how much milk to pour into the pancake batter, or how to peel a potato without cutting her thumb. And here I'd been mean to her over something so silly as sewing on buttons.

I got out of bed; I needed to say I was sorry, to tell Tess she could sew Daddy's buttons whenever she wanted.

As I neared the top step, I heard Daddy and Tess downstairs. Tess was crying, and as she spoke, her voice broke. "He'd wait until . . . my seizure . . . and then . . . Oh, Rupert . . . Awful . . . It was so awful . . ."

I listened from the stairs, hearing her terrible story, how she'd wet herself during her seizures, and afterwards, her father took off her panties and rubbed between her legs. How he scolded her for being a big girl and still wetting herself, and wouldn't let her have clean underpants unless she let him touch her down there. "He started keeping my panties out in his room, and told me I'd have to earn them. If I didn't . . . If I didn't do what he wanted, he hit me, and held me down."

I heard my father's voice say her name, over and over: "Tess,

Tess, Tess. You should have said something . . . You should have told me!"

Then, in a deep, fierce voice I didn't know Daddy had: "I'm going to kill him, Tess. I swear to God, I'm going to see that bastard dead!"

Daddy's voice was like thunder, and I hurried to my room, my heart beating so fast and hard it felt like a hammer against my chest. I didn't want to hear the rest of the story, even though questions filled my mind. Why did Mr. Reed do those bad things to Tess? And what would Daddy do now that he was so upset? Daddy's angry voice scared me. I knew he couldn't have really meant that he'd kill Mr. Reed, but his threat sounded so real.

Back in my bed, I held Jellybean tight. Even though my room was warm and my body wrapped in thick blankets, I couldn't stop shivering.

I tried hard to stay awake, to keep my eyes open. Why didn't Daddy and Tess stop talking? I slid over to one side of the bed, remembering that Tess would be sleeping with me. I kept wishing she would hurry; I didn't like being alone, not tonight anyway.

My eyes eventually closed, but only bad dreams swirled inside my head. Mama's voice called me, but I couldn't find her no matter which direction I ran. Her voice was like God talking: it filled the air around my head and yet, I could never see her face.

Tess must have had bad dreams, too.

When I woke in the middle of the night, I found her sleeping in Daddy's bed.

NINE

CHALK DOORS, CHOCOLATES, AND A KISS

THE NIGHT'S BAD DREAMS left a heavy fog inside my head. After finding Tess asleep in Daddy's bed, I went back to my room. I'd thought about nudging Tess awake and asking her to come back to my room where she belonged, but I was afraid of what I didn't know or understand. Her seizures scared me. The things her father did to her scared me, too.

When it started getting lighter outside, I felt a little safer. I fell asleep again, this time without dreams.

I woke later, not as tired, but still uneasy. I hoped I'd slept too late and missed the school bus. I wanted to go to the hospital to visit Mama instead. I hurried from bed, kicking the tangle of blankets from my feet.

I still felt unsettled, though—nervous and confused. I even had trouble brushing my teeth, ending up with toothpaste all over the place. I hoped breakfast would help.

Coming downstairs, Jellybean peeped inside his box and I almost tripped on the steps. As I crossed the floor, the whistle in the teakettle blew, and my heart jumped into my throat. I couldn't remember ever being so nervous. It was as if a wire had been wound too tight inside me.

When I finally joined Daddy and Tess at the kitchen table, I felt glad that the chair held me up.

The telephone rang. Daddy rose to take the call. I tried to hear what he said, but Tess blabbed on about the breakfast she'd cooked, making it hard for me to hear Daddy's voice.

When Daddy returned to the table, he said that some boys had broken into the school and shoved burlap bags and old shoes into all the toilets. The school was flooded, which meant our Easter holiday would begin today instead of Thursday. I was glad, because now I'd be able to see Mama.

Tess rose and went back to the stove. She asked if they knew which boys did it, but Daddy said no.

I knew it was probably Hank Shipes, the worst troublemaker at school. But I didn't day anything. Mama was all that mattered to me.

Tess placed a plate of food in front of me and stood at the counter grinding more beans for coffee. The smell was good, but the noise just made me more jittery.

Suddenly, someone knocked on the front door. Startled, I dropped my fork on the floor and nearly knocked over my glass of milk. What if Mr. Reed had come back for Tess? I thought about the gun in the shed and worried Daddy might use it to make Mr. Reed leave.

Daddy pushed his chair from the table and walked toward the door.

I held my breath.

But it wasn't Tess's father. It was Mr. Morgan, who owned Daddy's store.

Seeing him was like a smile had washed over me. I jumped from my seat and ran toward him. "Mr. Morgan! Mr. Morgan!"

"There's my girl!" He wrapped his arms around me and hugged me tight.

I was so happy to see him. Mr. Morgan was like a grandfather to me. He was old and twisted with arthritis, but I loved him with my whole heart.

I didn't have grandparents to call my own. Daddy's father ran off when Daddy was a little boy, and his mother grew lumps in her breasts and died. Afterwards, Daddy and his two sisters were put into separate foster homes and Daddy never saw them again. "I figure they got adopted by fine people and live some place real nice," Daddy would say whenever I asked him about my aunts, Kate and Suzanne. He seldom mentioned them, but when he did, they were always twelve and nine, the ages they were when their mother died.

Mama's parents both died in the accident; they'd lived in Georgia, and I'd never seen them. Their pictures hung in gold-leaf frames in the foyer. Mama had her father's fair skin and bright eyes; her mother's dark hair and round cheekbones.

If I couldn't have grandparents of my own, Mr. Morgan was the next best thing.

Daddy warned me not to squeeze Mr. Morgan so tight.

"Oh, you can't hurt an old codger like me." Mr. Morgan laughed. He tousled my hair with bony fingers that felt as light as stalks of wheat.

"Would you like some coffee?" Daddy held out his hand toward the kitchen table.

"That would be nice. Thank you, Rupert."

Tess greeted Mr. Morgan. "Morning, Pops. What do you take in your coffee?" She stood by the kitchen sink with Mama's apron tied around her waist.

"Sugar and cream. Loaded with both," he said as he eased himself into a chair. He'd brought a large shopping bag from Spangle's Gift Shop. I watched as he pulled out a yellow box of Whitman's candy. "This is for your mother," he said, then shook his finger at me. "Now don't you go and eat it up!" He winked at me as he sat the box on the middle of the table.

"I won't."

He reached back into his bag and paused. "Close your eyes now!"

I squeezed my eyes shut, listening for any sound from the bag that might give me a clue. "What is it? What is it?"

"Patience, my girl. Okay, now you can look."

I opened my eyes and saw a wooden box that looked almost like a dollhouse, with a shingled roof and shuttered windows painted on the front. Jellybean's name was printed above the door in bright gold letters.

"A house for Jellybean!" I squealed and kissed Mr. Morgan's face.

"Somebody told me you had a chick from my store," Mr. Morgan said, and winked at Daddy. "And well, you can't go around with him in an oatmeal box forever. He'll outgrow that in no time flat. Or worse yet, peck a hole right through and escape."

He showed me how to unlatch the door so Jellybean could walk in and out to suit himself. "Be sure to keep the latch closed like this when you're not watching him, or he'll open it up on his own and take off after some pretty hen."

"Here's your coffee," Tess said as she placed a steaming cup in front of Mr. Morgan.

"Thank you, dear." He sipped some coffee then returned his cup to the table and sighed. "Ah, that hits the spot, Tess. You sure do know how to make a cup of coffee. I was surprised to hear you'd moved in here to help out. It's mighty kind of you, but who's looking after your father now that you're staying here?"

"He can tend to himself, I imagine. Nothing strange about me moving in here. Lots of people have live-in girls to help out. Besides, I always wanted to live closer in town." Tess turned her back to Mr. Morgan and used one of my mother's sponges to wipe the kitchen counters clean. She scrubbed so hard her body shook, and I remembered her epilepsy, wondered if she could shake herself into a seizure. I was used to Mama's spells and knew how she might cry for days. I didn't know much about seizures. I'd have to ask Mary Roberts.

Mr. Morgan and Daddy didn't seem to notice any problem with Tess, so I took that to mean she was fine for the time being.

"Well, I hope he takes care of those tomato plants. I'm counting on having your fine tomatoes in my store front window again this summer," Mr. Morgan added, then cleared his throat.

Tess turned around and looked at Daddy. "I was thinking maybe I could bring the plants here, set them out back in the garden?"

Daddy nodded. "Of course. I'll go over in a day or two and get them."

"You must be planning on staying here awhile then?" Mr. Morgan added.

Tess started to speak, but Daddy interrupted. "Julia's going to take quite awhile to mend, and with her difficulties, Tess being here will help out more than you know."

Mr. Morgan nodded slightly, as if to say he heard but maybe didn't agree.

The idea of Daddy going to Mason Reed's house scared me, but I understood why Tess wanted to tend to her own plants. I felt the same about my chicks. Even though I knew Mr. Morgan would take good care of them, I wanted to go to the store and care for them myself.

Mr. Morgan gulped more coffee, then wiped his mouth with the back of his hand. He addressed my father. "Rupert, I want you to take as much time as you need to get Julia home and settled in. I'm getting old, but I can still ring the cash register and lift a few buckets of paint. Take care of your family first, you hear me?"

"Yes, Mr. Morgan. And thank you, sir. I appreciate it." Daddy extended his hand and shook Mr. Morgan's.

"Oh, don't mention it. And before I forget, I left a roll of wire by your shed. Make my girl a pen for that chick of hers."

Daddy nodded. "I think I can handle that."

"Now, I need a smoke after this fine cup of coffee. You still know how to roll a cigarette, Ellie?" Mr. Morgan had taught me when I was little.

I smiled. "Of course!"

"Well then, you put the little chick in his house and let's go outside. I don't want your Mama coming home and smelling my cigarette smoke in her pretty curtains. A woman can always tell when something in her house is amiss."

I SAT NEXT to Mr. Morgan on the front porch step and rolled his cigarette, just as he'd taught me, careful not to spill any brown tobacco bits. I handed it to him and watched him light the end, then drag on the cigarette. He breathed strands of white smoke into the clear sky. "Ah, perfect," he said.

"How are the chicks at the store?" I asked him.

"Oh, just fine, honey. Sold a couple just this morning."

"To good homes, I hope?"

Mr. Morgan chuckled. "Well, I don't reckon any of those chicks will end up in homes as fine as young Jellybean's, but I make sure they go to decent folk."

I nodded, satisfied. "How are the ones we put in the back office? Are they eating yet?"

"Oh, yes, they are gobbling that mash up like nobody's business. Be moving them out with the others tonight."

"Good," I said, glad Mr. Morgan would see to them.

"How are things with Tess living here?" Mr. Morgan asked, changing the subject.

"Fine," I said, twisting my shoelaces between my fingers and thumbs.

"You like her?"

"I like her okay, I guess. Daddy likes her more than I do."

"I can see that. Think your mother's going to like her?"

I pulled a dandelion from the cracked sidewalk and blew away its cottony head. "I don't know. She didn't seem to like the idea when we told her yesterday."

"I see." He flicked ashes into the grass. "Ellie, sometimes things work out when you don't expect them to, and other times, things that look perfect can just fall apart. Nobody's fault, really. Life is unpredictable. Understand?"

I didn't, not really. But I nodded my head, pretending to know what he was talking about.

Satisfied, Mr. Morgan moved on to another subject. "You still like to draw?"

"Yes."

"You got any chalk?"

I nodded. "Upstairs, in my room."

"Go fetch it while I finish my smoke."

I returned in a few minutes with my box of chalk. Mr. Morgan pulled out a long white stick and knelt on the sidewalk. He tottered a moment. I thought he might fall, but he caught himself with his hands.

Mr. Morgan drew a large rectangle, nearly as tall as me. Then midway down the rectangle, to the right, he drew a round circle, and colored it in.

Mr. Morgan had drawn a door.

"When I was a boy, Ellie, I stuttered. The other children, including my own brothers, taunted me. Called me Stuttering Stanley, Mumbling Morgan, and worse names I won't repeat in a young lady's company. They put gum in my hair, punched my back, and hid my books. I wanted to quit school. I wanted to hurt them back. Then my mother, God bless her, drew a door like this and said, 'Son, no matter how bad they treat you, remember you already have a way out.' She touched my forehead and said, 'Just use your mind. You draw a door, and see yourself step through it. On the other side, their words can't hurt you. On the other side of the door, you'll be safe.'"

"Did it work?" I asked, amazed at the idea of a magic door.

"Absolutely. The other children still teased me, but on the other side of the door, it didn't matter. And after awhile, when they saw their harsh words no longer bothered me, they stopped teasing me, and I didn't need the door anymore."

I nodded. "Will the door work for me, too?"

"Yes, of course. That's why I'm telling you about it. Anytime things get too hard, you draw yourself a door and step on the other side, you hear? You are always safe on the other side of the door."

Mr. Morgan stood up and handed me the piece of chalk. "Now, speaking of doors, I need to get back to the store before all my customers leave!"

Mr. Morgan hugged me good-bye.

AFTER MR. MORGAN LEFT, I went back inside to help Tess finish cleaning up the kitchen. I hadn't done any chores since Mama fell. Tess had scrubbed the stains in the kitchen, cooked breakfast, and washed the dishes. I needed to do more to make sure God didn't think I'd broken my promises. Toast crumbs and spilled sugar on the kitchen table only took a few minutes to sponge away. "Is there anything else I can do to help?" I asked Tess.

"You could sweep the floor if you want." Tess put the last of the breakfast dishes in the cabinets and lined up the teaspoons inside the drawer where Mama kept all the everyday silverware.

I took the broom and dustpan from the back porch and swept. Most housekeeping jobs I'd learned from Mama. She'd taught me how to sew on buttons, make sandwiches and deviled eggs, dust furniture, and make my bed. Sweeping was something I learned from Daddy. He believed in keeping the store spotless. That was no easy job. Rainy days meant farmers walked inside with mud on their boots. Children always seemed to step in messes and track them inside. Sweeping the kitchen seemed easy after cleaning up mud, chewing gum, cigarette butts, and wet leaves.

Sweeping made me think about Daddy. "Did Daddy go to the store with Mr. Morgan?"

"No, he's upstairs shaving. How's the floor coming?"

"Almost done."

Tess smiled. "You're a hard worker, Ellie."

Just then Daddy came down the stairs in his bare feet. He wore his undershirt and had wrapped a thick towel around his neck the way he always did when he shaved.

"You look like a boxer, Daddy," I teased.

He laughed and came at me with curled fists, pretending to swing punches at me. "You remember that match I took you to in Fairfield last summer? Well, I could have beaten both those featherweights!"

I leaned the broom against the wall and threw up my hands to defend against his make-believe blows.

Tess came to my defense. "Come on, Ellie, we can take this man down," she said as she came at Daddy, tickling him under the arms.

I scrambled to help her tickle Daddy. He pulled his towel from his neck and began swatting both our behinds.

We kept tickling Daddy as he backed into the living room and fell on the sofa. Tess and I jumped on top of him, laughing, and sat on him until he gave in, crying, "You win! You win!"

Then I remembered Mama lying in the hospital bed and suddenly felt ashamed for having so much fun. I crawled off the sofa and walked away. "I better go check on Jellybean."

DADDY WAS IN no hurry to go back to the hospital. He suggested I play with Mary Roberts while he and Tess picked up groceries and finished a few chores.

"But I want to see Mama," I pleaded.

"I know, Ellie, and we will in awhile. But I have some bills to pay, need to pick up groceries and do a few things around here. I already called Mrs. Roberts and she said you could have lunch with Mary. I'll pick you up in the cab when it's time to go to the hospital."

"Can I pack Mama's suitcase first?"

Daddy agreed, so I went upstairs and gathered things Mama

might want from home: her terry-cloth bathrobe, makeup bag, Jergens lotion, Noxzema, the McCall's magazine, and two books from her bedside table.

Mama would be happy that I remembered her Jergens. Before I slipped the jar into Mama's bag, I dabbed a little on the palms of my hands and rubbed the lotion into my skin until the white cream disappeared. I closed my eyes and breathed Mama into me.

MARY ROBERTS AND I stood on the steps of her front porch and ate the box of Cracker Jacks her mother had given us after lunch. Jellybean slept in his little house, his tummy full of the warm oatmeal Mrs. Roberts had made especially for him.

"Tess has seizures," I said, keeping my voice low so Mrs. Roberts couldn't hear through the screen window.

"You're kidding?" Mary asked, her eyes wide. "Have you seen her do it?"

"No, not yet. But sometimes, when she's mad, her body shakes a little, and I think she's going to fall on the floor and have one. It scares me. What do you suppose it's like?"

"Oh, it's awful, even worse than a woman's blood curse," Mary said, her angel-blonde curls bouncing because she spoke so fast. "A spell comes over you like a fog, and you have some sort of fit, foaming at the mouth like a rabid fox. It's like being in the electric chair when the warden zaps you full of electricity." Mary jerked her body to show me. "Sometimes," she pointed her finger at me, "you pee your pants and flop around like a fish on dry land. If it goes on too long, you might bite off your tongue. That's why you have to put a spoon in their mouth. Always."

No wonder Mama didn't seem too happy about Tess staying with us. Who would want to see someone flop on the floor, biting off her tongue?

Suddenly my stomach felt queasy, and I didn't want any more Cracker Jacks.

I sat on the front porch step and held Jellybean on my lap while I waited for Daddy.

Late afternoon, Daddy and I rode in the cab to the hospital. I wanted to take Jellybean, but Daddy had asked the cab driver to drop my chick off at the house first. Tess would keep him while we visited Mama. "We pressed our luck taking that chicken into the hospital the first time, so let's not try that again."

At the hospital, Daddy carried the suitcase in one arm, and Mama's box of candy in the other. I trailed close behind, keeping my arms at my sides to avoid touching anyone or anything. I hated the hospital and its bad smells.

After the brief elevator ride, we walked the long, dull tunnel until we came to room 311. I wished they'd put Mama on the first floor. I didn't like being in the middle of the hospital, floors of sick people over my head and under my feet.

Daddy shoved the door open with his shoulder. I followed close behind. In a rush to leave the corridor, I nearly stepped on his heels.

"Mama!" I squealed. I'd seen her only yesterday, but it felt like days.

Mama held out her arms to me, her fingers dancing in the air.

I climbed into her hospital bed and buried my head in her neck.

"Guess what?" Mama's voice was soft and happy.

I sat up and looked at her face. Her eyebrows lifted, raising the white bandage like a little flag. The blue-black bruise on her face was softening into greens and yellows. She looked at me, then at Daddy. "The doctor said I can come home in the morning!"

I clapped my hands and shouted, "Hurray!"

We wouldn't have to come inside this hospital anymore until Mama had her baby, and that would be a happy visit. I'd have Mama home, and she would make my bad dreams go away. I wouldn't even need the magic chalk door Mr. Morgan had shown me.

Daddy leaned down and kissed Mama's forehead the way he kissed mine good-night. "That's good news, Julia. But is Dr. Cline certain you're ready? It's so soon."

Mama frowned. "Rupert, you sound like you don't want me to come home."

"Of course I want you home, Julia. I just want to be sure the doctor isn't making a hasty decision. You took quite a fall. The bed rest can't hurt."

"Rupert," Mama spoke in her impatient voice. "I can rest just as easily at home."

"Yes, I suppose you're right," Daddy said, a look of concern on his face. He dropped her suitcase at the foot of the bed. "We brought your robe and gowns, a few other things from home, but I guess you won't be needing those if you're being released tomorrow."

"We can bring you a dress to wear home," I offered.

"That would be wonderful, Ellie. Why don't you pick a home-coming dress for me?"

"I will." I squeezed Mama's hands and smiled.

Daddy took the box of Whitman's candy and placed it on my mother's lap. "A get-well present." He kissed her forehead again.

Mama blushed. She ran her fingers along the edges of the box, admiring her gift. She thanked him and wrapped her arms around his neck. "You didn't need to get me anything, Rupert."

Daddy patted her arm, then lowered himself into the chair by her bed.

He never told Mama the candy was a gift from Mr. Morgan.

TESS WAS BEADING a necklace at the kitchen table when we returned. Jellybean sat on the table near her, pecking at a blue bead. "Isn't it pretty?" she asked as she held up the wire half-strung with colorful beads. Tess smiled at us.

"Julia's coming home tomorrow," Daddy said.

Her smile disappeared. "I thought you said she wouldn't be

back for days!" she screamed at my father. She picked up my mother's sugar bowl and threw it against the kitchen wall. The white porcelain shattered, leaving sugar and broken shards on the floor.

I gasped, sucking air into my lungs so suddenly it sounded like a noise an animal might make.

"Ellie," Daddy said, "I want you to take Jellybean outside and let him walk around in the yard."

My legs wouldn't move. I'd never seen anyone break something on purpose. Maybe a pencil or a toy that didn't work, but nothing that belonged to someone else. Nothing as pretty as my mother's porcelain.

Daddy didn't notice that I hadn't left. He didn't notice me at all.

He moved toward Tess, placed his hands on her shoulders, and whispered her name.

She turned her head as if she didn't want to look at him.

I watched Daddy take her face in his hands as if he held a precious shell. And then he kissed her.

Not on the forehead.

Not on the cheek.

Daddy kissed Tess on the lips.

TEN

RUNAWAY GIRL

SEEING DADDY KISS Tess made me want to poke out my
eyes. I'd never be able to erase it away. How could he do
such a thing? My ears rang like somebody had hit me, and I felt
light-headed.

I turned and ran outside, slamming the door behind me.
Daddy followed me into the backyard and called after me. But I
kept running, not sure where to go, just wanting to get away. I ran
across the street, slipping between the tall elms that bordered the
next yard. My movements disturbed birds that had nested for the
evening. I heard them flutter and caw in the trees.

Behind me, the thud of my father's boots on asphalt made my
heart race. Daddy was faster than me, but I was smaller and the
sun had almost set, making it hard for him to see me. I moved
behind trash cans and bushes until his footsteps no longer
followed.

I reached the church parking lot, and started to go inside. I
could sleep on the wooden pew, maybe find some communion
bread and grape juice for supper. But I was not in such good favor
with God and didn't want to push my luck.

Spending the night with Mary Roberts wasn't a good idea either. I'd have to walk a long way back and risk running into Daddy. Mrs. Roberts would feed me dinner and let me sleep in the white canopy bed with Mary, but she would also ask a lot of questions. What if I slipped and told her about the kiss?

I really wanted to stay with Mr. Morgan, to curl up in his lap and roll his cigarettes while he told me again about the special door. He wouldn't be at the store this late, and his house was too far to walk. I checked my pockets: one dollar and twelve cents. Not enough to pay cab fare to Mr. Morgan's house.

I decided to walk to school. There was no other place to go. Maybe the janitor had left a door open. Or maybe I could crawl inside an open window. I could even break a window if I had to. I knew how from watching Daddy break in our house the time Mama changed the locks and wouldn't let him inside. Daddy had wrapped his hand in his coat while he smashed the glass with a rock. I didn't have a coat with me, but I could rip part of my dress or use one of my socks.

You have to make do when you're a runaway girl.

Once inside, I'd have the building to myself. I could curl up in the library and read a book. Maybe eat leftover fish sticks in the cafeteria, then all the strawberry ice cream I wanted. If I cut myself on the way in, there were Band-Aids and peroxide in the infirmary. The brown plaid sofa beside the cola machine in the teachers' lounge might make a good bed. I could go to the music room and bang on the piano as loudly as I felt like it. If I stayed away long enough, Daddy would be sorry. He wouldn't kiss Tess again. He'd love Mama the way he did before Tess came.

I worried about Jellybean and hoped he'd forgive me for leaving. Early in the morning, I'd sneak back home and get him. I felt bad. He'd be cold, scared, and hungry. "Don't cry, don't cry," I repeated. The tears came anyway. I wiped my eyes with my fists, then pinched my arm.

Runaway girls need to be brave.

I walked a long time to reach the school yard, and had to cut through the trailer park where country music blared from radios, and there were beer cans scattered across some of the front yards. I'm not allowed to play in the trailer park or on Gratton Street where coloreds live, but I've gone to both places with Daddy to deliver screens and plywood. Seems there are always windows and doors needing repair in poor houses.

The backs of my legs hurt. My saddle shoes were tight and making my feet sweat.

Fireflies began their nightly dance in the darkening sky. To keep my mind off troubles, I counted green blinks as I walked to Granby Elementary.

I didn't expect to find anyone at the school, but when I stepped around the corner to see if the back doors were unlocked, I noticed two women on the playground. It was Miss Franklin and Miss Wilder. I never guessed they came to the school after hours. Miss Franklin pushed Miss Wilder on the swing, and they both laughed like girls.

Miss Wilder spotted me before I could back away. She threw up her hand and waved. "Ellie!"

I waved, then turned to leave.

"Wait," Miss Wilder called.

This time my legs were too tired to run. The backs of my knees ached. The soles of my feet burned and felt sore. My shoes probably had rubbed blisters.

"Hi Ellie, how are you?" Miss Wilder knelt beside me. She wore blue jeans and a yellow tee shirt. I was so used to seeing her in dresses, I couldn't help but stare.

"I'm fine."

"Are you here with your parents?"

"No, by myself. I don't live too far. Grace Street." A mosquito bit my forearm and I slapped it, smearing a drop of blood on my skin.

Miss Wilder pulled a tissue from her pocket, dampened it with her tongue and wiped the blood from my arm. I was grateful Mary Roberts wasn't here to see that. She'd be sure to say that lesbian spit rubbed on your arm would only lead a girl to trouble. But I didn't care. I was already in too much trouble to worry about spit.

"Well, it's nearly dark, Ellie. That's a long way for a little girl to walk alone at night. Can I come with you?"

"No, I can make my way back." I couldn't let Miss Wilder walk me home and run into Daddy or Tess.

"Does your mother know you're here?"

"Mama fell and is in the hospital. That's why I missed school yesterday. I was in a hurry to get to Daddy's store, and didn't stay home and get her onion, and she slipped. She's supposed to have a baby, but now the baby might die." I hadn't meant to say so much, but the words came anyway. I didn't want to cry in front of my teacher, but I couldn't stop the tears.

Miss Wilder wrapped her arms around me. She patted my back the way a mother burps her baby. Her hand felt warm and solid.

Miss Franklin walked over, too. "Is there anything I can do?"

"Ellie's having a hard day," Miss Wilder said. "Ellie, honey, Miss Franklin and I live near here, too. Just two blocks away. Why don't you come home with us now and we'll figure things out?"

I nodded and let Miss Wilder keep her arm around my shoulder. It felt good to have someone's hand steady me. As we walked back to their house, Miss Franklin followed close behind. She whistled a tune I liked but didn't recognize.

A vase of pink carnations decorated the kitchen table. By the window, a lime green parrot perched in a wrought iron cage. "Hello, Belle," the parrot screeched and turned its head to one side to look at me.

"We bought Belle when we went on a trip to South America two summers ago," Miss Wilder said.

At school, Miss Wilder kept clay pots and brightly colored

baskets on her desk, some filled with paper clips or apples. She reminded me of Mama, the way they both loved unusual things and were not afraid to be different, but Miss Wilder didn't suffer the moods Mama did. She might scold Belle for being noisy, but she wouldn't tape the bird's beak shut to quiet her.

"Does she know many words?" I tried to think of something to say to be a good guest. Seeing Belle reminded me that my little green chick was on his own unless Daddy or Tess remembered to feed him. I should not have left Jellybean. No matter how mad I felt at Daddy, or how much I hated Tess, my chick was small and helpless. New tears wet my eyes.

Miss Wilder guided me to a chair at the table where Lotus-shaped candles floated in a bowl of water. She handed me a box of Kleenex from the top of her refrigerator, then brushed my bangs away from my face. "Would you like some warm milk?"

Miss Wilder knows just what a person needs when they feel low. At school, when I stand at the blackboard and get the equations wrong, she touches my shoulder and makes me forget how stupid I feel. Once, when Mary Roberts tripped on the wet steps in front of the school, Miss Wilder brushed the dirt off Mary's dress. She checked and rechecked all the bones Mary swore she'd broken.

"Yes, milk would taste good."

Miss Wilder stood at the stove and heated a pan of milk, then stirred in nutmeg and honey before testing the temperature with her finger. After pouring the milk into a bright blue bowl, she handed it to me.

"In Europe, the people drink coffee in bowls, not cups. Did you know that?" she asked.

I shook my head and managed to smile.

"Drink this," she said. "It will make you feel better."

I sipped the warm, sweet milk. It soothed my throat and filled the sad place in my belly.

Miss Franklin went into another room and returned a few

minutes later with a drawing tablet and a box of colored pencils. "When I feel really down, it helps me to sketch pictures. The colors make me feel better again. Maybe you'd like to draw for awhile?"

I opened the drawing tablet. At first I made only a few random marks, but after a little while, pictures moved across my mind and I put them on the paper. Soon, three pages were filled. I drew Belle and my blue bowl. I drew my house on Grace Street with its wide front porch and shuttered windows, then a picture of Jellybean peeking from his oatmeal box.

I didn't draw Mama, Daddy, or Tess.

"You know, Ellie, I have to call your father and let him know you're here. I'm sure he's very worried about you," Miss Wilder said.

"No, he's not."

"Why do you say that?" Miss Wilder wrinkled her forehead.

"I just know." I drank the last of my milk, then wiped my mouth with the back of my hand. "Can I stay here?"

"Yes, I suppose. I mean, I'd love to have you spend the night, but I do have to ask your father, Ellie. Is that a deal?"

I thought for a moment. Teachers want permission slips for everything. Field trips and tardiness, even trips to the bathroom. She wouldn't understand that runaway girls don't bring notes from their fathers. I didn't want her to call Daddy, but knew she had to. I gave Miss Wilder my phone number.

She walked into the next room and called. Her voice was so low, I couldn't make out what she said. A few moments later, she stepped around the corner, the black receiver in her hand. "Ellie, here. Your father wants to speak to you."

I held the receiver.

"Ellie?" My father's voice sounded sharp and hollow like an ax against wood. This was a voice I'd heard him use at other people, but never at me.

"Yes." I stood in the living room and tightened my hand around the phone.

"I know you're upset with me, Ellie." His voice softened a little as he continued. "There are things you're too young to understand, things I don't know how to explain to you."

"I know what I saw, Daddy. You kissed Tess. I saw you." I tried not to speak so loudly Miss Wilder would hear.

Daddy sighed. I pictured him running his hand through his thick, dark hair. He'd have his glasses off; he'd pinch the bridge of his nose between his thumb and finger, trying to find the words he wanted. "Ellie, I'm coming to get you. We'll go to Joe's, have an ice cream float and talk, okay?"

"I don't want to come home, Daddy. I don't want to go to Joe's, and I don't want an ice cream float!" I wanted to slam the telephone down, like I'd seen people do in movies.

"Ellie, you're just going to have to trust me. You belong at home. I'm coming over to get you now."

"I don't want to come home! You can't make me!"

"Fine, Ellie. I thought you were more mature than that. You've always been my big girl, helping me at the store, sewing the buttons on my shirt. I thought I could count on you. Maybe I was wrong. And maybe I was wrong to let you have Jellybean, too. You just ran off and left him here. No food. No water."

"I was going to come back and get Jellybean." Tears stung my eyes.

My father used his firm voice. "You have a choice to make, Ellie. I'm calling a cab, and coming over to Miss Wilder's to get you. If you don't come home, Jellybean goes back to the store."

My voice broke. "Please, Daddy, I'll come home. Please don't take Jellybean away!"

Daddy didn't say another word. I heard the loud click in my ear which told me he'd hung up the phone. I stood in Miss Wilder's living room as long as I could, holding the receiver in my hand. Maybe I listened for Daddy's voice to come back and say something to make the hurt inside me stop. Maybe I just didn't want to return to the kitchen and face Miss Wilder's questioning looks.

I don't remember what ideas filled my mind, only that I waited there a long, long time.

Miss Wilder's voice startled me. "Everything okay?" She poked her head inside the door and looked at me with soft, worried eyes.

"I have to use the bathroom," I said, and placed the receiver back in its cradle.

INSIDE MISS WILDER's bathroom, I sank to the floor and leaned against the cold toilet. Tight knots twisted inside my stomach. Maybe this was my fault for letting Tess kiss me. I thought about the smoke kisses she blew against Daddy's neck a few weeks earlier while they talked inside her truck. That hadn't been my fault. This was all too confusing. My head hurt.

I stood up and ran my fingers over the gold bar of soap in the open shell on the sink. Then a knock came and Miss Wilder's voice. "Ellie, your father is here."

WHILE THE YELLOW cab waited in front of the bungalow, I said good-bye to Belle and thanked Miss Wilder for the milk. She kissed me on the cheek and told me to visit again. Daddy opened the cab door for me. He waved at Miss Wilder, who remained standing on her front porch, her arms folded against the chilled air. Miss Franklin stepped outside and waved, too.

I climbed into the backseat of the cab and scooted all the way to the door opposite Daddy. The cab smelled like leather and cigarettes. A wad of bubble gum and a crumbled potato chip bag lay on the floor. As the cab pulled away, Daddy slid next to me. He wrapped his arms around me, resting his chin on my head. He rocked me back and forth, saying my name over and over.

His breath smelled bad, like the whiskey he keeps in his toolshed. I'd known my father to drink only when he was worried about important things like bills, taxes, and my mother's moods.

"I was so scared, Ellie. Don't ever do that again," he pleaded. "Don't ever run away from me again."

Seeing Daddy hurt was more than I could stand. I told him I was sorry and promised never to run away again. "Don't worry, Daddy, everything will be fine. Mama's coming home tomorrow."

INVISIBLE THINGS LIVE in the air. Dust fairies. Whispers. The static of socks on wool. I felt something invisible the night I came from Miss Wilder's house. The fine hairs on my arms and neck rose like threads.

Daddy stood too long at the window, staring at the road in front of our house. What did he see that held his gaze so long? I tried to imagine looking through his eyes. No matter how long I stared, I saw nothing but the blue-gray pavement darkening into black before it disappeared.

Tess flipped through magazines, but had little to say. She looked at Daddy, then back at the glossy pages of girls wearing bright clothes and earrings that dangled above their pale shoulders.

No one mentioned the kiss. No one said a word about me running away. No one spoke about Mama coming home the next day.

But the words nobody said were like oily fingers staining everything.

I sat cross-legged on the floor and played with Jellybean, trying small doll hats to see which ones fit. Only the bonnets that tied under his beak stayed on when he shook his head. I left a yellow one on for his sleeping cap and excused myself to go to bed.

That night a spider came to me in dreams. It wasn't the leggy black insect that scared me, but the web, white like skeins of yarn. Caught in the sticky fibers, I struggled, twisting my arms and legs, shoving the long, white cords away. No matter how I twisted or pulled, I couldn't break free. The web tightened around me like a thick cocoon.

ELEVEN

BAD LETTERS

THUMPING SOUNDS WOKE ME. In my drowsiness, the spider's black heartbeat filled my ear.

I sat up in bed and screamed.

"Ellie?" a girl's voice came from outside my door.

I rubbed my arms. Only bed sheets. No spider webs. I felt my hair, running my fingers through tangles. I looked at my fingers. No spun web, only hair.

"Ellie? I'm . . . I'm out here." Tess. Her voice sounded strange. Was she hurt? Maybe she was having a seizure? Maybe Tess was on the other side of my door flopping on the stairs with her tongue trapped between her teeth, barely able to speak.

Remembering what Mary Roberts had told me, I rushed to the table by my bed and grabbed Jellybean's feeding spoon. I tried to scrap off the dried oatmeal with my fingernails, but had bitten them to the quick since Mama's accident. I couldn't get the spoon very clean. Surely Tess wouldn't mind a little dried cereal if it saved her tongue. I tiptoed to my door, pressed my ear to the wood, and listened. Another thump. Daddy had hardly ever left Tess alone in the days she'd been in our home, so where was he now? Not sure what I'd see or find, I took a deep breath and opened my bedroom door.

Tess stood partway down the stairs, wearing denim cutoffs and a pale pink tee shirt. She wasn't having a seizure. The thumping was Daddy's brown suitcase bouncing down the stairs, one step at a time. Maybe Tess was leaving after all. Maybe she'd decided to ask Daddy for train fare. She could go someplace new and different. Far away from here.

"Tess, where are you going?"

She dabbed the sweat from her forehead. "I'm not going anywhere." She looked at my hand. "What's the spoon for, Ellie?"

I tried to think of what to say. "Nothing. I . . . I'm bringing it downstairs to wash with Mama's Palmolive."

"Oh, we ran out of that. I had your father buy some Joy. It smells nicer."

"Mama always uses Palmolive."

"Well, your Mama isn't doing the dishes now. I am. And I like Joy."

I knew this would be just the kind of talk to start an argument, so I changed the subject. "Is Daddy taking his suitcase to the hospital?"

"No, he's moving into the sewing room, and there's no bureau in that room for his clothes."

I scrunched up my face. "The sewing room?"

"That's right," she said. "Can you give me a hand?"

"Hang on." I stepped back into my room, left the spoon on the table, then returned to grab one end of the suitcase. "Why is Daddy moving to the sewing room?"

As soon as I asked the question, I wished I could take it back. I knew it had an answer I didn't want to hear.

Tess didn't say anything until we landed on the bottom step. She stood up, brushed her hair away from her face, and sat on top of the suitcase. "Rupert is going to be sleeping in the sewing room, so he wants to keep his clothes in there."

I sat down on the bottom step. "But there's no bed in the sewing room. Where will he sleep?"

"Your father is out in the shed building a frame for a mattress."

Why would Daddy sleep in the sewing room? Maybe climbing the stairs would be too hard for Mama and a downstairs bedroom would be better. "Is Mama moving into that room because of her fall?"

"No, of course not. She's not moving into the sewing room." Tess looked aggravated.

"Mama is still coming home today, isn't she?"

"I suppose so."

"You will be nice to her, won't you, Tess?"

She shrugged her shoulders. "Sure. Aren't I nice to you? Don't I let you play with my makeup? Didn't I give you your first Kotex? Teach you how to kiss?"

"Yes, but . . ." I felt suddenly shamed.

Tess sighed and folded her arms across her chest. "But what?"

How could I explain to Tess about Mama's moods? She does things without thinking, like the time she went outside to water her flowers wearing only her bra and panties, and Daddy had to pull her back inside before the neighbors saw. Other times, little things upset her in deep ways. She once burned a cake and cried for hours, and then forced herself to eat the entire cake as punishment. These were stories I couldn't tell anyone, especially Tess.

"Mama gets sad sometimes. She cries for no reason. Daddy says she's like a lily caught in a hurricane."

Tess rolled her eyes. "Look, I made up her bed this morning and swept the floors. I made a pitcher of lemonade. I even packed her bag with clothes to wear home from the hospital."

"I was supposed to pick her dress."

"Well, I've already done it. See how nice I am?"

"I hope you picked something pretty." I didn't want to start an argument with Tess. She might throw more dishes or cry to

Daddy that I was being mean. But I was mad that she'd picked my mother's homecoming outfit.

"I took a dress from the ones hanging in your mother's closet. If she doesn't like it, don't blame me. Ugly dresses belong in the Goodwill bin."

"She's going to have a baby, you know." Even Tess couldn't be mean to a woman who was going to have a baby.

Tess raised her eyebrows. "The doctor doesn't think so. Not after that fall."

"Don't say that, Tess." My throat tightened. I swallowed to keep from crying.

"Well, it's true."

"Just don't talk about it. It's bad luck to say." Mama's baby had to live. I crossed my fingers and recited God promises under my breath. *I will be good, God. I will be good.*

"Okay. I won't say another word. Now, I've got some work to do before Rupert comes back."

She stood up and lugged the suitcase through the kitchen and into the sewing room where my father would sleep.

If I could have one wish at that moment it would be to see Tess disappear like a snowflake touching warm ground.

I FED JELLYBEAN before going to the kitchen to eat breakfast alone. Daddy continued to work in his shed while Tess busied herself in the sewing room. Every few minutes I heard the rustle of paper or thud of furniture as she rearranged the room to suit herself.

After my breakfast I cleared the table. With a damp sponge, I wiped away the coffee cup rings Tess had missed.

As I washed my bowl and cup in the kitchen sink, I stared at the plastic bottle of Joy. Something mean rose up inside me like a black balloon. I couldn't stop myself. I took a paring knife from the drawer and cut a narrow slit in the bottom of the plastic bottle. Yellow Joy leaked into the sink. I left the bottle there to drain. I dried my hands, returned the knife, and went out to the shed to see Daddy.

The shed stayed locked most of the time because Daddy kept dangerous things inside, like hammers, saws, and his gun. I knocked on the door. Two fast knocks, followed by three slow ones: our secret code.

"Come in, Ellie," Daddy called.

I shoved the heavy door open and saw my father kneeling on the floor. I walked over to him and wrapped my arms around his neck. He smelled of sweat and sawdust.

Daddy laid his hammer down on the bench next to him. He sat on the bench, brushed the dust from his knees, then pulled me onto his lap. "So what do you think of my bed, Ellie?"

I leaned forward and ran my fingers over the knotty pine slab. "It's nice, Daddy. But I don't understand why you want to sleep in the sewing room."

Daddy cleared his throat. "Your Mama's going to need her rest, Ellie. It will be better if she has the room to herself."

I brushed sawdust from his dark hair. A fine dust landed on his shoulders. "Is Tess going to be sleeping in your new bed, too?"

His dark eyes narrowed. "What made you say that, Ellie? Tess shares your room, you know that."

"Her things are in my room, but when I wake up, Tess isn't in my room. I've seen her pink nightgown in your room, too," I said, my head lowered to avoid Daddy's gaze.

Daddy placed his thumb under my chin and lifted my head. His eyes were as fixed as stone. "You misunderstood what you saw, young lady. I don't want to hear you say anything so foolish around your mother. I mean it."

"Yes, sir."

"I know it was a long time ago, but don't you remember when your mother came home from the hospital the last time? How happy she was until the letters came?"

I remembered.

I REMEMBERED WHEN my mother returned from the psychiatric hospital she brought a large manila folder marked "Poems by Julia Sanders." "It was part of my therapy to write poetry."

Mama wrote her poems on yellow legal paper. Scratching them out in pencil, she wrote at the market, in church, and between loads of laundry. I knew when she was working on a difficult line because her shoulders curled over the page, her cigarettes and coffee untouched.

"I was going to go to college," she once told me, "and be an English teacher, then maybe a writer."

"Why didn't you, Mama?"

"Why, silly, I met your father and had you instead."

She touched my hair and smiled when she said this, but her mouth dropped, the corners sagging with regret.

For her birthday, Daddy surprised Mama with a blue-gray Smith Corona typewriter so she could type her poems. My father's suggestion that she send some to magazines thrilled her. She found names and addresses to editors and mailed her poems.

For awhile I'd never seen Mama so happy. Then the letters started coming, bad letters that said my mother's writing was no good.

Daddy tried to explain. "Julia, look here, it doesn't say anything's wrong with your writing. It only says they were unable to use the poems at this time."

"Oh what do you know about poetry, Rupert? And what do you know about me, for that matter? Tell me? What?" Mama's face streaked red as the tears fell. "No, I'll tell you. You don't know a damn thing about poetry. You know even less about me!"

Mama went into another sad spell, crying a lot, angry at Daddy, ignoring me. It lasted a long time. And I never saw her write again.

• • •

DADDY SHOOK MY SHOULDERS. "You can't say careless things in front of your mother. Tess is here to help with the housework, and she shares your room. Understand? You can't tell that you saw me kiss Tess, or that Tess has slept in my bed, do you understand? Do you, Ellie?"

I nodded.

Tess was like the bad letters.

TWELVE

THE SEWING ROOM

While Daddy continued nailing legs on his new bed, I picked wildflowers for Mama's homecoming and carried them back to the house. I needed to trim some dead leaves and long stems, so I went to get Mama's scissors in the sewing room.

Tess was still hard at work to turn Mama's sewing room into a bedroom for Daddy. She'd shoved the black Singer into the far corner and draped all my mother's patterns and cut fabrics over a chair next to the sewing machine. Daddy's brown suitcase was near the door, and more of his clothes filled a cardboard box. On the glass-top table that had held Mama's thimble collection, Tess had placed Daddy's shaving cup and razor. She had taken down garments from the dress rack, replacing them with trousers.

Why couldn't Tess pack up her own things and leave? I wondered. I didn't want her to handle Daddy's clothes as if she were his make-believe wife. I hated the way she crammed all Mama's things against the wall as if they didn't matter.

Mama's sewing basket was on the floor under the window. Kneeling by the basket, I opened its woven lid to find the scissors.

"What are you looking for, Ellie?" Tess asked.

I wished with my whole heart that I could be brave and smart like Mary Roberts. She always had something smart and snappy to say, mostly learned from her older brother. I bit my lip and tried to think of something.

Tess must have thought I hadn't heard her. She repeated her question: "What are you looking for, Ellie?"

And then it came. "None of your beeswax," I said, then looked right at Tess.

"What did you say?" Tess's face turned red.

I picked up Mama's scissors. "You heard me," I said, and marched out of the room.

Mary Roberts could not have done better.

AFTER TRIMMING AND arranging the flowers, I carried them upstairs and placed the vase on the table by Mama's bed, then arranged her lamp and box of tissues. When I turned on the lamp, there was no way to avoid seeing Daddy's absence there.

The room looked sad and lopsided, like a person with only one arm. The table on Daddy's side of the bed was empty. The book he was reading, his wire-rimmed glasses, and alarm clock were all gone. His shoes and boots no longer lined the floor at the foot of the bed. His navy plaid robe had been moved from the bathroom door hook. Checking inside the bathroom, I saw that his toothbrush and shaving cream were missing. I breathed in, sniffing the room. Lysol and bleach covered the cigarette smoke and Old Spice that usually tinted the air.

Back in my parents' bedroom, I opened the cedar closet. Mama's dresses hung alone on the rack. No trousers, no shirts, no row of belts or neckties.

Every trace of my father was gone. I did my best to spread out the few things I could to make the room look better. I placed some of Mama's books on Daddy's side of the bed, and arranged Mama's toiletries across the dresser.

No matter how I moved items around the room, though, there was no way to fix what was wrong.

Daddy called to me from downstairs. He'd put up his bed in the sewing room and was ready to bring Mama home from the hospital. "Let's go," he called.

I bolted into my bedroom and fed Jellybean his second meal of the day. "We can do this, Jellybean," I whispered, then blew a kiss his way.

I dressed as fast as I could, then ran downstairs to wait with my father for the cab.

Tess had dressed and combed her hair. She'd put on a red-and-white-striped dress with red sandals and earrings to match. Her hair was tied back with a ribbon and she'd painted her lips and nails red. Tess looked prettier than I'd ever seen her. I was happy to see she'd fixed up for Mama's homecoming.

But maybe she looked too pretty. Daddy couldn't keep his eyes off her.

When the cab pulled up in front of our house, I yanked Daddy by his sleeve and led him to the door.

As the cab turned off Grace Street, I snuggled close to my father. The pine oil and sawdust smells from his toolshed lingered on his clothes and skin. He was quiet on the ride to the hospital, but I squeezed his strong fingers in mine and tried not to worry. The past few days had been difficult, and it had felt as if something fragile had been broken. Now that Mama was coming home, we'd put the pieces back together.

THIRTEEN

THE GHOST DRESS

A s soon as the cab slowed in front of the hospital, I grabbed the shopping bag with Mama's clothes and leapt to the sidewalk. "Daddy, come on!" My knees twitched and I could hardly stand still.

"Hold your horses, Ellie." My father stepped out of the cab and walked toward me. He smiled, but only for a second. It wasn't the smile he wore when he felt happy, but the quick smile he put on when his mind was in a different place. Miss Wilder called the look "preoccupied."

Knowing Daddy would catch up, I ran ahead, racing down the corridor toward the elevator. I looked straight ahead, barely noticing the smells and sights that usually scared me. After today, the bedpans, nurses, and awful smells would be a bad dream.

"Slow down, Ellie." Daddy tried to rein me in, but I wouldn't wait. His footsteps grew quick behind me.

He caught up with me at the elevator where I had to step aside for an orderly to push an old woman in a wheelchair into the corridor.

On the elevator, I started to wonder which outfit Tess had packed for Mama. I should have checked before leaving home. Some of her dresses might be too tight now that she was going to have a baby. I opened the shopping bag to take a peek.

Curled inside was gray, paisley fabric. Tess had packed the dark, plain dress that had belonged to my dead grandmother. Mama never wore that dress. It was a keepsake, like Mama's wheat china or my white baby shoes.

My knees folded, and I sank to the elevator floor, crying, tired of trying to be brave.

Daddy knelt beside me. "What's wrong? Ellie, what's wrong?" His hands gripped my shoulders. He shook me so hard the back of my neck felt like it might snap.

My mouth opened, but only sobs came out. When the elevator doors parted, a nurse stepped inside. My father asked her to hold the doors open while he scooped me up in his arms and carried me into the corridor.

Daddy asked the nurse if there was a quiet place he could take me. She guided him toward an empty examining room. He thanked her and carried me inside where he set me on a table and held me.

"Tell me what's the matter, Ellie. Please, please, tell me."

I pushed myself from his arms and sat upright so I could face him. Because the table was so high off the floor, my eyes were nearly even with his.

His furrowed brow glistened with sweat.

The whiteness of the room calmed my sobs, but words wouldn't come. I turned away from Daddy and stared at the chart taped to the back of the door. Fixing my eyes on the big black *E,* I pointed to the shopping bag.

The paper rustled as Daddy opened the bag. He pulled out the ghost dress and laid it in my lap.

"This?" Daddy asked. "This is what made you cry?"

I grabbed fistfuls of the dress. "Look at this! This isn't Mama's dress! Smell it!" I shoved the gray dress in my father's face. "This was Nana's dress, the one Mama was hemming at the time of the accident."

"Well, honey," Daddy said, taking the dress from my hands and dropping it back into the bag.

"Well, what?" I crossed my arms across my chest and poked out my chin. I wanted him to make this right.

"Tess didn't know, Ellie. She probably picked the first thing in the closet."

I shook my head. "No, Daddy! Tess picked the ugliest dress in the closet, and she did it on purpose!"

Placing his hands on my shoulders, Daddy stared into my eyes and spoke slowly. He picked each word carefully, the way he did in the hardware store when someone complained about a purchase. "Tess is not perfect, but she's not mean, Ellie. She made a mistake, that's all. Haven't you made mistakes, too?"

"Yes, but . . ."

"Of course you have. We all have. Now please, Ellie. I need you to handle this like a big girl. We talked about this. You promised you were going to take care of Jellybean, help out around the house, and not upset Mama. Remember?"

"I know, Daddy, but . . ."

He put his finger to my lips. "Hush, no more arguing. Tess made a simple mistake. It's not important. Your mother will understand. I'll explain it to her, all right? You don't want to upset her, Ellie. Seeing you cry will only hurt her, and we don't need that, do we?"

I shook my head.

"Remember what I said about your mother being like a lily caught in a hurricane?

"Yes."

"And the only way we can help her is to keep the wind and water around her calm. Understand?"

"Yes, Daddy. I'm sorry."

My father pulled out his handkerchief and dried my eyes and nose.

"Now, are you ready to take your mother home?"

I struggled to smile, then nodded and reached out to him.

Daddy's large, rough hand swallowed mine.

MAMA'S FACE BRIGHTENED when she saw us. I jumped on her bed and threw my arms around her neck, trying to be careful not to hurt her. All the while my heart felt like a balloon ready to burst.

"All set to go?" Daddy asked, leaning to kiss her forehead.

"Am I ever! I already signed most of the forms, and saw both doctors this morning. As soon as I get dressed, we can leave."

"I'll go check at the desk, see if there's anything else to sign while you dress. Should I get a nurse to help you?"

Mama waved her hand. "Oh, no. I can manage on my own."

She lowered her legs over the edge of the bed and sat up, slowly pulling herself into a standing position. "Are those my clothes? Which dress did you pick, Ellie? Shall I try to guess?"

My father answered for me. "I'm afraid there was a mistake, Julia. Tess packed your things, and well, she . . ."

"What, Rupert? What is it? Did you forget the dress? Well . . ."

He held the shopping bag out to my mother and looked down at the floor. I was reminded of the time I handed the librarian a book I'd accidentally dropped in the bathtub, ruining every page.

Daddy lowered his voice. "Tess didn't know, Julia. She just picked the first dress . . ."

Mama took the bag from his hand and looked inside, then she sat back down on the bed, her face drained of all color.

My stomach felt tight and weak all at once. I wanted to believe that God had somehow reached inside that bag and changed

Mama's ghost dress into something else, but one look at Mama's face told me He had not.

Daddy pushed her to speak. "Julia, please. Say something."

Mama didn't lift her head. She pulled the paisley dress from the bag and draped it across her lap. The ghost dress never looked more dark or ugly.

"Damn you, Rupert. Damn you."

FOURTEEN

CUCUMBER SANDWICHES

DURING THE CAB RIDE back home, my parents did not speak to each other. I sat between them, Daddy on my right, Mama on my left. I felt like the division mark drawn down the middle of a battlefield.

Daddy made small talk with the cab driver, making no effort to include my mother.

When did this bad thing happen? When did Daddy turn against Mama? Was it when Tess sat in her truck and blew smoke kisses on his neck? Or maybe it began when he first saw Tess walk into the store, a basket of tomatoes swinging on her arm.

While Daddy talked with the cab driver, Mama stayed perfectly quiet, picking at the stitches in her forehead, causing a thin red trickle of blood to run down her cheek.

My sad mama was coming back. I knew all the signs: the bowed shoulders, nervous fingers picking skin, and the drift-away look in her eyes.

I snuggled close, pulling her hand away from her face as gently as I could. "I've missed you, Mama," I whispered in her ear.

A half smile crossed her pale lips. "I've missed you, too, Ellie. Tell me about Jellybean. How is your little chick?"

Closing her eyes, she leaned her head against the back of the seat. Her bruised skin reminded me of the poem she wrote about shadows crossing a woman's face. In the end of the poem, the woman drowns, but her blue face blooms into a flower. It was a sad and beautiful poem, just like my mother.

Even in my dead grandmother's dress, Mama looked lovely. I wanted to tell her, "You are a queen compared to Tess," but she would not have believed me, and besides, I didn't want to mention Tess's name.

So I leaned close and told her about my tiny chick. Speaking in my best storytelling voice, I drew out the words to make them last. Mama's tight lips parted. Flickers across her eyelids told me pictures played in her mind. Words are magic that way.

I kept talking, stretching out my tale as long as I could, careful not to mention Daddy or Tess. The lines in Mama's face smoothed like an ironed shirt. I licked my thumb and rubbed away the red streak from her cheek.

"I will take care of you, Mama. Always."

It was a promise I meant to keep.

Tess greeted us with a plate of cucumber sandwiches piled on the Christmas tray Mama used for fruitcake and sugar cookies. She smiled with all the sincerity of a game-show hostess showing off a brand new Maytag.

I wanted to slap her.

"I don't care for any," Mama said.

"Me neither," I chimed in. "I hate cucumbers." *I hate you, too, Tess,* I said under my breath.

Daddy took one look at Tess's hurt face and grabbed up sandwiches in both hands. "These are really good," he said, as he crammed another sandwich in his mouth.

I hoped he would choke.

Tess beamed, her pink face aglow as she continued her gracious hostess act. "Well, I also made lemonade, or I could brew some tea if you want something hot."

"No, thank you," my mother said. Mama lifted her head and stared at Tess, her eyes narrow and pointed like darts. "I don't want anything from you."

Mama didn't wait for Tess to speak. She turned and walked upstairs to the room she no longer shared with my father.

MY HANDS SWEATED as I stood in the hallway outside Mama's room. Taking a deep breath, I twisted the brass knob, nudged the door open, and stepped inside.

Mama was perched on the edge of her bed like a child uncertain where or how she should sit. I almost expected her to run from the room, but she must have realized what I already knew: there was no place to go. Tess had already taken over most of the house, buying new brands of detergents, paper towels, and soaps; rearranging furniture to suit herself; leaving her books, cosmetics, and whatnots on tables in every room. This room was the only part of the house left for my mother, and that was spoiled now, too. Spoiled not by what was added, but by what had been taken away.

I sat on the bed and wrapped my arms around Mama's shoulders. Tears washed the faded bruises on her face. "She wants to take him, Ellie. She wants to steal your father." Spit formed in the corners of her mouth. Beneath my hands, the muscles in Mama's back stiffened.

"Daddy would never leave us, Mama." I patted her back, trying to smooth the tension away. "He'll get tired of Tess. You'll get better, and she'll go away for good."

Mama twisted a tissue in her hands. "When she leaves, your father will go with her, Ellie. Watch and see. I know him, Ellie. When we met, your father was a young man working as a field hand. He came to my papa's front door and offered to clear the back pasture for room and board plus wages. Papa gave him the job, and within three weeks, Rupert had cleared that land. When Papa handed him the wage he'd earned, Rupert said he didn't want the money, that all he wanted was a dance with the dark-haired girl he'd seen reading under the willow tree."

"And that was you, Mama?"

Mama smiled. "That was me." She wiped the corner of her eyes with her tissue, then continued. "My father wouldn't hear of it, of course. Papa would not see me married to a field hand. He shoved money into Rupert's hand and told him to leave, even had my brothers escort him to the train depot to be sure we'd seen the last of Rupert Sanders. But your daddy was a determined man, even then. He found his way back to me, and one summer afternoon, he caught me alone under the willow tree. He smelled so good, his arms felt so strong, and when he swirled me around under the perfect sky, I knew I'd go anywhere he'd ask. The next afternoon, I packed my things, and while Papa and Mama were visiting a sick neighbor, I rode away with my handsome prince, all the way to Memphis, where we were married at a little roadside chapel." Mama paused. "So you see, Ellie, I know how your father acts when he is in love."

Mama stared right through me, her mind so far away I felt alone even sitting right beside her.

AFTER HELPING MAMA undress and get into bed, I went back to my room. Jellybean had spent so much time alone and confined to his box that I felt guilty about ever bringing him home. He would have been better off sold to another girl, someone who would love him and tend to him the way he deserved.

Mama had barely touched her tray at the hospital, so she had to be hungry. I knew I was hungry, too, and decided to walk downstairs and find something to eat.

No voices in the kitchen or living room told me that Daddy and Tess had gone outside, maybe to Daddy's toolshed or to the store. I didn't feel like talking to them anyway. I wanted only to eat, and to feed Mama and Jellybean. Afterwards, I wanted a long, deep sleep.

I wanted to make something special for Mama, but I wasn't sure what ingredients or how much trouble I'd be in for messing up the kitchen. I was supposed to use the stove only with an adult present, but bending the rule this once seemed okay.

Mama kept three cookbooks on the counter beside the toaster. I pulled out the one with the red-and-white-checkered cover and sat down at the kitchen table to decide what to fix. The recipes I liked best were the ones with pictures beside them showing you what the finished dish would look like, assuming you got it right, of course.

I admired a plate of spaghetti with three perfect meatballs, covered with a layer of Parmesan cheese that looked like snow. The instructions, though, were a little long.

Deviled eggs were the most difficult food I'd ever made, and Mama had done the hard part: boiling the eggs. My job was to peel away the shells, cut the eggs in half, and fill the eggs with the yolk, mayonnaise, and mustard combination. The spaghetti meal would probably be too much for me to handle on my own.

I returned the cookbook to the counter and decided to find something easier. Soup and sandwiches might be good.

While cutting the tin lid from the Campbell's can, I noticed a note tacked to the pegboard by the telephone: *Ellie, we've gone to Tess's house to get her tomato plants. Will be back in an hour or two. Love, Daddy.*

A panicky feeling came over me. What if Mama was right? What if Daddy did leave? What if he said he was going to get Tess's tomato plants but was lying? I wondered what Mary Roberts would do, but couldn't picture her in a mess like this. She would have handled it long before it got to this point.

After emptying the soup into Mama's pot and adding a can of water, I turned the burner on low heat and sat down at the kitchen table to think.

I reasoned that if Daddy were going to leave, he'd take his clothes, wouldn't he? Unless they're really, really upset, no one runs away from home without taking their clothes. I jumped up from the table and ran into the sewing room to check. All

Daddy's things seemed to be there. His shaving cup, clothes, and alarm clock hadn't been moved since this morning.

I sighed with relief. Maybe there was nothing to worry about after all. Mama and Daddy had disagreed about things before, and they'd always worked them out. Maybe in a few days, they'd calm down enough to talk. Together, they'd decide what to do about Tess. Mama would understand that Daddy couldn't send Tess back to Mr. Reed's house because of the dirty things he did to her. Daddy might want her to stay, but he'd surely see that Mama's feelings had to be considered as well. Somehow, there had to be a better way. Maybe Tess could work in the store and use the money to rent a room? Or maybe she had relatives who lived far away. I would put all my sewing money toward buying her a bus ticket.

I smelled food burning and checked the stove. The soup was fine, but some bread that had fallen under the burner was sending up a thin thread of smoke. The heat and smell reminded me of stormy winter days when the electricity went out. Daddy always rigged up a small gas stove in the living room and Mama melted cheese on thick slices of stale bread, and warmed cocoa or soup in mugs. We curled up in blankets on the floor, the three of us under one cover. With my belly warm and full, I'd listen to their voices and dream until morning.

The soup gurgled on the stove, interrupting my daydream. I turned the heat back a little to keep the bottom of the pan from scorching. Many times, when first learning to heat soup or gravy, I'd left the heat too high and had to spend hours scrubbing pans clean.

Just as I reached for the spoon to stir the soup, Mama screamed.

FIFTEEN

THE BABY

MAMA SCREAMED AGAIN, a long shrill sound.
I couldn't breathe. For a few seconds, I stood frozen, then something broke inside my throat and I screamed, too. Her scream and mine became the same sound, so sharp I felt it slice through me.

Somehow my legs and feet carried me up the stairs toward the mother who needed me.

Lily caught in a hurricane.
Be the calm wind for her.
Be the still water, the gentle rain.

I stopped screaming and tried to breathe.

My legs kept moving.

"Mama! Mama!"

She wasn't in her bed. Shoved to one side, the sheets and covers were piled on the floor. A reddish stain spread out from the bed's center and darkened the floral sheet.

As I started for my room to see if she'd wandered in there, she cried out again. This time, her voice wasn't shrill, but deeper, as if she'd been hurt: a sound caught midway between a scream and a moan.

The noise came from the bathroom. I hurried in that direction, my hands shaking because I didn't know what I'd find. She may have fallen. Or she could have hurt herself on purpose. Sometimes Mama cries the hardest when she hurts inside. From living with Mama, I've come to understand that the places you can't see or reach can hurt most of all.

The door was closed, but knocking didn't seem important. I opened it and stepped inside.

"Oh, Mama!"

She was crouched on the floor between the toilet and bathtub, looking like a frightened animal. Her dark hair fell into her face so that I couldn't see her eyes. I needed to see them. A person's eyes tell everything.

As I moved closer, I looked down and saw a dull red puddle spread out under Mama. She was bleeding! This couldn't be the monthly blood Tess told me about, could it? No, there was too much. This was something bad. I wanted to look away, but couldn't. There was no one else to hand this to and say, "Here, you take it." Mama was mine.

I steadied my voice. "Mama, what happened?"

She moved a little, shifting her hips in the puddle of blood, causing her white nightgown to ride up around her thighs, the fabric soaked in blood. Mama's pale legs were smeared red, too. As I looked closer, I saw that Mama held something in her hands, something small and bloody.

"The baby, Ellie. The baby came out of me," she cried, her face twisted.

Sweat trickled down my neck. I couldn't swallow or breathe. It was as if all the air had been sucked from the room. I opened my mouth, gasping for one deep, clean gulp.

I wanted to erase the sight of Mama holding the bloody thing she called her baby. I swallowed again, and forced myself to kneel beside my mother. I hadn't been there when she fell down the stairs, but I wouldn't leave her again. "Oh, Mama, I'm so, so sorry. Please. Tell me what to do, Mama. What do I do?" My voice shook.

Mama closed her eyes and leaned against the toilet as if she couldn't sit up anymore. As she cradled the baby to her chest, she began to sing a lullaby, her voice quivering.

"Mama, please! You have to tell me what to do. Should I call for the ambulance? Daddy's not here . . ." I'd never called the ambulance, but had practiced at school. Why did Daddy have to pick now to go for Tess's tomatoes?

Mama's mood changed from sad to mad. "He's off somewhere with that slut, isn't he?" She spat the word *slut* the way a snake hisses at passing ankles.

"I don't know," I lied, "I can go find him . . ."

"No, Ellie. He mustn't know about this." She looked worried.

"Mama . . ."

"Promise me, Ellie. Promise me you won't tell Daddy that I bled out the baby. If he finds out, he won't love me anymore, not ever . . . he'll go away with her and . . . and we'll never see him again. Do you want that to happen?"

I kneeled beside Mama and touched her damp hair, brushing a stray wisp from her brow. Her skin felt moist, but cool. "Mama, Daddy will understand. You need a doctor. I'm scared!" *Be the still, calm water.*

"No! I just need you to help me, Ellie." She held out her hand, red with blood. "Please help me."

I nodded. "I'll help you, Mama. Just tell me what to do. How do I help?" *Be the gentle rain.*

"Go downstairs and bring the Reynolds Wrap." Mama's voice sounded sure.

"Reynolds Wrap?" I wondered out loud.

"I can't put him in the ground, I just can't. We'll keep the baby in the freezer. He'll be safe there. Then we'll clean up. Daddy can't see. He can't see this, Ellie!"

Unsure, but anxious to be out of that bathroom, I hurried downstairs for the aluminum foil. The tomato soup I'd left on the stove had boiled over, splattering the stove and counter with red drops.

As soon as I saw the red, I ran to the sink and threw up.

BACK UPSTAIRS, I HANDED Mama sheets of aluminum foil. I might have torn the pieces too big, but I didn't want to measure the baby. I didn't want to touch it, didn't want to know what its skin felt like in my hands.

While Mama wrapped the body, I looked up at the white swirled ceiling, not wanting to see the dead baby again until it was wrapped in foil. Waves moved inside my stomach. I swallowed the sour taste that tried to climb my throat.

Mama spoke to the baby. Over the crinkle of foil, her soft voice cooed. "It will be all right, lovey. Ellie will take you to a safe place. It will be cold and dark, but you mustn't be afraid."

When she finished, she handed me the bundle and told me to take it to the basement and lay it in the freezer. "Put the baby in a nice place, Ellie. Near the cakes and strawberries, not near the beef and venison."

I wanted to tell my mother the baby was dead and wouldn't care where I placed it, that it couldn't hear her singing, couldn't hear her words. But Mama has places in her mind that no one else can go, places where things that make no sense to anyone make perfect sense to her.

Taking the dead baby into my hands, I promised to lay it where she wanted.

The walk to the basement never seemed so long. I wanted to run, to get the baby into the freezer and be done, but my knees felt like rubber. Falling down scared me. I didn't want to drop

Mama's baby. I hurried down the stairs and outside to the sidewalk.

The cellar stairwell scared me more than ever now that Mama had fallen there. I'd never come here in the dark without Daddy. The shadows and cool brick seemed to close in around me. I hurried to open the door and flipped the switch to turn on the overhead bulb. Light filled the center of the room, chasing shadows to the edges. My legs shivered as I stood in the damp, dimly lit space. The single lightbulb flickered above my head. Please God, don't let the bulb burn out and put me in blackness.

Knowing the freezer lid was hard to open, I carefully placed the baby on the floor and pulled the lid up with both hands. A blast of cold air hit my face.

Then as I had promised Mama, I tucked the dead baby between plastic bags of strawberries and a box of honey-glazed donuts. He would be happy there. It was silly to talk to the baby since dead things can't hear. Still, it seemed the right thing to do. Mama would have said something to reassure the baby, so I did it for her. "Rest here, little one. We won't be far away."

I closed the heavy freezer door and hurried back upstairs where my mother soaked in the tub, washing the blood from her hands and thighs. She looked up at me. "You put him in a good place?"

"Yes, Mama." I'd never watched my mother bathe. I noticed the scars across her belly, and wondered if the baby had stretched her skin somehow. Mama's eyes looked glassy, but I didn't want to stare or watch her cry. Afraid to upset her more, I looked away.

"It's so cold in the freezer, Ellie."

"I know."

"And so dark. He'll be afraid, won't he? I shouldn't have sent him to the freezer. That's not a good place." Her voice broke as if she were going to cry again.

"No, Mama. The baby won't be afraid."

"How do you know?" Her eyes widened.

I tried to think of something to say, anything to keep her from sending me back to the cellar to bring up the baby. If Daddy came home and saw her rocking it, he'd have the doctors take her away, maybe this time for good. Daddy might not care now that he had Tess. I couldn't let that happen. I needed Mama.

Using the sponge, I washed Mama's bowed shoulders. "Because I told him. I told the baby not to be afraid."

Her face looked hopeful. "You did?"

I kept talking. When you love somebody, the words you need come as sure and easy as rain.

"Yes, I told him not to be afraid, that his mother loved him, and that he was in a safe place. I told him about Jellybean, and how the Easter bunny was coming soon."

Mama leaned back in the tub. "You did good, Ellie. I don't know what I'd do without you."

After her bath, Mama dried off with a towel. While she went to her room to dress in a fresh gown and get into bed, I cleaned the rust-colored stains from the bathroom floor.

I thought about my God promises, how I'd tried to be good and God still killed my mother's baby. I figured all the talk in church about God being good and loving was just a lie. The truth is, God didn't need Mama's baby half as much as she did. Why couldn't He do that one thing? Was it too much for God to spare a little baby? Maybe God's like the rest of us, doing bad things sometimes just because we can. Only with God, it's not little things like sneaking into the boys' bathroom or stealing an extra cookie when your mother's not watching. With God, it's sending tomato girls to steal your father's heart; it's killing your mother's baby to make her mind go.

DADDY'S VOICE CAME from downstairs and startled me. He couldn't learn about the baby, at least not yet. Mama wasn't ready for him to know the baby died. Maybe Mama was right, that pretending the baby was still alive meant she could make things work again.

I hurried to hide the Reynolds Wrap and Mama's stained clothing, shoving them both to the bottom of the clothes hamper.

A moment later, Daddy tapped on the bedroom door before he stepped inside. "Feeling better, Julia?" His voice was as even as butter. He tiptoed around Mama as he tested her mood. He didn't mention Tess, which meant he wanted to make peace.

Feeling grateful that he was trying, I walked over to my father and wrapped my arms around his waist. His strong body felt as solid as a tree. A bit of happiness washed over me.

Mama sat up in bed and smiled. "Yes, Rupert. I'm just a little tired."

Daddy tousled my hair and moved closer to Mama's bed. He sat down beside her. "What's this?" he asked, pointing to a bulge under the cover next to her.

Mama smiled again. "It's for the baby, Rupert."

She pulled out a skein of pale blue yarn and knitting needles. A half-knitted bootie dangled in her hand.

Tess stood in the kitchen and scrubbed the red soup stains. I remembered how she'd done the same thing the morning after Mama's accident, cleaning the stove and floor where the stew had burned.

"Let me do that," I said. "I'm the one who made a mess." Really, I felt so tired and sad that I wanted to curl up on the sofa, and yet something in me made me take the sponge from Tess's hand. I wanted to clean up the spill myself. Maybe to show Tess I didn't need her, that I could clean my own messes. We could manage fine if she just went away.

While I cleaned, Tess set plates for the sandwiches and macaroni salad she and Daddy bought. She tried to make the table look nice, arranging napkins under each wrapped sandwich and piling chips and pickle slices to the side. I hated her for trying to make my mother's place her own.

Daddy had decided some things. He explained at the table how he thought we needed a schedule, a routine. He said he would sleep on it, and tomorrow give us each a schedule and chore list. There was plenty for everyone to do, and we would all pull together and make this work. Tess would do most of the cooking and laundry. I would do the sweeping, dusting, and washing dishes. Daddy would tend to Mama, but I'd be expected to take her food up to her room and spend some time each day reading to her. He'd spell it out in black and white sometime tomorrow, post a schedule right on the refrigerator where everyone could see.

The rest of the evening was like standing outside someone's house and looking in through the window. You see what goes on: the meals being cooked, eaten, dishes cleared away; the father watching television while the mother darns socks; the children fighting over marbles or playing Old Maid. But you aren't a part of it, you can't taste the lemon cookies or feel the cool, blue marbles in the palm of your hand. You are an outsider, looking in on a world that isn't yours. That's how I felt watching Daddy and Tess. I didn't belong.

At the kitchen table, I bit off pieces of crusty bread and spooned macaroni into my mouth.

Tess and Daddy talked. Their voices sounded so ordinary, as if they'd always drifted across the kitchen table and I just hadn't noticed before this day. Daddy was at ease with Tess in a way he never seemed with Mama.

After dinner, Daddy played the radio low and set up the Scrabble board on the coffee table. Tess twirled her pale hair around her fingers and made words from tiles.

They asked me to join them, and I declined, but I don't remember what excuse I gave. I do remember feeding Jellybean his bedtime gruel and trying hard not to think about the dead baby in the cellar.

No matter how hard I tried, though, I could think of nothing else.

SIXTEEN

PANSIES

MARY ROBERTS CAME BY the next day with a coffee cake covered in golden crumbs and bits of buttered brown sugar. "A get-well gift for your Mama," she said. "My mother wanted to come herself, but she has to finish making coconut cream pies for the church bazaar."

Mrs. Roberts made award-winning pies and had a wall covered with blue and red ribbons from county fairs. I wondered if Mama would be happier if she had something people admired the way they did Mrs. Roberts's pies. Mama had plenty of talent, but her ideas came from places no pie judge would understand.

I thanked Mary for the cake and invited her inside. Tess and Daddy had already finished their morning coffee and gone outside. The smell of coffee hung in the kitchen a long time because Tess used more beans, fixing it the way she said Europeans drink their coffee. She told us she planned to vacation in Paris when she made it big selling Avon. Daddy had smiled, nodded, and said that would be just grand.

"Could we buy you a ticket now?" I'd asked in a tone so smart even Mary Roberts would have been impressed.

"Ellie!" Daddy had scolded me, his voice so disapproving I left the room.

"We should make a special tray for your mama," Mary said as she followed me around the kitchen.

"That's a good idea."

Mary fixed a cup of tea by using hot water from the tap. You're supposed to boil the water on the stove, but tap water works when you are in a hurry, and doesn't taste so bad if you don't mind weak tea.

I cut two cake squares and placed them side by side on Mama's plate, then looked through the cabinets for the silver tray. Maybe using something pretty to serve Mama's food would make her feel a little better.

Mary, who had learned origami at church camp, folded the paper napkin into the shape of a bird, and I hurried to the garden to clip pansies from Mama's flower bed. We found a bud vase for the flowers and carried the finished tray upstairs.

"I'll take it in myself," I told Mary. "You could go get Jellybean ready to play outside. He's in my room, on the bed." The idea of Mary talking to Mama scared me. The dead baby was an awful secret.

"Oh, we have all day. I'm in no hurry. Besides, my mother will want to know if she liked her cake. It's made from a new recipe; this one has walnuts in it."

My forehead dampened. My knees felt like hinges ready to fold.

Mary knocked lightly on Mama's door.

No answer. Good. Maybe Mama was in the bathroom. We could leave the tray and slip out before she noticed.

Mary cracked the door, a little at first, then a bit wider, and we both stepped inside. Mary first, then me.

Mama was sound asleep, her arm curled around her head. Her eyelids looked pink and swollen, which told me she'd been crying.

"Let's not wake her," I said, trying not to cry myself.

We left the tray by her bed and tiptoed away.

Mary and I went across the hall to get Jellybean. He'd tipped over his box and sat on the middle of the bed. I scooped him up in my hands and nuzzled his soft head.

"So these are her things?" Mary asked as she walked around my room looking at Tess's clothes and belongings. Mary opened the lid to the small suitcase where Tess kept all her Avon and other cosmetics. She pulled the lid from one of the small white sample tubes and traced her lips in a deep plum color. "My mother still can't believe that the tomato girl is living with you," Mary said, rubbing her lips together the way women do. Without a tissue to blot the excess, the dark color smeared outside the lines of her lips.

"Yes? What did she say?" I knew Mrs. Roberts would have an opinion.

"My mother said she didn't want to pry or make your Daddy mad, but she said opening your home to that girl will bring more trouble than you ever dreamed. She said the whole Reed family has bred nothing but drunks and whores."

"Let's go," I said and headed for the door with Jellybean cupped in my hands. I didn't want to talk about Tess and her drunk father.

In the kitchen, Mary and I cut ourselves thick slices of cake and poured glasses of cold milk. Mary took the tray to the crab apple tree. I carried Jellybean.

Settled in the grass, Mary fed Jellybean yellow crumbs from her cake. "I wish I could hold my mother's finches," Mary said, "but they are so fast they get away, and so small that if you squeeze them too hard, all their bones will break."

The mention of tiny bones breaking made me feel sick. I tried to get my mind off the dead baby and onto something else. It felt good just to sit cross-legged in the tall grass. So much had happened in the past few days, happy times seemed far away.

I missed being in school, passing notes to Mary Roberts, or listening to Miss Wilder read. But I missed times after school most of all, going to the store to help Daddy, or visiting Mary Roberts's house.

I suggested we play a game, but then we couldn't decide which one. Mary wanted to play catalogs, but with all the trouble over Tess and Mama's dead baby, picking husbands and babies didn't seem like so much fun now.

"I'm tired of catalogs," I said, brushing the cake crumbs from my lap. "What about checkers?"

Mary stroked Jellybean's head. "Nah, checkers are boring."

"We could play store. I could bring out some Jell-O boxes and cans. You can be the grocer."

"You left your Monopoly game at my house, remember? We can't play store without money."

Mary Roberts thinks of everything.

"Well, let's just walk around until we get an idea."

Mary agreed. She carried Jellybean while I ran our plates and glasses back the kitchen. I almost went upstairs to check on Mama, but didn't want to risk waking her.

I hurried back outside to find Mary walking toward my father's shed, where he and Tess stood watering tomato plants on Mr. Morgan's truck bed. I ran to catch up.

"You girls want to help us set out these tomatoes in the garden?" Daddy asked, smoothing his hair back with his hands. His nails were black with dirt.

Tess hardly noticed us as she traced her fingers along each green leaf, checking the pale undersides for aphids. She pinched off yellow leaves and tossed them to the ground.

Normally, I loved working in the garden. Knowing seeds would take root and send up tiny green tendrils was the closest thing to magic I knew. But I didn't want to help plant a garden for Tess.

Lined up on the back of Mr. Morgan's truck, the potted plants covered two thirds of the bed. This would take up most of our small garden. I didn't understand why Tess needed so many or why they had to be planted at all. She didn't live with us and had her own home. "Why do you need to set the plants in the garden if Tess is only going to be here until Mama is well?"

Daddy picked up a plant in each hand. "This is Tess's home for as long as she wants to stay. Besides, we have no idea how long your mother may need help. While Tess is living here, I want her to have a garden."

"Well, I don't want to help," I said.

"Me neither," Mary agreed.

Daddy frowned and shrugged his shoulders. "Suit yourselves."

MARY AND I CLIMBED into my tree house and sat on the braided rug my mother had given me to cover the rough wood floor. We played Go Fish while Jellybean napped. My hands began to fill with cards, and I knew I'd soon lose the game.

Mary peeked through the pink curtains. "Looks like your Daddy's planning to keep that tomato girl around for a long time."

After losing, I dealt us both a new hand. "I don't know, Mary. I've seen Daddy kiss her." I felt ashamed to tell the secret, but needed someone to give me advice. "What if that means he loves her?"

"Well, don't worry." Mary picked up her cards. "He can't leave your mother with a baby on the way."

I couldn't bring myself to tell Mary how the baby had been born dead. She was my best friend and knew many secrets, but I just couldn't tell Mary we had a dead baby in the freezer. I couldn't tell anyone.

"Besides," Mary added, "once your daddy sees that girl have a seizure, foaming at the mouth like a mad dog, he's not going to want her."

A little reassured, I picked up my cards and waited for Mary to arrange hers the way she wanted. While she spread her cards into a fan, I looked out my tree house window into the yard. I saw Daddy grab his hoe. He walked to the garden and drew long furrows in the ground, then plowed through Mama's blue pansies as if they weren't there.

SEVENTEEN

MAMA'S ROOM

BLACK CROWS PICKED at bits of blue flowers. Their oily feathers shone as they tossed around Mama's pansies in search of food.

"I think you should go now," I said to Mary Roberts.

She leaned across my lap to look through the window. She gasped before dropping her handful of cards. They swirled in a current of wind and fell to the ground like small kites. Startled, the crows cawed, flapped their wings, then continued to chew on Mama's plowed flowers.

I'm not a superstitious girl. My ears don't burn when somebody talks about me. I've never been afraid to walk under ladders and don't fret over broken mirrors. The only superstitions I ever believed were ones about luck: rabbits' feet, four-leaf clover, found pennies, and first stars. But as more black crows gathered, a strange feeling came over me. The dark feathers, the eyes that looked like stones: these were bad signs.

A few crows waited in the trees while others flocked on the ground to peck at the flowers. Three times they cawed to each other, then grew still. My skin prickled at their silence.

TESS DIDN'T WANT me to move into Mama's room. She threw herself on my bed and stretched out on her stomach. "Why don't you like me?" she asked, her lower lip poked out as if she could make me feel sorry for her.

I folded my nightgown and shoved it inside a grocery bag. "It isn't that, Tess. It's just . . . well, I need to go."

"If you liked me, you'd stay."

"I just want to be with Mama."

"It's because of the pansies, isn't it? Your daddy already explained they were going to die anyway. Mites had gotten into them. We had to spray my tomato plants just to plant them in the same bed. Besides, your mama needs rest. She won't be able to tend to a garden this spring."

"I could have watered Mama's pansies for her. And there are sprays to kill mites. Daddy sells them at the store."

"Your daddy just didn't think of that, Ellie. He's had a lot on his mind." Tess frowned again.

I wanted to come back with something clever, but couldn't think of anything, so I kept packing. Only so many things fit inside a paper bag, so I chose the most important, knowing I could always come back tomorrow. Down the hall is not far to travel.

Tess could pout and brood on her own. "I want to be with my mother. It's where I belong."

"Well, I don't want to sleep in here by myself. There's too many strange noises. Tree branches tapping on the window and Jellybean scratching the floor of his box. Just the other night, a mouse was chewing on the lamp cord. I heard his little teeth hit each other."

She was making up excuses. The tree limbs barely reached the window; we didn't have any mice; and Jellybean never woke in the dark. Still, I didn't want to argue. "Well, Jellybean will be with me, so you won't hear him. Daddy can set a mousetrap and trim back the tree limbs. Just ask him. He'll do anything you want." I tried not to say the word *you* louder than the other words, but couldn't help myself. None of this would have happened if Tess hadn't come to our home. Daddy would be caring for Mama, sleeping in the room with her. Her pansies would be blooming in the garden. Maybe, just maybe, the baby would not have died.

"You don't understand." Reaching over the edge of the bed, Tess grabbed the paper sack from my hand and turned it upside down.

My clothes, shoes, and toothbrush fell to the floor.

"Tess!" My hands went to my hips and I stood there like a mother scolding her child.

"Don't be mad at me, Ellie," she begged, tilting her head to one side and wrinkling her forehead. "I don't like to be alone in the dark. Don't you ever feel afraid when you open your eyes and see nothing but black? Afraid to reach out because you don't know what's there? Don't leave me, Ellie."

Kneeling on the floor, I picked up my belongings and crammed them back inside the paper sack.

My feelings were as jumbled as a shoebox full of crayons. I hated Tess for the way she treated Mama, taking over the kitchen and garden, moving Daddy into the sewing room, sending the ghost dress to the hospital. I hated her cucumber sandwiches, her pouty red lips, and the way she drew my father's eyes like a magnet.

And yet, Tess wasn't all bad. She'd been like a big sister, playing Avon Lady and dress-up. She'd given me kissing lessons and my first Kotex. She could be mean, but with the epilepsy, no mother, and a dirty father who did awful things to her, maybe she didn't know better.

Still, my mother needed me. More and more, Tess had my father, leaving only me to care for Mama.

If not for Tess, maybe Mama wouldn't have gone back into her sad world or sent the baby to the freezer. Even if Daddy couldn't have saved the baby, he would have been here when it died. He'd have known what to say to Mama. He would have buried the baby in the ground where dead things belonged.

"Well?" Tess waited for an answer.

My eyes stung, but hard blinks kept me from crying. Yes, I knew what it was like to be scared. I felt scared all the time. My whole life I'd been afraid of Mama's dark places taking her for good, scared that those same places might live inside me. Now I feared that Tess would take away my father, and my mother might grow so sad I wouldn't know how to make her smile again.

But I didn't owe Tess an answer. She'd taken too much. I wouldn't give her anything else. Sometimes you have to hold onto what you have, even if the only thing left is fear.

I grabbed Jellybean, dragged my sack down the hall, and moved into Mama's room.

"HAVE YOU SEEN the baby, Ellie?" Mama asked. She lay in the bed and stared at the ceiling.

I tucked my bag inside one of Daddy's empty dresser drawers. The unfinished wood smelled of his aftershave. I inhaled deeply, as if I could breathe Daddy back into this room. "No, Mama. I've spent the day playing with Mary and Jellybean."

The saucer by the bed told me she'd hardly eaten any of the cake. "Mama, you have to eat something. Didn't you like the cake? Mrs. Roberts made it for you, a get well present."

She touched the blue pansies on the tray, her fingers stroking the skirt-shaped petals. "I'm worried about the baby, Ellie. So cold, it's so cold in the freezer. And the basement gets completely dark; there's only that slit for a window. Babies are always afraid of the dark."

"It's not too dark. Daddy put a new lightbulb in the freezer about a week ago."

Seeming satisfied, she settled back against her pillow and looked at me. Her brow furrowed, which meant something troubled her. "He's got to have a name, Ellie. I haven't been able to think of one. It's like my head's thick with clouds," she said, scrubbing her temples with her fists.

Climbing on the bed, I placed my hands over hers. "Easy, Mama. Your head will feel better if you rub like this."

Her hands slowed under mine.

"There, that's better. You'll think of a good name later, Mama. Try not to worry about that right now." I offered her some cake. "You have to eat to keep up your strength." I said it steady and firm, just like she used to tell me to eat my chicken soup when I had a cold.

She opened her mouth and took a bite of buttery cake. Mama didn't bother to take the fork in her hand or to wipe the yellow crumbs from her lips, but let me feed her the way a mother feeds a baby. This is how her mind works, wrapping itself so tight around a thought or idea she cannot remember simple things like feeding herself.

After finishing the cake, Mama wanted to know about Daddy and Tess. Her eyes darted around the room as if she expected to see Tess standing in a corner, eavesdropping. "She doesn't come around me, did you notice?"

I placed the empty saucer on the bedside table and walked into the bathroom to get a wet cloth to clean her mouth. The clothes hamper with the bloody gown and panties reminded me I'd need to move them before Tess did the laundry. Maybe I'd sneak them to the basement or to the trash can beside Daddy's toolshed. Washing them myself would be too risky.

"You know why that slut stays away from me, don't you?" Mama asked as I came back into her room. If she kept up this way, she'd soon worry herself into a crying spell. After Mama's anger rises so far, the tears follow.

"Daddy said it would be best if he and I look after you." I walked over to Mama and dabbed the crumbs from her lips.

"Yes, and what will her job be? As if I didn't know." Mama's brow wrinkled.

"Tess will help Daddy at the store and do the cooking and cleaning here." I folded the damp cloth and covered her forehead.

"They're up to no good, the two of them. You understand what I mean, don't you, Ellie? They're sleeping together, I know it."

"Mama, please. I don't want to talk about Daddy and Tess. I just want you to get better so she can leave and we can be like we used to be."

My face warmed with shame to think what Tess and my Daddy might be doing. I didn't understand it all, but knew a little. Mary Roberts had given me the birds and bees talk. She'd undressed Barbie and Ken and rubbed them together, face to face. I didn't want to think of my Daddy like the naked Ken doll on top of Tess.

Mama pulled the cover up under her chin. "We won't ever be like we used to be, Ellie. Not as long as that whore lives here."

"But she'll leave, Mama. When you're better."

She shook her head. "No, no, no! You don't see. You don't know your father. He won't let her go. I see it in his face." The quiver in her voice told me she was about to cry.

"Here, Mama, we need to play with Jellybean." I placed him on the bed. Mama's words made me want to cry, too, but if I broke down, who would hold Mama together?

She smiled and cupped her hands around him. I sighed, glad to see her attention shift to my green chick. "Have you taken him to show the baby?"

Talking about the dead baby gave me a sick feeling, but talking about Daddy and Tess was worse. That hurt went all through me like a dull butter knife. "I haven't, Mama, but will tomorrow."

"You're a good girl, Ellie. I don't know what I'd do without you. I'm counting on you to look after the baby for me. Go and check on him, tell him he's going to be fine. I know he's frightened. I heard him cry."

"Cry?" My skin prickled and felt cold.

"Yes. While I was napping, he kept crying for me. It was awful, Ellie. I need to see him. You'll bring him up to me soon, Ellie? When your Daddy goes to work?"

"Mr. Morgan's going to fill in for Daddy for awhile. Try not to worry, Mama. You need to rest. We'll figure this out. Promise."

I curled up beside my mother and rested my head beside her face. For awhile, I lay on the bed beside Mama, the two of us curled into each other like question marks.

"There has to be a way to get rid of her, Ellie. It doesn't matter how. She needs to leave. I was thinking maybe if I wrote to her father. Yes, that's what I'll do. I'll write him and explain why she can't stay. Or maybe I'll telephone him. He's bound to have a phone out there, if I can get the number . . . in the phone directory . . . or maybe the operator will know . . . "

Mama's voice trailed off.

The room soon darkened. Storm clouds blew in and spilled rain. I fell asleep to the sound of raindrops on the tin roof.

I DREAMED THE dead baby crawled out of the freezer to find me. His blue body shivered from the cold. Pulling himself up the stairs, he squirmed his way from step to step, not so much crawling, but moving the way an earthworm does.

Daddy walked in and found the baby, then snatched him up in his arms. Covering the baby's mouth with his, Daddy breathed the baby back to life. Mama and I watched as the baby's tiny chest expanded like a thin balloon, the delicate ribs bending like stems. The frost melted away and pink skin showed through. The baby didn't shiver or struggle, but curled in Daddy's arms.

Mama smiled and held out her hands. She wanted to hold her baby. Her eyes filled with hopeful tears. I held my hands out toward the baby, too.

Daddy didn't give the baby back to my mother or me. He said we'd killed his son.

Mama screamed, "No, Rupert! Please! Give me my baby."

Daddy shook his head and turned his back to us. He walked to the opposite side of the room and handed the baby to Tess.

A loud bang woke me. It had been raining as I fell asleep, but the noise that woke me was too loud to be thunder. My heart burned like a hot coil. My ears rang.

I knew that sound, had heard it up close once before. Last fall, while walking in deep woods with my father, we'd found a deer caught in barbed wire. Her neck, sliced open, spilled so much blood that Daddy said nothing could be done. He had to put her out of her misery. I'd turned away, not wanting to see. Even with my hands pressing my ears, the noise had pounded inside my head.

In the dark room, I touched my mother's side of the bed. My hand felt a cold sheet where her body had been.

EIGHTEEN

THE GUN

I SAT UP IN BED, frozen in place, too afraid to go downstairs. The blasts had sounded so loud, rattling the walls and
floor.

The thought of Mama or Daddy, lying dead on the kitchen
floor, made me shudder with fear. "Let it be Tess," I prayed as I
sat in the dark.

I knew that was a bad thing to say. It's always wrong to wish
somebody dead, even your worst enemy. I didn't care. "Please,
God, don't let it be Mama or Daddy. I won't ever ask another thing
as long as I live. If somebody was shot, please let it be Tess."

I wondered if Mason Reed had come for Tess, and he and
Daddy had fought. Neither Tess nor Daddy had said anything
about their trip to pick up Tess's tomato plants. Had Mr. Reed
been there? And where was Mama? Had Daddy found the baby
and argued with her about it? Would Mama shoot Tess to keep
Daddy?

Maybe this wasn't even about Tess or the baby. Maybe a rob-
ber had broken in to steal the few nice things we owned, Mama's
good china or Daddy's radio.

But in those few long, dark seconds after the shots fired, I heard Tess cry, and then Daddy's voice as he swore out loud.

I didn't hear Mama. I strained to listen, but the floorboards muffled their voices. I heard dull, scuffling noises like furniture moving across the floor and glass breaking, but no sound from Mama.

Somehow, I had to make myself go downstairs. The phone was there, by the kitchen table. If Mama or Daddy were hurt, the ambulance wouldn't know to come unless someone called.

I crawled out of bed and tiptoed in the dark, feeling my way with my hands to the door and into the hallway. A little light from downstairs made it easier to see going down the steps.

There, in the kitchen, Tess leaned against the stove. She pressed a dish towel against her face and sobbed.

Daddy lay on the floor, pinning my mother face down under him.

I couldn't move. I'd never seen my father hurt my mother on purpose.

"Give me the gun, Julia." His hands pressed Mama's body against the black and white tiles.

My hands shook.

Sweat dripped from Daddy's forehead. His shirt, stained with sweat and dirt, clung to his wide back.

Mama struggled against my father. "Get off me, Rupert!" She gripped the rifle under her belly.

Daddy managed to pull the gun from beneath her and shove it across the slick floor, out of reach.

As Daddy stood up, Mama pulled herself to her knees and tried to crawl away, but Daddy grabbed a handful of her nightgown to hold her in place. He locked his arms around her waist and held her. She kicked and screamed, her eyes so glassy and wide they scared me. Dirt covered the front of her gown, dark smudges the size of her hands. My mother's blue pansies scattered on the floor.

Everything happened so fast, I didn't know how to make sense of any of it. Maybe Mama went to the cellar to visit the dead baby. Maybe she couldn't sleep and wanted to take a walk, or had come downstairs to find Mr. Reed's phone number. She must have gone outside and seen the flowers Daddy dug up to make room for Tess's tomato plants. Had Mama gone to the shed to get Daddy's gun? Maybe Daddy heard her outside and thought she was a prowler. Or maybe . . .

Just then, Mama saw me on the bottom step. "Ellie," She reached out her hands to me. "Help me, Ellie, don't let them put me away, please. Please help . . . don't let them . . ."

"Daddy, don't hurt her." I came closer and tried to touch my mother, but Daddy shouted, "No!" His harsh voice startled me, making me cry.

Daddy dragged Mama to the pantry near the back porch. After shoving her inside, he grabbed a chair and wedged it under the doorknob to keep her there.

I moved toward the door.

"Don't you touch that chair," he ordered, pointing his finger at me.

"I can't . . . I can't . . . take this, Rupert," Tess said between sobs.

"It's okay, honey. Just relax." Daddy went to Tess and wrapped his arms around her.

Tess pointed at the wall where there were two black holes. The bullets had wedged in the kitchen wall near her.

Mama banged and kicked inside the pantry. Kneeling on the floor, I tried to talk to her through the tiny keyhole. "Mama, don't." But she kept pounding and kicking, making too much noise to hear my voice.

She said bad words, too. Awful words. And her voice sounded so hard.

Tess wrapped her arms around my father's neck and cried. "She's mean, Rupert! I don't want to stay in this house with a crazy, mean woman."

Daddy stroked her hair and told her not to fret.

I tapped on the pantry door. Using my knuckles, I kept tapping, slow and gentle like a heartbeat.

Mama quieted down.

Daddy saw me by the door. "Ellie, get away from there. Come on, we're going upstairs," he said.

"But, what about Mama? We can't leave her here." Determined not to leave, I held onto the doorknob.

"She needs to calm down, Ellie. Just for awhile." Daddy knelt beside me and held out his hand.

"You'll let her out later?"

"Yes, of course."

"Tonight?"

"Tonight."

"You promise?"

"I promise."

I put my hand into my father's and let him pull me up. I didn't want to leave, but knew the sooner I did what Daddy wanted, the sooner he'd open the door and let Mama out of the pantry.

Upstairs, Daddy helped Tess into my bathtub so she could soak. He poured her a drink from his whiskey bottle and told her to finish it all. "This will make you feel better," he said.

I wished there was a pretty amber drink that would make me feel better, but Daddy never let me even sip from the whiskey bottle.

I sat on the floor outside the bathroom and chewed on my cuticle. As soon as I could stand up, I'd check on Jellybean, and then I'd talk to Daddy about Mama. She wouldn't spend the night in the pantry. Daddy had promised.

Just as the house quieted, someone knocked on the door downstairs. At first, I thought it was Mama, but Daddy looked out the window and swore. "Goddamn, it's Sheriff Rhodes."

"A neighbor must have heard the gunshot," Tess said.

"Shit, this is all I need. Christ!" Then he turned to me. "I want you to keep Tess company for awhile, Ellie. Read to her or something. Everybody just needs to relax a little, okay?" Daddy wiped the sweat from his face with his shirt sleeve.

I tried to offer a smile, but couldn't. I nodded, then walked to my room and pretended to look at a book.

Daddy went downstairs. The back door slammed.

I waited a moment, then tiptoed into the hallway. I didn't want to be seen.

Down the hall, Tess refilled the bathtub.

The sound of a car pulling away told me Daddy had lied. If Sheriff Rhodes knew Mama was locked in the pantry, he wouldn't have left her there. The sheriff thought the world of Mama. Once, when he'd said his wife made fun of his charcoal drawing of eggs, bowls, and apples, Mama kissed his smudged fingers and told him he had Picasso's hands. He'd adored my mother since.

A few minutes after the car drove away, Daddy came in carrying something. When he turned on the light, I saw the syringe and brown jar in his hand.

NINETEEN

SNOW ANGEL

I KNEW WHAT WAS going to happen, so I sat on the stairs with my eyes closed and covered my ears with my hands. But I couldn't keep out the sounds or the pictures inside my head: Daddy's dirty work boots kicking away the chair that held the pantry door closed . . . hinges creaking as he opened the door . . . scuffle noises as he held my mother down . . . Mama screaming when she saw the syringe in his hand . . . her sobs as the needle broke her skin . . . the soft thud when her body folded on the floor.

After she quieted, I opened my eyes and uncovered my ears. I heard Daddy come out of the pantry.

A long, long time had passed since Daddy last tranquilized Mama. She had been getting better, her bad spells were coming less often. Now, like a strong wind that suddenly changes direction, they were back . . . Mama's tears and screams . . . Daddy holding her down to put the needle into her skin . . . The lines on Daddy's face . . . The voices inside Mama's head . . . And the sad, sick feeling that churned in my stomach like sour milk.

Daddy turned at the foot of the steps. Mama's body was a limp dishrag in his arms. He was coming upstairs.

I was supposed to be with Tess, who was soaking in the bathtub, and there wasn't enough time for me to get back to my room, and no hiding place on the landing.

The thud of Daddy's boots on the steps matched the beating of my heart.

"Ellie, I thought I told you to stay in your room and read to Tess?" He spoke softly, but his anger was clear.

I nodded, and opened my mouth, but no words came.

"You disobeyed me."

His stern tone made me shiver.

"Come with me, Ellie."

I followed him into Mama's room, where he laid her on the unmade bed. Her head sank into the pillow. She looked like a broken doll, and her blistered face was red, swollen, and bruised. The stitches on her forehead had broken open in the struggle, and dried blood streaked down her cheek. Garden dirt soiled her white nightgown.

At the foot of her bed, I stood and watched Mama breathe. As long as she breathed, she couldn't be dead.

I wanted to wash her, make her pretty and whole like she was on the day I left her alone to get my chick. If only we could go back to the time before her fall. Tess wouldn't have come, and the baby wouldn't have died. We would not be facing this awful, awful night.

Sitting on the edge of Mama's bed, Daddy motioned for me to climb onto his lap.

I paused. The syringe might still be in his pocket. Needles scared me. Lately, my father scared me, too. Who knew what the medicine in the brown bottle might do with Mama so weak from losing the baby? Daddy didn't know about the blood she'd lost. What if he'd given her too much?

Mama's chest moved up and down, but the rest of her body stayed perfectly still. She didn't seem to hear. Her eyelids didn't flicker the way they did when she dreamed. Except for the rise and fall of her chest, Mama looked dead.

Daddy stood and placed his hand on my shoulder. His touch startled me. My body jerked. Had he stabbed me with the needle?

As if reading my thoughts, Daddy pulled the medicine and syringe from his pocket and set them on the bedside table. "I'd never do anything to hurt you, Ellie. Never." When Daddy motioned for me again, I climbed onto his lap, sinking into his arms.

Not so long ago, Daddy's lap was a place to hear stories, steal kisses, or beg for help with homework. Now his lap was where he explained hard and awful things. Maybe Daddy could make sense of it all, but to me everything was coming apart.

"Ellie, you have to know I wouldn't hurt your mother on purpose. I couldn't just leave her locked in the pantry. She wasn't going to calm down by herself. You saw how she acted. Now, what if she really hurt Tess badly? What if the ambulance and police had to come?"

"You mean Mama might go to jail?"

"Well, that's one possibility. That would be really bad, don't you think?"

"Yes, but . . ."

Daddy cleared his throat. I smelled the whiskey smell as he talked. "So I did what I had to do to calm Mama down, make her sleep." He paused before continuing. "Remember when you bought Mary Roberts that glass ballerina and accidentally knocked it off the table?"

"Her head broke into pieces. She was ruined."

"Exactly. And it was Christmas Eve. We couldn't glue the broken head back together because there were so many small pieces. And all the stores were closed . . ."

"So we went out to your toolshed and made Mary a cradle for her ragdoll."

"Yes. And remember what we said?" Daddy's face looked hopeful.

"It wasn't the fanciest cradle . . ." I recited.

". . . and it wasn't the gift we'd wanted for her . . ." Daddy chimed in.

"But we'd done the best we could . . ."

". . . and no one can do better than that."

Daddy smiled and hugged me for remembering. "That's all I did, Ellie. The best I could do. I wish your mother understood and handled things better, but she doesn't. And I can't let her hurt Tess or herself. So I gave her medicine that will keep her asleep. Maybe, just maybe, she'll be calmer when she wakes up. Understand?"

I nodded, but still didn't like what he'd done. Maybe he'd given Mama shots in the past to help her. This time it was different.

This time wasn't about Mama.

This was about Tess.

Daddy hugged me again, harder, burying his face in my hair. I loved him and hated him all at once. So many feelings swelled inside me. I wanted to stay the night in Mama's room to watch over her, but Daddy said no. "Not until she's better, Ellie. The tranquilizer will wear off tomorrow and you can see her then."

Too tired to argue, I nodded. "Can I kiss her good-night?"

"Of course."

I climbed down from his lap and walked to the head of Mama's bed. Careful not to jar the mattress, I leaned forward and kissed her soft, damp cheek. "'Night, Mama."

"You go on to your room now. I'll be there in a minute."

I left the room to get ready for bed, but knew somehow I'd find a way back to Mama before morning.

Tess wouldn't let Daddy sleep downstairs in the sewing room. "I can't sleep up here alone, Rupert. I'm afraid of her."

Daddy didn't tell Tess he'd given Mama a shot to make her sleep through the night. He put his arms around Tess and said, "Don't worry. I'll stay right here with you."

The three of us slept in my bed.

Tess wore her pink baby-doll nightgown and curled up against my father who'd taken off his clothes down to his white boxers.

Sleeping in bed beside Daddy and Tess felt all wrong, like wearing somebody else's underwear. I scooted to the bed's edge and faced the wall. I tried to pretend they weren't there, but it was useless. The ointment Daddy had rubbed on Tess's shoulders mixed with her honeysuckle perfume and made a thick, sickening smell. The sour whiskey on Daddy's breath tinted the air, and each time he moved, I smelled sweat from his body.

I placed Jellybean beside me and wrapped my arm around him so he wouldn't tumble off the bed. I inched as close to the edge as I could without falling.

There wasn't any sound from Mama's room. She didn't cry, scream, or call out for anyone. The medicine had put her into a deep, deep sleep. At least if the dead baby cried, she wouldn't hear it. If she slept, she couldn't prowl the house in search of Daddy's gun. But the quiet worried me, too. What if she stopped breathing? I didn't know how far it might be from deep sleep to dying. That scared me.

I didn't want to sleep. Too many bad dreams might come: Daddy shooting me with the syringe . . . the dead baby chasing me . . . Tess's father with dirty hands . . . Mama pointing a gun . . .

Daddy snored, tossing from side to side. With so little room in my bed, his face ended up against the back of my neck, his warm breath dampening my skin.

My stomach felt queasy. Quickly, I slipped out of my bed, taking Jellybean with me.

Maybe I intended to go to the bathroom and drink water or put a wet cloth to my face. Maybe I had no plan in my mind at all. But as soon as my feet touched the floor, I wanted only one thing: to go to my mother.

The hallway was so dark—dead babies, dirty hands, tomato girls, guns.

I shoved the door open and rubbed the wall to find the light switch.

When I saw Mama, my knees folded. I had to lean against the wall to steady myself.

Daddy had put a rag into her mouth. Her hands, bound with bedsheets, were pulled up to the headboard. Stretched out on the blanket, Mama looked like a snow angel tied to a tree.

TWENTY

BRAIDS

Mama didn't stir when I pulled the rag from her mouth. I kissed her lips; they were dry and chafed. How could Daddy do such a thing? Part of me wanted to run back to my room and shake him as hard as I could. Didn't he know that what he was doing was wrong? What had happened to the Daddy who took care of Mama?

The knots on Mama's wrists were as tight as fists and had turned her hands blue. I tugged and twisted, tried to find a gap to slip my finger through, but the knots wouldn't give.

I'd need something sharp to cut Mama loose. Scissors, even a knife might work, but that meant going downstairs.

I put Jellybean inside a clothes basket in Mama's bathroom closet. Then I hurried back to Mama. I placed my palm across her mouth and nose to make sure she was breathing. Warm breath kissed my skin.

I didn't want to leave her side, but I needed the scissors to free her.

I walked softly, trying not to make the floorboards creak. A sure way to get caught in a sleeping house is to make too much noise. If I imagined myself going to the kitchen for an ordinary reason, like getting a glass of milk, the trip downstairs wouldn't frighten me. I'd gone to the kitchen many times during the night, never afraid unless thunder cracked outside the window or a spider crawled across the floor.

But now, thinking of milk reminded me of baby bottles, and the frozen baby wrapped in tinfoil. So many bad pictures came to my mind, no amount of pretending could erase them.

I chewed on my bottom lip and kept walking. I had to fight the bad pictures.

I pushed myself forward, down the dark stairs.

In the kitchen, my feet stepped on something damp, cool, and soft. I clamped my hand over my mouth to keep from screaming, then remembered the pansies scattered on the floor. I'd need to sweep before Mama woke in the morning and saw her wilted flowers again. Sometimes, after the shots, Mama didn't remember too much. Maybe she'd forget her ruined pansies.

I'd left one pair of scissors in the kitchen drawer when I trimmed flower stems, but I'd need bigger ones to cut the knotted bedsheets. Those scissors should have been in Mama's sewing basket, but nothing was in its usual place since Tess had rearranged the room for my father.

I hunted through Daddy's clothes and shoes, bumping into the table that held his razor and shaving cream. I was afraid to turn on the light, but the moon glowed through the window and made it a little easier to see. The black-handled shears lay on the chair by the bed. As I reached for them, I heard gurgling sounds from upstairs as someone flushed the toilet.

Daddy or Tess must have awakened. I prayed it was Tess. She wouldn't notice me gone, and if she did, she wouldn't care.

Footsteps moved across the hall, maybe into Mama's room. I couldn't tell whose footsteps. Bare feet don't make much noise.

"Ellie?"

Daddy's voice, coming downstairs.

Think. What would Mary Roberts do? Whenever she got caught, she twisted the story or left something out. She was clever that way.

I'm not such a fast thinker. Sometimes I need more time than I have.

What to do? What to say?

"Ellie?" Daddy's voice grew louder. The pad of feet against wood told me he was almost there.

I crawled into Daddy's bed and shoved the scissors under the pillow.

"Ellie, what are you doing down here?"

I peeked out of one eye. Daddy leaned against the door frame, a cigarette in his hand. His dark hair stood up on his head.

Rubbing my eyes as if I'd been asleep, I explained there wasn't enough room in my bed. "I want to sleep down here, Daddy." I faked a yawn, hopeful that Daddy would think twice about making me return to my bed.

"Okay, angel." He stepped into the room and put out his cigarette in the bottom of his shaving cup. As he leaned to kiss my forehead, I smelled the cigarettes and whiskey on his breath. "I'll stay with you until you fall asleep," he said, crawling into the bed with me. As his arm fell across my belly, he whispered good-night. His breathing slowed in my ear. A few minutes later, Daddy's mouth opened in a snore. What scared me most was that Tess would wake and find Daddy gone. She might scream and wake Mama, and I didn't want Mama to wake up and see her tied hands.

Inch by inch, I slid down the bed. Daddy snored again, pausing for just a second when my hand fished under the pillow for the scissors. I kissed Daddy's rough cheek. Despite all the bad things he'd done, I still loved him. He wouldn't have done these things if not for Tess. She was like a witch casting an evil spell on him. If only I could make her leave. I wanted my father back.

MAMA NEEDED ME. I hurried back upstairs, walking down the hall on tiptoes to avoid waking Tess. Asleep, she'd be less trouble. I held my breath as I passed my room. The bedsprings creaked, then were quiet again.

Wet with sweat, my hands made the scissors slippery to hold. I nearly dropped them before opening the door.

Inside Mama's room, I sank to the floor and leaned my head against the dresser to watch her breathe. Her chest rose and fell under her dirty nightgown. Sleeping, only sleeping, I reminded myself.

Cutting the knots worried me. Mary Roberts would call this a bona fide dilemma. If I cut the knots, Daddy would be furious. Who knew what he might do? He'd already locked Mama in the pantry, given the shot to make her sleep, and tied her to the bed. What if Daddy decided this was the last straw and called the police or the asylum, and had them take Mama away for good? Or what if I let Mama go, and then she hurt herself? She'd done that before, taking too many aspirin, and Daddy had to shove his fingers down her throat until she threw up.

And yet, it wasn't right to leave Mama like this. She looked dirty and smelled bad. Dried blood stained her face. Her arms, pulled over her head, were sure to get stiff and sore. She'd grow thirsty, hungry, and need to go to the bathroom.

If I cut her loose, maybe we would have to run away. Mama, Jellybean, and me. Where would we go? What would we eat? The night I ran away, Miss Wilder looked after me. Could I go back there with Mama? No—Miss Wilder would call Daddy.

Without Daddy, could I handle Mama on my own? I'd practiced all my life, knew all her moods, how to go slow and easy when she grew upset. There were the times, though, when only

Daddy knew how to handle Mama, times when she grew out of control and only someone bigger and stronger could stop her. Sometimes the shots were the only way.

My mind was a spinning top of worries. I blinked my eyes and tried not to think anymore.

This was my mother tied to the bed. Not a stranger, not Tess, not some madwoman. My mother. No matter how mad Daddy would be, I could not leave her this way.

I climbed onto the bed to reach Mama's wrists. My knees sank into the soft mattress, and for a second, I feared falling forward with the scissors. Quickly, I balanced myself by standing on my knees. I slid the blade between the knots and Mama's skin and began to cut the sheets. I had to use both hands to cut the fabric because Daddy had twisted it like rope, making it hard to tear.

Finally, the knots opened. As Mama's arms fell free, I lowered them to her sides. Red marks circled Mama's wrists. I rubbed them with my fingertips, but the marks were deep and couldn't be wiped away. Mama would know. She'd wake up when the medicine wore off and see. She'd know Daddy had tied her to the bed.

Tears filled my eyes. Even though she looked and smelled bad, this was my mother. I wished I were big enough to hold her in my arms.

I curled up in bed beside her, the scissors still in my hands. No matter how hard I tried to think of better, sunny days, I couldn't make the sadness leave.

I cried until the darkness in the room swallowed me. Sleep came, and soon the dreams.

WHEN I OPENED my eyes, a pale light filled the room, telling me it was barely morning. I turned over on my side, wanting to be closer to Mama.

She was no longer in the bed beside me. I patted the mattress, the pillows, and sheets. The sewing shears were gone, too.

A creaking noise came from the corner. I looked across the room and saw Mama sitting in the rocker by the window. At her feet lay the missing scissors, their shiny blades open in a *V.*

Mama's hands moved in her lap, her fingers braiding strands of long, blonde hair.

TWENTY-ONE

THE RIVER PICNIC

T ESS LOOKED LIKE a raffia doll. Yellow tufts stuck out all over her head. She cried and pulled at what was left of her hair. Some pieces were longer than others. Seeing her made me think of a scarecrow.

"Oh, honey, don't worry." Daddy smoothed her hair with his hands. "We'll take you to the salon and have it trimmed. You'll see. It will be fine."

Tess leaned over the edge of my bed and reached for her purse. She dug through her makeup bag and pulled out her brown compact. Looking into the small round mirror, Tess saw her sheared hair and cried all over again. Red splotches bloomed on her face.

I stood in the doorway, afraid to move. Please God, don't let them see me.

Daddy wrapped his arms around Tess's shoulders and rocked her back and forth on the bed. "You're still my beautiful girl, Tessy. My beautiful, beautiful girl." He repeated the words like a lullaby, and held her until her sobbing stopped. "Now, go get dressed. We're going out. We're getting you a new hairdo."

"There's no way to fix this," she complained.

"Oh yes, there is. You look sexy with short hair. Very European."
Her face brightened, and she kissed Daddy on the cheek.

Daddy noticed me standing by the door. "Get dressed, Ellie. I
want you to come along."

"But Mama . . ."

"I don't want to hear a damn word about your mother right
now," Daddy barked. "I know you brought the scissors upstairs,
Ellie. There's no other way she could have gotten them. I thought
we'd talked about this last night."

Ashamed, I looked at the floor.

Daddy walked over, lifted my chin, and stared into my eyes.
He didn't blink, not once, as if he could will me to see things his
way. "Your mother's not well. I don't know how much more I
can take. I know you were trying to help, that you didn't want to
see her that way, but you have to trust me, Ellie. She's dangerous
when she gets this angry. I don't want to hurt her, but I can't let
her hurt Tess either, or you, or herself for that matter. Do you understand? You can't second-guess me, young lady. Someone could
get hurt."

I swallowed hard, not sure what to say. So much of what Daddy
said was true, but Tess was only the tomato girl. He was supposed
to be worried about Mama, not Tess. I didn't know how to make
Daddy see. He was blind when it came to Tess.

When Daddy released my chin, I walked to my closet and
pulled out a blue sun dress. After I dressed and combed my hair, I
gathered Jellybean and went downstairs to wait for the cab.

Going with Tess to the salon was the last thing I wanted to
do, but Daddy was not in a mood to hear my complaints. I'd
go along, wait for Tess to get her hair trimmed, then come back
home and look after Mama the rest of the day. She'd need to
eat, take a bath, and dress in a clean gown. The pansies and dirt
should be swept up from the kitchen floor. The cut sheets had to
be thrown away, and Mama's bed made fresh and clean. I would
do it all, too, every single chore. Daddy would soon see that we

didn't need Tess. I'd take care of the house and Mama. I'd take care of everything.

I'D NEVER BEEN to the beauty parlor before and wasn't sure what to expect. I wore my hair long, with bangs straight across the front. Mama trimmed them for me every six or seven weeks, or whenever I complained about my hair getting in my eyes. When she suffered bad moods and couldn't be trusted with shears, I used a plastic barrette to hold my bangs to one side, or I trimmed them myself. Mama wore her hair long, too, but sometimes permed or colored it, which she did herself.

The cab took us downtown, past the post office and drugstore, to the little beauty parlor with wigs and shampoos on display in the front window. A bed of plastic grass filled the window well with pink, orange, blue, and purple eggs scattered through the green. I lifted Jellybean from my purse to show him the pretty scene. "Today is Good Friday," I whispered in his ear.

"I want the works for both my girls," Daddy told the lady at the cash register.

She smiled at Daddy. Sky-blue eye shadow creased in her lids. "Sugar, they just don't make enough men like you."

Daddy blushed and handed the lady a wad of money. Tess squeezed his hand.

"Well, okay then. I'm going over to the store, see if Mr. Morgan needs a hand. I'll be back in an hour or so," Daddy said, kissing both Tess and me before walking back to the cab.

How I missed the store. I wanted to tend to the chicks and help set out the phlox, marigolds, and snapdragons for spring. I'd rather sweep the dusty aisles or water plants than have my hair styled, but Daddy wanted me to do this with Tess. I'd already angered him by cutting Mama free. In a way, Tess's bad haircut was my fault. Crossing Daddy now would only make matters worse. He seemed to be determined that Tess and I be friends, like we'd been on the first day, when that seemed possible. It wasn't possible now, but I wanted to smooth things over with Daddy as best I could.

Tess and I sat in chairs near the window and waited for our turns.

A woman came for Tess. "My name's Ester." She had wide hips that strained under dark stretch pants, and her small head was covered in red ringlets. "Lord, child, who did this to you? It looks like a butcher cut your hair," she said, running her thick fingers through the pale wisps of Tess's hair.

"I'd rather not say," Tess told her.

I looked down at the floor, hoping Ester wouldn't ask me what happened to Tess's hair.

Jellybean peeped inside my basket purse. I whispered to him to hush while I waited. Almost immediately, the woman with blue eye shadow came for me. "My name's Bunny," she said, leading me to the back room to shampoo my hair. I figured her name was a good omen with it being Easter weekend.

While Bunny's fingers scrubbed my scalp, I listened to Tess complain to Ester that a crazy and jealous woman had come into her room in the night and chopped off her long blonde hair. I was glad when the rinse water filled my ears so I didn't have to listen to the rest of her story.

AN HOUR LATER, Daddy returned as he said, greeting us both with a single carnation. Red for Tess, pink for me. I didn't ask, because I already knew he bought no flower for Mama.

Tess's hair was a cap of soft blonde curls with bangs like fringe coming to the middle of her forehead. My hair looked almost the same as it did before, only a little shorter and curled on the ends.

Daddy said we looked beautiful. He thanked Bunny and gave her a tip. We walked out to the sidewalk, Tess on one side of Daddy and me on the other.

"Where's the cab?" Tess asked.

Daddy pulled keys from his pocket and dangled them in the air. The brass keys glinted in the sun.

"You bought us a car?" Tess squealed, smacking her hands together as if she could hardly believe it, as if Daddy had bought the car just for her.

"Mr. Morgan made me an offer on his son's Pontiac. I couldn't pass it up," Daddy said, pointing to the corner where he'd parked a pale yellow car with a black roof.

He shook the keys again. "Now, it's not every day a man buys a car. Let's go for a drive."

"What about Mama?" I asked, wanting to get home. We'd already been gone for over an hour.

"Oh, we've got plenty of time. We'll get back soon, don't worry. Just a quick little spin, Ellie."

"Okay." I went along; it was easier not to argue.

Tess walked over and stroked his face with the back of her hand, then giggled. She snatched the keys from his hand and said, "Let's go!"

Tess wanted to drive.

"Give me the keys, Tess." Daddy held his open hand toward her. His voice sounded half-serious, half-playful.

Tess was already buckling herself into the driver's seat. She clutched the keys in her hands. "I know how to drive!" She'd driven the old pickup truck to the store, so I knew this was true.

I sat in the back and held Jellybean. The faded plaid seat cover smelled like cigarettes, but was still in good shape. I rubbed my fingers over the chrome door handles and the black vinyl.

Daddy and Tess kept on about the keys.

"I know, honey, but you don't have a permit, and I don't need you getting a ticket while you're with me. Give me those keys."

"If you want them, take them," Tess said as she tucked them down the front of her shirt.

I watched through the rearview mirror as my father slipped his hand inside Tess's blouse and fished for the keys.

She squirmed, giggled, and pushed at his hands. Daddy reached in further, and I blushed to see my father's hand disappear inside Tess's bra. A few seconds later, he pulled out the keys. "Ta da!" he said, just like a magician pulling a rabbit from a hat. Daddy held the keys in front of her face. "Here, honey, go ahead and drive. I just pray the sheriff doesn't see you driving with me."

"It's a dumb rule anyhow that I can't get a permit on account of my epilepsy. I haven't had a seizure in so long."

"I know. Sometimes rules don't make sense," Daddy agreed.

I thought it sounded like a pretty good rule myself. If what Mary Roberts had told me about seizures was true, there would be no way to avoid a wreck.

Tess started the car and pulled onto the street. She pressed too hard on the accelerator and caused the car to jerk forward, almost spilling Jellybean to the floor. "Let's get out of this town," she said, "and never come back."

I didn't pay any attention to what Tess said. She was only dreaming out loud. My father would never leave Granby.

As the road unrolled toward the next town, I wondered if Tess had a destination in mind, but soon realized she just wanted to drive.

I tried to imagine living in a house without a mother and only a father who did dirty things to me. That would never feel like home. I'd probably want to keep driving, too.

After what seemed more than an hour, I leaned over the seat and tugged at my father's sleeve. "Let's go home, Daddy." We'd been out far too long; Mama needed food and a bath. The haircuts had taken long enough. I wanted to go home.

"Rupert, I have an idea." Tess said before Daddy could respond.

"What is it, hon?" Daddy asked.

"Let's drive to the river, have a little picnic before we go back. Please, Rupert? I'm just not ready yet. Not now, not after last night."

Daddy hesitated and looked at his watch. He knew we'd already left Mama home alone for too long, but he couldn't refuse Tess.

WE STOPPED AT A market and bought ham sandwiches, potato chips, pies, and Cokes. I'd never been inside or even heard of Galen's Convenience Store, so I figured we'd traveled a good distance outside of Granby. Walking the aisles of stocked goods made me miss Daddy's store more than ever.

Tess held the bag of food on her lap and gave Daddy the keys so he could drive the rest of the trip. Then, after parking at the boat dock, we walked up a steep hill to a flat gray rock that stuck out in the water like a hitchhiker's thumb. As we sat on the sun-warmed rock and ate, Tess and I hardly said a word to each other. She'd tried to get me to comment on her haircut while we were at the salon, but I'd forced a half smile and looked away. I felt bad for her life, but couldn't forgive her for trying to steal my father's love.

I just didn't want to be there, out with Tess. I still loved Daddy, and didn't understand how he could behave this way, but I knew Tess was to blame. If she'd go away, Daddy would become himself again. Mama would be important to him the way she used to be, and with Daddy focused on her, she would get better. If only Tess would leave.

While Daddy and Tess talked about the store and places we could go now that Daddy had a car, I looked out across the river. Waterbugs skidded across the surface, their black bodies like seeds floating on water. Brown cattails bent toward the water. Any other time I might have gone exploring to find something interesting to show Mary Roberts, but today, all I wanted was to go home.

This morning, as we left, I saw that Daddy hadn't cleaned up the pansies in the kitchen. He said he'd fed Mama, but I wanted to see with my own eyes that she was clean and had eaten her food. If she heard the baby cry again, she might try to go to the cellar to get him. After one of the shots, she doesn't walk so steady, and might fall.

I shoved the last bit of sandwich into my mouth. "Let's go, Daddy," I said, my mouth still partially full of food.

"We've got more time, Ellie. Don't worry," Daddy said.

I lifted Jellybean out of my purse so he could walk around the flat rocks. He chirped and fluttered his baby wings. "You love the sun, don't you Jellybean?" I stroked his head with my finger. His green color was fading now, as it always does when chicks grow.

Tess held out a bit of her pie for Jellybean. He stumbled over the rocks to reach the treat, nibbling one piece, then another. When the crumbs were all gone, he climbed into her hand. Tess laughed. "You greedy boy." She stood up and walked with him toward the river. If Daddy hadn't been there, I would have reached out and taken back my little chick. I didn't want Tess to hold anything that belonged to me.

Trying to ignore her, I gathered up the empty Coke bottles and paper wrappers, and then put them inside the brown bag. This was the first car we had owned in a long time, and I didn't want it to get dirty.

Daddy swigged the last of his Coke, then called to Tess. "Don't go too close to the edge. I don't want to end up fishing you out of the river."

Tess blew Daddy a kiss and shook her behind in his direction to make him laugh. She took a few more steps, then yelled, lifting her right foot suddenly, as if she'd stepped on something sharp. She tottered, her arms spread away from her body to help her gain her balance.

I watched Tess's hand open and my chick fall.

His small body hit the dark rock, slid into the river, and was gone.

TWENTY-TWO

DROWNING

JELLYBEAN'S PALE GREEN HEAD surfaced, then disappeared again as he bobbed like a rubber bath toy in the swirling water.

Daddy yanked off his boots and socks and jumped into the river. His arms made large arcs in the river, but he couldn't keep up against the swift current. Like a seed or leaf tossed into wind, Jellybean's small body followed the water's flow.

Tess ran along the edge of the bank. "Please hurry, Rupert, please!" She dug her fingers into her short hair.

At first, I didn't do anything: didn't cry, or scream, or run along the bank. I felt numb, like a thousand bees had stung me all at once. Inside my head, I heard the blood hum in my veins. Then the humming in my head swirled and broke into a gushing noise. My knees trembled, and I stumbled forward, taking a few small steps before I broke into a run. I headed up the hill, toward the woods.

Stumps and fallen branches slowed me. I brushed against pine needles, scratching my arms and legs. I thought of Hansel and Gretel and the bread crumbs they scattered so someone could find them. It didn't matter that I had no bread crumbs. I didn't want to be found.

The woods, however, were not deep, and I quickly came out the other side and found myself back at the water's edge, at a point where the river made a bend. Too tired to return, too numb to turn in a different direction, I ran down the sloped bank, slick with mud, then waded into the water.

Without thinking, I kept moving, going out further, letting the water take me. I wanted to be carried to some other place. Any other place. Not here.

Face down in the river, I let myself float like a piece of driftwood. Everything was cloudy, dreamy, and not quite real, just like a slow-motion movie. There were no sounds at all, and yet voices filled my head. Hymns, poems, and chanted words I couldn't understand. I didn't even recognize the voices, but somehow that didn't seem strange to me.

For the first time in days, I didn't feel afraid anymore. Here, there were no dead babies, tomato girls, or sick mothers. In the river, I could float myself to sleep.

Behind closed eyes, my mind drifted. I could hear voices, but the loudest noise was the water, roaring as it filled my body, pulling me down.

I don't remember Daddy lifting me from the river. I don't remember his large hands holding onto me so tight I would find bruises on my arms two days later. My body on the bank, spitting up water and coughing—I do remember that—and Daddy's mouth over mine, blowing breath into me. Tess stood or knelt somewhere to my side, crying, "Breathe, Ellie, breathe."

The blue sky came back to me in pieces, like a jigsaw puzzle, then the green undersides of leaves, and my father's face.

I hurt all over. My arms and legs ached, and deep inside, my lungs and throat felt raw.

I coughed again and tried to swallow. "Jellybean is dead," I said.

Daddy nodded. He already knew, of course. I just needed to say it. Words made it real. Words made sure I couldn't pretend it was another way. Make-believe is a dangerous game. I'd learned that from watching Mama.

"I didn't mean for it to happen, Ellie. I stepped on broken glass, and lost my balance. I am so sorry. Oh, please forgive me." Tess spoke between sobs. She showed her bleeding foot as proof.

What could I say? As awful as Tess could be, I knew she'd loved Jellybean, too. She hadn't dropped him on purpose. But my little chick was dead, and he was all I had. Mama had secret worlds inside her mind and Daddy had Tess. Jellybean had been mine. Now he was gone.

Anger rose in me like a serpent's head, and I spat words at Tess. "You should've been more careful. When you're holding something that belongs to someone else, you don't take chances."

On the ride home, I curled up on Daddy's lap while Tess drove. I moved in and out of sleep. I felt cold, even with Daddy's shirt wrapped around me.

My stomach churned with a sick feeling, but I was too weak to cough up more water. Too numb to cry, I buried my face in my father's neck and tried to remember to breathe.

BACK HOME, DADDY told Mama to stay away. "I'm not going to let you upset her, Julia. Ellie needs rest."

Mama leaned against the wall, rubbing the sides of her head. She hadn't bathed while we were gone. She wore the same dirty nightgown and hadn't combed her hair. Around her neck, she'd tied the pale, blonde braid made from Tess's hair. When she saw me in Daddy's arms, she yelled at Tess, "What did you do, you whore? What did you do to my child?"

"Just keep walking," Daddy told Tess.

With me in his arms, Daddy followed Tess upstairs. Mama trailed behind us, her voice shaking. "You tell me what she did! Rupert, tell me!"

Daddy didn't answer as he kept walking.

Over his shoulder, I saw Mama, her face tight, her lips drawn inward. As she came up behind Daddy, she tripped on the hem of her gown and fell. Mama groaned, and then began to sob. I squirmed in Daddy's arms. The sound of Mama crying called to me. Even though I felt weak and numb, I needed to go to her.

Daddy held me. "No, Ellie, don't fight."

His firm hands and voice stilled me.

Tess started back down the stairs as if to help, but Daddy wouldn't let her. That seemed cruel at the time, but maybe Daddy knew that would be worse. The wrong person's touch when you are hurting can set loose something wild inside you. I'd seen times when my father had walked around Mama, careful not to touch her until she calmed down.

"Leave her alone," Daddy told Tess. "I'll take care of Ellie and come back to help her."

UPSTAIRS, TESS HELPED Daddy pull off my wet clothes and lower me into the bathtub. Tess offered to bathe me, but Daddy said no, he'd come too close to losing me to leave me just yet. Tess kept apologizing. "I didn't mean it . . . It was an accident . . ."

Daddy reassured her. "I know. Nobody is blaming you. Please, just go rest and let me take care of Ellie."

Tess didn't leave the room. She sat on the toilet and waited while Daddy bathed me.

As the hot water poured over me, I began to cry again, tears for my drowned chick and for the dead baby in the cellar. I cried for Mama, left alone at the bottom of the stairs, and for Daddy's worried eyes. I even cried for Tess, sitting on the toilet with her hopeless face in her hands.

Daddy cried, too.

He washed me gently, as if I were a new baby, rubbing soap in my hair, and over my skin. His hands made my blood flow under my skin, and I began to feel warm again, at least on the surface. No amount of warmth could reach the places inside where I felt hollowed out. If someone peeled away my skin, I knew they'd see a rib cage and nothing more, just a dark empty hole where my lungs, stomach, and heart used to be.

After drying me with a clean towel, Daddy dressed me in pajamas and combed the tangles from my wet hair. He tucked me in bed, wrapped me in thick quilts, then kissed me before he went downstairs. He didn't try to explain or say anything to make it all better. He knew he couldn't. There are times when words won't make a bad thing better. Those are the saddest times of all.

As I began to fall asleep, I heard scuffing sounds and voices arguing. Daddy's voice deep and even; Mama's shrill and rising, always rising. Mama said all the bad words. Faster and louder. She wouldn't be quiet. Daddy shouted, "I'm warning you, Julia. You have to control yourself." More bad words, loud and sharp.

I plugged my ears with my fingers as Mama's cries rose through the floorboards and threatened to drown me again.

The rest of the afternoon and evening, I floated in and out of sleep. Several times I heard Mama wander into the hallway, asking to see me.

Daddy kept watch in the hallway. Each time Mama came near, he guided her back to her room.

In a way, I was glad he kept Mama away. Part of me wanted to run to my mother, to climb onto her lap and have her stroke my hair and tell me everything would be fine. But that mother had disappeared like a magician's dove. I didn't know the magic words to bring her back.

DADDY BROUGHT ME chicken soup in a blue bowl with saltine crackers and a glass of milk. He propped me up in bed, my head against my pillow, and spooned the noodles and broth into my mouth. The soup tasted good and familiar. I felt safe with Daddy beside me. I wanted to tell him everything then, about how I hadn't gone to the cellar to get Mama the onion, how the baby had died and I'd put it in the freezer. I wanted to tell him how sad I felt about Jellybean, and how hard I wished Tess would go away.

Instead I swallowed the warm, salty soup and tried not to cry again.

THE NEXT MORNING, Tess brought a shoebox into my room. Wearing a black dress and a dark scarf tied around her head, she climbed onto my bed. Bright sunlight shone through the window telling me I'd slept very late.

"I think we should bury Jellybean. Seems only fitting, but I'll leave it to you to decide," she said.

"He's inside there?" I rubbed my eyes, still swollen and sore from the tears.

Tess nodded. "Last night, after everyone went to sleep, I took the new car back to the river. I walked the edge of the water until I found Jellybean's remains."

I sat up in my bed. The way she said *remains* made me scared to look. Sometimes turtles and fish feed on small, dead things. "Does he look bad?"

"Oh, no, not at all," Tess assured me. "I got to him before anything else did. I fixed him as good as I could, Ellie." She almost sounded proud of herself, and I wondered if she could even see her own fault.

I took the box from her hands and steadied it on my knees. Part of me didn't want to see, and I almost decided to tape the box shut and not look. Maybe it would be better to remember my chick as he'd been only days before. Another part of me wanted to see him inside the box, to make myself face the hard good-bye. My little chick deserved that much.

Opening the cardboard lid, I peeked inside, slowly at first, until I saw Jellybean, his tiny body laid out on a bed of Daddy's white handkerchiefs. Tess had tied a little black bow around his neck and placed one of my embroidered doll pillows under his tiny head. I touched him lightly, tracing his cold, stiff body with my fingers.

"I thought we could bury him beneath the crab apple tree." Her voice sounded hopeful, like a question.

I nodded. "That's a nice place. He'll like it there."

Tess left the room to make plans with Daddy for the funeral. She came back a short time later and gave me the details. I heard her voice, but my mind could barely focus on words.

While I brushed my teeth and dressed in dark clothes, Daddy put Mama in her room and went for Mary Roberts.

MARY GAVE A fine eulogy, the best one since the summer we'd buried the gray tomcat we'd found dead in the road. She recited lines from the Bible, and the parts she could remember of a poem that began, "I heard a fly buzz when I died," which didn't exactly fit, but was a nice gesture.

Daddy took a shovel from his shed and dug the grave, a perfect little rectangle under the crab apple tree. I wished Mama could have been there, but Daddy said no, and I knew he was right. Still, I wished she was there.

Tess held the box until my part came, which was the hardest. Because Jellybean belonged to me, I had to lower him into the open ground and throw in the first fistful of dirt. No one else could do it, only me.

My hand shook as the grainy, black soil slipped through my fingers to pepper Jellybean's box. This is the part where everyone most wants to cry, when the dirt covers the coffin. It is final then. The one you bury in the ground isn't coming back.

Mary Roberts wrapped her arms around me, and I hid my face in her soft hair.

Daddy shoveled the rest of the dirt in place while Tess arranged wildflowers in a blue Maxwell House can and sang "Amazing Grace," her high, clear voice lifting through the leaves.

For a long moment, I closed my eyes and wished a heaven for my little chick filled with yellow sunflowers and perfect blue skies.

Then I heard a door slam, and I opened my eyes. Over Mary's shoulder, I saw Mama walk out of the house, still dressed in her soiled gown.

Before the funeral, Daddy had wedged Mama's door closed. Somehow, she'd worked her way free.

Mama ran across the backyard, toward us, her arms lifted in the air like a bird about to fly. She screamed, the sound sharp and deep, like a wild animal. Her voice startled us all, even Daddy.

For a moment, no one breathed. That is what happens when you see something you know is true, but cannot believe. The blood doesn't want to move through your veins. Your lungs don't want to take in the next breath. You forget to swallow and nearly choke on your own soft tongue.

At the grave, Mama fell on her knees and plunged her hands into the loose dirt. "I told you not to put my baby in the ground. You lied to me," she yelled, looking at me, her eyes glassy and wide. Her hands scooped away dirt from Jellybean's grave. She spoke into the ground, softly, her voice quivering. "It's all right, baby. Mama hears you. Mama will take you from this dark hole."

TWENTY-THREE

AT THE GRAVE

Daddy's eyes narrowed into dark slits above his unshaven cheeks. His hands tightened on the shovel handle, stretching his knuckles white.

Mama pressed her face into the dirt, loose soil muffling her cries.

Daddy looked up and threw the shovel, hurling it high into the tree. It caught on a branch and dangled there, swinging back and forth.

"Why are you doing this, Julia? Why?" Daddy fell to his knees and leaned over Mama's body. He clenched his fists and spoke to the back of her head. "How much more of this do you think I can take?" Tears ran down Daddy's face.

I'd never seen my father so broken. No matter how Mama behaved, Daddy had always been the calm one. He and I had always worked together, handling her moods. We did the cooking and cleaning, and answered the door and telephone. We kept people far away when she had her spells, talked softly to her, and didn't argue or scold. What would happen if Daddy gave up?

Mama clawed at the grave where she thought we'd buried her

baby. She dug quickly, pawing the dirt with both hands the way a dog digs up a bone. "I just want my baby, Rupert," Mama cried. "Why did you bury my baby?" Her face was caked with dirt.

"I don't know what you're talking about, Julia. I don't know what you mean!" Daddy's voice sounded more hopeless than angry.

"You do know, you all know." Mama looked at each one of us; her accusing eyes moved from face to face. "Standing around here like you don't know you put my baby into the ground." Then she looked back at Daddy, "You brought your whore into my house, and now you want to take my baby from me. I want him back, Rupert." Her voice cracked as she spoke. "I want my son back!" Tears flowed down her face, leaving furrows on her dirty cheeks. Her trembling shoulders curled forward as she struggled to dig.

Tess and Mary Roberts stood under the crab apple tree, their faces pale. Tess chewed on her thumbnail, while Mary's knees turned inward like they do when she's afraid. Daddy hung his head, defeated by my mother's words. No one seemed to know what to say or do.

I knew. The baby wasn't a mystery to me.

Kneeling beside Mama, I whispered. "The baby isn't in the grave, Mama. Look, I'll show you."

Her sobs quieted. A puzzled look crossed her face.

My hands shook as I dug into the cool, black dirt. Putting Jellybean into the ground was hard enough. Bringing him up from his grave to show Mama was almost more than I could stand, but I couldn't fail. Not this time. I kept digging.

When my fingers hit cardboard, I wiped the fine layer of soil away with the back of my hand, then opened the lid. "Here, Mama, look," I said, scooping up my dead chick. His stiff little body felt light as I lifted him to my lips to kiss his head.

I still loved him, and could imagine how Mama felt losing her baby. But I knew Jellybean was gone for good and belonged in the ground. Mama didn't know how to let her baby go. Maybe she'd see Jellybean and understand.

"Jellybean drowned," I explained, handing her the chick. "It's Jellybean we buried, not your baby. Your baby is still safe. He's in the same place you told me to lay him, sleeping like an angel."

"What the hell?" My father's eyebrows knitted together as he tried to make sense of what he heard and saw.

Mama smiled a little, rubbing Jellybean's dead body. Her hands smudged his clean body with dirt.

I wanted to cry.

I wanted to take him away from her.

"Oh, Ellie," Mama said, her bottom lip quivering. "You lost your baby."

I swallowed hard. "Yes, I lost my baby."

Mama turned her head to look at Tess. "You! You came to my house and cursed it! You, you baby killer!"

Tess trembled under my mother's words. "I'm not a baby killer!" she screamed. "Jellybean was an accident. I didn't mean for him to drown. You're nothing but a crazy woman, and you want to drive everybody else crazy!" Tess spat words in a shrill, shaky voice.

"Tess, don't," my father's voice snapped.

Tess broke into tears. She wasn't used to my father speaking harshly to her. She hid her face in her hands and ran toward the house.

"I'll be right back," Daddy said. He stood up and followed Tess inside, leaving Mary, Mama, and me alone.

With each step he took, I felt my heart sink lower in my chest. I wanted to call after him, "Please, Daddy, stay with us. Mama needs you. I need you." I kept quiet, though. I knew what he'd say, and wasn't ready to hear those words.

Mama pressed Jellybean to her breast and hummed. She looked at Mary and offered a half smile. "That's a lovely dress you're wearing today, Miss Mary."

Up until then, Mary hadn't said anything. When she finally spoke, her words stuck to her tongue. "Th-thank you, Mrs. S-an-Sanders."

"I'm sorry I look such a mess, Mary. I haven't been well, you know."

Mary nodded. "Ellie t-told m-me about your f-fall." I hadn't heard Mary stutter since first grade.

"Oh, yes. And I meant to thank you for the lovely cake." Mama combed her fingers through her hair, tucking a tangled strand behind her ear. "You will tell your mother how much I appreciated it, won't you?" Mama suddenly laughed, then covered her mouth with her hand. "Your mother is an amazing baker," Mama said, her voice too loud and high pitched.

"I'll t-t-tell her," Mary struggled to speak. "Do-do you want m-me to br-bring you the r-recipe?"

"How nice. Yes, I'd like that, Mary." Mama giggled again.

Mary looked down at her leather T-straps. She seemed not to know what else to say. "I g-guess I sh-should be going h-h-home now."

Mama smoothed the front of her gown as if trying to appear more presentable. She looked at Mary, then paused. Her eyebrows raised as she spoke. "Mary, would you like to see my baby before you go?"

Mary stuttered, "W-well, uh, well, yes, I g-g-uess so." You could tell from Mary's voice that she didn't want to see the baby. Her words came out flat and tight. It's only a matter of habit that when a grown-up offers to show you something, you agree to look.

Mama looked at me and smiled. "Ellie, be a good girl, and take Mary to the cellar to see the new baby."

MARY AND I HELD HANDS as we walked down the basement stairs. I didn't want to leave Mama alone, but I knew she'd only become angry if I didn't take Mary to see the baby. By the way she'd laughed and played with her hair, I wasn't sure about Mama's mood or which direction it might take.

"Does your mother really have a b-baby down here?" Mary asked. Away from Mama, Mary's stutter was not as bad.

"Yes, but it almost doesn't look like a baby."

"What happened to it?" she asked, her voice a whisper.

The air at the bottom of the stairwell felt cool and damp.

I held the door open for Mary. "She was bleeding. It died inside her somehow, and came out dead. She wouldn't let me tell Daddy or even call a doctor."

Mary stepped inside and reached for the light switch on the wall. The bright bulb burned overhead.

"Why didn't she bury it? A b-ba-baby should have a funeral, Ellie."

I shrugged my shoulders. "In a way, Mama seems to know it's dead. She cried, and didn't want Daddy to know. But another part of her doesn't believe the baby is gone. She thinks it's safe here, but then she worries about it being cold and afraid in the dark. I know it doesn't make sense."

"This gives me the creeps," Mary said.

"It gives me the creeps, too, but I don't know what to do."

Mary didn't answer, having finally come up against a problem she didn't know how to solve any better than I did.

I felt grateful that she'd agreed to come with me. I'm not sure I could have been so brave if it had been Mrs. Roberts's dead baby in the cellar. I patted her shoulder. "You don't really have to look at the baby if you don't want to."

"I think I'll go home now," Mary said. She turned around and walked back upstairs. The door shut behind her.

I sat cross-legged on the cold floor and sucked my thumb. It still fit perfectly in my mouth. My skin tasted like dirt from digging up the grave, but the feel of my thumb against the roof of my mouth comforted me, and I needed comforting now more than ever. *Mary probably won't want to be friends anymore,* I thought. Who would want a friend whose mother keeps a dead baby in the freezer?

No one. Not a girl like Mary Roberts, that was for sure. She could do better.

She'd tell her mother, who'd tell the whole town, and everybody would point at me and say, "There goes the girl with the crazy mother." I'd be laughed at like the retarded boy at school. I'd be the girl nobody wants to sit next to, the girl who never gets a valentine, the girl nobody picks to play games with.

In my whole life, I'd never felt so alone.

I curled up in the corner and closed my eyes. For once, I wasn't afraid of what bad dreams might come while I slept. I knew now that bad dreams can find you even when you're awake.

TWENTY-FOUR

THE JAR

I WOKE TO SOMEONE knocking on the cellar door. I thought maybe Mama had wandered down the stairs to see the baby, too.

"Ellie?" a girl called my name.

Was I still dreaming?

"Mary?" Mary had come back. I hurried to my feet and opened the cellar door wide. "Mary!"

She smiled and held up a Mason jar filled with clear liquid. "Here," she said.

"A jar of water?" I didn't quite know what to say. Still, she'd come back when she didn't have to, so I pretended to be pleased. "Thank you."

Mary smiled and sat down on the floor. "No, silly. It's not water. It's formaldehyde."

"Formaldehyde?" I felt even more confused as I sat next to Mary.

Mary nodded. "Remember my brother's biology set? The jars he keeps on his bookshelf?"

"The ones with the crayfish and fetal pig?" Remembering the stiff little creatures made my skin prickle.

"Right. He has a black snake now, too; its skin is partly shed. And there's a toad with one mashed leg from when we ran over him with the wheelbarrow. Anyhow, I emptied out the formaldehyde, then put water in so my brother wouldn't know."

"What do I need it for?"

Mary rolled her eyes. "For your mother's baby, of course. I brought enough for Jellybean, too, if you want to keep him."

I shook my head. "No. I don't want to keep Jellybean in a jar." The idea of my sweet little chick floating in formaldehyde made my throat tighten.

"What about your mother's baby?"

"I don't know, Mary. A baby in a jar?"

"Well, if she wants to keep it, a jar is better than the freezer."

Mary had a point. Besides, I was so happy that Mary was still my friend that at the moment I would have agreed to anything. "Sure, I guess so," I said, although I was anything but sure.

"If your mother doesn't like it, we can bring him back to the freezer."

I nodded. The idea of unwrapping the dead baby and putting him inside the jar made my stomach feel funny, but I figured it couldn't be any worse than what I'd been through already. Besides, I didn't know what Daddy might do about the baby in the freezer. What if he decided to throw the baby away? Or what if he insisted on burying the baby in the backyard? I didn't want to imagine how Mama might react. At least in a jar, I could hide the baby in different places.

"Are you scared?" Mary asked.

"Yes. But I'm glad you came back."

As it turned out, Mary had been far more afraid of my mother than the dead baby. Her hands shook a little as she held the jar for me, but she didn't stutter the way she had around Mama. "I never knew your mother acted that way. I mean, I knew she was different than most mothers, and sometimes did unusual things, but never anything like this."

"She has spells, Mary. She cries a lot for no reason, or for little things like spilled pepper. Sometimes she stares out the window, just looking at the same piece of sky. She says strange things, and sometimes she tries to hurt herself."

"What's the matter with her?"

"Nothing is the matter with her," I said, but I knew I was lying. Something was terribly wrong with my mother; I just didn't know how to explain.

"Then why did she put the baby in the freezer?"

"I don't know why. Most of the time, she's not like you saw her today. Only sometimes."

"She's been this way before?"

"Yeah, but never so bad as this. Tess makes it worse, and then the baby dying . . ."

"Does your Daddy really love Tess?"

"I don't know." I shrugged my shoulders. "I'm afraid of Tess staying here much longer. I don't think Mama can take her being here. But I don't know what Daddy will do if she leaves, and I don't think Tess can even go back home."

"Why not?"

"Because when she has seizures, her father does dirty things to her."

Mary scrunched up her face. "Yuck."

"I know. Because of that, Daddy won't let Tess leave. He was so angry when Tess told him, he swore he was going to kill Mr. Reed."

"Maybe you and your mother could move to another house."

"I don't think it's that easy, Mary. Mama doesn't have any money."

Mary nodded. "I forgot about that." She paused a moment, then said, "What about the money in your jar under the bed?"

"It wouldn't be enough." Sometimes I thought Mary Roberts knew everything. Other times I found myself amazed by the things she didn't know. My sewing money would maybe pay for one night in a motel or maybe one week in a run-down boarding house. That's it. There wouldn't be enough for food or coffee or even bars of soap.

"Okay," Mary agreed. She sighed, as if trying to solve the problem wore her out. I knew that feeling. I carried it with me all the time.

Mary moved onto a problem she could handle. "Will we need a bigger jar? My mother only had this one and a pickle jar, but if I go back and look in my father's garage, I bet I could find something bigger."

"No, that will be big enough. It's a small baby. Nowhere near the size a baby is supposed to be."

I walked over to the freezer and forced open the lid. I quickly took the little packet from the ice vault, then let the freezer lid slam shut. The Reynolds Wrap felt cold in my hand, stinging my fingers. "I need to lay the baby down," I told Mary.

She knelt on the floor and motioned to me, "Here, sit." She patted the cement.

I sat on the floor and faced Mary, then placed the wrapped baby between us. We both stared at the frosted package as if we expected the silvery paper to open like petals.

Mary twisted off the lid and sat the jar beside the wrapped baby.

"Should we wait for the baby to thaw?" I asked.

"No, I don't think so." Mary's eyes darted from the tinfoil to the jar.

"What if its skin peels off when I unwrap it?"

"It won't." Mary didn't sound as certain as she usually did, and her words gave me little comfort.

"How do you know?" I wanted proof or at least some explanation.

"Well, I don't know for sure, but I don't think it will because skin comes in layers. When you get a sunburn, and peel off skin, there is more skin under it. So even if some of its skin peels off, there will be another layer beneath it."

Reassured, I picked up the tinfoil and, bit by bit, I unwrapped the baby from its shiny blanket.

Mary gasped when the baby's pale blue skin was exposed. "It's so small," she said.

"It wasn't done growing," I explained, pulling away the last layers of foil.

We stared at the frozen baby lying on the floor, tiny ice crystals glistening on its skin.

I waited for Mary to say something, but she only stared. I tried to think of something to say myself. "It doesn't look much like a real baby, does it?"

Mary shook her head no. I hoped seeing the baby wouldn't make her stutter worse.

We couldn't sit there forever. Mama could still be outside alone, and I didn't know if Daddy would return for her. I wasn't even sure how long I'd been asleep before Mary returned with the formaldehyde. "Well, let's just put the baby in the jar," I said, picking up the little corpse with both hands. It felt stiff and cold, and fit easily into my hands. The baby was no more than six inches long, with a large head and small body. It had eyes, but they weren't open, and looked more like black seeds wedged under chalky blue skin. The mouth was a slit like a papercut, and the nose, just a tiny bump. The baby had arms and legs, but there were short stubs with little webbed nubs where fingers and toes belonged. A thin, dark piece of ropelike tissue hung from its belly. Some of Mama's blood had dried on its bluish skin.

"It needs a bath," Mary said.

"I don't want to wash it," I said. I remembered Mama in the bathtub the night the baby died, how the water turned pink with blood.

"Well, the formaldehyde should clean it some," Mary offered.

"Right."

She held the open jar out to me. The sharp smell of the chemical burned my nose and eyes, and I blinked to keep back tears. I tilted the baby so he'd go into the jar feet first. Even though small, he took up most of the room in the jar and caused some of the formaldehyde to spill over the edge and wet Mary's hands. She screwed the lid back in place, put the jar on the floor, and wiped her hands on her dress. Mrs. Roberts would scold her if she got her dress dirty. I hoped Mary had the sense not to tell her mother what we'd done. We needed to keep this our secret. Forever.

As Mary had guessed, the formaldehyde washed some of the blood from the baby's skin. Soon, the liquid inside the jar turned pink and little red flecks settled to the bottom. The baby in the jar reminded me of the snow globe I'd gotten for Christmas.

Just then, the cellar door opened and let in a tunnel of light. "Ellie?" Daddy called. His boots made heavy thuds as he walked down the steps.

Mary and I looked at each other. "Hurry!" I whispered.

I wadded up the tinfoil and held it in my hand. Mary grabbed the jar and hid it behind the onion bin just as my father's legs came into view.

Daddy sat down on the bottom step. He nodded at Mary, then looked at me. His eyes were deep, sad pockets. "I want to know about the baby, Ellie. I need to see for myself."

TWENTY-FIVE

THE WATERBABY

I THOUGHT DADDY WOULD be mad about the baby, but he looked more sad than angry. He hadn't shaved in two days; black stubble darkened his face. Circles hung like half moons under his bloodshot eyes. His hair stood on end the way it did when he first woke in the morning.

Mary stood near the onion bin. From the way she looked at her feet and picked at the hem of her dress, I knew she was nervous. She didn't want to get in trouble for her idea about the formaldehyde.

I walked to the bin, dropped the wadded tinfoil I'd been holding, then picked up the jar. The glass felt cool and moist. Carefully, I took the few steps from the onion bin back to my father, then placed the jar in his hands. Something caught in his throat when his fingers touched the glass, causing him to make a sound like choking. He swallowed, then took a deep breath and slowly let it out. I sat close to him.

My father turned the jar to look at the baby from different angles, finally tilting it to stare at the baby's face. "Such a wee thing," he said, then repeated it. A tear slid down his unshaven cheek. He handed the jar back to me.

"Can I give it to Mama?" I asked.

"I don't know, Ellie," he began, rubbing his face with both hands as he hunted for an answer, maybe many answers.

"Please, Daddy, this is all she has left."

He nodded, swallowing again. His voice shook as he spoke, "Of course. Yes, you're right. Give her the baby, Ellie."

Daddy stood, then walked back up the stairs, leaving open the cellar door.

"I d-don't want to come when you give the b-baby to your m-m-mother," Mary said. She stepped out of the corner. "I want to g-go home."

I walked over to Mary and hugged her. "It's okay, you don't have to come. Let's go."

It felt good to leave the cellar. The day had turned overcast. Pale shadows softened the trees and turned the last few pansies in the garden a navy blue.

At the top of the stairs, Mary gave me a quick hug and took off running toward her house, where her mother would scold her for staining her good dress and her father would remind her that money doesn't grow on trees. For a moment, I wished that I could trade places with Mary Roberts. Being scolded for a soiled dress was easier than being a girl with a dead baby in her hands.

Mama wasn't under the crab apple tree, so perhaps Daddy had helped her inside. I looked for Jellybean's body, but it was gone, too. His open grave still held the cardboard box we'd buried him in, but it was empty.

Overhead, Daddy's shovel still hung in the tree. Holding the Mason jar in one hand, I picked up a huge piece of sod in my other hand and threw it, knocking the shovel to the ground. A surge of anger swelled up in me, and I began hurling clump after clump of sod, throwing as hard as I could, pulling my arm back so far my shoulder hurt. I needed to hear the thud of dirt against the tree, to see the clumps break apart and fall to the ground.

"Hey there, young lady," a man yelled from the front of the house.

Startled, I dropped the last clump of dirt and turned around. The postman walking toward me. "Hi," I said, quickly picking up the jar and hiding it behind my back.

The postman noticed the small grave under the tree. "Burying a pet, are you?"

"Yes, my baby chick died."

"Well, I'm mighty sorry to hear that, Ellie. My girl lost her kitten last summer, and we buried it in our yard, too. I made her a real nice cross from tree limbs. Say, I got my pocketknife with me. I could whittle you up a cross for your chick in no time at all," he offered.

"Uh, no, that's okay. We're going to put a stone marker on his grave."

"I see." He looked around the yard. "Somebody plowed up your mother's pansies? Well, goodness, I can't imagine that. To plant tomatoes?"

"The tomato girl is living with us now, and she needed a place for her plants."

His eyebrows lifted, and he scratched his ear. My story didn't seem to make sense to him, but it was true and I couldn't think how to make it sound any better.

"The tomato girl? That would be Mason Reed's girl, I reckon?"

"Yes," I said. I wanted to say no, she's my Daddy's girl now, but held my tongue.

"I thought so. I got a letter here from her father."

Why would Tess's daddy write her? Was it because she'd taken the tomato plants? Or had Mama telephoned him like she planned? What could he want?

The postman continued. "Mr. Reed doesn't write too good,

and I wasn't sure about the address." He dug in his bag, pulled out an envelope, and held the letter out to me.

I adjusted the jar behind my back, moving it so I could hold it with one hand and take the envelope in the other. "Thank you, I'll see she gets it," I said, smiling. I hoped he would leave soon; I couldn't hold the jar for long, and if I dropped it, the postman would see the dead baby. Or worse, the jar might break and spill the baby on the ground.

"Well, I guess I'll be going. Here's the rest of your mail," he said, holding up the newspaper.

"Thanks." I didn't move.

"Seems you have your hands full," he said when I didn't take the newspaper. "Want me to put the mail on your front porch?"

I nodded yes.

"That your chick behind your back?"

I nodded again, wondering if a nod was really a lie.

"You don't have to be afraid to let me see. Death is nothing to be ashamed of, Ellie."

"I don't want to," I said. The jar was beginning to slip. I couldn't hold onto it much longer.

He tipped his hat. "Okay then, Miss Ellie. I'll leave these on the porch. You make sure you deliver that letter," he said, pointing to the envelope in my hand. "Give my best to your folks. And once again, I'm real sorry about your chick."

"Thank you." I waited for him to leave, then placed the jar on the ground beside my feet. Not wanting to be seen by anyone else, I quickly tucked the letter inside my sock, picked up the jar, and walked into the house to find Mama.

THE HOUSE WAS so quiet I could hear the clock ticking on the kitchen wall. I checked all the rooms downstairs. No one was there. The house looked a little cleaner. Someone had swept the pansies and dirt from the kitchen floor and placed the furniture where it belonged. The dishes hadn't been washed, but were piled into the sink. I knew that somebody had been smoking, because I could smell it in the room. At first I thought Mr. Morgan had visited while I slept, then remembered both my parents sometimes smoked when upset. Coffee cup rings darkened the counter where a pack of matches and ashtray rested.

Upstairs, the door to my room stood ajar. Carefully, I tiptoed closer and peeked through the crack. Daddy was lying in my bed, his arm wrapped around Tess. They faced the window, but Daddy's deep even breathing told me he was asleep. I started to place the letter on the bed beside Tess, but decided to wait. What if Daddy woke first and found the letter? Would he be angry that Mr. Reed wrote Tess?

I walked a little further down the hall and went into Mama's room. She rested in her bed, propped up against pillows. Mama's eyes were closed, her breathing so slow and shallow her chest barely moved. Her eyelids looked as milky blue and thin as the skin covering the dead baby, and suddenly I felt afraid. Is this the way people die, turning blue at the edges, in tiny places like eyelids and earlobes?

"Mama?" My voice came out sharper than I wanted, and surprised me.

She opened her eyes, blinking a few times as if to focus. "Ellie?"

"Yes, Mama, it's me." I sat down on the edge of the bed and faced her, but left the jar in my lap with my hands covering it so she couldn't see it right away. "You're all clean," I said, touching her gown.

"Daddy took care of me," she said and smoothed the front of her bodice. "He bathed me and changed my gown, even put a bandage on my head." She pointed to her forehead. "He still loves me, Ellie. Deep in his heart, he does. Even though he did a bad thing when he tore up my flowers and gave me the shot, he didn't mean it. It's the stress, you know. Stress can make a man do strange things. It's because of that girl. She puts lies in his head.

She's trying to turn him against me because she wants him for herself."

I nodded, not knowing what else to do or say.

"Oh, I brought Jellybean back inside for you," she said, pulling back the cover to show me. My chick lay on the pillow next to her, his green and yellow feathers speckled with dirt.

I didn't understand why God killed little things like Jellybean and Mama's baby. Mrs. Roberts once explained that God takes someone good when He needs an angel. But it seems so unfair. Why would God send little souls into the world just long enough to let somebody love them, then snatch them away? Didn't God know how much Mama needed her baby? Didn't He know how much I needed Jellybean? With His own hosts of angels, why take away those we love?

"I brought you something, too." I placed the jar on the bed so she could see.

Mama's eyes widened when she saw the baby floating in its pink-tinged bath.

"Oh, Ellie. The baby! You brought the baby for me." She picked up the jar and pressed it to her breast. "Can I open it?"

"No, no, Mama. The jar has to stay closed. The water he's in is special, and he has to stay in the jar."

"I see. It's like magic, isn't it?" She smiled.

"Yes, Mama. That's exactly right. You can't open the jar, but you can keep the baby near you this way."

"He's a little waterbaby. Remember the story, Ellie? How the fairies take the chimney sweep and make him into a waterbaby?"

"Yes, Mama. I remember."

"What was the boy's name, Ellie? Sam?"

"Tom. His name was Tom."

Mama smiled. "Yes, Tom. And that's what we'll call the baby. Tom."

She lifted the jar to her pale lips and kissed the glass.

I took Jellybean's body back outside to bury. After shaking the loose dirt from the handkerchief, I smoothed the fabric and pillow. "Good-bye, little friend," I whispered, then placed him back in his box. Using Daddy's shovel, I covered the grave, patting the soil into place with the palms of my hand. I wanted to make sure nothing ever disturbed his grave, to protect him the way I hadn't when he was alive.

Satisfied that the dirt was packed over his box casket, I hunted through the fence row for some honeysuckle and a flat gray rock to mark his grave. I felt too tired to pray, too tired to cry. I leaned my head against the crab apple tree and closed my eyes.

I didn't hear the back door close or Daddy walk up to me. His voice startled me.

"Ellie," he said, then cleared his throat.

I opened my eyes and saw Daddy beside me, his hands shoved into his pockets. "Tess heated up some ravioli and bread. Why don't you come inside and eat?"

He turned around, expecting me to follow.

I dreaded going back inside, but knew I had no choice. "I'm coming, Daddy."

He waited for me to catch up, then took my hand in his. His rough fingers circled mine, and he looked at my hand as if this was the first time he'd seen it. "After dinner, Ellie, we need to talk about your mother."

His eyes never left my hand.

TWENTY-SIX

WHITE LIES

TESS STOOD IN THE KITCHEN, making a tray for Mama:
ravioli squares on a blue plate, a slice of buttered bread, a
glass of milk, and a cored apple cut into quarters.

"Can I take Mama's food upstairs to her?"

Tess looked to Daddy for an answer.

He nodded. "Go ahead, but don't take long. You need to eat,
too, Ellie."

"Here's a napkin," Tess said as she lifted the silverware and
placed the folded cloth beside Mama's plate. She'd found Mama's
good linens, the beige ones embroidered with small pink tulips.
These were for Sunday dinners and not used for canned ravioli
and sliced apples. Tess didn't ask, she just took what she wanted
and used it the way she pleased. *No wonder I was growing to hate
her. She didn't care about what belonged to anyone else. To her,
everything in reach was hers.*

Tess handed me the tray, then reached for a bottle of pills from
the window sill. She set the bottle beside the glass of milk. "Tell
her to take two of these. They're for pain."

Daddy picked up the bottle and shook two white pills into his hand, then plopped them on the tray. He looked at Tess as he spoke. "Don't ever give her a full bottle of pills, for Christ's sake. If today's events didn't teach you that much . . ."

"Don't snap at me," Tess said, parking her hands on her hips. "I've never played nursemaid to a crazy woman before."

"Mama isn't crazy," I yelled at Tess. "You take that back!"

"Hush, both of you. God knows we've had enough turmoil for one day."

Daddy's voice quieted us both.

Tess's mouth tightened into a thin line. I wished I could take my needle and thread and stitch her mouth closed so she couldn't say another word. Ever.

Daddy pointed to the table. "Tess, go ahead and set out the plates. And you," he said as he placed his hands on my shoulders and turned me toward the stairs, "need to take this food to your mother before it gets cold."

I walked slowly, careful not to spill the milk as I carried the tray upstairs. Warm tears slid down my cheeks. I blinked, and took a deep breath so Mama wouldn't know I'd been crying.

The door was closed, so I had to set the tray on the floor to open it. I stepped inside and placed the tray on the edge of her bedside table. "Here's your food, Mama." When I moved the vase aside to make room for her food, daisy petals fell from the arrangement and scattered on the dark wood.

"They're wilting, Ellie." Mama's voice sounded sad. "Why do pretty things have to die?"

I wondered that, too, and didn't know the answer. "I'll pick you some new ones in the morning, Mama."

"Don't you see, Ellie? What's the point? Those flowers will die, too, in a few days. Everything pretty dies."

"Are you hungry, Mama? I brought you food."

Mama looked at the plate. "Did she make it, Ellie? Did she make the food?" Her voice sounded harsh and angry. She pulled herself up so that she was sitting in bed, wincing a little when she moved. On the pillow next to Mama, Baby Tom floated in his jar, his stubby fingers open toward her.

"Well, yes, Mama. But it came in a can, so she didn't really cook it. All she did was heat it up."

"It's poison, Ellie," she whispered. "She wants me dead so she can have your father."

"Mama, it's not poison, really. Here, smell it." I lifted the plate and held it close to her.

She leaned forward a little and sniffed. "Rat poison. It's in the tomatoes. She put rat poison in the sauce. I'm not eating this, Ellie." Mama shoved the plate back into my hands.

"At least drink the milk and take your medicine."

She took the glass from me and smelled the milk.

"Tess didn't touch the milk, Mama. I promise. I watched her the whole time. I know to keep an eye on her."

Mama hesitated, as if unsure, then held her hand open to receive her pills.

"These will make you feel better," I said, placing the pills in her hand.

She shoved the white ovals to the back of her tongue and washed them down with milk, swallowing huge gulps until the glass was empty.

"I wish you'd eat something, Mama. You have to be hungry." I reached for the napkin and blotted the milk away from her lips, grateful that she didn't notice her good linens.

"I can't eat any food that girl prepares, Ellie. Don't you see she wants me dead? She wants to kill me just like she killed Jellybean." Mama reached over to adjust Baby Tom, propping the jar up against the pillow. His little bald walnut-shaped head tilted to one side. "You keep sliding down, don't you, love?"

I tried to ignore the baby, and instead looked back at Mama's face. "Jellybean's drowning was an accident, Mama. Tess didn't really mean it."

Mama placed her hands on my face and tilted my head. She stared into my eyes as she spoke. "Girls like Tess don't do anything by accident. You watch her, Ellie. Don't turn your back on her for a minute." Mama's thumbs dug into my skin, hurting my cheeks.

I nodded.

Mama let go of my face and pointed to the tray. "Here, take this food back downstairs and tell her I don't want it."

"Mama, can't I just flush the food down the toilet? This is only going to start an argument with Tess. I'm tired of fighting with her." I didn't mean to whine, but couldn't help myself. This was all too hard for me, trying to keep Mama calm, doing what Daddy wanted, not stirring up trouble with Tess. I felt like a bandage being stretched to cover too many places at once.

Mama reached out her hand and stroked my hair. "I know this is difficult, Ellie, but you can't let her frighten you. Now, you take this food right back to her and tell her not to send any more of her garbage."

I picked up the tray and started to leave.

"Wait a minute," Mama called.

I walked back to the bed. Maybe she'd changed her mind. Maybe she'd eat the apples at least. "Yes, Mama?"

She leaned forward, lowered her head over the tray, and spat on the food. "There."

After leaving Mama's room, I sat on the top step and tried to think of what to say. Tess would have a fit if she saw that Mama spat in her food. Maybe I could mix it up, make the spit disappear in the tomato sauce. Still, Tess would see that Mama hadn't eaten. I could say Mama had an upset stomach and wanted poached eggs and milk toast instead. Mama wouldn't have to know Tess cooked the egg. I could tell her I cooked it. Sometimes a little white lie isn't a bad thing, not if the lie helps someone. If it got Mama to eat, I'd tell white lies and not even ask God to forgive me.

While sitting on the step and going over what to say, I caught Daddy's voice. "You just don't understand, Tess. I can't send her away."

"Why not, Rupert? You sent her before." Tess said, her voice shrill and impatient.

"Because I've been giving her the tranquilizers again. They'd show up in her blood."

"Oh, God, Rupert . . ."

"I love you, Tess. You know I do. I just don't know how to do this. I don't know how to make it right."

"Maybe you can't."

"What's that supposed to mean?"

"Rupert, I'm not staying here and waiting for your crazy wife to hurt me."

"Tess, don't . . ."

I'd heard all I could stand. I couldn't just sit on the step and listen to Tess talk Daddy into putting Mama into the hospital. I couldn't sit by and let Tess take Daddy away.

I ran down the stairs. "Daddy!" I tripped on my shoelaces and fell, dropping Mama's tray. The ravioli splattered the floor. The empty milk glass shattered. When I reached out to steady myself, my hands pressed on the glass, cutting my palms.

"Ellie?" Daddy called. "Oh, Ellie." He ran into the hall and knelt beside me. Taking my hands in his, he turned them over to look at my bleeding palms. A piece of glass glittered in my skin.

"I've got to clean this, Ellie." Daddy scooped me up and carried me into the kitchen. He sent Tess upstairs to get cotton, antiseptic, and a pair of tweezers.

"Put your hand under the stream," he said as he turned on the cold water faucet.

My palms burned, and I couldn't help crying. "Promise you won't leave, Daddy. Promise you won't send Mama away," I sobbed.

"Don't you worry, honey. Let's talk about this later. Right now, we need to take care of your hand."

Tess walked back into the kitchen and handed Daddy the tweezers. She touched my shoulder. "Poor Ellie," she whispered. "Don't worry. You'll be fine."

Daddy struck a match and held it to the tweezer tips, turning the ends black. "Sit here on the table where the light's good," he said.

I stepped up on the chair and sat down on the edge of the table.

Tess began to clean up the broken glass and spilled ravioli, putting everything into the garbage pail.

Daddy held my hand in a firm grip. "Be still and this won't hurt," he said. Bending forward, he fished the glass sliver from my hand.

I held perfectly still, just like he told me, but it did hurt.

"The cut isn't deep. You won't need a bandage." After he pulled out the glass, Daddy dabbed on the alcohol, which stung sharply for a moment, then cooled when Daddy blew across my palm. When he was all done, Daddy said, "There now, didn't hurt a bit, did it?"

"No," I said, figuring even somebody as strong as my daddy needed white lies sometimes, too.

"That's my girl," he said, patting my knee. Moving down my leg, Daddy's hand brushed the corner of the envelope sticking out of my sock. "What's this?"

My face grew warm. I'd forgotten all about Tess's letter. She'd think I'd done it on purpose, to pay her back for drowning Jellybean and being mean to Mama.

Daddy pulled the envelope from my sock and studied it.

I scratched my leg where the letter had been.

Tess chewed her thumbnail and looked at Daddy.

The vein on my father's temple darkened. He looked at Tess. "It's for you."

TWENTY-SEVEN

THE LETTER

G IVE ME THE LETTER, Rupert." Tess held out her hand, palm up. "I mean it."

Daddy looked at Tess, then back at the envelope, turning it over in his hand. "Who else knows you're living here, Tess? And who would be writing you?" Daddy stared at her, his eyes full of angry questions.

"I don't know. Don't look at me like that, Rupert. It's not a crime to get a letter, is it?"

"No." Daddy smacked the envelope down on the table. "There's no crime in it, but I still need to know who's writing you. You are living in my home now. You're my responsibility."

"Don't speak to me like I'm a child." Tess's milky skin showed red patches.

My father studied the writing on the front. "This doesn't look like a girl's writing. Letters are too large, sloppy. A man wrote this. Or a boy." Daddy nodded his head as if he'd suddenly figured out who'd written Tess. "It's that Cline boy who used to come looking for you at the store, isn't it? What's his name? The prick with the guitar on his back who thought he was headed to the Grand Ole Opry?" Daddy faked a laugh.

"Roger, but . . ."

"You been writing to Roger, Tess?" Drops of sweat shone on Daddy's forehead. "You planning to run off with Roger and live in some two-bit trailer with a kid who sings for his supper?" He slapped the table. "Tell me, Tess!"

Tess and I both jumped. I suddenly needed to go pee, but was too afraid to move.

"No, of course not. I can't even stand Roger Cline. I don't know who it's from, honey, I swear. Go on and open it if it means so much to you." Tess wiped the corner of her eye as if she didn't want Daddy to see her crying. She looked so broken I almost felt sorry for her.

"It's from her daddy," I said, looking down at the tiled floor. "The postman brought the mail today while I was outside. He said the letter was from Mr. Reed, and I forgot to give the letter to Tess when I came inside."

"Daddy wrote me?" Tess asked, her voice quivering. She seemed shocked and afraid, not happy to hear from her father, but then he was not the kind of father anyone would miss.

I thought I'd be in trouble for keeping the letter in my sock, but neither Daddy nor Tess paid attention to me. A heavy quiet settled in the room.

"You want to read it?" Daddy finally said. He looked at Tess.

She shook her head. "No, I don't want it. Throw it away, Rupert. Just throw the damn thing away. I don't want to hear a word he has to say."

Daddy placed the envelope back on the kitchen table and didn't say anything, just kept staring at the envelope.

Tess's eyes darted from Daddy to the envelope on the table. Did she want him to open it? Did she care what it said, or did she wish, as I did, that Daddy would rip the letter into pieces so small no one could read the words?

Even as I wished differently, I knew Daddy would read the letter. Mama likes to hide from the hard things, but Daddy is more afraid of what he doesn't know than of anything he can see.

Finally, Daddy spoke. "That bastard wants something. I don't trust him. I want to know what he has to say. No need to be operating in the dark, now is there?"

Before Tess had time to speak, Daddy shoved his thumb under the loose corner flap and ripped open the envelope. He pulled out the piece of notebook paper, unfolded it, and read. He mouthed the words to himself.

Tess and I waited.

"That bastard!"

I covered my ears, but could still hear my father cursing.

"That no-good fucking bastard!"

"Rupert, what is it?" Tess stepped forward, reaching for the letter.

Daddy shoved the paper into her hands. He stood up and pounded his fist against the wall.

Tears filled my eyes. Daddy's loud voice and glaring eyes scared me. "Daddy?"

"I'll be back," Daddy said. "You both go ahead and start supper without me." He ripped his keys from the hook on the wall and stormed out of the house, slamming the door so hard the table shook under me.

"Rupert, please don't," Tess called after him. She wadded up the letter and threw it down, then ran out the door behind Daddy.

Would Tess be able to calm my father? I wondered. Or would he pace the sidewalk or go into his shed and chisel wood until the last angry sparks inside him were gone?

I looked around.

The letter lay on the floor.

Reading somebody else's mail is wrong. Still, I had to know what Mr. Reed had written. I wanted to know what upset Daddy so much.

I picked up the crumpled paper and spread it flat on the table. The letters were fat and black. They slanted downhill like mine had in first grade. Some were even backwards. I read the letter as fast as I could, but Mr. Reed spelled most of the words wrong, and I had to think hard to figure them out:

deer Tess,

    i seen you com here and took your tomatos. Look here, young ladie, I want you to com home rite now. i wud com git you mysef but i turnd my ankl on the porch step when i seen them tomatos gone. you hav staid with that man long enuff. so i wrute to you to tel you to com hom rit away. you is my gurl Tessy. com home to yur daddy. i need you with me. i miss your voice and your purty pink skin.

    If that man you is with don't let you com home I wil sind Raymund Witters out ther to git you, Tessy.

    al my lov
    yur daddy
    Mason Reed

My hands shook as I crumpled the letter and tossed it back on the floor.

I knew Daddy would never let Tess go back to live with Mr. Reed. Even if the man had treated her right and Tess wanted to go back, Daddy might not allow her to leave. What would happen if Mr. Reed's ankle healed and he showed up to take Tess home, or if he sent someone for her like he'd said in his letter? Daddy would do anything to keep her. I knew it in the way he looked at her, watched over her, and kissed her.

I walked to the kitchen window and looked at Daddy and Tess. They stood in front of Daddy's toolshed, arguing. I couldn't hear their voices, but I knew they were angry. Daddy's clenched fists hung at his sides. Tess leaned toward him, tugging at his shirt, her face red and shiny.

I didn't know what to do. Hide upstairs with Mama? Go out-side and try to stop Daddy and Tess from arguing?

Deciding that keeping busy was the best thing to do, I began to clear the table. I moved the plates and glasses first, a habit I'd gotten into because leaving glass out in the open too long made Daddy nervous, especially when Mama was upset.

As I picked up a bowl to carry to the sink, the door opened. Tess walked in, crying. "Oh, God, Ellie. I couldn't stop him."

I turned, startled. "Where's Daddy? Stop him from what?"

"He left. I begged him not to go," she sobbed, collapsing on a chair. She buried her face in her hands and leaned forward until her head landed on the table.

I rushed to the window and looked out to see Daddy's car gone.

"What are we going to do?" Tess said. "He took the gun, Ellie. He took the gun!"

TWENTY-EIGHT

SPOON

I KNEW WHAT IT meant that Daddy took his gun. Tess knew, too. She paced the kitchen floor and chewed her nails. "What are we going to do?" she asked.

"Why did you have to come here, Tess? Why couldn't you leave Daddy alone? He isn't yours! He belongs to Mama and me! Why couldn't you pick Roger or somebody else? Why couldn't you sell your tomatoes and buy a bus ticket to some other town?"

"Please, Ellie. Don't be mean to me," she pleaded like a child. "I didn't plan for things to turn out this way. I love your Daddy, I really do. I never wanted anything bad to happen. I tried to stop him. Honest, I did."

"But you didn't stop him, Tess. He's gone, and we don't know if he's coming . . ." I couldn't finish. My words turned to sobs. I sank to the floor and cried, pressing my face into my hands.

Tess sat down beside me and touched my hair. "Oh, Ellie. Don't cry. Please don't."

I pushed her hand away. "Leave me alone, Tess. You were supposed to help my mother, but that's not why you came, was it?

You stole Daddy, and made Mama sad. You dropped . . . you dropped my chick in the river. You . . . you're bad!"

Tess frowned. "I didn't do it on purpose, Ellie. I mess up things sometimes. I don't know why."

"I don't want . . . to talk about it . . . anymore. Just leave me . . . alone," I said between sobs.

A siren blared outside, and Tess and I both ran to the door, then out onto the porch.

We watched an ambulance drive by, headed toward someone else's house, down Grace Street.

Daddy was still safe. At least for now.

Tess walked back inside, but I stayed on the porch. Before Tess came, Daddy and I would take walks on evenings like this. Sometimes, Mama came along, too. There were whole weeks when Mama acted like everyone else's mother. No tears or broken things, no giggles that wouldn't end, only cookies and a quiet voice.

I tried not to think about Daddy and Mr. Reed arguing, but whenever you try not to think of something, you always do. Tess lived out in the country, so the drive would take Daddy some time even if he drove fast, which I figured he would do. Maybe the drive would calm him down and give him time to think. The car might even run out of gas and Daddy would have to hitch a ride back into town. Maybe Mr. Reed wouldn't be home.

When I came back into the house, I noticed Tess washing the dishes. *She's probably right to keep busy,* I thought. I picked up a towel to dry the plates. Their smooth surfaces reflected my face and showed me how worried I looked.

"Thanks, Ellie." Tess spoke in a low voice, barely a whisper. Her pale blonde hair lay flat across her head, all her salon curls washed away.

The clock told me Daddy had been gone for just under an hour. He'd be at Mason Reed's house by now, walking up to the front door.

Tess rubbed her forehead the way grown-ups do when they have a headache, pressing fingers against their skull. She pulled the plug in the sink, and I heard the dirty water run down the drain.

The clock ticked, sending the red second hand around and around.

Daddy would be knocking on the screen door by now. He'd be running his fingers through his hair, waiting for Mason Reed to pull himself up from his sofa and limp to the door on his twisted ankle. The inside of his house would surely be filthy with Tess gone.

Maybe Daddy would walk inside this nasty house and decide Mr. Reed wasn't worth the trouble. Not even for Tess.

I tried to focus on the plate in my hand, the china smooth and warm against my skin.

Tess leaned against the sink, her flat belly pressed against the counter. She moved both hands to her head and groaned. All the arguing must have given her a very bad headache.

Mama's bottle of pain pills were on the window sill. I thought about offering Tess one, but decided not to.

Tess wobbled at the sink. I glanced at her face to try to figure out what was the matter. Her eyes blinked fast, again and again, and all I could see was the white part. It was as if her eyes had rolled into her head and locked there. A few seconds later, Tess collapsed on the kitchen floor, falling like a marionette with cut strings.

"Tess!" I screamed. Could a girl stand at the sink washing dishes and seconds later drop dead? Kneeling beside her body, I touched her arm. She felt stiff.

What was happening?

Her skin turned pale and splotchy, then her legs twitched, both legs at the same time, as if they were joined to a single wire. Next, her whole body jerked. She thrashed on the floor.

Epilepsy. Seizure.

Mary Roberts had described what they looked like, but seeing Tess this way frightened me.

Her body rose a few inches, then slammed against the floor, flopping like a fish tossed on the river bank. Her head made a thud every time it hit the floor. Her arms flew out, hitting me. I lost my balance, landing on my back.

I turned and quickly stood up. How long would this last? What should I do?

Just then, I remembered the spoon. "You have to put a spoon in their mouth or they'll bite their tongue off," Mary had said.

I thought if the time came, I wouldn't care if Tess bit off her tongue, but I was too scared to be mean to her now. "Don't let her die, God," I prayed. If Daddy came home and saw I'd let Tess bite off her tongue, he wouldn't love me anymore. Not ever. He might even go to that place in his mind where Mama goes.

A spoon. I had to find a spoon and get it into her mouth. As Tess thrashed on the floor, I reached into the sink, pulled out a teaspoon.

Kneeling beside Tess, I saw drops of blood coming from her mouth. *Oh, God, don't let me be too late. Please.*

Her face was gray, and her skin felt cool now. I couldn't help but think of Jellybean, cold and stiff in his little grave, and Baby Tom, floating in his jar. Tess couldn't die.

"I'm sorry, Tess. I didn't mean those bad things I said. Please don't die."

It took all my strength to lift her head onto my lap. My hand hurt from my own cut palm, but I tried to hold her still. Her head thumped against my legs so hard I thought my knees would crack. I tried to slip the spoon inside her mouth, but her teeth clenched down.

I remembered how Mama got me to take medicine when I'd refuse to open my mouth. She'd pinch my nose closed until I opened my mouth to breathe, then in with the spoon.

Maybe that would work with Tess. I reached for her nose, but her head wouldn't stay still for more than a second. Every time I tried, her head rocked in my lap and I lost my grip. My fingers, wet with blood, slipped when she moved. I pressed my hand across her nose like a cup, hoping to force her mouth open for air.

A few seconds later, I saw a small opening and shoved the spoon inside. Her teeth clamped down hard, and she almost bit the tip of my finger. I barely managed to hold onto the spoon, but gripped with all my might and pushed it deeper until her tongue was under it.

I sat on the floor with Tess and waited for the thrashing to stop. My arms hurt from holding her so tight. Sweat ran down my face, burning my eyes, but I didn't dare move my hands.

I looked at the clock again. Only a few minutes had passed. It seemed much longer. I wished Daddy would come home and tell me what to do.

Floorboards creaked overhead. I prayed Mama would stay upstairs. She'd only make this worse. She might even be happy to let Tess die.

The toilet flushed, and the soft thud of feet followed. I held my breath, listening for the door. The creak sounded more like bedsprings. *Good,* I thought.

Tess jerked one final time in my lap, then grew still. At first, I thought maybe she'd died, but then she groaned. Her eyes searched the room as if she didn't know where she was. I slipped the spoon from her mouth, glad to see her tongue move as she licked her blood-smeared lips.

"You'll be okay, Tess," I whispered.

She didn't seem to hear or see me.

I eased her head from my lap and let it rest against the floor. "I'll get you a blanket."

As I laid the spoon on the floor and moved to stand up, I noticed a yellowish puddle spread on the floor under Tess.

"I'll bring some clean clothes, too."

I hurried upstairs and found clean panties and a blue dress for

Tess. I didn't want to go to the hall closet for another blanket and risk Mama hearing me, so I pulled the quilt from my bed, and carried the bundle back to the kitchen.

When I saw Tess, I dropped the blanket and clothes.

She sat on the floor, leaning against the stove. Her eyes seemed to look right through me, as if she couldn't see. She'd taken off her wet panties, and her skirt was pulled up over her knees. Her hand smacked between her legs. "Please, Papa, don't. It hurts, it hurts," she cried.

When I saw Tess, I thought about the dirty things her father had done to her after her seizures. I swallowed hard, forcing the sour taste down my throat.

"Tess, please don't," I said as I stepped toward her.

"Ellie?" Tess said my name like a question. She acted like she hardly knew me. Her eyes moved around the room as if seeing it for the first time. At least she'd stopped hitting herself.

Kneeling beside Tess, I tried to comfort her. "It's me, Tess. It's Ellie. Don't you remember? We played Avon Lady in my room, and you braided my hair. You gave me kissing lessons. Remember?"

She studied my face. Her eyes moved as she looked at me. She reached up with one hand to touch my arm. "I remember, Ellie. Ellie with the Jellybean bird."

"That's right." I made myself smile.

She wrinkled up her forehead. "Oh, no. The funeral. There was a funeral, wasn't there? Jellybean died, and we buried . . . and then she called me the baby killer . . . and Rupert? . . . Where's Rupert?" She tried to sit up more, then winced. Her body must have hurt from banging so hard against the floor.

"Papa, he . . . he hurt me down there."

"He wasn't here, Tess. You had a bad dream, that's all."

"No, no. I remember. I fell, and then he was on me, pushing me. And . . ." She sobbed, and started clawing between her legs as if she could feel her father there.

I managed to pull her hands away and to make her stop. Then I placed the blanket over her body, and stroked her face, wet with tears. "Tess, please. You have to believe me. You had a seizure, but your papa isn't here. He was never here."

"I hurt too much. I want Rupert. Where's Rupert?"

"Oh, Tess, I want him, too, but he's not here." If only someone could tell me what to do.

I stood up and walked to the telephone. Maybe I should call someone. Mr. Morgan? Miss Wilder? Maybe the ambulance?

Without knowing who to call or what to say, I picked up the receiver and took a deep breath.

Just as I placed my finger in the dial, a screeching noise came from outside the front of the house. Then a car door slammed. "Daddy?" I called.

I dropped the phone and ran toward the door. As I pulled the door open, Daddy stepped inside.

My father looked right past me. When he saw Tess on the floor, his face turned white. "Oh, God, what happened? What happened?" Daddy ran to Tess and knelt at her side. He took her face in his hands and kissed her mouth, her cheeks, even her eyes.

"I tried to help her, Daddy." My voice broke as I explained. "She started shaking, and then she fell."

Daddy looked up at me. "A seizure? How long?"

"Yes. I don't . . . It seemed long, but . . . and . . . and I put a spoon in her mouth, but she'd already bit her tongue a little."

Daddy looked at Tess's mouth. "Open, let me see, baby."

Tess opened her mouth for Daddy to check the cut.

"Not too bad. Just a little cut." Daddy wiped the blood from her lips. Then he looked at me and said, "You did fine, Ellie. You took good care of her."

Tess cried. She gripped Daddy's shirt. "I thought he was on me, Rupert. I could feel him, smell him."

"Hush, it's okay."

She nodded, wiping tears from her face.

"I was getting ready to call the ambulance when you came, Daddy. I didn't know what else to do."

"No, no ambulance. I'm here now. I'll take care of her."

"I tried, Daddy. I was scared."

"You did good, Ellie. It's okay."

Daddy yanked away the blanket covering Tess. There was pee and a small amount of blood on the floor under Tess. Daddy looked at me. "Ellie, go upstairs and bring Vaseline, bandages, and clean towels."

I hurried to the bathroom and gathered the things Daddy wanted. I was glad Tess had brought her own Vaseline, so I didn't have to go into Mama's bathroom and take it from her medicine chest.

Back downstairs, I handed Daddy the jar, bandages, and towels, then curled up in the corner to stay out of his way.

Daddy didn't notice me. He busied himself tending Tess, cleaning her. As he did it, he talked softly. "You're okay now, don't worry. I'll take care of you. Don't worry. Mason Reed can't ever come near you again. I made sure of that."

Tess looked at Daddy with wide eyes. "Oh, Rupert, what have you done?"

"Only what he had coming. What somebody should've done a long time ago."

Tess grabbed Daddy by the arms as if she wanted to shake the truth from him. "Tell me you just hit him, Rupert. Tell me you only gave him a piece of your mind. You wouldn't . . . you didn't hurt him, did you?"

Daddy picked up the Vaseline jar and threw it against the kitchen wall. The glass broke, smearing the wallpaper.

"I'm sorry, Tess. Look, you hush now. Just rest, and let me handle everything."

Daddy looked across the room and saw me in the corner. His eyes darkened like wet stones.

TWENTY-NINE

LEAVING

DADDY AIMING THE GUN at Mason Reed . . . His finger pulling the trigger . . . Mason Reed falling to the floor . . . Blood in a dark red puddle . . .

These pictures played in my head as if I'd stood in the room and watched Daddy shoot the man.

Still seated on the floor, Tess leaned against the stove. She put her hands over her face and cried, her shoulders curled inward. She pulled her knees to her chest as if trying to ball her body into something tight and closed.

I wanted to tell her, "You should be glad," but that would've meant saying out loud that Daddy was a murderer.

When Tess stopped crying, her voice was sharp and high. "How could you, Rupert?"

"Tess, shut up," I yelled. Daddy had done this awful thing for her, because of her. How could she blame or question him? "You know Daddy wouldn't hurt anybody. Just shut up!" The word *kill* almost came out instead of *hurt*. No, no, I couldn't say it. I squeezed my fists tight and reminded myself to be careful.

Still, my voice must have startled Tess. She stared at me, a stunned look on her face. She made a sniffling sound and wiped her nose on the back of her hand. "You're right, Ellie. I'm just upset. So much has happened . . . and I . . . I'm not thinking straight . . . my head," she said, rubbing her eyebrows.

I wanted Daddy to deny what he'd done, but he didn't say another word about Mason Reed. He didn't even ask us to keep this night's events secret. He didn't have to. I'd never tell anyone—not Mama, not Mr. Morgan, not even Mary Roberts.

Tess complained again about the pain in her head.

"Let's try a compress," Daddy said as he walked to the sink. He pulled out one of Mama's dishrags from the drawer, held it under running water, squeezed the excess into the sink, and returned to Tess. He knelt beside her. "Hold it right there and close your eyes," Daddy said, pressing the wet cloth to her forehead and positioning her hand to anchor it.

While Tess rested, Daddy came over and sat on the floor next to me. "You did good tonight, Ellie." He picked up my hand and kissed it.

"I didn't do it for her, Daddy. I hate Tess." I whispered so Tess wouldn't hear me. If we started arguing, Mama might wake up and come downstairs. Mama couldn't know about the spoon, or the letter, or about Daddy going out with the gun. Not ever.

"Don't hate her, Ellie. It breaks my heart to even hear you say that." Daddy looked at me with eyes so sad I wanted to take back my words, but I didn't. Tess had ruined everything. I did hate her. I wanted to hate her for the rest of my life.

"You better get some sleep, Ellie." Daddy stood up and walked to the front window. He pulled back the tan curtain and looked outside, his eyes searching. I knew from his furrowed brow he wasn't looking for stars or the moon. He was looking for something else, something eyes can't see.

"Can I sleep down here on the sofa?" Going upstairs seemed too far from Daddy.

He turned toward me and nodded. "Tess will sleep in the sewing room on my bed."

"Where will you sleep, Daddy?"

"Oh, don't worry about me. I'll nap in a chair. I'm not too sleepy anyhow."

I stood up and moved to the sofa, curling up on my side so my skirt covered my legs. Daddy pulled off my shoes and massaged my feet in his large hands, warming them. He took the afghan from the sofa's back to wrap around me, careful to tuck the edges under me.

"Will you check on Mama before you go to sleep? She hardly touched her supper." I hadn't eaten either, but didn't feel hungry.

Daddy pulled the cover under my chin and rubbed my shoulder. "Yes, I'll check on her. I'll take her some saltines if she's hungry."

"Promise?" I yawned. My eyelids felt heavy.

"I promise. Don't worry now."

"The baby in the jar, his name is Tom. You have to remember that, Daddy. Mama will want you to notice Tom."

"I will, Ellie. I'll say something nice about Tom. Now go to sleep."

"I love you, Daddy."

Daddy leaned close and kissed me good-night. "I love you, Ellie."

SLEEP CAME, BUT it was fitful and broken. Doors creaked. The car engine moaned outside. Thumping sounds hit the floor. Lights flickered on the porch and glowed in the window. In my sleep, I couldn't tell which sounds came from dreams and which were real.

Tess's voice woke me. "Please, Rupert, you've got to help me! The headache . . . the pain . . . it won't stop."

"Daddy?" I called from the sofa.

Sunlight streamed in the front window, making the room bright. I must have slept for hours. "Daddy?" I called again, rubbing my arm awake.

When Daddy didn't answer, I got up from the sofa and followed his voice into the sewing room.

"Not the hospital, Tess. We can't go to the hospital. Not now. I know a man not too far from here. He's good. He'll know . . ."

"Rupert, I need a doctor, not some man."

"He is a doctor, honey. He got in some trouble, lost his license for a little while, but he'll know exactly what to do. And he'll keep quiet."

"Daddy?" I stood in the doorway and looked into the room. Tess sat on the makeshift bed, dabbing a cloth at her head. Pieces of the night flashed in my mind: the letter, the spoon, the broken jar of Vaseline.

Daddy turned around. "Ellie."

"What's the matter, Daddy?"

"Ellie, Tess had another seizure. She needs a doctor. I'm going to have to leave for awhile and take her to see someone who can help."

"No, Daddy. No!"

"Honey, I have to . . ."

"Why can't the ambulance come and take her like it did when Mama fell?"

"There's another doctor that'll look at Tess. Now, I'm going upstairs to check on your mother. You wait here, keep Tess company."

"But Daddy!"

"Hush now, Ellie!"

After Daddy left the room, Tess reached out her arms to me. "What's going to happen, Ellie? I'm so scared."

Ignoring her, I hunted for Mama's sewing basket. "I'm going to sort buttons."

"Buttons? You're going to sort buttons?" she repeated.

I didn't answer. I had to stay in the room because Daddy said to, but he hadn't told me to talk to her.

"Reds in the corner. Blues in back." My fingers separated buttons into little piles. "Three green buttons . . ."

"God, would you shut up about the damn buttons!" Tess screeched. She stood a few feet from me.

"Seven black buttons. One more makes eight . . ."

"Jesus Christ!"

"One canary yellow . . . three off-whites."

"You're just jealous. Jealous because your daddy loves me. Go ahead and count your stupid buttons."

Something dark and fierce rose inside me. Nothing I could do would stop it from escaping. I picked up handfuls of buttons and threw them at Tess.

She screamed and tried to cover herself with her hands.

Blacks, reds, blues . . . I grabbed fistfuls and threw them as hard as I could. Buttons hit her legs, arms, and face.

Daddy came downstairs and ran into the sewing room. He wrapped his arms around my waist. "Ellie, don't! Stop it!"

I thought Daddy would be angry, but he just held me tight and carried me to the sofa. He sat with me on his lap and rocked me back and forth while I cried. As soon as my sobs quieted, Daddy looked into my face and spoke in a firm voice. "I'm going to be gone for awhile, Ellie."

"Daddy, no!"

"I have to, Ellie, just for a little while. Not long, I promise. And I'll be back . . . but I have to go."

"I don't want you to go!" I sobbed into his shirt.

"I know, Ellie, but I can't just let Tess have another seizure, not after two already tonight. It's too dangerous. You know that. She has to get some medication. And I've done some terrible things, things I could get in trouble for, awful trouble. I have to go away for awhile until I can figure everything out."

"Why can't you stay here and figure them out?"

Daddy held my face in his hands. His eyes never looked more serious. "Because if I stay, Sheriff Rhodes is going to come looking for me, then I will have to go away for good. So you see, it's better that I go away now for a little while, then come back when I figure out a safe way."

"Why can't you take me? Maybe I can help you figure out things. I want to come with you!"

"Ellie, honey, Mama isn't well, and I can't bring her along. If you come with me, she'll have no one to take care of her. Is that what you want?"

"No, but . . ."

"Oh, Ellie, I know this is hard. You and I, we've never been apart, have we? And that's the way it will be again, angel, you'll see." Daddy wiped my tears away with his calloused hands. He kissed the top of my head. I could feel his warm lips tremble against my scalp.

"Promise, Daddy? Promise me you'll come back? Promise me, Daddy!"

"I promise. Cross my heart and hope to die," he said, drawing an invisible *x* over his chest. He forced a smile. "Now, have you forgotten that it's Easter Sunday?"

My eyes widened. "I did forget!" Although part of me didn't care that it was Easter. After all that had happened, chocolate bunnies and dyed eggs didn't matter anymore. But Daddy was trying hard to make me feel better, and I loved him so much, I pretended to care.

"Well, run upstairs while I carry Tess's things out to the car. Wash your face and comb your hair. And don't forget to check at the foot of your bed." Daddy winked.

I wrapped my arms around Daddy's neck and hugged him. He held me for a moment, then let go. "Scoot, now," he said, swatting my bottom with his hand.

"You'll be here when I come back?"

Daddy nodded. He looked away.

UPSTAIRS IN MY ROOM, every sign of Tess was gone: her clothes, makeup, and stack of books. Only the smell of her perfume hung in the air. I wanted to open every door and window to rid the house of her, but somehow I knew it was useless. Tess was now a stain soaked into the bones of our house.

Daddy had left a large wicker basket at the foot of my bed.

Pink and yellow ribbons circled the handle and formed a bow on top. Rows of chocolate bunnies wrapped in tinfoil peeked over the edge. Right in the middle, next to a sugary marshmallow egg, sat a little green chick so much like Jellybean that my voice caught in my throat when I saw him.

My hands shook as I scooped him from the basket and untangled plastic grass from around his thin legs. I sat on my bed, held my new chick, and cried all over again.

I never knew my eyes could make so many tears.

DOWNSTAIRS, THE DOOR CLOSED.

"Daddy!"

I dropped the chick on my bed and ran as fast as my legs would move. Partway down, I called to my father, even though I could not see him. "Daddy! No, Daddy! Please don't go!"

I crossed the floor quickly and pulled the front door open. I ran onto the front porch and down the steps. The morning sun shone in my eyes, causing me to squint. I saw Tess sitting in the front seat of Daddy's car. She looked in the mirror. Wrapped in a quilt, she'd left one hand free to put lipstick on her mouth.

"Ellie."

Daddy's voice spun me around.

"Do you like your chick, angel?" He wore his best gray coat and carried his brown suitcase. "I know it's not Jellybean, but . . ."

I nodded. My voice stuck in my throat.

"I have to go now, Ellie." His eyes looked so calm they frightened me. This was not how things were supposed to be. *My father can't just leave,* I thought. *He can't get into the car and drive away. It's not possible.* I knew this could not be possible.

And yet it was.

Everything inside me broke. "No! No! No!"

Daddy hugged me with one arm, never letting his suitcase go. With his hand on my shoulder, he nudged me toward the house. "Go back inside, Ellie."

I dropped to my knees and grabbed the hem of his coat. "Daddy, please don't go. I'll do anything you want," I begged with all I had inside me. "I'll be good. I'll be nice to Tess. Please don't leave me, Daddy!"

"I've got to go, Ellie." Daddy pulled his coat from my hands and walked to the car.

I ran behind him, my arms reaching for him, my voice crying, "Please, don't leave me, Daddy!"

Daddy slipped into the car and locked the door. I banged on the window, screaming for my father to stay.

The engine started, the slow vibrations tingling my hands.

All my tears and pleading couldn't make Daddy stay.

The car pulled forward, a sudden lurch that almost threw me off balance. I stepped back quickly. Loose gravel dug into the bottoms of my socks, hurting my feet. A wave of exhaust fumes hit my face.

Daddy drove away. He didn't wave or look back.

I ran after him as far as I could. The gravel and asphalt tore through my socks and cut the soles of my feet.

I tried to keep up, but the car grew smaller and smaller as it turned onto Gratton Street, then went up the steep hill. When the red taillights disappeared, I fell facedown on the asphalt and pounded the road with my fists.

I screamed for my father, but he'd gone too far for my voice to bring back.

THIRTY

CLARA AND JERICHO

L ORD, CHILD, WHAT are you doing laying in the middle of the road?" Fingers tugged at the back of my dress. I tried to see who stood beside me, but could only make out two scuffed shoes a few inches from my face. "Come on now, let's get up from here before a car hits you and me both."

My arms and legs felt numb from kicking and pounding on the road.

"Come on now," the woman said again.

I tried, but didn't have the strength to push myself up.

"Jericho! Jericho! Get out here and help me with this child. Mercy, who left this girl in the street?" The woman's voice rose louder. "Jericho, come here!"

A door slammed and footsteps came toward me.

My eyes and nose stung from crying. I squinted to see who stood over me. Their voices sounded like ones I'd heard before, maybe in Daddy's store, maybe in the market.

A wing-shaped shadow opened above me as two wide arms

lifted me from the road. My head felt dizzy. I tried to breathe deeper, wanting to stop the pinwheels spinning inside my head.

The man smelled like familiar things, tobacco and coconut, and I looked at his huge face. His skin was the dark brown color of coffee beans, his eyes black like my ragdoll's button eyes. When he smiled, a gold tooth glinted from behind his lower lip.

As he took a step back, my head felt light and dizzy. "I'm Jericho," the man said.

"Tess . . . no, Ellie . . . I . . ." My head and eyes burned, my throat felt dry and scratchy.

"Well, which is it, honey? Are you a Tess or an Ellie?" When he chuckled, his Adam's apple bobbed up and down in his wrinkled neck.

"Ellie. My name is Ellie." I licked my lips. "Are you an angel, Jericho?"

"Well, I don't know if I'm quite that good, but I sure ain't a devil, Ellie."

"Come on, Jericho, let's get her inside," the woman said.

Jericho held me close to his chest as he took long strides down the sidewalk, and even though I didn't know this man and should have been afraid, I wasn't. He was solid like an old tree, a tree that had lived through storms and harsh winters. You can lean all your worries against a tree like that.

Up two steps, we entered a pink clapboard house with white shutters. I smelled coffee, and something like roasted corn. A dog barked, and from far away, in another room, gospel voices sang on the radio.

"Hush up, Leo!" the woman hollered. "Go on, get outside!"

The door opened, then slammed shut on the barking dog.

"Put her in our room, Jericho."

He carried me down a narrow hall. I saw a picture of the crucified Jesus on the wall, and a calendar from Daddy's store. I swallowed hard, not wanting to cry. Somehow I knew there'd be more tears, that I was a long way from finished, but my body hurt so deep I couldn't cry again. Not yet.

Jericho carried me into another room and laid me on a bed. "There now. You rest, gumdrop."

My body sank in soft down. "Are you leaving, Jericho? Don't go!" I reached up to wrap my arms around his neck.

"Aren't you something?" he laughed. "Attached to me already."

The woman swatted Jericho's leg with a towel. "Don't flatter yourself, old man."

She sat next to me on the bed, and I looked at her face a long minute while she looked at mine. Gray hair ran in plaited rows across her head. Her skin, not as dark as Jericho's, glowed with tiny sweat beads. Her eyes looked more gold than brown, and lines spread out from her eyes and lips.

"Jericho ain't going nowhere, child," she said. "I couldn't get rid of him if I tried."

"Who are you? I've seen you before." I studied her face.

"Why, I'm Clara. Jericho's wife. This is Gratton Street, where me and Jericho live."

I knew that mostly colored people lived on Gratton Street, and maybe one or two families from Mexico who had come here to work at the poultry plant on the edge of town. Mary Roberts and I weren't allowed to play on Gratton Street, but it wasn't far from my house.

Clara turned to her husband. "Jericho, don't you have some work to do?" she asked.

"It's Easter Sunday. I'm not working on the day our Lord rose from the grave."

"You going to be in your own grave soon enough if you don't get out of my way and let me tend to this child." Clara laughed as she scolded her husband.

Jericho leaned over and touched my cheek with his finger. "You rest up, little Ellie. Clara's just fussing at me 'cause she loves me so." He winked and added, "Don't pay her no mind."

Clara pushed Jericho toward the door. "Find something to do

while I clean up this child." She turned around to face me. "Now, let's get you washed up," she said, then disappeared into the next room. I heard water running and she returned with a basin and towel in her hands.

Clara dipped the cloth into the water, rubbed on soap until she worked up a good lather, then reached for my hand. "What happened to you, honey?" She rubbed the warm soap over my dirty knuckles, then over the palm of my hand. She noticed the red line where yesterday the glass sliver had cut my hand. "What happened here?"

"I fell and broke a glass," I explained.

Clara kept washing, careful not to scrape my wound. Soon, the cloth turned gray.

"I see," Clara said as she wiped my face. She stared at me a moment as if studying my features. "Why, I know who you are now." She nodded, sure of herself. "You're the little Sanders girl, right?"

"Yes. Ellie Sanders. But how do you know me?"

"Rupert Sanders is your daddy? Runs the store down on Henders Lane?"

I nodded.

"Well, it sure is a small world, Ellie. I was just down there not two days gone to buy mousetraps and penny nails. Your Daddy's a fine man, but he charges too much. I've seen you in there on Saturdays a time or two, I believe."

"I'm there after school sometimes, too. I help Daddy sweep floors and look after the chicks." I remembered her now, the colored woman who asked about Mama and bought dried corn cobs to feed birds in winter. I'd seen her there only a couple times. Daddy said she knew magic and could read people's futures.

Clara left to refill the basin with clean water. When she returned, she sat next to me and continued to wash my hands, face, and arms. She pulled off my dirty socks and washed my feet. "How are your folks? Somebody told me your Mama had taken sick, is that true?"

"My mother fell . . . and, well . . . I don't . . ." My bottom lip quivered.

"It's all right, go on, you can tell Clara. Won't be much I haven't heard in the sixty years I've been walking the earth. I've got ears for listening, now you tell me."

"My daddy . . . he . . ." I couldn't finish. There was so much to tell, too many places to begin the story and all of them made me sad.

Clara lifted my head and held it between her hands. "Your daddy didn't hurt you, did he? That's not why you ran away, is it?"

"No . . . he . . . Daddy went . . . I don't even know where he went. He left with the tomato girl!"

I bit down on my lip, but the tears came anyway. I dropped my face in my hands and cried.

"Oh, honey, you're going to be just fine. Whatever it is, don't matter how bad, Clara's right here. You just cry it out." Clara sat close and wrapped her arms around me. "I got you now, you just let it all out. Spill those tears, little one."

I cried so hard my whole body shook. My eyes and throat burned, and my stomach ached. I cried so hard I gagged. Through it all, Clara held me like she'd promised. She didn't flinch, or move, or let me go, not for a second.

I don't know how long I cried, but it felt like hours. For the first time in days, I felt clean inside. It had taken so much of me, trying to be good for God and to keep Mama from sinking into her sad mood. I'd held so much inside, I couldn't hold it any longer. I needed somewhere to let my worries go. Clara's arms was just the place.

When my sobs slowed, Clara wrapped me in a heavy blue quilt covered in stars. My fingers traced the gold stitches. "This quilt belonged to my mother," she said. "Whenever I have a hard day, I curl up in Mama's quilt and dream my troubles away. You give each worry you have to one of the stars. Remember that. Don't matter how many worries you got because there are always more stars than worries."

I closed my eyes and prayed Clara's quilt would bring Daddy back to me.

In the moments before I drifted off to sleep, Clara's voice floated in from another room. She spoke to Jericho. "Go down to Tucker's house, see what you can find out about Rupert Sanders who runs the store on Henders Lane. When y'all find Mr. Sanders, tell him we've got his girl here. And you tell him Clara says he's got a heap of explaining to do."

THIRTY-ONE

CLARA'S ROOM

CLARA RAN HER hand across my cheek. "You nearly slept the whole day away, child. Don't you want some food? I baked an Easter ham, some potato salad, all kinds of pie."

"I'm not too hungry, Clara."

"Maybe something to drink, then? Jericho bought Coca-Cola last night. He won't miss a little."

I nodded. My throat felt dry.

Clara squeezed my hands. "I don't know what all happened to you, Ellie, but I know you going to be all right. You don't need to worry." Clara smiled, then left the room to get my drink.

I pulled myself up in Clara's bed and rested my back against a pillow. The soft down made a nest for my head. From now on, whenever somebody said the word comfort, I would think of Clara's room, lying on her thick mattress under a quilt patterned with stars.

My eyes circled the room. Beside the bed, a tall wardrobe rose in the corner with folded blankets lined up on top. Next to the wardrobe stood a table covered with shells, feathers, beads in bowls, and cards.

I looked toward the light coming from the window, which was

covered in yellow sheers that matched the walls. A lady's straw hat rested on the sill, propped against the screen.

Clara's room reminded me of Miss Wilder's house, where objects had special meaning if only you knew what and where to find it. Like Clara's shells, and her bowl of beads, she'd have stories about them. Maybe one day she'd tell me.

But this was no time for stories. Daddy could be anywhere in the world by now, and no story could bring him home.

The front door slammed and Jericho's voice rose from down the hall. "Clara?"

"In here," Clara answered. She sounded like she might be in the kitchen, because I heard the sound of a spoon or spatula scraping a skillet.

I tossed the quilt back and tiptoed to the door to hear what Jericho said. Maybe he'd heard something about Daddy. I smelled the food Clara mentioned, warm ham and bread, and something sweet like coconut. My stomach growled and I suddenly wished I hadn't turned down the meal Clara offered.

"Lord, Clara. It ain't good news, that's for damn sure."

"Hush up, Jericho. Don't be using bad language in my house. Go on, tell me. What is it? Did you find Rupert Sanders or not?"

"Nobody's going to find that man, unless it's Sheriff Rhodes."

"Sheriff Rhodes? What do you mean?" Clara's tone was serious. "And don't speak too loud now," Clara added, lowering her own voice.

"I went down to the store. Course it was closed, but there was a man feeding them dyed chickens they got . . ."

I remembered leaving my nameless chick alone on my bed when I ran out of the house after Daddy. I closed my eyes, praying he'd be safe until I got home. I worried even more about Mama. What might she do when she saw everybody gone? The dimming light outside the windows told me the day was almost gone. I needed to go home, but not before I heard what Jericho knew about Daddy.

"That'd be Mr. Morgan. He owns the store, Jericho."

"Nope. Morgan headed down to his little place in Florida. According to his son, Fred, he goes there every spring for a short spell."

"And?" Clara's voice rose.

"Fred come down from Philly to run things. He the one I talked to when I went to the store. I asked him about Rupert Sanders. He told me he ain't never met Mr. Sanders, but knows that he's the man that usually manages his father's store."

"Well," Clara interrupted, "did he say why Rupert Sanders wasn't there feeding the chickens instead of him?"

"I'm getting to that, woman, hold your horses. He says Mr. Sanders's wife suffered a fall down the cellar, and he needed the time off to tend to her."

"Well, he certainly ain't tending her now, is he?"

Jericho continued. "I thanked him, got ready to leave. That's when the man asked if I happened to grow tomatoes or knew somebody who raised enough extra to sell . . ."

"Maisy Jones once tried to sell tomatoes to the store, but they didn't need hers, said they had plenty. Doesn't that little Reed girl sell her tomatoes in there?"

"Yep, but he says the girl who sold them produce moved in to help Mrs. Sanders, and they weren't sure she'd be bringing in tomatoes this year."

Clara grunted like she didn't believe or like what she heard. "Did Mr. Morgan's son know where Rupert Sanders might be now?"

"He didn't know, but then Sheriff Rhodes showed up as I was leaving."

"What'd he want? I figured Millie Rhodes would have him in church all day."

"Seems Mason Reed shot himself last night."

The words sounded like a hammer in my head.

"Dear God," Clara said. "Dear sweet Jesus!"

Jericho continued. "Sheriff Rhodes was looking for the girl,

Tess, to tell her the news. I didn't stay to hear no more. I'm guessing we found that child in the road 'cause her daddy done run off with that girl."

"Lord have mercy, that poor child. She can't stay home alone with her mama. What are we going to do? You know Julia Sanders ain't well . . ."

"Clara, now that was a long time ago when you read for her."

I didn't know what she meant by reading, since Mama could read on her own.

"You don't know what I saw when I took that woman's hand in mine and turned it over, Jericho. The dark places inside her mind. I took to the bed for three weeks after that, don't you remember?"

"Course I remember. Who you think fed you broth from a spoon when you was so weak you couldn't lift your head to eat?"

"Well, if you remember, then you know why I'm not sending her back there."

"Clara, have you done looked in the mirror? You think a colored woman can just up and keep a white woman's child?"

I didn't wait to hear more. Sheriff Rhodes would go to our house looking for Tess. The letter might still be on the floor. What if the sheriff read it? Would he know what Daddy did? What if Mama came downstairs carrying Baby Tom?

I had to hurry home.

The window. There was no other way to leave without being seen.

I moved Clara's straw hat and pushed on the screen, the folding kind Daddy sold at the store. It fell away with one hard shove. Careful not to knock over Clara's beads and shells, I stepped up onto the table, climbed through the window, and fell to the ground.

A sharp pain ran through my arm. My elbow had hit a rock and split open, but there was no time to worry about that. I pulled myself up, brushed the dirt from my dress, and ran home.

THIRTY-TWO

SHERIFF RHODES

THE SHERIFF'S BROWN police car was parked in front of my house. I looked into the car's back window, half expecting to see Daddy handcuffed and Tess crying at his side, but the car was empty except for Bubba, the sheriff's black and tan hound.

I took a moment to say hello to Bubba, and then walked up the sidewalk toward the door. Up the first step and I heard Mama's laughter through the screen door—the shrill, loud laugh when she is in her too-fast mood. I remembered Jellybean's grave, how she'd laughed and fretted with her gown and hair. The signs had been there. The changes when she goes from the dark, sad place, into the light, giddy place. This place seems like a happier one, but like spinning tops and bubbles, is impossible to control.

I should have left with Daddy and Tess. If only I could go back, wrap my arms around his ankles and hold tight. Handling Mama without Daddy scared me enough to make me want to run away, just like Daddy.

Then I thought about Mama lying in the basement stairwell after she fell, how her pretty face was smeared with blood, and

I'd believed she was dead. I remembered how scared and alone I felt.

I ran inside the house. "Mama? Mama?"

"In here, Ellie," Mama's voice came from the kitchen.

Sheriff Rhodes and Mama sat at the kitchen table, two brown mugs and a carton of milk between them. The room smelled like coffee and aftershave.

"Ellie, where have you been?" Mama asked. "And what happened to your arm?" Mama noticed the cut where I'd fallen from Clara's window. "And where are your shoes, young lady?"

"I . . . I went to see . . . Mary Roberts." Bringing up Clara and Jericho seemed a bad idea, and too much to explain. I ignored her question about my shoes.

"Hey there, little gal. You sure are growing into a pretty young lady," Sheriff Rhodes said. "You're almost as pretty as your Mama." He laughed and looked at Mama.

Mama smiled back, then pursed her lips. "Why, George, you know Rupert could walk in that door any minute now and hear you flirting with his wife." Mama had put on a clean dress, but the top buttons had come undone and her lacy bra showed. She'd brushed her hair and covered the cuts and bruises on her face with a layer of makeup. She almost looked like the Mama before Tess came, but not with her dress undone, not with red lipstick smeared on her mouth as if she'd colored out of line. Her fingers twisted a paper in her hands. I knew it was the letter from Mason Reed because I could see some of the large-print words.

"Actually, I do need to speak with Rupert. Is he around?" the sheriff asked.

Mama reached out her hand and touched Sheriff Rhodes's tan sleeve. "And I thought you'd come by to visit me."

Sheriff Rhodes's plump cheeks turned red. He laughed again. "That, too. But got to earn my keep, you know." He pulled back his chair and said, "Excuse me a minute." He stepped toward the back door.

"Of course." Mama looked at me as she picked up the carton of milk. "Want something to drink, Ellie?"

"No, Mama. I'm fine. I'm glad to see you're all better."

"Oh, and I am, Ellie. I woke up this morning, and no one was here. At first, I sat on the steps and cried, but then it was as if a huge gray cloud floated away from me. Why, I think I could climb out on the roof, spread my arms and fly, I feel so good. Don't you feel it, Ellie? There's an electricity in the air, passing through my veins, my skin, my hair." Mama left the crumpled paper on the table. She ran her fingers through her hair and shivered.

"I don't feel it, Mama."

Mama pouted. "That's too bad, Ellie. You're too serious. Just like your father. Learn to fly, Ellie!" Mama lifted her hands up in the air and tossed her head back, giggling.

Sheriff Rhodes stood by the kitchen door. He held it open, spat dark juice into the bushes, then came back to the table.

"Chewing is a bad habit, George." Mama rested her arms on top of her head. "I'd think that wife of yours would make you give it up."

"You know I don't let Millie tell me what to do."

Mama laughed. "I see. Yes, I see. Now why don't you tell me what you want?"

"Uh, yes." Sheriff Rhodes pulled a handkerchief from his pocket and wiped his forehead. He seemed more uneasy around Mama than I'd ever seen him. "Well, it appears there's been an accident." He paused.

"Accident?" Mama frowned and gasped. "Rupert?"

"No, no. Rupert hasn't been in an accident. It's, well . . . Maybe we shouldn't talk about this in front of little ears," he said, nodding in my direction.

Mama looked at me. "Ellie, honey, why don't you go upstairs, play with the new chick. I saw the Easter Bunny left you one."

Arguing would do no good, so I said good-bye to Sheriff Rhodes, and pretended to go to my room. Instead, I knelt behind the railing at the top of the stairs and listened to what the sheriff said.

"Julia, I'm going to be frank. A neighbor found Mason Reed dead in his house this morning."

"Dear God!"

My stomach tightened. I didn't want to hear the rest, but listening was the only way to find out what Mama and Sheriff Rhodes knew.

"Yes. Shot in the head," the sheriff continued. "Looks like a suicide, but we won't know until the autopsy report comes in. Thing is, I needed to let his girl know, and folks tell me she's been staying here."

"I see. Well, that's sad news, George. A man taking his own life."

"Yes, it is. Of course, the man drank like a fish, and folks can do foolish things when they're drunk. Things they later regret."

"I suppose Mr. Reed won't have the opportunity to regret now, will he?" Mama said, then giggled.

"Well, that's right. But damn, Julia, I didn't mean it that way. You should show a little respect for the dead."

"Of course!" Mama laughed. Loud laughter that lasted too long. Yes, this was the Mama that came sometimes after the sad Mama went away.

Sheriff Rhodes waited for Mama to quiet before he continued. "I don't know what comes over you at times, Julia. I swear I don't. Anyhow, I'm looking for his daughter, Tess. She's a minor, so I have to follow up on her, see that she gets placed with relatives if we can find any. Is she here?"

"Well, no. She's not here. She came to help when I fell. That's where the bruises came from in case you're wondering."

"I did wonder. Didn't want to ask, but . . ."

"Did you think Rupert beat me?"

"No, of course not, Julia. I've never pictured Rupert as the kind of man . . ."

"You have no idea what kind of man Rupert is, or what he might do. He screws her, did you know that? His little tomato girl? Right here in my house!" Mama smacked the table.

"Julia, get ahold of yourself. Do you need a drink?" Sheriff Rhodes walked toward the cabinet where Daddy kept bottles of liquor. "What's Rupert got around here, any Scotch?"

"What are you trying to do to me, George? Do you want me to get drunk so I'll blow my brains out like poor Mason Reed?" More laughter.

My eyes blurred with tears.

"Of course not, Julia. Don't be ridiculous. Now listen . . ."

"Do you still think I'm pretty, George?"

"Yes, you know . . ."

"How pretty?"

"Damn, Julia, I need you to cooperate. I've got to find the Reed girl."

"Here, read this. The little whore's father apparently wrote to her, telling her to come home, which I'm sure didn't set well with Rupert. Find my husband. The girl won't be far away."

I ran down the stairs, screaming, "No! No! No!"

Sheriff Rhodes looked at me. "Ellie, what on earth?"

Tears streamed down my face. "Don't read that letter! It's not like you think! Daddy didn't do anything wrong!"

Sheriff Rhodes took the letter from Mama's outstretched hand. "Ellie, honey," he said, "I think you better tell me exactly what's going on."

THIRTY-THREE

HOLES

SHERIFF RHODES PUT his thick fingers around my wrist and pulled me close. Three times he asked me to tell him what I knew about the letter from Mason Reed, but I wouldn't answer. I didn't lie. Didn't tell only part of the story. I just didn't say anything at all. You can never get in trouble for saying the wrong thing if you say nothing.

"I suppose your Daddy got mad when he read the letter from Mr. Reed?" Sheriff Rhodes asked again. "Did he seem upset in any way?"

I didn't answer.

"Did he and Tess argue?" He scratched his ear. "I need your help here, Ellie."

I shook my head no.

Mama tapped the kitchen table. When she was in her too-fast mood, she didn't like life to go slow. "I need a cigarette," she said, her voice much too loud.

"Here," Sheriff Rhodes said, tossing her a half-empty pack of Winstons. "Matches are inside."

"Come on, sweetheart," he said, "you know you can trust Sheriff Rhodes." Still holding my wrist, he guided me onto his lap. "Here, you sit with me and just think for a minute. Close your eyes and think."

I closed my eyes, but all I thought about was my daddy, and how I had to protect him.

Sheriff Rhodes's voice broke my thoughts. "Sometime yesterday, Ellie, the postman brought a letter from Mr. Reed. It's clear somebody opened and read it. Your Mama said she found it crumpled up here on the floor, so I figure somebody didn't like what the letter said. Now, your Daddy and Tess have disappeared and Mr. Reed is dead. What's Sheriff Rhodes supposed to think, huh?"

I didn't say anything.

Sheriff Rhodes sighed.

Mama ran her fingers through her hair. "For God's sake, George, let her be. She'll never tell you. She's a daddy's girl through and through. Daddy, Daddy, Daddy. I'm surprised she didn't leave with him."

"Mama! How can you say that?" My voice came out louder than I meant for it to, but I couldn't stop myself. "I took care of you, Mama, the best I knew how!" I thought about the night Mama lost Baby Tom, how I'd helped her clean up and taken the Baby to the cellar for her. When Daddy had tied her wrists to the headboard, I'd cut her free and slept by her side. All the times before, making her tissue paper flowers and soup, keeping people away when she felt sad, doing chores when she couldn't manage, and telling white lies to keep her happy. I'd always taken care of her.

Mama pressed her hands against her ears to shut out my voice. The cigarette dangled between her lips.

Sheriff Rhodes scratched his head. "Wait now, let's not pick a fight here," he warned me.

I stopped talking and waited to see if Mama had anything else to say, but she simply removed her hands from her ears and put her cigarette out on the table before dropping it into her coffee cup.

I wiped my eyes with the back of my hand.

"Well, I can see I'm not getting anywhere here," Sheriff Rhodes said. "Julia, I know Rupert does some hunting. Do you know where he keeps his shotgun?"

"Out in the shed. Why?" Mama's eyes darkened.

"You won't mind if I take a look around?"

"No, of course not. But you're not leaving, are you?" Mama asked. She twisted the buttons on the front of her dress.

"I'll come back in before I go," he said.

Sheriff Rhodes put his hand on my chin and looked into my eyes as he spoke. "Ellie, honey, I don't know what your daddy's done. However this turns out, I'll do all I can to look after you and your mama."

"I don't want you looking after us. I want Daddy!" I said, almost shouting. "And you leave my father alone! Don't you dare shoot my daddy! Promise me you won't shoot him!"

Sheriff Rhodes wrapped his arms around me. "I won't shoot your daddy, Ellie. I promise I won't hurt him."

As my sobs turned to hiccups, Mama came over and rubbed my hair. Her hand moved quickly, the way it does when she's nervous.

WHILE SHERIFF RHODES went out to the toolshed to look for Daddy's gun, Mama made supper. I helped stir the mashed potatoes while Mama finished frying the pork chops and salted the green peas. Mama talked and talked. She rambled on about Baby Tom and planting new pansies; about how I shouldn't fret because Daddy would forget Tess and come back; not to worry about Sheriff Rhodes because she could keep him from putting Daddy in jail. "You'll see, Ellie. We'll all be a family again, Daddy, Mommy, you, and Baby Tom."

The sheriff returned to the house just as Mama finished setting the food on the table. "There's no gun out there." He leaned against the kitchen wall and looked at Mama. "Only strange thing I saw was some equine tranquilizers and a couple of syringes. I know Rupert doesn't keep horses. Any idea what he'd be using them for?"

Mama looked at the floor. Her eyes focused on the black and white tiles. She studied the pattern as if it were a giant chessboard and she needed to decide her next move.

The sheriff paused, watching Mama stare at the floor. He gazed at me. I wanted to look away, but I didn't. I stared back at him, not blinking once. He had to see I was strong. I wouldn't be the place he could find a crack. Daddy had taught me that you never tell people too much, and you keep your eyes focused when they get close to the truth.

"Well, I'll have to call the coroner, see if they find any trace of tranquilizer used on Mason Reed." The sheriff spoke to Mama, but looked at me. He knew I knew, but I would not give.

"Don't bother, George." Mama looked up, her face tense and flushed. "They weren't for Mason Reed. He used them on me, understand?"

"Jesus Christ!"

Sheriff Rhodes stepped forward and put his hands on Mama's shoulders. She pulled away. He didn't know Mama's moods like I did. She needed to move, not be held still.

"Let's eat," Mama said, pacing from the stove to the table, from the cabinets to the sink. She gathered spoons, salt and pepper, anything to keep moving. Most folks would see a busy woman preparing the evening meal, but if you knew Mama as I did, you'd see the spiral inside like whirls of color trapped under her skin. Her hands shook as she placed each item on the table, spilling a few peas from the bowl. Every few minutes, Mama paused, wound the same strand of hair behind her ears, and gazed at the road through the window.

WE SAT AROUND the table, Sheriff Rhodes in Daddy's chair at the head of the table. I wanted to ask him to move, but instead kept quiet. An argument might get him back to questions about Daddy.

Besides, I was hungry. I'd been too upset to eat at Clara's house and now my stomach ached. I speared a thick pork chop and cut it into pieces on my plate, then added a large scoop of mashed potatoes with extra butter on top. I spooned a few peas beside my potatoes. I hate green peas almost as much as carrots, but grown-ups make a fuss if they see no vegetables on your plate.

The pork chop tasted salty; Mama had sprinkled too much on them while they fried. The inside was tender and moist, though, and I ate it, savoring every bite.

"I fed your chick earlier today, but you might want to take him some of these mashed potatoes after we're done," Mama said, piling too much food on her plate. Mounds of peas covered Mama's potatoes.

"Got you an Easter chick, hey?" Sheriff Rhodes asked, shoving pork then buttered bread into his mouth. He looked at Mama as she played with her hair and stirred her peas into her potatoes.

I nodded and drank my tea.

"What's his name?" He talked from the corner of his full mouth.

"I haven't named him yet." I almost told him about Jellybean, but didn't want to talk about any more dead things. Besides, Tess had named Jellybean and that reminder might upset Mama. During her sad times, she mostly cried when she got upset, but during her too-fast times, she sometimes threw things and had fits. She said dirty words and made faces that scared me. For now, she seemed able to eat and stay seated. At other times, she might not be able to settle down enough to eat or sleep or stop crying. Those were the times Daddy gave her the shots. Would I be able to calm Mama without them?

I understood how Daddy could use them. When you are desperate, you do things you'd never imagine. Is that how Daddy felt when he killed Mason Reed? Maybe Tess made Daddy desperate that way.

Mama swallowed her food and licked her fingers, one at a time. The sucking sounded loud in the quiet kitchen.

"What about Easter? That's a good name for a chick," Mama suggested.

"Thanks, Mama. I like that." I hadn't cleaned my plate, but didn't think Mama would notice. She forgot many of the rules. That had mostly been Daddy's job. "Can I go up to see him now?"

Mama nodded. "I couldn't find a box, so I cleaned out a coffee can and put him in that. The coffee shouldn't hurt him, just a few grounds left in the bottom."

"Okay." I pushed my chair back from the table and stood. My scraped elbow burned when I bent my arm. "As long as you remembered to poke lots of holes."

Mama dropped her fork and put her hand over her mouth.

My knees almost buckled, then I caught myself. "No, Mama, please don't say you forgot the holes."

I ran upstairs, my tired legs stretching to take two steps at a time. I threw open the door to my room. Mama and Sheriff Rhodes were right behind me.

The blue Maxwell House can stood on my bed. *Please God,* I prayed. How long ago had she put him in the can? There would be enough air for awhile, but I'd been gone for hours.

My hands shook as I pulled the plastic lid from the can. The air inside felt warm and smelled bitter from the chick's droppings and leftover coffee grounds.

The green chick lay on his side.

"Easter?" My eyes filled with tears. He didn't even know he had a name.

Mama placed her shaking hand on the small chick. "He's breathing, just a little, Ellie. Here, feel." Mama took my hand and rested it on the chick.

I was so afraid the breathing Mama felt was her own tremble. But no, I felt it, too! A tiny movement, a flutter. I had to do something to try to save him. And then I remembered what I had overheard that afternoon. "We have to take Easter to see Clara, Mama. She knows magic. Please, Mama. Clara can save him, I know she can."

THIRTY-FOUR

YELLOW BIRD

I RODE IN THE BACKSEAT of Sheriff Rhodes's car and held the coffee can on my lap. Even with the window rolled down partway, the inside of the car smelled like sweat, pee, cigarettes, and dog. I worried that the bad air would make it even harder for little Easter to breathe. I cupped my hand over his soft body to make sure he was still alive. His tiny chest barely moved.

Tears wet my face, but I didn't dare take my hands off Easter to wipe them away. Bubba sniffed at the can, trying to find the chick he smelled but couldn't see. "Bubba, stop!" I had to grip the can tight to keep him from knocking it out of my hands.

"Lay down, Bubba!" Sheriff Rhodes looked into the rearview mirror and made a stern face.

The scolded dog flopped down on the seat and rested his head on his paws.

Mama sat up front next to Sheriff Rhodes and stared out the window. She had grown quiet at the mention of Clara. She didn't ask how I knew her; she didn't say anything. She twisted a strand of hair between her fingers, winding it tight against her head.

This would hurt anyone else, but when Mama's in her too-fast mood, she doesn't seem to feel pain.

Sheriff Rhodes adjusted his hat. A roll of fat on the back of his neck rested on his dark brown collar. "We'll be at Clara's house in no time," he said. "Right down the street, and we'll be there."

I wondered if he said the same thing to criminals as he drove them to jail. I could hear him saying, "We're almost to the jail-house now, boys." No wonder they sweated and peed all over the backseat.

He said a few more things, but I only half heard them. When your heart is breaking, sometimes you just want everyone to hush.

I focused on my mission. Clara could save Easter. Yes, she could. She had to save him, because the thought of him dying hurt too much to imagine. I could not stand in the yard and put another small thing into the cold ground. *Please, God,* I prayed, *let her know the right magic. Let Easter live.*

Sheriff Rhodes parked in front of Clara's house. I looked out the window and saw Jericho sitting in a rocking chair on the porch.

Sheriff Rhodes raised his hand at Jericho. Jericho waved back.

I tried to find a door handle to let myself out, but there wasn't one. I had to wait for Sheriff Rhodes to let me out.

Finally, he opened the door for Mama, then me.

I ran ahead of Mama and Sheriff Rhodes, up the path to the porch. Yellow light glowed from inside one window, and I imagined Clara inside, reading or making evening bread.

Jericho stood up when I reached the porch. "What you got in that coffee can, Ellie?"

"My chick . . . Mama forgot the holes . . . and . . ." I started crying again. I felt like pinching my own face for not being brave. Crying wouldn't explain how I needed Clara's help.

Somehow, Jericho knew.

"Come on in, honey. Clara's got her bag of tricks. She ain't going to let your bird die."

Jericho opened the front door to let us in. "Clara?" he called. "We got company. They need your medicine."

Clara stepped out of her bedroom and walked toward us. She'd tied a purple scarf around her head, but had on the same blue-gray dress with white flowers splattered on it that she'd worn earlier in the day.

I expected her to ask me why I'd run off this afternoon without saying thank you or good-bye, but she didn't. She didn't say anything to me at first.

Clara walked past Sheriff Rhodes and me and went straight to Mama. "Miss Julia," she said, "I'm so glad you came to my home." Clara held onto Mama's hands while she spoke, her dark thumbs rubbing Mama's palms. "I hoped I'd see you again. Remember I read for you once, when you were feeling poorly?"

Mama's skin paled as she nodded.

"I fell ill myself for a spell, then had to go back to Georgia and look after my mother until she passed," Clara said.

Even as Mama's eyes darted around the room and her shoulders twitched, Clara held onto her hands and kept talking.

Just as Jericho somehow knew about my dying chick even when I couldn't get the words out, I knew not to interrupt Clara.

"Me and Jericho haven't been back here long, Julia." Clara led Mama to a chair by the window. "Here, you sit."

Mama sat down and opened her mouth to speak. Clara touched Mama's lips with her finger. "Hush now, let me finish." Clara stood beside Mama's chair and continued talking. "I stopped in the store a few times. I saw your girl a time or two. I asked your husband about you. He said you were doing fine, but you know, I like to see things for my own self. I kept hoping I'd run into you, but he said you didn't come to the store much. I sure am glad you came to me now." Clara rubbed Mama's arm.

Mama's eyes grew watery and her lips trembled. She started to speak again, but Clara stopped her again.

Clara pinched a small green leaf from a plant in the window.

"Hush now. You don't need to tell me a thing. I know you remember things you don't want to. Not now. You don't need to speak now. Here, put this under your tongue."

Mama opened her mouth like an obedient child.

"Now don't chew or swallow, just leave it under your tongue, and be still."

Mama did as Clara said.

"Now then, seems I got a sick bird to mend." Clara walked to me and took the can from my hands.

How did she know? Had she heard Jericho and me talking on the front porch?

"Follow me," she said as she walked toward the next room. She stopped in front of Sheriff Rhodes. "Jericho can see these two ladies back to Grace Street. Why don't you go on home? Millie's wondering where you been."

Sheriff Rhodes shifted on his feet. "I reckon you saw that in your crystal ball?"

Clara laughed at Sheriff Rhodes. "Don't need no crystal ball to know a man's wife got to wonder why her husband's car been parked outside another woman's house all evening. You do as I say, and go on home."

Jericho laughed, rose from his seat, and walked toward Sheriff Rhodes. "You best quit while you is ahead. Come on now, let's you and me go have a smoke." Jericho placed his hand on Sheriff Rhodes's shoulder and led him out the front door.

I thought Mama would put up a fuss when he left. Instead, she leaned against the back of her chair. Her eyelids flickered, but didn't open.

I followed Clara into the kitchen. A large black stove sat in one corner and in the center of the room was a narrow table.

Clara handed the can back to me. "Hold this," she said. While I held the can, Clara untied the scarf from her head and smoothed it flat on the table. "Now you watch," Clara said, "but do not cry or speak unless I ask you a question, understand?"

I nodded.

Clara reached inside the can and lifted the little green chick. "And his name?"

"Easter," I said, careful not to let my voice quiver.

Clara laid Easter on the center of her scarf. He didn't move, so I thought he must be dead, but Clara held up her hand to warn me not to speak.

As she moved about the room and gathered items from a cabinet by the sink, Clara spoke directly to Easter. "You are a fine bird, Easter. All green like a lime, with a nice layer of baby fat. I knew a chicken like you, only he was yellow." Clara sat down. She reached into a white bag and pulled out a handful of yellow powder. She moved her hand around Easter, sprinkling what looked like cornmeal. When she was done, a thin yellow line circled Easter's body.

"Put this away." Clara handed me the bag without looking at me, and I returned it to the cabinet, making as little noise as possible. Goosebumps rose along my arms.

She lit a green candle and placed it outside the circle. "Yes, Yellow Bird used to follow me around the yard when I was a girl. Anybody come near to bother me, Yellow Bird pecked their feet. He saved my backside many a switching, yes he did. Now here you are with a girl of your own to look after. You can't let her down, you hear me?" Clara put her ear to his beak as if to listen for his answer.

A moment later, Clara reached into her apron pocket and pulled out four flat black stones. She placed one at Easter's feet, one at his head, and one on either side of his body. Speaking to me, she rested her hands over Easter's body. "Go into my backyard and find a feather from the right wing of a bird."

"But it's dark outside. How will I find a bird?" I wondered, too, how Clara expected me to make a bird hold still while I took a feather.

"You came here for me to raise this bird, right?"

"Yes, but . . ."

"If you believe I can raise this bird, then you have to believe I can call a bird to you for its feather. Now, go out back, look in the lilac bush. There will be your bird."

I did as Clara told me. Just outside her back door, a lilac bush grew against her house. Although it was dark, a street lamp shone bright enough for me to see the small clusters of blooms. I heard a cooing sound, then saw small gray wings flutter in the middle of the bush. When I reached out to touch the bird, she flew away. As she lifted into the sky, I held my hands up to try and grab her. Her wings beat faster, and she flew out of reach. She called out once more, and then, a single pale feather floated into my hands.

My fingers felt its warmth, like a soothing ointment.

Back inside the house, I handed Clara the feather.

Taking deep breaths, Clara blew across Easter's body and waved the feather in circles around him, her hand moving faster and faster. Seconds later, Easter's wings twitched. At first, just one sudden twitch, barely noticeable, but then the twitches grew stronger, until his tiny green wings fluttered and he rose up on his feet.

"Welcome back," Clara said, then laughed. She turned toward me. "Well, girl, are you going to pick up this bird or not?"

I hugged Clara's neck, then scooped up Easter with both hands. His soft body felt warm and alive. His tiny heart thumped against my palm.

Clara pinched some cornmeal from the table and sprinkled it into the palm of her hand. She spit on the yellow powder and made a paste. Little by little, she fed Easter the damp cornmeal.

"He sleeps in my oven tonight to keep his blood warm," Clara said.

Clara's words confused me. "But I want to take Easter home."

"No!" Clara snapped. "You cannot take him home yet. There

is a dead spirit in your house, no? I can see it, but not clear. It's trapped somehow, behind water, or mirror, or maybe a glass." Clara squinted as if trying to make out what she saw. She rose from her chair and opened her oven door. She looked at me. "An unsettled spirit might take his life away. Your chick cannot go back there until the dead thing rests."

THIRTY-FIVE

HOME

CLARA PACKED A BASKET of butter cookies and jars of dark red jellies. She wrapped a gray knitted shawl around Mama's shoulders and brushed the hair away from her face. "Spit," she said, and put her hand under Mama's mouth to catch the leaf she'd placed under her tongue when we first arrived. After Mama spat, Clara shoved the wet leaf into her apron pocket. She looked into Mama's eyes. "If you need anything, Julia, you send the girl, and Jericho or I will come, do you hear? Don't care if it be day or night. Don't care how bad a thing is, if you need me, send the girl."

Mama nodded and licked her lips.

"I forgot to cover these cookies," Clara said. She took the basket from Jericho and carried it toward the kitchen. "Come with me," Clara motioned to me.

Once there, Clara turned to me. "I know you want to take the chick with you, but he's better left with me for a time. He's too weak to handle the pull of a restless spirit."

"When the spirit finds rest, can Easter come home?"

"Yes." Clara wiped her hands on her apron and covered the basket of cookies with a checkered cloth.

"But how does a dead spirit find rest, Clara?"

"Different ways, child. Depends on why the spirit don't rest. Sometimes, it's because the spirit don't want to leave what it knows. Sometimes the living won't let the dead go. Either way, the chick needs to stay here to be safe."

I knelt by the stove and kissed Easter's soft head. The oven's heat warmed my face and hands. "He won't get too warm here, will he?"

"I'll watch him, don't worry. I ain't going to cook no bird I brought back from the grave." Clara laughed and patted my head.

"Can I visit him while he's here?"

"Yes, you come, you hear? You come every day after school. If you don't come, I'll know something's wrong and send Jericho. You come every day, rain or shine, you understand?"

"Yes, I'll come. I promise."

Clara smiled. "That's my girl."

"Clara?"

"Yes, child?"

"Will Daddy come home again?"

Clara's eyes narrowed. Her forehead wrinkled as if she felt pain. "He will come back, yes. But it will not be the way you picture it. It will be a darker thing, I'm afraid."

Clara's words sent a chill through me.

"Don't ask no more, girl. Me and Jericho will look after you as best we can. Now, you have school in the morning. It's time for you to go home and get to bed."

I nodded, then wrapped my arms around Clara's neck and kissed her soft, warm cheek.

AFTER JERICHO WALKED us home, Mama stayed awake most of the night, pacing the kitchen floor with Baby Tom in her arms. I sat at the table and nibbled on Clara's butter cookies while trying to figure out how to make Mama settle down.

"God, why won't this child sleep?" she screamed. She grew angry and shook the jar. "Go to sleep, Tom! I can't take any more!"

Baby Tom bobbed up and down in his formaldehyde bath, his little body bumping against the glass. In a way, Baby Tom was lucky he'd been born dead. Otherwise, he'd surely end up retarded. I'd heard from Mary Roberts that if a baby is born fine and becomes retarded later, it's because their mothers shook them or dropped them on their heads.

Suddenly, I felt sorry for Baby Tom. "Let me hold him, Mama." I held out my hands to take the jar.

Mama let go of the glass so suddenly, I nearly dropped it on the floor. My fingers shook as I wrapped them around the jar. Wet from Mama's sweaty palms, the sides felt slippery in my hands. I hurried to the chair by the window so Baby Tom could rest on my lap.

Mama paced and smoked. Sheriff Rhodes had left a full pack of cigarettes, but now, all but two of the cigarettes were gone. Somehow, I'd have to find her more tomorrow.

"He's just like you, you know?" Mama spoke to the wall. Her bare foot tapped the floor as if keeping time to music.

"Like me?" I asked, not sure who or what she meant.

"Yes," she puffed the cigarette, then mashed the butt on a saucer. She used such force, the saucer rattled on the table, spilling ashes. "When you were a baby, you refused my milk, just like Tom."

"Mama, Tom is . . ." I couldn't finish. I couldn't tell Mama that dead babies don't drink milk.

"Tom is what, Ellie?" Mama stepped closer.

"Nothing, Mama."

"You don't believe me? Here, watch." Mama unbuttoned her dress and pulled out her breast. She grabbed Baby Tom from my hands and pressed the jar against her pale flesh. She tried adjusting herself so that her nipple met Tom's face, but her movements were too rough. Baby Tom floated the other way.

Mama's eyes filled with tears. "See? He doesn't want me. You did the same thing. Why don't my babies want me? I knew it would be that way. See what kind of woman I am? Even my own children don't love me."

"But I do love you, Mama. I do! And so does Baby Tom."

Mama looked down at Baby Tom. When she moved the jar, his tiny face turned further from her breast.

She let out a sob that came from some place so deep it scared me. The veins in her neck rose like vines that might choke her. She fell on the floor, hunched over Tom, and cried, her body heaving as if she might throw up.

I quickly walked over to Mama, and knelt close to rub her shoulder. "Don't cry, Mama. Everything's going to be okay. Just give Baby Tom a chance. He'll learn. He came out of you too soon, so he doesn't know all the things a baby is supposed to know. Why, he doesn't even know how to suck his own thumb, Mama."

Her sobs slowed and she breathed more evenly.

"Here, Mama. Sit up and let me show you."

After she sat up on the floor, I placed my hands around the jar and slowly turned it until Baby Tom leaned toward Mama's breast. "See, Mama, he's doing a little better. Baby Tom loves you, just like I do."

Once she saw the baby facing her breast, Mama quieted down. After a few minutes of holding the jar against her breast, she seemed calm again, and let me take her hand and lead her upstairs.

I tucked Mama and Baby Tom in bed, pulling the thick covers around them. I looked at Tom, wondered how his spirit would ever be free if he had to stay in a glass jar, cared for by a mother who could hardly look after herself.

Finally I went to my own room. Too tired to brush my teeth and get undressed, I kicked off my shoes and climbed into my bed. With my eyes closed, I listened to night sounds: the faraway bark of a dog; the house creaking as floorboards settled; water gurgling though the pipes.

In those dreamlike moments before falling asleep, I felt Daddy kiss me good-night.

THIRTY-SIX

SCHOOL

My MIND MOVED in and out of sleep. Night sounds caused my eyes to open to the dreamy dark of my room. Shadows threatened to step off the walls and come after me.

Noises stirred that night. I woke many times to the creaks and whines of floorboards and pipes. It was as if our house missed Daddy, too.

Worry made sleep difficult, too. Taking care of Mama felt like buckets stacked high on my shoulders. How long would Daddy be gone? Would Mama and I make it until he came home? What would happen if Sheriff Rhodes found proof that Daddy shot Mason Reed?

Mama's moods could be unpredictable and change direction in a matter of days, even hours, sometimes with no warning. What would her mood be when she woke?

I wondered about the things I'd heard from Clara. She talked in riddles about spirits, and what she said about Daddy returning in a darker way made little sense to me.

When the alarm rang on my dresser, I climbed out of bed and stumbled downstairs for breakfast. Only days before, the morning kitchen had smelled like coffee and bacon. Now, cigarette smoke hung in the air and made the room seem dirty and strange.

I looked for Mama in the kitchen, then figured she must have been too tired to wake. Her cigarette butts were scattered on the floor. Gray ashes covered one side of the table. I wet a sponge and wiped up as best I could. When Daddy came back, he'd see that I'd tried to keep up appearances.

Breakfast was usually oatmeal with cinnamon sugar, or eggs and bacon. Weekends were cold cereal days. This was a school day, which meant oatmeal or eggs, but I didn't feel like cooking, and anyway, I wasn't supposed to use the stove without a grown-up nearby. So today cold cereal would do. I figured that until Daddy came home, there would be a lot of cold cereal days.

AFRAID I'D BE LATE for school, I hurried to dress. No one had done the laundry in days, and the only clean outfit in my closet was my Easter dress. Mama had bought it weeks ago, before she fell down the steps. A beautiful pink dress with a wide sash around the waist and puffed sleeves with lace trim, it was the sort of dress for church or a party, not school.

I almost decided to stay home sick, but being home with Mama seemed harder than going to school in the wrong dress. Tonight, I'd wash clothes and get things organized. Today, if anyone asked, I'd tell them I'd been invited to a party after school and wouldn't have time to go home and change.

Not a single noise came from Mama's room while I dressed and ran the comb through my tangled hair. I listened for the soft thud of her feet, the creak of bedsprings, the flushing toilet, a cough, anything at all to tell me Mama was there.

Nothing.

Maybe I should have tiptoed into her room to check on her, or to at least let her know I was headed to school. Instead, I carried my book satchel outside and waited for the bus.

In a way, I felt glad Mama hadn't come downstairs and waited with me for the bus. What if she brought Baby Tom? Everyone would have laughed at me, the girl whose mother keeps a dead baby in a jar.

The cold rain fell, dotting my pink dress.

The one good thing about standing in the rain is nobody can tell you've been crying.

BEING BACK AT SCHOOL felt good. This was the one place where grown-ups handled everything. The worst things you had to figure out on your own were equations at the blackboard and where the decimal point should go.

When I stepped into Miss Wilder's room and took my seat in the third row, I breathed in the familiar smell of crayons, pencils, and chalk, and I felt safe.

When Mary Roberts looked up and saw me, she walked over to her desk, which was right next to mine. "Why weren't you in church yesterday, Ellie? You missed the program, and the egg hunt, and . . . Wait a minute, isn't that your Easter dress?" She picked up the hem of my skirt to check the frilled border.

I pulled my dress from her hands. Mary Roberts can take only a few clues and figure out an entire story, so I had to think of something to distract her. "Mama wasn't feeling well, so we didn't come. But," I tried to use my most excited voice to take her mind off my dress, "Daddy gave me a new chick!"

Just as Mary's mouth curled to ask another question, Miss Wilder stood at the front of the room and rang the small brass bell. Everyone quieted and faced her.

For the next few hours, my head filled with fractions, pronouns, and pictures of the basic food groups. When lunchtime came, I realized I had forgotten to pack a lunch and didn't have any money to pay the cafeteria lady. When everyone lined up to go to the cafeteria, I stayed behind.

"Aren't you coming?" Mary Roberts asked.

"Not today. I'm not very hungry."

Mary shrugged her shoulders. "You must be catching cold or something," she said, then went to the cafeteria without me.

"Are you sick, Ellie?" Miss Wilder asked. "You look a little pale. Would you like to go to the infirmary?"

"No, ma'am. I ate too much breakfast." Lying to Miss Wilder made me feel ashamed.

Alone in the classroom, I walked to the window and looked outside. My stomach hurt. My head felt as light as a balloon.

Next to me, Nutmeg, the class's pet hamster, scurried about in the pine shavings lining the bottom of his cage. He walked the perimeter of his cage, stopped at his shallow food dish, then picked up a sliced sweet potato.

My stomach growled. The faint smell of sweet potato filled my nose. I could almost taste the thin, orange bits.

I couldn't stop myself. After checking the door to make sure no one would see, I quickly reached into the hamster's plastic bowl and scooped out a handful of his chopped sweet potato, sunflower seeds, and alfalfa. I shoved the stolen hamster food into my mouth and chewed it as fast as I could. The grainy pieces tasted raw like earth.

Had this been something Mary Roberts and I had decided to do on a dare, it might have been fun, something to laugh about on the playground. On my own, I was scared to think that anyone would see. As soon as I swallowed the chewed food, I hurried to the water cooler in the hallway to rinse the taste from my mouth. I drank gulp after gulp from the fountain, but no amount of water rinsed away my shame.

A tiny seed wedged between my lower front teeth. I dug at it with my fingernail, making my gums bleed.

I walked to the bathroom down the hall and hid in a stall. I dug at my gums until my mouth filled with blood. In a strange way, the bleeding made me feel clean.

Of course, it also made me feel guilty. Mrs. Roberts once

told me that causing yourself to bleed on purpose was a mortal sin, and things like tattoos, pierced ears, and any kinds of self-inflicted mark or wound are evil. Digging your gums until they bleed is certain to be on that list, too.

To prove it, God sent me the curse the very same day.

AFTER LUNCH WE HAD story time, and then recess. I felt embarrassed by my Easter dress and hid near the broken merry-go-round, away from most of the kids. Mary Roberts came with me.

"Does she still have it?" Mary asked.

"Does who have what?" I asked. Sometimes Mary Roberts thinks I can read her mind.

"Your Mama. Does she still have that baby in a jar?"

"Hush," I nodded and looked around to make sure no one heard. "I don't want to . . ."

"Hey, Ellie," a boy's voice called to me.

I turned around and saw Hank Shipes, a sixth grader who lives on my street, and his friend, Marvin Gregory. Hank had failed sixth grade twice, and was the oldest boy at our school. He hardly ever spoke to me, and I couldn't imagine why he wanted to talk to me now. I tried to act natural. "Hi, Hank."

"So what are you all dressed up for, Ellie? You got a boyfriend?" He grabbed my dress and pulled it up to my waist.

"Stop it, Hank!" Mary Roberts yelled.

Marvin came at Mary and held her so she couldn't move.

I bit my lip, trying not to cry, but couldn't help myself. Both boys could see my panties. My face burned. "Please Hank, leave me alone." My voice shook. I tried to push my dress back down, but Hank slapped my hands.

"You all dressed up for your Mama's nigger?" His breath hit my face and smelled bad. "I seen you and your Mama walking home late last night hanging on that colored man's arm."

"Jericho . . . He's just my friend . . . He . . ."

Hank put his hand between my legs and squeezed hard. It hurt, and I cried out, trying to push Hank away.

"What's going on here?" Miss Wilder stormed up behind Hank, surprising us all.

Both boys took off running.

Miss Wilder put her arms around me. "Are you all right, Ellie? Did he hurt you?"

I tried to speak, but my throat felt too tight to make words.

Miss Wilder led Mary and me back inside the school. She wiped my eyes with tissues and helped me straighten my dress. "Can you tell me what happened, Ellie?"

I shook my head. I was afraid if I told one thing, all the rest might spill out of my mouth, too. How could I tell Miss Wilder or anyone? Not just about Hank, but about Jericho, or why I wore my Easter dress to school, or why I ate hamster food for lunch? How could I tell her Mama carried around a dead baby, and that Daddy ran away with his tomato girl?

Miss Wilder turned to Mary. "Can you tell me?"

"All I know is Hank came over and pulled up Ellie's dress. He said a bad thing."

"What bad thing did he say?"

"He called some colored man Ellie knows a nigger."

Miss Wilder flinched. "I see. Thank you, Mary. Can you stay here with Ellie while I speak to the principal and collect the other children?"

After Miss Wilder left the room, Mary patted my arm. "It's okay, Ellie. You don't have to worry. Hank Shipes is a stupid boy with a grease monkey for a father. His mama doesn't even have real teeth. I've walked by their house and seen her dirty dentures sitting in a glass on the window sill."

I smiled, the way you do when you know somebody's trying to make you feel better but can't.

"Is it true what Hank said, Ellie? Were you and your mama out with a colored man last night?"

"Yes, but not like Hank said. Jericho and his wife, Clara, are my friends." I told Mary how Clara had saved Easter, and how Jericho had walked Mama and me home.

Mary shook her head. "They might be nice people, but they're still colored, Ellie. You can't let people see you in the colored part of town and especially not with a colored man. Doesn't your mama know better?"

"It's not like that, Mary. They helped us."

"I know, but white girls just can't be friendly with colored men."

When Miss Wilder came back, I asked for a bathroom pass. My stomach hurt and I wanted to be alone. I felt so ashamed and dirty. Even though no one saw Hank Shipes touch me except Mary Roberts, Marvin, and maybe Miss Wilder, I felt the whole world could take one look at me and know.

In the bathroom, I pulled down my panties and sat on the toilet. I saw Hank's dirty fingerprints where he'd grabbed me, and on the inside of my panties, a dark red stain the size of a dime. When I wiped, there was more blood on the tissue. Had Hank hurt me there? Or was this the bleeding Tess had told me about when she gave me the Kotex? I felt too ashamed to ask the nurse. I wadded tissue in my panties to soak up the blood and walked back to my classroom. My belly hurt in a deep, low place. I felt sore there the rest of the day, through history and science, and right into library time. The warm trickle between my legs stayed on my mind until the last bell rang.

I CLIMBED ONTO the bus and took the first seat. I usually sat further back, but walking with a wad of tissue in my panties made my legs spread too far apart. I wanted to go home, and hoped Mama didn't start fussing right away about Baby Tom not breast-feeding. *Please, Mama, be okay for this one day.* All I wanted at the moment was to wash my panties, eat a thick slice of buttered bread, and walk to Clara's house to see Easter.

When the bus stopped in front of my house, I waddled down the steps and stood on the sidewalk. Right away, I noticed Sheriff Rhodes's car parked out front. Maybe he'd heard news of Daddy.

Suddenly, something hard and sharp hit my leg. On the sidewalk, a flat gray stone lay at my feet.

I looked in the direction the stone came. Next door, someone stood behind the oak tree in Mrs. Preston's front yard. When I saw the plaid shirtsleeve and the muddy brown boots, I knew who hid behind the tree.

I dropped my books and ran into my house.

Hank Shipes had come back for me.

THIRTY-SEVEN

MAGIC

SHERIFF RHODES CAME DOWN the stairs, tucking his shirt into his pants. "School out already?" he asked when he saw me standing in the middle of the floor.

"Yes, sir." I tried to catch my breath. "Have you found Daddy yet?"

"No, not yet, honey. But I'll find him. Don't you worry." He adjusted his belt buckle.

"Is Mama upstairs?"

"Yes," he said, and wiped his forehead. "But she's resting now. Maybe you should let her be for awhile."

I nodded as I pushed my hair behind my ear and tried to think of something to say.

Sheriff Rhodes sat down on the steps and motioned to me. He used his whole hand as if he were guiding a small boat toward shore. "Come here, sweetheart. I need to have a talk with you."

I walked closer, not sure if I was supposed to sit or stand. He took my hand. "Sit here," he said, guiding me onto his lap.

When my bottom pressed against his legs, the tissues in my panties shifted. I prayed he wouldn't feel the wad on his knee and ask me about it.

"Honey, when I was upstairs with your mama, I noticed something strange, and, well, I just wanted to ask you about it, see if you might help me figure it out. Think you could do that?"

"I can try."

"That's my girl." Sheriff Rhodes patted my leg with his rough hand. "While I was visiting with your mother, I felt something hard under her pillow. Something like glass. When I tried to see what it was, she became right upset with me." He turned his head and showed me some scratches along the side of his neck. "See here?"

I swallowed hard and stared at the red lines, four matching rows down his neck. "You didn't take it, did you? You didn't take the jar away from Mama?"

"No, of course not, honey. Your mama . . . I realize she's got . . . well, she's got some problems, doesn't she?"

"Bad problems," I whispered. "Very bad problems."

"Yes. That's why I thought maybe you could help me."

"How can I help?"

"Well, maybe you could tell me what she's got in the jar and why she's so afraid to let me see it."

"I can't tell. Mama would be so mad . . ."

"It's okay, Ellie. This will be a secret, just between you and me. Maybe if I knew, I could help. You want me to help, don't you?"

I wanted anyone's help, but telling anyone about Baby Tom scared me, so I kept quiet.

Sheriff Rhodes sighed. "Tell you what, how about we play a little guessing game? I'll guess what's in the jar, and you just nod when I'm getting closer."

"You won't be able to guess. Nobody would guess right. It's too awful."

"Is it something stolen?"

"No." I said, pushing Sheriff Rhodes's arms from around my waist. "I don't want to play this game." As I stood up, the tissues inside my panties fell, landing on the floor between my feet.

Red splotches showed on the white paper. My neck and face grew warm.

Sheriff Rhodes looked at the blood-spotted tissues. His face turned red, too. "Ellie, honey, did you . . . Well, honey . . . Uh, I mean, is this . . . Are you having your time?" He stressed the word *time* as if it somehow was a whole story or world of its own.

"I don't know." My voice quivered. "Hank hurt me down there, but I don't know if it's that or . . ." I bit my lip to keep from crying.

"Wait a damn minute. Hank? Hank Shipes? He hurt you?" Sheriff Rhodes's eyebrows raised like dark flags.

"Yes, on the playground." I felt like a tattletale, but somehow, it was a relief to see the sheriff switch his focus from Mama to Hank Shipes.

"What did he do, honey?" Sheriff Rhodes's round face glowed even deeper red. "Tell me what he did to you!"

I wouldn't tell on Daddy, or give away Mama's secrets, but telling on Hank Shipes suddenly seemed easy, as if it was one awful thing I could let go. "He pulled up my dress and pinched me. Hard. Down there." I looked at the floor. "Then I went to the bathroom . . . and saw blood."

"He ever done anything like this to you before?"

I shook my head. "No. Hank saw Mama and me walking home with Jericho, and didn't like that because Jericho is colored." I swallowed hard, then blurted out, "I'm afraid, Sheriff Rhodes! Hank got suspended from school for what he did, and now he's really mad. He hid by the tree and threw a rock at me when I got off the bus."

"Which tree?"

I walked over to the window and pointed next door.

Sheriff Rhodes bolted up like a startled rabbit and looked in the direction I pointed. He quickly shoved the blood-stained tissues into my hands. "Throw these away, honey, and stay put. I'll see to it that boy doesn't mess with you again."

He stormed out of the house and let Bubba out of the car. The sheriff and dog then walked toward the tree next door where Hank was still hiding, maybe thinking I'd come back outside later. When Sheriff Rhodes neared the tree, Hank ran, but Bubba soon caught up with him and knocked him to the ground.

I couldn't hear what Sheriff Rhodes said, but by the way he yanked Hank up by his shirt, I knew he meant business. Whatever Sheriff Rhodes said, the boy must have agreed with most of it because his head nodded every few seconds. When the sheriff let go, Hank ran down Grace Street.

After he put Bubba back in the car, Sheriff Rhodes came back inside the house. He handed me the books I'd dropped, and told me to let him know the next time Hank Shipes even looked at me. "Now," he said, "we need to get you over to Clara's house so she can check you out."

SHERIFF RHODES SAID I could ride up front with him, but I wanted to ride in back in case I left a blood spot on the seat. I tried to keep my legs together and take slow, even breaths, believing if I kept still enough, the blood might not drip so fast. But my head began to feel light from taking too many shallow breaths, so I breathed deeply, and sure enough, felt a trickle between my legs. Even though Sheriff Rhodes couldn't see the drop of blood, my face still colored with shame. This was something a girl needed to share with her mother, not the sheriff. But when your mother is in her room, rocking a dead baby, you have to make do.

In the end, having Sheriff Rhodes help was better than being on my own. I felt suddenly sad and grateful all at once. I looked at him in the rearview mirror and when our eyes met, I smiled. He smiled back, then quickly looked away.

"Sheriff Rhodes?"

"Yes, honey?"

"If this is the monthly curse, does that mean I'm a woman now?"

He cleared his throat. "Well, uh, yes. Yes, I suppose that's exactly what it means."

Sheriff Rhodes cleared his throat again, then drove a little faster.

You can always tell when someone's glad to see you by the way their face opens at the first sight. That's how Clara's face looked when she saw me. But then her face turned worried, and she wrapped her soft, dark arms around me and held me close. "You look flushed, child. What's the matter?" She put her hand on my head as if checking for a fever.

"How's Easter?" I asked.

"See for yourself." Clara pointed to a small box by the stove.

I crossed and knelt beside the box. Inside, my small, green chick looked up at me. When I placed my hand over him, he pecked at my thumb.

While I cooed and hummed to my chick, Sheriff Rhodes pulled Clara aside and talked to her in a low voice. I heard Hank Shipes's name and figured they were discussing what happened on the playground. I felt embarrassed all over again, and hoped the sheriff hadn't told her the reason for Hank's anger.

"You go out back with Jericho," Clara told Sheriff Rhodes. "We got women's business."

After the sheriff went outside, Clara led me back to her bedroom and told me to rest on the bed. She propped the pillow under my head and turned on the lamp. "We got to check you, honey, since the sheriff said you're not sure if you bleeding because that boy hurt you or if your time has come on."

"Okay." I swallowed hard, feeling ashamed and scared all at once.

"Now, you just look up at the ceiling. I'm not going to hurt you, I promise." Her voice was steady and soothing.

I did as Clara said, let my mind imagine pictures as she spoke.

"You see the bird up there? How his wings open to fly?"

I looked for the bird, saw the outline of wings in the cracked plaster above me. While my eyes stared at the ceiling, Clara took off my panties.

"See how the branches run like a tree?" Clara's hands parted my legs. Her fingers touched me while I looked for the branches. I thought about Mama bleeding out the baby, and my legs tightened again.

"All right then, you're all right," Clara said. "Just look at the bird on the ceiling. Just look for the wings, the tiny feather lines."

I looked back at the bird, fixed my eyes on the faded crack lines to keep from crying. Clara didn't hurt me, but I didn't want anybody to see or touch me down there.

"Well, you got a bruise, that's for sure, but the blood is your time." Clara pulled my dress back down. "Now, we got to clean you up and find you a rag to wear."

I blinked away a tear and took a deep breath. Clara returned with a damp washcloth from the bathroom and wiped the blood from between my legs.

She tossed the cloth into her clothes hamper, then opened her bureau. "I haven't bled for years, you know? You're lucky I don't ever throw nothing away. I'm sure to have that belt in here somewhere."

"Belt?" The only belts I knew about where the ones men wore to hold up their trousers.

"You got to have a belt to hold the rag, sugar."

"Tess left me something she said to use when this happened."

"Ah-ha!" Clara shouted, then pulled out a white strap that must have been the belt she wanted. "No, girl, you don't never use them store bought things, you hear me? You put anything inside you before you're married and you ruin yourself. You go home and throw whatever she gave you away. Besides, the blood is magic. And you don't never throw magic away."

Clara showed me how to fit the belt and how to fasten the

small white rags in place to soak up the blood. "I don't have any underpants to fit you, honey. Lord knows you'd be drowned in a pair of mine. But this will cover you up plenty until you get home." She gave me some spare rags to change, then patted my belly. "You feel bad here? Any burning or tight feeling?"

"A little."

"Well, I got roots you can put in some tea that will take that away. Now, come to the kitchen. You're too pale. I'll fry you some liver and onions. You need something hearty and rich on a day like today. And something special, like warm spoon bread."

I never liked liver and onions, but I was so hungry, I ate every bite. Clara fried them both until they were caramel in color and tasted sweeter than any I'd ever eaten. I drank two glasses of milk and ate a large chunk of spoon bread spread with butter. After my meal, Clara gave me a cup of tea with a white root floating in the cup. The taste was spicy like horehound candy.

Jericho and Sheriff Rhodes came back inside just as I finished the last of my tea. Jericho leaned down to scoop Easter from his box and hand him to me. My chick fluffed his feathers and settled into the bowl of my hands.

"Feed him some of Clara's spoon bread," Jericho said, "and that chicken will gets as fat as a Thanksgiving turkey in no time."

"You should eat some yourself, old man, you and that skinny backside," Clara teased as she wiped the crumbs from her table.

Jericho grinned and handed me a piece of spoon bread from the bowl. "Don't you love a bossy woman?" he asked the sheriff.

Clara interrupted. "Looks like from them scratches, you been in a cat fight." Clara pointed at Sheriff Rhodes's neck.

"Well, I . . ." Sheriff Rhodes leaned against the kitchen doorframe.

"Don't even try that with me. You a good man, George Rhodes, but you don't knows whose bed to leave your boots under, do you?" Clara chided him.

Sheriff Rhodes cleared his throat.

"Sit. Let me put some salve on there before you go home to Millie and end up sleeping with Bubba tonight."

Sheriff Rhodes sat on a chair in the middle of Clara's small kitchen as she shoved his head to one side and dabbed blue salve on the scratches Mama had made on his neck.

Before we left, Clara fixed a plate of food for Mama. "You makes sure she eats it. And there's some extra spoon bread in there for you," she told me. She handed the wrapped plate to Sheriff Rhodes.

I kissed Easter's green head and gave him back to Clara.

"Don't worry about your chick. He's doing good, real good," Clara said. She put a brown paper bag in my hands, then whispered in my ear so Jericho and Sheriff Rhodes couldn't hear. "There's special magic in a girl's first blood. Tonight, you plant this in the ground outside your window, and a wish will come true."

BACK HOME, I GAVE Mama her plate of food in bed. She looked better after she'd eaten a few bites. A little pink color brightened her cheeks, and her eyes seemed less dull and sunken. She lit one of the cigarettes from the pack Sheriff Rhodes left and took a long, slow drag.

While Mama smoked, I sat on the edge of the bed and told her about my day at school. Nearly everything I told her was made up. I couldn't bring myself to tell her about eating hamster food, or what Hank did to me on the playground, or how my first blood had come. While I talked, Mama puffed on her cigarette, then put it out on the edge of her plate. She reached under her pillow and lifted Baby Tom. "You haven't said a word about the baby since you came home."

"I'm sorry, Mama."

Adjusting the jar in her arms, Mama unbuttoned her night gown and pressed the jar to her breast to nurse him. "I think he's growing a little, don't you, Ellie?"

I patted her arm. "Yes, Mama. He's growing." Really, he'd shriveled some and turned darker. His wrinkled face looked like a walnut.

I kissed Mama and Baby Tom good-night, then went into the bathroom and washed by hand a pair of panties, socks, and my yellow school dress. I hung them on the shower rod to dry overnight.

Before going to sleep, I sneaked outside with the bag Clara had given me. With the spade from Daddy's shed, I dug a hole in the ground, directly under my window.

Inside the paper bag, Clara had placed my blood-stained panties, folded neatly. I took them from the bag, laid them in the shallow hole, and stared for a moment at the moth-shaped stain. I covered the panties with dirt and packed the soil with the palms of both hands to make it hard for any animals to dig there. I made a wish with closed eyes, just as Clara told me.

With my blood magic, I'd bring Daddy home again.

THIRTY-EIGHT

SAD CONFETTI

THE NEXT DAY went a little better. I didn't miss Daddy any less, and still worried about Mama, but somehow I woke with a clearer mind. Maybe becoming a woman the day before made the difference. I stayed in bed a few minutes and tried to imagine my bones inside my skin. Woman-bones inside woman-skin. I felt new and grown-up. Maybe this afternoon, I could even tell Mama my news. She might even be happy for me. We could go to Joe's for ice cream or buy a cake mix and have a party. No boys allowed, not even Baby Tom.

The day before had taught me one lesson: to think ahead. Before I'd gone to sleep, I'd washed out clothes to wear. And after carefully fixing my belt and cloth in place in the morning, I dressed and went downstairs, quietly, so as not to wake Mama.

For breakfast, I ate part of Clara's spoon bread. I wanted to eat the entire piece of bread. Instead, I left some on a saucer for Mama, and slipped the rest inside my pocket for the hamster whose food I'd stolen. I put three tea bags in a jar of water and sat it in a sunny window so Mama and I could have tea for dinner.

I'd found enough quarters in the bottom of Daddy's junk

drawer to buy the cafeteria lunch, so when I sat at my desk in the afternoon, I almost felt like the same old Ellie. Almost.

The hardest part of the day was making up with Mary Roberts. At lunch, she started talking to me. "Hank Shipes shouldn't have done that to you," she wagged her finger at me as she spoke, "but you should have more sense than to go around with coloreds. Especially a colored man, and at night!"

Mary warmed up, though, after I told her I was a woman now, and not to be bossed around anymore. In the bathroom, I pulled up my dress to let her see the belt and rag Clara had made for me. She didn't believe me at first, and thought I was wearing it for show the way we sometimes tried on our mothers' high heels. When I pulled down my panties and showed Mary the red stain, her mouth opened like a window.

MATH EQUATIONS ON the blackboard. Roll calls and hall passes. Books, markers, and the sound of shoes scuffing the floor. There were whole minutes as perfect as new pennies. In those moments, I didn't miss Daddy or worry about Mama at home alone with Baby Tom.

When the day came to a close and we lined up to board the yellow bus, the sad feelings came back. I sat near the rear of the bus and looked out the window. Purple clouds swelled like bruises over the peaked mountain. If only my wishes could bring Daddy back the way the wind drew dark clouds.

I missed Daddy, missed the sound of his voice, and the way he smelled like cedar and aftershave. I missed his strong hands lifting me off the ground, a smile hidden in his eyes. I wanted to go to the store and sweep up the dust for Daddy, then come home and sit next to him on the sofa while he read the newspaper. I wanted to hold his shirt on my lap and sew found buttons on his sleeve. The ache in my heart grew because I could do none of these things.

The yellow bus slowed, screeching to a stop in front of my

house. I climbed down and stood along the curb. The air smelled crisp and new, and I looked up, noticed the thick clouds overhead, and heard distant thunder.

Sheriff Rhodes's car wasn't parked in front, but I knew he'd been there because his car leaked oil. I stepped over a fresh black spot as I walked toward the house.

"Ellie?" Mama's voice came to me from the side of the house.

"Mama?"

"I'm over here, Ellie."

I looked around and saw Mama walking from the direction of Daddy's shed. Her hair stood out around her head, and she wiped her hands on her pink housecoat, leaving dirt stains.

"Mama, what are you doing out here?" I didn't want the neighbors to see Mama looking this way. "Where's Baby Tom?"

"Why, he's in the house, of course, taking a nap." Mama ran her fingers through her hair.

I nodded. When Mama's in one of her moods, I know better than to argue or ask too many questions.

"I've been out here looking for your father."

"Daddy? He's back?" I dropped my books on the ground and pointed toward the shed. "Where? In there?"

"He's not there now. I heard him, though, while I was inside with Sheriff Rhodes. He kept calling to me 'Julia, come to me. Julia.' Of course, I couldn't say anything, for fear the sheriff might arrest him. So I had to wait until Sheriff Rhodes left." She smoothed the front of her housecoat.

"Mama, how did you hear Daddy from inside? Did you have the window open?"

Mama's jaw tightened. "Don't question me, young lady."

I felt the weight pressing down on me. Daddy hadn't come home. Mama heard him inside her head, the same place she heard Baby Tom crying.

A man's voice called out to us. "Hello, there. Fine day, isn't it?"

Mama and I turned toward the voice. The postman stood on the sidewalk. He handed Mama a newspaper and three or four envelopes, then scratched his sunburned ear. "I was wondering if Rupert was in? I stopped by the store, but he wasn't there. The wife's collie is getting old, leaves puddles all over the house, so I need to fence in part of the yard. Thought maybe Rupert could give me a hand."

"Your wife's pissing dog is not my husband's problem," Mama snapped. "Besides," she added, thumbing through the mail, "he isn't here right now."

The postman's face turned as red as his ears. "I see. I'm sorry . . . didn't mean to . . ."

I looked down at the grass. I felt sorry for the postman, but didn't know what to say. If I apologized with Mama right there, she'd get mad at me. The postman could go home, forget all about Mama. I had to stay.

"Well, thank you just the same," he said, then turned and walked away.

Mama dropped all the mail on the ground except for one blue envelope. She looked at the writing, turned it over in her hand. "It's to you," she said.

"Me?" Who would be writing me? I wondered.

Mama recognized the writing. "It's from your daddy!" Instead of handing me the envelope, she ripped it open and pulled out the letter. Paper money floated to the ground.

I waited impatiently for her to finish reading the letter and give it to me.

"That bastard is never coming home!" Mama screamed as she ripped up the letter and threw the pieces into the air.

"Why, Mama? Why?" I knelt in the grass to pick up the pieces of blue paper. "The note was to me! Daddy wrote the letter to me!"

Mama stormed off toward the house without a word. She'd torn up my note from Daddy, the only thing that might tell me where he'd gone or when he was coming home again. I didn't want to follow her.

A gust of wind carried away the money and pieces of Daddy's note, and I chased after them.

One of the twenty-dollar bills blew into the neighbor's yard, but I didn't care. Losing the money didn't even matter; I wanted to know what Daddy had to say.

I shoved the pieces into my dress pocket and ran down Grace Street. If anyone in the world could read a torn letter, Clara could.

"You brought me a jigsaw, did you?" Clara stood in her yard as I came running up.

"How did you know?" I looked at Clara with amazed eyes.

"Oh, I see things. Pictures inside my head." Clara held out her hand and I gave her the blue pieces of paper. "Come inside. We'll get to work."

While I fed and cuddled Easter, Clara spread out the scraps of paper on her kitchen table. She lit a candle, then sprinkled salt on all four corners of the table. She sat down, spread her hands over the scraps and began to rearrange the pieces. Clara didn't read the words to know where the pieces belonged. She circled the paper slips with her hands as if she could read them with her fingertips the way blind children read Braille.

I watched from my seat by the stove. Before long, Clara called me to the table.

When I saw the letter, my mouth fell open. The blue paper on the table was a perfect rectangle. No rips. Not a single tear.

"Clara . . . how? I mean . . ."

"Hush, child. Sit here and read this letter. Your Daddy's got something to tell you."

Clara rose from her chair and motioned me to sit, which I did. My hands shook. I gripped the edge of the table to keep them still as I read.

Dear Ellie,

Here's a little money. I know it's not much, but it'll buy some groceries. I'll send you more when I can. I sent this to you because I don't know if your mother can handle a letter from me. I know I let you both down. I can't ever make it up to her, but I'll try to make it up to you if you let me.

Tess is in the hospital, but I can't tell you where. The doc stitched up her cut, and gave her some pills, but infection set in, and a bad fever, a fever so high she doesn't even know my face. But she'll get better. If I didn't believe that, I don't know what I'd do.

When I can, I'll come like I promised. But it will be a little longer than I thought, honey.

No matter what, Ellie, you'll always be my girl.

Love,

Daddy

When I finished reading Daddy's letter, Clara tossed the page into the air and blew a long, deep breath under it.

All around me, blue shreds fell like confetti.

THIRTY-NINE

THE WEEKS

THE FOLLOWING WEEKS brought more notes from Daddy.
After the first one, I waited every day after school for the
postman's delivery.

As time went by, Daddy sent less money and wrote shorter
notes. I tried to give the money to Mama, but even mentioning
Daddy made her angry. I put the cash in her pocketbook or in the
cookie jar on top of the refrigerator so we'd have money for trips
to the market. Daddy never sent enough though, and some of the
bills went unpaid.

I went to the shed to read Daddy's letters. Each time, I hoped
he'd tell me about the day he planned to return, but he wrote
mostly about Tess. I kept his letters in a shoebox under my bed
to read over again at night. I reread them so many times, I knew
them by heart.

He never put a return address on the envelope, and the post-
marks came from different towns. Still, I had things to tell Daddy,
so I wrote him back and kept my unsent letters in the box along
with his.

Dear Ellie,

Tess has healed up from the infection. The doctor says she will be well enough to go home in another day or two, but her fever went so high, he's not sure how much it damaged her mind. Some of what she lost is sure to come back in time. She's got good color. Remember how pink her cheeks turned when she laughed? She's still a little pale, but the color coming back is a good sign. Even the doctor said so and he doesn't know her like I do. I'll know when she's close to well again. She's not there yet, but she will be, and then I'll come for you, Ellie.

I know you're taking good care of your mother. I wish I knew how to help her, Ellie, but honest to God, I tried everything to cast out the demons in her head.

Right now, getting Tess back to normal takes every waking moment. I sit by her bed and talk to her, trying to help her remember the things she forgets. What hurts the most is that she sometimes doesn't seem to recognize me.

Love,
Daddy

Dear Daddy,

I don't know where you are, but I miss you. I know Mama misses you as much as I do. Sheriff Rhodes comes by nearly every day. He is looking for you, Daddy, but he's promised not to hurt you. He says it would be better in the end if you turned yourself in. He knows about the letter from Mr. Reed, and he knows I know about it, but I swear not to tell. I will never tell. Not even Mary Roberts.

I'm packing my bag, Daddy. I put in some clean underwear and two dresses so far. Mama doesn't wash clothes anymore so I can't pack much. I'm a woman now and have my own bra even. I haven't packed that yet, since I only have the one. Clara took me shopping to buy it because of how Mama is right now. You remember the colored woman, Clara, who reads cards and palms and knows magic? We've become friends, Daddy. The day you left, she and Jericho took me in and they look after me now.

*I miss you, Daddy. I'm really sorry about Tess, but Mama is grow-
ing more angry over little things. I'm afraid of her sometimes. Please
come home. I'll do anything you want if you just come home. I promise to be good.*
    Love,
    XOXO
    Ellie

Dear Ellie,
    *Today is a special day. May 2, 1969 — remember this day. It's the day
Tess came home from the hospital! She's out of the woods now, but she
doesn't talk yet. She sits by the window and watches the birds, and I bring
her food to help her regain her strength. She doesn't remember how to feed
herself, and sometimes the sight of the spoon makes her cry.*
    *There was a little flicker in her eye today when she saw a robin
on the window sill, and she tried to speak. She made a sound like
"je-je" and at first, I thought she meant jay, as in blue jay, but then
she looked away, and I kept guessing wrong. She reached out her hand
to the jar of jelly on the table. Then I knew she was remembering
Jellybean. When I said his name, tears came to her eyes, and it nearly
broke my heart. I know it will do Tess good to see you, Ellie, and to
hear from your own mouth that you don't blame her for what happened. I know one day you are going to love Tess as much as I do.*
    I hope the new chick is doing all right, honey.
    *I'm sending a little money. I know it's not much, but I can't go
out to work just yet and leave Tess like this. I met a man who needs
somebody to drive his pulpwood to the next state, so as soon as I can
figure what to do about Tess, I'll have a job and then I will be able
to send more.*
    *If you or your mother need anything, you ask Mr. Morgan's son.
Don't say anything to the sheriff. You are my girl. I know I can count
on you.*
    Love,
    Daddy

Dear Daddy,

Easter is doing fine. He's lost most of his green color now that his new feathers are growing in. He stays with Clara and Jericho, but I go over to visit him every day, and Clara is teaching me how to bake pies. She's also teaching me how to read cards and which herbs work magic on the sick. I cured a blister on my foot with just a dab of gray powder.

We had a little accident with the new chick when Mama put him in a can and forgot to poke holes. He was nearly dead, but Clara brought him back.

I keep asking her to make her magic work to cure Mama's mind and bring you home again, but she says there's a limit to how much magic she can do unless a person wants it to work. The magic only worked on Easter because he wanted to live. That makes me wonder if you do want to come back? You do want to, don't you, Daddy? Please say you do.

I would ask her to bring back Baby Tom, but I worry that Mama would hurt him. The way Mama acts, maybe it's better she has only a dead baby to take care of, and not one who needs love.

Love,
XOXOXO
Ellie

Dear Ellie,

I had to take the job or risk losing it, so now I'm driving the pulpwood truck between states. I take Tess along. Some words are coming back to her, but her recovery will be slow. She had a seizure last night, and I sat up with her until morning. She's grown afraid of the dark.

I take Tess along on all my runs. I tried to find a woman to look after her, but the only one I could afford said no when I told her about Tess's seizures.

I'll send you a little money when I get paid.
Love,
Daddy

Dear Daddy,

Mama keeps trying to nurse the baby. She keeps me up sometimes all night. Last night, she sat up and smoked cigarettes. I went for a walk and got sick. All the smoke and no sleep made my head and stomach hurt. I threw up in the cemetery. I leaned up against somebody's headstone and cried myself to sleep.

There's been rumors about you, Daddy, about how you ran off with the tomato girl. People say you shot Mason Reed so you could have his girl for yourself.

Mr. Morgan taught me about chalk doors before you left, when Mama was in the hospital. He showed me how to draw a door and close out words that hurt. Being behind the door helps, but I'm still scared.

I try to make things look normal, but can't keep up. Clara makes sure we get supper, but we have so many bills, and Mama is getting worse. She yells at me for every little thing I do. Sheriff Rhodes says that the autopsy report came back, and that he has to bring you in. It sounds bad, Daddy. He even knows about the pulpwood truck. He promises he won't hurt you, Daddy, as long as you don't run.

Love,
XOXOXO
Ellie

Dear Ellie,

I'm running loads of pulpwood nearly every day, trying to keep a roof over our heads and pay the hospital bill. I send what I can. I hope you understand.

Tess is getting better. She smiles and squeezes my hand. The truck rides are long and hard, but we manage. I stop to let her walk around. Today, I bought her a tomato plant. She holds it on her lap while we make our runs.

Be a good girl, Ellie. Make sure you do your homework and look after things until I come.

Love,
Daddy and Tess

Dear Daddy,

I haven't been able to study like I'm supposed to, and my grades are getting bad. I try hard, memorizing words on the front porch while I wait for the postman. But when the test comes, I forget them. I hope you won't be mad when you see my report card. I can't think straight when I'm hungry, sleepy, and scared. Mama keeps me up late, fretting about Baby Tom, and we never really have enough to eat. I worry what's going to happen now that Sheriff Rhodes knows where you are.

I'm seeing a counselor at school. I have to go because of my bad grades. I sit in Mrs. Milby's office and draw pictures or play with dolls. I'm supposed to talk to her, but she only wants to know my secrets. When I step into her office, I just can't speak. She is nice to me, but I hate her. She wants me to talk about you.

My bags are all packed for when you come.

Love,

XOXOXO

Ellie

The next blue envelope came with no note, only three twenty-dollar bills folded inside.

Dear Daddy,

Thank you for the money, but I miss your letters. Tell me when, Daddy? When are you coming home? Tell me about the route you will take, how you have mapped it out, how you have filled the tank with gas, and found somebody to look after Tess. Oh, Daddy, I need good news.

Because we had money, Mama decided this would be market day. Sometimes, she sends me alone to pick up bread, milk, and a few tin cans from the bins marked "Half-price, dented," but not this time.

Today, she put on her dark coat over her dirty nightgown and told me to come along. She stood in the market and smashed yellow squash on the floor. She yelled at the vendor over the price of his rotten tomatoes. I couldn't take his side, or explain how the tomato girl had taken you away.

Please, Daddy. We need you. I need you. This is too hard to do alone.

Love,
XOXOXO
Ellie

FORTY

THE SCARECROW MOTHER

WHEN WE COME home from the market, Mama drops the paper bag on the kitchen table. Her elbow bumps a glass of juice left from breakfast, spilling the juice on the floor.

"Clean that up!" Mama slaps my face.

I jump. My cheek stings, and I am too shocked to know what to say. I don't remember the last time Mama struck me.

Mama paces the floor and runs her hands through her tangled hair. She used to comb it behind her ears, curling the ends under with her fingertips, her brown bangs swept to one side. Sometimes she'd take tortoiseshell combs and pull the sides up, or use a ribbon from her sewing box to tie her hair in a ponytail. She hardly washes it anymore. It's like straw now, and when she rakes her fingers through it, pieces stick out. Mama has turned into a scarecrow, and I'm the bird she frightens away.

"Why didn't you drink your juice? You think we can afford to pour juice on the goddamn floor?" Mama's hands rest on her hips. The blue vein in her neck rises like a snake trapped under her skin.

Hearing Mama curse makes me want to cry. Once she wouldn't allow bad words. Now I hear her at night in her rocking chair, chanting bad words about Daddy and Tess.

It's not only the bad words. Mama's voice is changing.

Her voice used to lift. She might say, "We're having boiled cabbage for supper," and it would sound like an invitation. Her smooth voice made me want to eat the cabbage, even though I hate it.

Now Mama clenches her teeth when she speaks. Her voice is thick and dark like cough syrup.

"I'm sorry I didn't drink my juice, Mama." I don't argue. I hadn't finished my juice this morning because she wouldn't wait for me. She'd walked into the kitchen wearing her coat and said, "Come on, Ellie, we're going to the market, now."

I stay quiet. Left alone, Mama might settle herself, maybe pick up her knitting needles and work on the blue blanket for Baby Tom. That sometimes calms her.

I move to the sink. Dirty dishes are piled on the counter and fill the sink. A dead fly floats in the dishwater that's been standing for days.

I'm falling behind on the housework; there is so much to do.

I squeeze a green glob of Palmolive onto a dishrag.

"Don't use so much! They don't give the damn soap away!"

"Yes, Mama." I kneel on the floor and wipe up the spilled juice. I bury my face in my hands and sob. I miss Daddy and don't understand how he could just go away. I miss Mama, who has gone away without leaving.

Mama walks around the kitchen, putting the groceries away, slamming cabinet doors. Then she goes into the living room to sit in a chair by the window. I watch her nervous fingers pick at a mole on her neck until it bleeds.

I go into the living room and whisper into her ear, "Mama, don't hurt yourself." My mother smells bad. Her hair, her breath, even her skin has a sour smell. She hasn't taken a bath or changed clothes in days.

In the upstairs bathroom, I find a clean washcloth, wet it with warm water and soap. I wring some of the water into the sink, then walk back downstairs to the living room where Mama sits. I move slowly, trying my best not to say or do anything to upset her. She's been tense all day, and the outburst in the market didn't seem to calm her. Her knuckles are white, and she keeps digging at the mole on her neck. I hum to her. Then gently, like peeling a Band-Aid from tender skin, I pull Mama's fingers away from her neck and lay the warm wet cloth where she's bleeding.

The small mole on Mama's neck hangs by a thin piece of skin. I don't know how to take it off without hurting, so I leave it to dangle. Clara says some wounds heal themselves. I hope she's right.

A knocking sound startles me. Somebody's at the door. "I'll get that, Mama," I say.

Three days ago, Sheriff Rhodes said he knew Daddy's whereabouts, then left for Tennessee. Maybe the sheriff's brought Daddy home instead of putting him in jail. Or maybe Daddy's come back like he promised, with his hands too full to reach into his pockets.

But it isn't Daddy. It's only Miss Wilder.

I try to smile. I don't want her to think I'm unhappy to see her, but I've had my bag packed for weeks. I want my daddy so bad, it hurts. I close the door partially so she can't see too far inside.

"Hi, Ellie. I just wanted to visit for a bit. Maybe see how your counseling sessions are going, talk with your mother. She hasn't answered the notes I've sent, so I thought we could all talk together. Is this a good time?" she asks.

"No, it's not a good time, not really. My mother is napping. She doesn't feel well."

"Oh, I see. I hope it's nothing serious."

Miss Wilder knows I'm lying. I can tell by her face, the way it seems torn between a smile and a frown.

I know that Miss Wilder's noticed changes in me. She watches me when she's at her desk grading papers or standing on the playground near the swings. Last week, I missed six of my spelling words and she'd asked, "Is everything all right at home?" I told her yes, but she hadn't seemed to believe me. She'd asked again, "Ellie, are you sure? You know you can come to me . . ." and her voice trailed to that worried sound.

I've tried so hard, but I know I'm not the same girl. I don't even look the same.

"Maybe you can visit another time." Miss Wilder mustn't see Mama, or the unswept floors, or the dirty clothes piled on the stairs.

"That would be nice." Miss Wilder smiles again. "I really would like to visit. And please, I think the visit should be soon. The school year's almost over, and we need to talk."

Part of me wants to scream out to Miss Wilder, to tell her all the awful things that are happening, but I only nod. I've got to keep quiet. If anyone finds out how Mama behaves, the doctors will take her away. I'll be sent to an orphanage or foster home, and Daddy won't know where to find me when he comes back.

"Oh, I brought a cake," Miss Wilder says. "It's nothing much. Lemon-vanilla swirl. Just trying a new recipe." She hands me a white Tupperware, and I open the door a bit wider to squeeze the container inside.

"Thank you, Miss Wilder."

"You could bring the container back to my house if you like, Ellie. You remember where I live? I'd love your company. Belle has learned a new trick or two."

I nod and thank her again. My bag is already packed for Daddy, and I can't leave until he comes home, but for a moment, I think about going with her. I think about grabbing my bag and my sweater and walking to Miss Wilder's house, where everything is clean and warm.

Instead, I close the door and lock it so no one can come inside. My mother needs me, and soon, my father will be home. I can wait a little longer.

After Miss Wilder leaves, I sit on the floor and open the Tupperware. Inside is a perfect cake, swirled white and yellow, and covered with glaze. The cake smells like lemons and butter, and I am hungry, but I feel too sad to eat it. I look at the pretty cake and remember the parties Mary Roberts and I had when we were friends. I think about the Sunday school picnic coming up this weekend, and how much I'd love to go.

A car engine rumbles outside and brings me back from daydreams. It sounds as if someone has parked in front of our house. I wonder if Miss Wilder came back? Or maybe Mrs. Roberts sent over the minister like she said she might. I leave the cake on the floor, then stand up to peek out the window.

Sheriff Rhodes opens his car door and steps out. He adjusts his wide-brimmed hat, but before he shuts the door, leans inside his car to speak to someone in back.

I cup my hands around my eyes to block the sun so I can see. The person is too small to be a man. I see the pale blonde hair, and I know.

Sheriff Rhodes has brought Tess, but where is Daddy?

FORTY-ONE

ONION SANDWICH

I DON'T WAIT FOR Sheriff Rhodes to come inside. I pull open the front door and shout, "Where's Daddy?"

Tears stream down my face. "I want Daddy!" I pull on Sheriff Rhodes's shirt. I'll make him tell.

"Ellie, honey, please calm down." Sheriff Rhodes places his large hands on my shoulders.

"You promised you'd bring my daddy back safe! Where is he? And why did you bring her? She doesn't belong here!" I point at Tess.

"Now hush, Ellie. You don't want the neighbors to come outside and see you acting this way, do you?" Sheriff Rhodes kneels in front of me and looks into my face.

I shake my head. I know about things you can't let people see.

"That's a good girl." He pauses. "In just a minute, we'll have to go tell your mama the news. But I'll tell you first, give you a chance to let it sink in before we go inside, okay?"

"Okay," I whisper. My stomach tightens.

"I found your daddy, and I didn't hurt him," Sheriff Rhodes explains. "I kept my promise, Ellie. But he refused to come with me, said he was the only one who knew how to take care of Tess. He wouldn't leave her. I had to get assistance from the Tennessee deputies to bring him in. He and the deputies got a little scuffed up in the process, but your Daddy is okay. Just a few bruises."

"But where is he?" I wipe tears from my eyes. I'm glad Daddy was found safe, but don't want to think of him struggling to break free. I don't want to picture him bruised or hurt.

Sheriff Rhodes clears his throat. "Ellie, honey, your daddy is in jail. You know I had to . . ."

"No, you didn't! You're the sheriff. You don't have to lock anybody up unless you want to! You just don't like my daddy."

"No, Ellie." He stares into my eyes. "I locked up your father because he killed a man."

I forget about the neighbors. I hurt so bad inside I have to hurt someone back. I start hitting Sheriff Rhodes. "That's not true! It's not true!"

He doesn't yell or smack me. Instead he puts his arms around me and holds me tight. And I cry. I cry until I think my face may break open like a shell.

"Good God, Julia, what have you done?"

Sheriff Rhodes rubs his unshaven beard with both hands. He stares at Mama as if he sees a ghost.

In the days that Sheriff Rhodes has been gone, Mama hasn't bathed, changed her clothes, or combed her hair. She's hardly eaten and can't sleep because Baby Tom is colicky and cries all night. She looks thin, sick, and dirty.

Mama picks at the mole on her neck, making it bleed again. She tugs at the mole, then touches her face, smudging blood on her cheek.

Mama stares at the sheriff. "Did you find him, then?"

"Yes, Julia."

Mama wraps her arms around herself as if the room suddenly

turned cold. She looks out the window, doesn't say anything for a few minutes, then turns toward Sheriff Rhodes. "Where's his little whore? Did you find her, too, George? Go on, you can tell me. Was he with his whore when you found him?"

"Mama!" I cover my ears with my hands. I don't want to hear.

"Julia, listen to me." Sheriff Rhodes kneels by Mama's chair. He pulls his handkerchief from his pocket and wipes Mama's neck, then takes her hand in his. "This is important, honey. Rupert is in trouble. We found the gun. There's enough evidence to convict him. God knows, I wish that wasn't true, but it is. He's going to need a good lawyer, and I'm not sure you're in any shape to take care of this. You've got to come up with the retainer. Might have to take out a loan, mortgage the house. You've got to pull yourself together. Maybe you should call your brothers in Georgia, ask them to help."

Mama laughs. "If you think Charlie and Hunter are going to come up here and help Rupert Sanders, you're a fool. They can't stand him. Hunter would rather see Rupert fry in the electric chair than buy him a cup of coffee."

I gasp. "Mama, please!"

"Hush, now. Nobody's going to the electric chair. Not over a drunk like Mason Reed, that's for damn sure." He pats Mama's hand. "Listen, I got the girl out in the car, Julia. She's hardly able to speak, drools all over herself. Hell if I know what happened to her, some kind of brain damage, I think. I got to check her into the hospital, then find a social worker to see if she has any other kin to look after her."

"I don't care what you do with her." Mama spits out her words.

"I understand that. All I'm saying is, I have to make some arrangements for her, and afterwards, go check on Rupert. Let's see how he's thinking after he's had time to cool down. By then, it'll be too late for me to come back tonight. Millie's already been complaining." He clears his throat. "But I'll be here first thing in the morning. I'll bring Clara, ask her to draw you a bath, maybe give you something to help you sleep. Then if you don't call Charlie or Hunter, by God, I will. They might not care what happens to Rupert, but somebody's got to look after you."

"Ellie's looking after me."

"She's a child, Julia."

I take my hands away from my ears. "I need Daddy. He knows how to take care of Mama. He knows how to take care of me!"

Sheriff Rhodes stands up. "Everybody's nerves are on edge. We all just need to take a deep breath. Ellie, soon as I leave, I want you to fix your Mama a cup of hot tea and a sandwich. Can you do that?"

I nod.

"Good." He turns toward Mama. "Julia, honey, I hate seeing you like this. Things are going to get better. I promise you that. Just hang on another night, and we'll sort this all out, first thing in the morning."

Mama's eyes fill with tears. "Go home to your wife," she says, and turns her head away.

Sheriff Rhodes's shoulders drop as he walks to the door. He stops and pats my head. "You'll be all right tonight, Ellie? I'm going to find somebody to come in here and help. Clara. Maybe a nurse from the health department. Somebody. She can't go on like this. I've seen her moody, know she has her rough times, but never like this."

"Not a nurse. No! Have Clara come in the morning. She'll know what to do," I say, then add, "When can I see Daddy?"

"Soon, honey. Maybe in a day or two. I'll be back in the morning with Clara," he says, then walks out the front door.

I remember the cake Miss Wilder left and hurry to take it to Sheriff Rhodes.

"What's that?" he asks, staring at the Tupperware in my hands.

"It's a cake. I want Daddy to have it. Maybe it will make him feel better."

"You didn't slip a file in here, did you?" He smiles, but his eyes are sad.

"No," I whisper. I know he was only joking, but I can't smile. I'm trying hard not to cry again.

"I'll make sure he gets it."

I can't say thank you. My voice is like a splinter stuck in my throat.

Sheriff Rhodes turns and walks to his car.

I watch Tess in the backseat. She presses her pale face against the glass and smiles.

I don't smile back.

I DO AS SHERIFF RHODES asked, and make Mama tea and a sandwich. The tea is no problem, but there's no meat in the house, and no mayonnaise or mustard. The peanut butter in the bottom of the jar is barely enough to cover one slice of bread. I could stretch it if we had honey or applesauce, but we are out of those, too. Mama bought so few things at the market, and most of those were the wrong things. So I end up smearing butter on bread and adding thin slices of sweet onions, and a little salt and pepper.

Mama only nibbles her food, spitting out most of the onion as if it is too bitter to eat. She chews a bit of bread and sips her tea. After she shoves her cup and saucer aside, she paces the floor and picks at her mole.

I don't know Mama's brothers but I hope they will come and help. I'm tired of trying to take care of everything. I'm tired of keeping secrets and looking after Mama and Baby Tom.

"ELLIE, HONEY, GET UP. There's something the matter with the baby." Mama's cold hand shakes me awake.

I rub my eyes and try to focus in the dark. Moonlight through my window gives my room a milky glow. I see Mama's white skin, then the jar with Baby Tom inside as she shoves it toward my face. In my half sleep, I see his mouth open.

"What, Mama? What's wrong?"

"Well, he keeps fussing. I try to rock him, but he won't settle. Look at his face. See how pained he looks?" Mama winces as if she herself feels Baby Tom's pain. He's like the tree she feeds from, her moods somehow tied to his.

"Maybe he's hungry." I don't like seeing Mama press the glass against her naked breast, but feeding Baby Tom sometimes makes her sleep.

"I tried that. He didn't want my milk. I think it was the onion on that sandwich. It made my milk bitter. Why'd you feed me onion, Ellie? Are you tying to turn my baby against me?"

"Of course not, Mama." I need to think of another idea before Mama goes on about the onion. She scares me when she blames me for something bad. Recently, everything is my fault; I don't want to be blamed for Baby Tom turning against her.

Still trying to wake up, I search my mind for an idea, and offer the only one that comes to me. "Well, he could be cold, Mama."

Mama holds up one hand as if testing the room's temperature. She must decide for herself, since she doesn't trust me because of the onion sandwich. "Yes, that could be it." She smiles slightly, then tells me she's going to wrap Tom in the blanket she's been knitting. "Good night, Ellie."

" 'Night, Mama."

After she leaves my room, I close my eyes, but can't get back to sleep. I think of Daddy in a cold jail cell with only a thin blanket to keep him warm. I think, too, about what Sheriff Rhodes said, how Daddy didn't want to leave Tess. I remember the day he went away, how he didn't look back. It was easy for him to leave me. What had I done to make Daddy stop loving me?

A sudden noise startles me. My voice catches in my throat. I know the sound right away. I've heard it many times, in the kitchen and in Daddy's store.

Glass.

Breaking.

FORTY-TWO

TOO MUCH RED

Mama is in the hallway, screaming. "No, no, no! Not my baby!"

I don't have to see it to know what's happened. She's broken the jar with Baby Tom inside.

My stomach twists tight like a knotted rope.

Get up, Ellie. Walk into the hall and help Mama back to bed. The broken glass and formaldehyde must be cleaned up before she gets cut. Someone must pick up Baby Tom and find a place for him: another jar, a shoebox, a tin can with holes.

No, no, no.

"Why wouldn't you stop crying? Why wouldn't you just stop?" Mama yells. The blame shifts from me to Baby Tom. It isn't my onion sandwich, but Tom's own fault. He is dead, but still to blame. I'm glad, but ashamed. I'm more afraid than I ever knew I could be.

Thoughts flood my head. After I get Mama back to bed, I'll have to make up with Mary Roberts to get more formaldehyde. Or maybe I could put him in vinegar. Or maybe salt water.

Clara will come in the morning. Maybe she'll know how to keep a dead baby from going bad.

Mama screams again.

I need to go to her, but I can't make myself move. I feel frozen in place.

In the hallway, Mama's screams turn to sobs. There's a dull banging sound, over and over, as if she's hitting her head against the wall.

I have to go to her. There's no choice. No one else can go for me. I am on my own.

My head spins when I stand. Please, God, don't let me faint. I'm so afraid of what I'll see on the other side of the door, I can barely breathe.

I reach for the doorknob. My hand shakes.

What if the hall is too dark for me to see? What if I step on the baby?

I take a deep breath, open the door, and step into the hall.

Oh, God. Mama, please. No!

Red. There's too much red.

On the floor, and the wall, all over her gown. Nothing but red.

I've never seen so much blood. Ribbons spill from Mama's wrist. She sits on the floor, her head and shoulders propped against the wall. Pieces of glass lie on the floor. She holds a large piece in her hands, uses it to cut a deep gash across her other wrist. Blood sprays from her new cut.

"Mama!" I don't know what to do. There is too much red.

I hurry, grab Mama's hands, make her give me the piece of glass. She doesn't want to let go, but I pull hard, until her fingers give. While taking the glass away, I cut my hands.

Mama tries to reach for other pieces. I have to gather them up so she can't get them. My bleeding hands are soon full of glass.

Baby Tom lies facedown on the floor in a puddle of formaldehyde, but I have to leave him there for now. I'm holding too much glass to pick him up. I'm afraid I'll cut him.

My legs take me back to the bathroom. I need to think fast. I throw the glass into the sink and grab all the towels I can carry.

I kneel beside Mama, press the towels on the places she's cut.

I press hard, try to get Mama to help. "Please, Mama, hold the towel. Why, Mama, why did you do this?"

"The baby wouldn't stop crying, Ellie. I couldn't listen to him cry another night."

"Oh, Mama. What am I supposed to do? Tell me what to do?" There is blood on my hands and my nightgown. I keep pressing, but don't know how to make the bleeding stop.

Mama's eyes open and close. Her skin is pale and cold.

"He doesn't love me, Ellie. I just wanted him . . ."

"Wanted him what, Mama?" I press a clean towel over each of her wrists. Red soaks the towel.

"I just wanted him to stop crying." She winces.

"He's not crying now, Mama."

"He's not?" Mama shifts her head as if to listen.

"No, he's not." I crawl on my knees and pick up Baby Tom. He's stiff, slippery, and cold, like a rubber doll left out in the rain. He smells bad, like the formaldehyde.

"Here, Mama." I place Baby Tom on her chest. My bloody hands leave prints across his tiny back. "He's not crying, Mama."

A weak smile crosses her lips. Mama's eyes flood with tears. "You're right, Ellie. He isn't crying." She swallows hard. "He isn't crying anymore."

There is too much blood on the floor, on the towels, on the front of Mama's gown.

I stand up to leave Mama and Baby Tom. I have to go downstairs and call for help.

Mama cries, "Don't go, Ellie. Don't leave me alone."

I remember crying those words in the middle of the road the day Daddy went away. I know how bad it feels when someone leaves you alone.

"I was never going to leave you, Mama. I'm sorry about packing my suitcase. I just wanted Daddy to come back for me. I didn't want to leave you. Not ever."

Mama's eyelids flicker, then close.

FORTY-THREE

DREAMS

MY EYES SEARCH OUT cracks in the ceiling. If the roof splits open, I'll see stars.

I stare without blinking, practice widening the cracks with my eyes. The white plaster crumbles. Dark rafters fall away.

I see a black sky dotted with stars.

If I find Mama's face, I might sleep again.

I DREAM OF a baby with blue veins. He's like a worm trapped inside a jar. A girl's hands put him there.

Mine.

IN THE KITCHEN, there is spilled flour, onion peels, a vat of lard on its side. No tone on the telephone, the bill unpaid.

I knock over a chair, a coffee can.

Upstairs, Mama's body slumps on the floor. No noise, no breathing. She doesn't move.

Her wrists split open. She is all bled out.

I'm the girl they found standing on the table. The girl who traced the cracks in the wall with her mother's blood.

A COLORED WOMAN tends to me. I sleep in her house, but I'm not her kin. She brings me food in a wooden bowl and teas with powders in them.

I hear a man in the next room. He reads aloud the book of Job. His boots tap on loose floorboards.

God the Father.

Daddy is not here.

MY BED DRIFTS over drowsy seas. The colored woman kisses my brow good-night.

She tucks a quilt under my chin, a quilt patterned with stars. To keep from drowning, I swallow a fistful.

The stars melt on my tongue.

A HAND SHAKES my shoulder. The same woman leans over me. Her gold-brown eyes are wet with tears.

I remember now.

"Clara?"

She found me before the ambulance came.

"Wake up, child, you can't stay in this bed. We got to bury your Mama."

I SOMETIMES THINK all my days from now on will seem as far away and fitful as my dreams.

I remember Mama's funeral in bits and pieces — the navy blue dress Clara ironed and pulled over my head, following a dark car to the cemetery, standing over Mama's open grave, the minister taking my hand to toss the first fistful of dirt.

Dressed in black suits, Mama's tall brothers stood beside me and stared at the open grave. One folded his hands the way Mama sometimes did. His slender fingers laced together like hers. The same bent thumbs curled inward.

Mary Roberts came, too. She tucked a white handkerchief in

my fist and said, "Don't cry, Ellie. Please don't cry." Miss Wilder stroked my hair and blinked back tears. I'd never seen her so lost for words.

Sheriff Rhodes brought Daddy. As soon as I saw him, I struggled to break free, but Jericho held me close. Clara's cool hands smoothed my face. "Not yet, child. Not this day."

As Mrs. Roberts sang the last hymn, I searched for Daddy's face in the thin crowd. Sheriff Rhodes was leading him away, toward the sidewalk lined by parked cars.

"Daddy!"

He turned, and his sad eyes met mine. Daddy smiled, tried to wave, but the shackles held his hands down. Sheriff Rhodes nudged him forward.

I dropped to my knees.

Daddy grew smaller and smaller, then disappeared like a drop of rain.

"You remember a little bit, don't you, child?" Clara's voice brings me back to the kitchen.

I nod. The eggs on my plate have grown cold. I'm not hungry and want to go to sleep, but Clara won't let me stay in bed. "I remember, but I don't want to."

Clara puts the iron down on the board and leans over to hug me. "I know, Ellie. I know."

"You came for me, Clara? The night Mama . . ." I can't finish the sentence.

"Yes, honey." Clara sits at the table and sips coffee. "Sheriff Rhodes stopped by, told me he found your daddy and that girl he run off with. I asked him if you'd be all right. He said not to worry, you was fine for the night, but could I be ready in the morning to go to stay with you and your mama until he contacted relatives or a social worker. I told him 'Of course.' So I packed my bag with clean underclothes and what have you, then settled down to feed Easter—at least, I tried to feed him. He wouldn't hardly eat for me. That worried me, but Jericho said that bird just missed you."

Clara drinks more coffee. "I went on to bed, but couldn't sleep. Easter kept scratching on the bottom of his box, even in the dark. Everybody knows a bird roosts when the lights go out, but Easter wouldn't go to sleep no matter what I did. Later in the night, my wrists burned. They burned real bad, like scalding water had been poured on them. I could hear Easter in his box, flapping like something wild. And then I knew. I saw the blood," Clara says, pointing to her forehead. "I saw it in here." She looked at me with tear-filled eyes. "I came, but Lord, it was too late. Too late. Child, I'm so sorry."

"But you brought back Easter, Clara. Why didn't you bring Mama back?"

Clara shakes her head. "I told you before. I can only bring back them that want to live."

"But why, Clara?" I don't understand. "Why didn't Mama want to live?"

"Some people are born sad." Clara leans forward as if she wants to make sure I'm listening. "You can't change the way a person is, Ellie. Not when it is deep inside them. You can only love them just as they are. A sad person is hard to love sometimes, but they need it most of all."

I remember the times when Mama looked out the windows with tears in her eyes. When I asked her why she was so sad, she'd said, "The rain makes me lonely." I would have given anything to make the rain go away, to reach through the clouds and paint the sky blue again.

"Did you see Baby Tom? When you came to the house?" I ask Clara.

Clara nods. "I made sure Miss Julia's baby got placed in the grave with her. I figured from the smell of him, she'd been keeping him in the jar that broke?"

"Yes." I feel ashamed that I hadn't told Clara about him, but it is good to know Baby Tom got buried with Mama. I don't want to think of her alone.

"Most women lose a baby, they put that baby in the ground, say good-bye. That's too hard for your mama. She had to keep him, couldn't let him go 'cause it hurt her so bad. A person got to know when to let go, you hear me?"

I don't say anything.

Clara puts her finger under my chin and turns my head until our eyes meet. "I said, do you hear me?"

"Yes."

"Good. I'm glad you understand that, 'cause now that your mama is in the ground and your daddy in jail, you have some letting go of your own to do."

"What do you mean?"

"Honey, this is hard for me to tell you, but sometimes it's best to just spit out the truth plain and simple. With your mama gone and your daddy locked up, the judge had to make a decision about you."

"About me? I don't . . ."

"About where you live, honey. You can't stay back at your house alone. The judge has say over where you go. He tried to get your mama's kin to take you, but they said no, least not until your daddy's trial is done. So the judge, he ordered that you go to a foster home."

"But Clara . . ."

She spoke over me, her voice steady and firm. "Miss Emily is a good woman, and she's going to take good care of you. She'll be here in a spell, so you best eat your eggs and wash up."

I push Clara's hand away and stand up. "I don't want to go, Clara. I don't want to leave you and Jericho."

"I know, Ellie, and believe me, Jericho and me would love to keep you. But you know well as me that colored folk can't keep a white child. Nobody is going to allow that, are they?"

"But what about Daddy? I can't leave Daddy. He needs me nearby."

Clara stands up and wraps her wide arms around me. "Miss Emily doesn't live too far away. And child, you listen to me. You weren't the one who left. He was."

Deep inside, I know what Clara says is true. "Daddy told me to take care of Mama, but I didn't know how, Clara. I let Mama die."

"No, Ellie, you did the best you could. Your daddy left you a job too big for one little girl. That was his job, and he's the one who didn't do the right thing. Not you, honey. Not you," Clara says, holding me tight.

"That bird is gonna die if you don't feed him."

"I don't care!" I yell at Clara.

"I didn't bring that chicken back from the grave so you could starve him." Clara unties her apron and puts it on a hook by the kitchen door. "I got laundry to hang," Clara says. "Miss Emily is a good woman. I ain't never lied to you, have I? She coming to pick up you and that bird, too. But if you don't want him, so be it." She picks up a basket filled with damp clothes and walks outside.

I squat on the floor and look at Easter. Most of the green has grown out, replaced by white feathers. He's lost so much weight in the days since Mama died, he's almost half the size I remember. Clara feeds him every few hours, but she says he won't eat right for her.

"That bird knows who his mama is," Jericho says as he steps into the kitchen. "He ain't going to live unless you want him to. Clara be right about that."

Jericho opens the door and goes back outside.

I stare at Easter. He flaps his thin wings and pecks at my fingers. His little black eyes stare at mine.

My heart feels like a fist that can't open. I think of everybody

I've lost. I don't want to love this chick. If I love him, he'll just go away or die.

Clara walks back inside. "You going to feed that bird or not? He ought to eat before his car ride."

"I'm not taking Easter with me. You can keep him, Clara."

Clara slams her basket down. "I got enough trouble without a half-starved chicken running around my feet." Clara cracks the screen door and yells to Jericho, "Brings me an ax, old man."

"An ax? Clara, what do you need an ax for?" I ask.

Clara stares at me. "I aim to kill this chicken and eat him for supper tonight."

My eyes fill with tears. "No, you can't do that!"

"And why not, child? I tell you the bird won't eat and needs you to feed him. You won't feed him, won't take him with you. Now, I am an old woman and don't need a chicken to tend, and he won't eat for me now no how. Why should I let him starve to death in my house? I'm not going to let him suffer."

Jericho walks in, a rusted ax in his hands.

I scoop Easter up in my arms. Tears run down my cheeks. "I'll feed him, Clara, I will. Please! I want Easter to live."

The fist inside my heart opens enough to let Easter in.

FORTY FOUR

CHALK ON THE RIVER

E MILY RANDOLPH IS a widow with three grown sons and no daughters. One son, Abe, is a doctor in Charlotte, and the other two, Stephen and James, practice law nearby.

I live with Miss Emily in a blue two-story house with white shutters and a porch that stretches the entire front and partway down one side. She has barns and all the other makings of a farm, but doesn't raise livestock anymore. There are three tabby cats, though. Two gray and one yellow. The yellow one, Daisy, is due to have kittens any day now. Miss Emily tells me I can choose a kitten to be mine, but I don't know if I want to just yet. Taking care of Easter seems like enough.

Each morning, before I join Miss Emily in the kitchen, I carry Easter outside, feed him cracked corn, and refill his water dish. At night, I put Easter inside an old wicker picnic basket lined with straw so he can sleep on the floor beside my bed. I keep a towel over the basket to darken his nest; otherwise, he'd stay awake and peck his way through the basket.

Jericho came by a few days ago to build a pen in the backyard so Easter can walk around without the cats getting to him. "Next week, I'll get some plyboard and build him a little house," Jericho told me. "He can't be out in the rain but so long; all God's creatures needs a place to keep dry and warm."

The thing that upset me about coming to Miss Emily's house was leaving Clara and Jericho. I wasn't sure the judge would let me see them. He said he couldn't rightly order visitation with people who were not my kin, and not even my own race, but he left it up to Miss Emily's discretion who visited me. "Of course you can see them, Ellie," she'd said. "One thing you can never have enough of is love. Clara and Jericho love you, and they are welcome to visit you whenever they like, and you them." She says Mary Roberts can visit when she comes back from camp, and Mr. Morgan is welcome, too. Even Miss Wilder is welcome to come by when she wants. Miss Emily says her doors are open to anyone who loves me.

Miss Emily is good to me. She treats me like the daughter she never had. She even says that to me: "Ellie, you are like the daughter I never had. I love my sons, but I always wanted a girl." She places her hands on my face when she says this, and looks at me as if she is searching for some family resemblance, a curve of cheek or color in my eyes to match her own.

I just smile. I don't want to hurt Miss Emily's feelings, but I don't want to be anyone else's daughter. I had a mother. I want her back.

But that's between God and me, not Miss Emily. I know she'd bring back Mama if she could. She can't, so she does the next best thing and takes care of me the way a mother should.

At Miss Emily's house, there is always plenty to eat and I don't have to cook, wash dishes, or do any of the laundry unless I feel up to it. I pitch in when I can and find that work passes time. I don't know exactly what I am waiting for, but I always have that feeling. Maybe I am waiting for Daddy's trial to be over and for the sheriff to unlock the cell to set him free. Maybe I am waiting for Mama to walk through the door and braid daisies in my hair.

Sometimes I think I will spend the rest of my life waiting for familiar arms to hold me.

I tried to learn the rules right away so I could stay with Miss Emily, but she didn't seem to have many, so I did all the normal things like, walk—don't run—in the house, and don't touch anything that looks expensive, like her collection of clocks.

The only thing Miss Emily is particular about is that no one comes to the table without first washing their hands. I wash mine ten, maybe fifteen times a day, so that is never a problem. In fact, Miss Emily says she'd be real happy if I forgot to wash my hands. That isn't likely. No matter how many times I wash, I see Mama's blood on my hands. Some stains you can never wash clean.

My bedroom is on the second floor. Miss Emily decorated it with dried sunflowers and big wicker baskets, then bought some paint and brushes and told me to cover the walls with pictures of my own. "Sometimes picture making is the best therapy," she'd said. I didn't want to argue with her, but the pictures inside my head aren't the pretty ones a girl can paint on walls.

So I paint pictures of Easter instead: Easter sitting in my doll carriage. Easter eating kernels of corn. Easter standing on the bureau looking at himself in the mirror. Mary Roberts will be surprised when she sees how well I can paint now.

Mary hasn't seen my new room because she's spending the summer at church camp near Richmond. Every week, her short letters arrive on pale pink paper with matching envelopes.

I wanted to go to camp, too, and pretend none of the bad things happened. Only I couldn't go because of my therapy sessions. I don't much care for therapy, but that's the only way I'll be able to visit Daddy. The judge who sent me to live with Miss Emily says I have to go, it is an order, and more important than summer camp.

Daddy writes me, but Sheriff Rhodes gives the letters to my therapist, Miss Cassidy, so we can read them together. In his letters, Daddy always says how sorry he is for leaving. He says he's talking to a new lawyer to handle his case. When he gets out of jail, he promises things will be different. He's coming to get Tess and me and make a home for us.

I want to go home with Daddy, but I don't want Tess to live there.

Tess stays at Mildred Rogers's convalescent home where invalids and retarded people live. I haven't told anyone, but I walk by there sometimes, just to look at her. I don't know why. It's as if I need to see her for myself so I can remember what is real. It would be so easy to live in a make-believe world like Mama's, to imagine things entirely different than they are. When I see Tess, I know the difference between make-believe and real.

Tess is not the same girl. She doesn't look as pretty now. I have walked right up to her a few times, but she didn't seem to know me. When she laughed, ribbons of spit unfolded in the corner of her mouth.

Last week, I dug up one of Miss Emily's tomato plants, put it in a pot, then left it on Mrs. Rogers's front porch with a note that read, "To Tess." Daddy, I know, would want me to help her in any way I could.

The next day, I saw Tess pacing the sidewalk in front of Mrs. Rogers's house. She had the plant in her arms. Her thin fingers stroked the leaves.

That is all I can do for Tess. I don't want to see her anymore.

In his letters, Daddy keeps asking me to check on Tess. This makes my therapist angry. She says she is going to visit the jail to speak to him about it, but no, I cannot go along.

Miss Cassidy doesn't understand how much Daddy lost because of Tess. He will never give her up now.

Miss Cassidy's office is like a classroom with a big chalkboard and shelves lined with books. But it's different, too, because there are sofas instead of desks, and large, woven pillows piled on the floor. On her desk, she keeps pens, a scented candle that always burns, and large white cards with inkblots on them. The cards are not like Clara's, which predict your future; these cards tell about your past. I don't like them.

I try to like Miss Cassidy; she is soft and kind. But it is hard when she tries to make me talk about all the things I want to forget.

The first time she brought up Mama, I walked to the chalkboard, picked up a stick of chalk, and drew a door. I moved my chair so I could sit behind the door where Miss Cassidy's words couldn't reach me.

Now I keep a box of chalk with me all the time, and use it whenever she wants to talk about something that makes me hurt inside.

She asks me to draw pictures of a person, a tree, and a house. She hands me a set of cloth dolls and wants to watch me play with them. Sometimes, she shows me the white cards with inkblots.

I look at the cards, but try to see nothing

I won't draw a house, tree, or person.

I won't play with her dolls.

I draw another chalk door. I'm safe there.

On Tuesday afternoons, Miss Emily gets her hair done at the salon, then shops for groceries. While Miss Emily is at the salon and market, I spend the afternoons with Clara. I don't know if Miss Emily would let me visit Clara if she knew about the magic, so I keep quiet about it.

Clara teaches me all the magic—about the lines inside the palms of my hands, and how to swirl tea grounds in the bottom of a cup and read meaning in the patterns they make. She talks to me about colors and words, and how spirits live in stones, a handful of dirt, or the branches of trees. She's helping me grow an herb garden in a window box, and tells me which leaves and roots work to cure sickness, which ones bring good fortune, which ones lead to a long life.

Today is a special Tuesday. We are meeting beside the river. I haven't wanted to be here since Jellybean drowned, but Clara says it is important not to blame the river. "Water nourishes. It cleanses. It is good magic for carrying troubles away. Water washes away fears, regrets, and is a fine place to get rid of things we don't need," Clara says. She stands on the bank with her feet placed apart, and her eyes fixed on the water. "Sometimes, magic is a light thing, like planting a found coin in the time of a new moon to bring on luck or more money."

"Or burning pink candles while holding a rose petal on your tongue to bring love," I add, remembering the spinster who visited last week for Clara's advice on how to draw and keep a man.

"That's right. And sometimes, magic calls us to do something hard, to give up something we don't need, so we can grow." Clara looks at me. "Like that box of chalk you carry."

I look into Clara's gold eyes. My hand reaches inside the pocket on my dress to touch the box. I open my mouth, but don't know what to say. Finally, I tell Clara about Mr. Morgan and the chalk door, how he told me I could be safe behind the door, and it was like magic to go there.

Clara listens. She nods as I speak. When I finish she lets out a deep breath. "I understand," she says. She walks nearer the river, gazes across the water, then turns to face me again.

I look at Clara with questions in my eyes.

"The chalk door is good magic to shut out cruel deeds and words from others. That was a gift from Mr. Morgan, something he wanted you to use to protect yourself from rumors and name calling. But you use the chalk door to hide. To learn real magic, you have to face things that scare you. You have to face the hurt inside here," she says, pointing to my heart, "if you are ever to be rid of it." Clara walks away from the river, away from me. "You decide," she says over her shoulder.

I look out over the river. Behind a curtain of cattails and bent reeds, the water is a ribbon unfolding itself. It flows in ripples downstream, moving like something alive and determined. I take a deep breath and smell the water. It reminds me of moss, wet bark, and old shoes, but there is something reassuring and safe about it.

I reach inside my pocket again and touch the smooth box. Without the chalk door, I might tell Miss Cassidy about all the sad things that have split my heart into pieces. I might tell her about all the bad dreams and voices, or even spill secrets I'd promised to keep. I'm afraid of how much that will hurt, afraid of what it may cost.

But I know Clara is right. I am tired of carrying so many dark and broken things inside me. I can never do magic with so many fears, hurts, and secrets. They weigh down my heart like a stone.

I kneel at the edge of the river. I pull the box from my pocket and open the lid. Five pieces of chalk. Five smooth, perfect pieces. When I turn the open box upside down and shake it, the chalk drops into the water. I watch the thin white sticks bob in the blue-green river, then come together like a hand, to float quietly away.

ACKNOWLEDGMENTS

My deepest gratitude goes to the many people who made this book possible:

To my husband and children, for inspiring me to dream while keeping me grounded.

To my parents, who indulged my early love of books and never censored what I read.

To the members of the Internet Writing Workshop, who read and critiqued the first draft and gave me encouragement as I stumbled through the process. Their ongoing support is a blessing.

To my editor, Chuck Adams, who not only showed unwavering enthusiasm for the book but worked magic to make the story clearer and whole.

To my agent, Sandy Choron, who is a champion without rival and the best reader a writer could hope to find.

To good friends and amazing teachers, not only for encouraging me to write but for daring me to take greater risks on the page.